SOULMATCH

SOULMATCH

REBECCA DANZENBAKER

SIMON & SCHUSTER BFYR
NEW YORK   AMSTERDAM/ANTWERP   LONDON
TORONTO   SYDNEY/MELBOURNE   NEW DELHI

An imprint of Simon & Schuster Children's Publishing Division
1230 Avenue of the Americas, New York, New York 10020
For more than 100 years, Simon & Schuster has championed authors and the stories they create. By respecting the copyright of an author's intellectual property, you enable Simon & Schuster and the author to continue publishing exceptional books for years to come. We thank you for supporting the author's copyright by purchasing an authorized edition of this book.
No amount of this book may be reproduced or stored in any format, nor may it be uploaded to any website, database, language-learning model, or other repository, retrieval, or artificial intelligence system without express permission. All rights reserved. Inquiries may be directed to Simon & Schuster, 1230 Avenue of the Americas, New York, NY 10020 or permissions@simonandschuster.com.
This book is a work of fiction. Any references to historical events, real people, or real places are used fictitiously. Other names, characters, places, and events are products of the author's imagination, and any resemblance to actual events or places or persons, living or dead, is entirely coincidental.
Text © 2025 by Rebecca Danzenbaker
Jacket design by Lucy Cummins
All rights reserved, including the right of reproduction in whole or in part in any form.
SIMON & SCHUSTER BOOKS FOR YOUNG READERS
and related marks are trademarks of Simon & Schuster, Inc.
For information about special discounts for bulk purchases, please contact Simon & Schuster Special Sales at 1-866-506-1949
or business@simonandschuster.com.
Simon & Schuster strongly believes in freedom of expression and stands against censorship in all its forms. For more information, visit BooksBelong.com.
The Simon & Schuster Speakers Bureau can bring authors to your live event. For more information or to book an event, contact the Simon & Schuster Speakers Bureau at 1-866-248-3049 or visit our website at www.simonspeakers.com.
Interior design by Hilary Zarycky
The text for this book was set in Adobe Caslon Pro.
Manufactured in the United States of America
First Edition
2 4 6 8 10 9 7 5 3 1
CIP data for this book is available from the Library of Congress.
ISBN 9781665963701
ISBN 9781665963725 (ebook)

To Chase and Clara

"Face your fears! Be brave! Just do it!" —Evan J. Corbitt

Dear Reader,

Please be aware that *Soulmatch* contains content that may be triggering. For a list, please visit RebeccaDanzenbakerBooks.com.

—Rebecca

My Last Letter

Dear me,

This letter is the only thing I'm leaving you, my next life. I know you're annoyed, probably even mad, but you'll get over it. We love a good challenge.

Instead of an inheritance (I'm bequeathing every last valut to a good cause), I offer only this advice. Trust your instincts. Yes, you've got a few people to watch out for, but far more on your side than against.

So go out there and play the game. It's what you do best. You won't always win, despite what you may think. That's okay. Each loss teaches you more about yourself . . . and how to beat your opponent in the next match.

I believe in you. I believe in us.

Carry forth,
XO
[undated]

Kirling

kirling—(CURL-ing) n. The government-mandated matching of a soul from a former life (foli) to a current life (culi).

Friday, August 24, 236 A.K.—Ashburn, VA

I'm not a bad soul. The mantra plays through my head as I scan my bedroom for items to pack. *Not a bad soul. Not a bad soul.* It would be easier to believe if not for the constant reminder coating my bedroom walls.

My eyes squeeze shut, blocking out the perpetual swirling of rainbow colors—the mural Mom painted five years ago after finally caving to my pleas. She can read auras, the palette of energy each person emits, which she depicts in one-of-a-kind portraits for her rich and famous clientele. But mine looks nothing like her usual work, and not just because of the sheer scale of it. Normal people have one to two colors in their auras. I have them all.

We don't know what that means.

Stop thinking about your messed-up aura and focus on packing. What will you need for your visit to the institute? No matter how many times I've checked my list, I can't shake the feeling I'm forgetting something.

Restless fingers twist my long brunette locks as I scan my room, waiting for something to pop out and scream, *Take me with you!*

I definitely won't need any of my old art projects—paintings, holograms, luminous tapestries. Not even sure why I still have them except for their one common attribute: The center of each depicts the symbol I dream about each night, a circle with an X inside of it. I don't know what that means, either, but I bet my past lives do.

Three more days. I clasp my hands together, using my thumbs to draw the familiar crossroads symbol into my palms. Only three days until my mandatory kirling, when these questions and more will be answered. What's up with my abnormal aura? Who was I in my previous lives? What should I do for a living? Do I have a soulmate? I yank my hands apart, groaning. Or am I a bad soul, destined to leave the institute in handcuffs?

I flop into my hovering desk chair and spin, taking in the walls again. If I'd inherited some of Mom's artistic talent or my father's prowess with numbers and computers, my uncertain future wouldn't keep me up at night. Unlike me, they didn't need their kirlings to decide what to do for a living. Dad died before I was born, but Mom said several companies recruited him based on his past lives' successes. He ended up accepting the generous offer from the same government institute I'll report to this morning.

I wish he still worked there. It would be nice to see a familiar face.

The notification of yesterday's notable kirlings pops onto my specs, the high-tech glasses Mom gave me at graduation. I place my foot on the floor, coming to a stop. *Maybe, just maybe....*

"Sivon, are you ready?" Mom calls up. Her footsteps echo off the wooden stairs, accompanied by her whistled rendition of "Happy Birthday." The serenade sounds more like a funeral dirge than well wishes.

Hurry, before she gets up here.

Brows furrowed, I wave my finger to scroll through the announcements, searching for one name and one name only—Flavinsky.

Please and *Please no* simultaneously whisper in my head, vying for dominance.

Almost two years have passed since Flavinsky's expected kirling. Maybe they'll finally show up today, and I'll have one less thing to worry about. Not that I want someone else to be Flavinsky. No one wants to learn they're the most notoriously tragic soul in kirling history. In a perfect world, Flavinsky would never appear on this list again.

I find the *F*s.

> F1NA7TC—CFO—three lives
> F4521F4—Surgeon—five lives
> FAR3ZNH—Celebrity Pastry Chef—three lives
> FY201O0—Comedian—four lives

No Flavinsky. I pull in a relieved breath, then hold it through the sinking terror. Is that what my unreadable aura means? Am *I* Flavinsky?

Mom reaches my doorway. To hide my panic, I turn my back to her, but after eighteen years, I should know better. She can see my aura from any angle.

"*Whoa.* What's wrong? You're like a big gray cloud." Though my colors constantly shift, like the paint on my walls, she can pick up hints to my mood based on their intensity.

I remove my specs and shove them into an outside pocket of

my red duffel bag. With sweaty palms, I tug the sides together and zip it shut. "I'm nervous."

She approaches and hugs me around the waist, plopping her head onto my shoulder. "I get it. Feels like yesterday I was heading to my own kirling."

Her sage-like scent of kinetic paint will be sorely missed this week. I fill my lungs to lock it inside.

Mom turns me to face her, offering a compassionate smile. "But you've looked forward to this for *ages*." She jiggles my shoulders. "And finding out who you were in your past lives won't change who you are, Sivon. You'll go in my little Indigo and come out my little Indigo."

"A grayish Indigo, apparently." I wish my aura were actually indigo blue and that wasn't just an endearment.

I was too young to remember, but Mom says she started calling me Indigo after teaching me the colors of the rainbow. She was explaining that most people can't distinguish indigo light from its neighboring blue and violet. "Kinda like how I can't interpret your many colors. You're my little Indigo."

The name stuck, and my aura is still indecipherable. Mom tells me not to worry about it, but how can I not? If my erratic colors mean I'm a bad soul, these could be the last minutes I'll spend in my bedroom, and the last time I'll ever see her.

Mom cups my jaw with her terracotta hands, exactly two shades darker than mine. "I see past the haziness to that beautiful heart of yours. And nothing you learn this week will change how much I love you."

"Aw, I love you, too, Mom." I wrap my arms around her shoulders, slipping my hands into her soft chestnut curls. "If I hit the jackpot this week, I promise to share my fortune with you."

She scoffs and pulls back. "I wouldn't dream of it. The valuts from your former lives are yours to keep. Don't you think I would've had more kids if I wanted a share of their inheritance?"

"I know, I know." I nudge her with my elbow. "But a brother or sister would've been nice."

"Psh. You have Vivi and Corah. I couldn't have given you anyone better if I tried."

I bite my bottom lip to hold back a smile. Vivi, Corah, and I have been practically inseparable since they moved to our neighborhood ten years ago. Their parents became my second parents, and their older brother treated me the same as his twin sisters—like a nuisance.

But Vivi and Corah left to attend the North American Intelligence College two months ago. And my other friends have started their new lives as well. It sucks being the youngest in my class, the last to be kirled.

My heart twinges. It's finally my turn. If I'm a good soul, like Vivi and Corah, like most people, I'll leave the institute with my career path and inheritance, maybe even a soulmate.

But something tells me I'm not like most people, and that something is the mural swirling around my room. I lace my fingers together and knead a circle across my left palm, then cross it with a deep X before switching hands.

"Are you sure you don't want me to come into the city with you?" Mom takes my hands to stop my nervous habit. "I can push back my next sitting."

I force a smile, hating myself for worrying her. "No, no. I'll be okay."

This is it, then. I lift my duffel from the bed, taking one last look around before my gaze settles on the walls. *Not a bad soul. Not a bad soul.*

Mom embraces me, squeezing harder than she has in years. "I love you, Sivon. No matter what."

I close my eyes and shudder. *Maybe not a good soul either.*

Meteor

Meteor—n. The high-speed, electromagnetic, subterranean shuttle that replaced Washington, DC's Metro system during World War III reconstruction. Around the same time, the city's name changed from the District of Columbia to the Coalition District, now referred to as Washington, CD.

Heart thundering, I step onto the express Meteor, slide my bag under the first available seat, and strap in. The morning commuters quickly find alternative rows and buckle up. As soon as the last harness clicks, the shuttle surges forward, pushing me into the hard seatback.

I fill my lungs to fight the uncomfortable pressure while trying to block out the overpowering scent of sweet vinegar. I've ridden the Meteor plenty of times but never got used to the smell or the way my soul practically rips free of my body. Can they find a way to strap down that part as well?

Across from me, the screen embedded in the curved white wall switches from a commercial to a recent interview with Janus, the prime minister's nephew. The sight of him perks me up, as it has since he began making public appearances six years ago. At the time, his handsome face, sandy blond hair, and intelligent gray eyes drew my admiration. Now that's inspired by his community outreach, infallible rhetoric, and casual grace.

Janus wears a white shirt, the sleeves rolled up to reveal his bronze forearms, and he's effortlessly perched on a stool, laughing at something someone said off camera. He passes a hand over his face to regain composure and beckons for the next question. No sound plays, but after watching this interview a half-dozen times already, it's easy to superimpose his silky voice on the subtitle bubbles.

The camera cuts to the reporter. "Your uncle's Advancement Party maintains only a small lead over the Improvement Party led by Senator Fahari, well within the margin of error. What's his strategy ahead of the September twelfth election?"

Janus threads his fingers and grins at the camera, his adorable dimples popping. "Uncle Mirovnik is the most selfless man I know. He cares about only one thing." His steely eyes lock with mine, as if he's speaking to me alone. "You, the North American people. Your safety. Your prosperity. And that starts with ensuring the kirling system works equally for all."

My pulse quickens at the mention of kirling. I'm less than ten minutes from the institute now. At least I have Janus to keep my mind off my unknown future. Since I'm eligible to vote for the first time this election, I should probably stop focusing on his flawless delivery and pay attention to what he's actually saying.

"You're referring to the special exceptions given to Fringe communities?"

"Yes, exactly." Janus leans forward. "Our forefathers did what was necessary to end the war, and for that, I'm grateful. But the doctrine meant to protect Fringe rights only holds them back. Fringe residents are North Americans too. They deserve to reap the rewards of our collective success.

"We are a peaceful nation. We are a peaceful world."

I whisper the words along with him.

He nods as if he knew I would. "We have been for almost two hundred years, thanks in no small part to international acceptance of the kirling system. Our Fringe communities have nothing to fear. We are one country. It's time we act like it."

The Advancement Party slogan, "Free the Fringe," flashes on the screen. I'm sold.

A Vast Valuts lottery commercial comes on, promising more money than the winner could spend in three lifetimes.

Hmm.... Would I rather win Vast Valuts or match with Janus as a soulmate? Vivi and Corah asked me that question when we were thirteen, and my answer remains the same: *I'd choose Janus. Because not only would I have eternal love, but he's already rich. Win-win!*

They agreed my logic was sound, but that led to years of playful teasing. They love pointing out how close mine and Janus's birthdays are—only eight days apart—which, in their estimation, must mean we're soulmates.

When I remind them that millions of people share the same birthdays, Corah changes gears, saying something along the lines of *I think your soulmate will end your undefeated streak at Chessfield.*

Vivi will disagree. *No, because soulmates don't care about beating each other at games. Your soulmate will make it easier for you to win, Sivon.*

And if Mom is around, she'll say, *Your soulmate will be the one who grounds you, who calms your aura.*

Then I remind them that most people don't have soulmates, so I probably won't, either, and they need to stop worrying about my love life and worry about their own. That puts a stop to it all, at least until the next time Janus comes up.

The Meteor slows to a halt at the next station, and the restraint presses into my chest. *Ow.*

"Fairtax and shuttles south," announces a crisp male voice as a dozen more people enter and strap in. "Next stop, the Semyon Kirlian Institute. Washington, CD."

My heart flips. Oh gosh, I'm so close. Why in the world did I insist on taking the express shuttle? I could've met Mom's client this morning instead. Who was it this time? Oh yeah, the singer-songwriter Lavonne. On my way out the door, Mom made a joke about our names rhyming. Lavonne and Sivon. Sivon and Lavonne.

I can't believe I passed up my chance to meet Lavonne. *Idiot!*

Maybe I'll end up with a soul so famous, she'll want to meet *me* someday. The thought almost makes me laugh out loud. No chance. I have not a lick of talent—artistic, musical, athletic, or otherwise... unless you consider winning games like Chessfield a talent.

Nah. That's all instinct.

Besides, celebrity life sounds horrid—the cameras and public appearances, the gossip and scrutiny. I love my privacy, time to think, and relative obscurity. Nothing and no one could lure me into that world...which *might* present a problem if I do end up Janus's soulmate.

Ha. That's ridiculous. Janus will not be my soulmate. He spends his days bouncing among meetings with the most influential people on the planet and paying goodwill visits to inmates and their families. He will likely succeed his uncle someday to become the next prime minister.

But me? I'm just a girl from the suburbs whose only skill is winning games of Chessfield. I'll consider myself lucky if my kirling yields a comfortable inheritance and interesting career. And sure, I'll take a soulmate. Who wouldn't?

The train lurches to a stop.

"Semyon Kirlian Institute. Washington, CD. Next stop, the Smithsonian Museum of the United States of America."

I'm here. I freeze in panic for a second, then rush to unbuckle and dart toward the doors. Three steps later, I realize I've left my duffel bag under the seat and hurry back for it. I manage to make it out a split second before the doors shut. The Meteor takes off again, creating a gust of stale wind that pushes me toward the escalasteps.

One by one, the metal slabs rise through the magnetic conveyor, floating toward the sun several stories above. The magic of hovering stairs wore off years ago, but every time I step on one, I still worry I've chosen the first-ever escalastep that fails. Wouldn't it be just my luck to make it this close to my kirling only to die in a freak accident?

I can see the Sociaty headline now—*Death by Escalasteps*. I'd come back to life just to die of embarrassment. Worse still, I'd never find out who I really am. It's that thought, and the person clearing their throat behind me, that has me stepping onto the next riser. *Up we go.*

Squinting into the sun, I remember my specs and unzip them from my bag. The lighting equalizes when I slide them on, and a missed call notification pops up from Vivi.

Damn! I can't believe I missed her. I wave my finger to play the video message.

"Hap—" Vivi begins, but Corah clamps her hand over Vivi's mouth.

"Happy birthday!" Corah shouts, then releases her twin sister. "Ha! Said it first."

Vivi narrows her eyes at Corah, then faces the camera. "Happy eighteenth, Sivon." She playfully flicks Corah's cheek.

"Ow!" Corah rubs the spot and tries to flick Vivi back.

Their antics escalate. Vivi sweeps Corah's leg out from under her but falls to the floor herself, leaving only grunts and laughter issuing from the speaker.

I dissolve into giggles. My goofy best friends are exactly the distraction I needed today. Why oh why did I pack my specs instead of wearing them?

"Quit it! We'll be late for Cryptography."

I'm pretty sure that was Vivi.

"Oh shit." Corah reappears and tugs Vivi up beside her.

Vivi smooths her long black hair, then helps Corah fix hers. They're identical from their russet-toned skin to the birthmarks on their shoulders, but I have no trouble telling them apart. Vivi's eyes hold empathetic concern while Corah shoots it straight. They face the camera, bearing matching smiles.

Vivi tilts her head. "You're gonna love the institute, Sivon."

The reminder wipes the grin from my face, clenching my insides. The top of the building is visible above. With every centimeter I ascend, another meter of granite comes into view, cold and looming. I walk off the escalasteps and take in the full monstrosity, stretching two blocks long and ten stories high. Unless I'm the monstrosity. Maybe my fear of kirling stems from evil lurking in my subconscious.

"Stop overthinking," Corah says. "You're not a bad soul."

I press my lips together. They know me so well.

"You are *not* a bad soul," Vivi echoes. "Relax and try to make friends while you're there, okay? It'll make the visit go faster. And don't forget our bet!"

She winks, and they disappear.

I chuckle, recalling the terms of our ridiculous bet, until a familiar chant draws my attention to kids jumping a holorope outside a nearby apartment building. Not long ago, that would've been the three of us.

Cinderella, dressed in yellow,
Went to SKI to meet her fella,
Made a mistake, no soulmate.
How many kirlings did it take?

As they start counting, I slowly lower my chin, taking in my yellow Soul Sisters tee. I huff and roll my eyes. *Well, that was dumb of me.*

I shake it off. It's fine. I'll change as soon as I check into my room. Surely the color of my shirt won't affect my results. I pull back my shoulders to face the entrance half a block away. If my friends, parents, and billions of others can do this, so can I.

No sooner do I take my first confident step than the institute doors slide open, and a boy my age, wide-eyed with terror, is led out in handcuffs.

The Semyon Kirlian Institute

The Semyon Kirlian Institute (SKI)—n. Established 2 A.K. in Lisbon, Portugal. Now over ten thousand SKIs exist worldwide, kirling a combined 2.5 million souls each week.

Friday, August 24, 236 A.K.—Day One at SKI—Washington, CD

After three wrong turns in the maze of hallways, I finally find my assigned room. I blow out a relieved breath and rest my fingers on the knob. Knowing my luck, it won't unlock. But a second later, its red light changes green, and the door swishes open. Thank goodness. My heart has been in my throat since witnessing the scene outside, and I could use a minute to process everything.

"Ah, good. You've arrived," the clipped feminine voice issues from the large screen embedded in the left wall.

Crap. Am I already late for my first meeting? I hurry to the foot of the double bed, head swiveling right to take in the bathroom door and dinette with two chairs. Like the jumble of halls I got lost in, everything in my room is solid white, down to the couch under the expansive window ahead of me.

The woman clears her throat, drawing my attention. Salt-and-pepper bangs skirt her old-fashioned tinted specs. Though her eyes are obscured, her pursed lips reveal her impatience.

"Um, hi! Sorry, got turned around on my way here." My voice wavers with nerves. I drop my duffel bag onto the bleached comforter and perch on the edge of the bed, inhaling the potent smell of disinfectant.

She pushes her specs higher and settles against a warm brown sofa that matches her skin. A gold-framed painting hangs behind her, only the bottom of which is in view. "Welcome to the Semyon Kirlian Institute, and happy birthday . . ." She pauses, no doubt checking my name on her roster. "Sivon."

She rhymes my name with *Simon*, like teachers did at the beginning of each school year.

"It's pronounced sih-VAHN."

Her eyebrows peak over the rims of her specs. "Very well. You may call me Windrose." She aimlessly waves a finger to the bold letters displayed above her head. "I'll be your counselor for the entirety of your visit."

Under the name WINDROSE, her soul ID appears in smaller font—3I2DR5E. As is typical, she created her soulname from the computer-generated ID assigned to her soul. She changed the *3* to a *W*, the *2* to an *N*, and the *5* to an *S*.

Not bad as far as soulnames go. I used to scroll through kirling announcements, trying to guess everyone's soulnames. Windrose's ID could've as easily created *Mind Race* or even *Mind Erase*, but a SKI counselor obviously wouldn't want either of those.

Along with my past lives, I'll learn my soul ID and soulname at my kirling. As long as mine doesn't make the "Worst Of" list on Sociaty, I'll be happy. Some poor souls are going around with names like Dreadful, Frizzle, and Gazpacho.

Vivi and Corah now go by Kitsune and Raposa in public. Their soulnames mean *fox* in different languages, fitting their intelligence careers. But they'll always be Vivi and Corah to me, and I'll always be Sivon to them.

Windrose waves her finger to scroll through content on her specs, occasionally tapping the air to open new files. I assume she's looking through my school records and family history, but she could be staring me down, making notes about my demeanor, and predicting my outcome. I squirm on the bed and trace the crossroads symbol across my palms.

After what feels like a century, she lowers her hand. "Over the next few days, I'll prepare you for your kirling and the public debut of your new identity. In addition to daily group meetings, we'll have three one-on-one consultations—the first tomorrow night, the second after your kirling on Monday, and the third on Tuesday. Your visit will conclude with the delivery of any inheritance, and the meeting with your government-assigned estate attorney."

My heart thumps into my throat, and I swallow to force it back down. *This is really happening. I'm finally at SKI.*

"I'll let you settle in." She swishes her finger, and a schedule appears on my screen. "Our first group meeting will be in two hours, and your camera will automatically turn on after the three beeps unless you adjust the setting.

"Please watch the Intro to SKI video beforehand but brace yourself for the holo on the right. He always catches people off guard." She disappears.

I blink at the smooth white wall, stunned by her departure, then spin in a slow circle. Like the screen, the overhead lights and opaque window are embedded into the ceiling and far wall. The sterile hotel room looks nothing like the dark prison cell of my nightmares, but I feel caged in all the same.

The sole decoration, a painting hung beside the door, brings on a sudden rush of déjà vu. *Whoa.* After going off-kilter for a second, the room rights itself.

I guess I wasn't expecting to see any of Mom's paintings at SKI, much less in my bedroom. Are others of hers on display here, or was this a stroke of luck? Mostly a deep indigo blue, vibrant silver threads radiate from the center, representing an intuitive and wise soul. Beautiful.

I wonder who Mom's subject was. Maybe it was my dad. He worked at SKI until his death, after all. Or perhaps it's her self-portrait? That would explain why she often adds *little* before my Indigo nickname. I'll ask when I get home.

I didn't pass any of her pieces in the halls, but a few other works adorned the ivory walls, all featuring butterflies. Even the elevator had a large butterfly etched into it, one wing on each door.

The symbolism isn't lost on me. We've entered a "chrysalis" of sorts and will emerge with our kirling results, ready to fly. Well, not all of us. Bad souls sometimes have prison sentences to complete, like the boy who left in handcuffs today. I slump onto the bed at the reminder of his tears and pointless pleading.

Please, that wasn't me. I would never do something so disgusting. You have to believe me!

What an ominous start to my SKI experience. What a traumatic end to his.

I gulp, wishing I could call Mom for reassurance. *Tell me again that I'm not a bad soul.* But SKI doesn't allow contact with anyone on the outside while we're here, so I had to check in my specs upon arrival. My thumb again circles and crosses my palm, massaging away the worry.

I've just switched to the opposite hand when the words *Start Here* flash across the large screen. I tap play on *Intro to SKI* and nearly jump out of my skin when a hologram appears to my right. So much for Windrose's warning.

"Welcome to the Coalition District's Semyon Kirlian Institute," announces the famous actor, Cadence.

Mom is a huge fan, especially of his early work, but he's not my favorite. His soulmate, Abernathy, was the more talented of the two. Sadly, they passed away last year on the set of their latest movie.

"Hi?" Wasn't expecting to converse with a dead guy today.

"We're excited to have you with us, Sivon!" Cadence also rhymes my name with *Simon*. Wonderful.

"Let's review the history of kirling, shall we? In 1939 A.D., Russian scientist Semyon Kirlian created the camera and methods to photograph what he thought were human auras. Unbeknownst to him, he was capturing the first photos of souls."

"Skip." No need to review stuff I already know.

"Of course. A century later, Drs. Alejandro Sanchez and Henrietta Esteban adapted Semyon Kirlian's technique with emerging camera technology, creating 3D models of subjects' soul IDs, also known as soulids." Photos of the scientists flash across the screen. "Their database, the Sanchez–Esteban Index of Kirlings, or SEIK, matches your soulids from life to life, body to body."

"Skip." We studied this in every history class I've ever taken.

"Here's a helpful fact. In the year 1 A.K., the Global Coalition of Governments, formerly known as the United Nations, mandated kirlings worldwide, creating a universal identification database.

When you receive your kirling results, you'll only learn your lives since 1 A.K. No official soulids were recorded prior—"

"Stop."

Cadence vanishes, and eerie silence envelops my ears, amplifying the accelerated drumming of my heart.

Two hundred and thirty-six years of past lives await me. If I screwed up in any of them, my life will change for the worse. But, I remind myself for the bazillionth time, most people have three to five completely normal former lives. Why not me?

I flop onto the bed and stare at the indigo aura on the wall. The kinetic paint swirls inside the frame, mocking me with its perfection. *You're not normal, Sivon. You never have been.*

Groaning, I push myself up and cross to the portrait. *Sorry, Mom, but I can't deal with this reminder all week.* My attempts to take down the frame go unrewarded, only increasing my frustration. I stomp over to my bag, rummage through it until I find my lightweight black cardigan, then toss it over the top. That's better.

Now to find a way to pass the next 112 minutes before the first meeting. I tap the calendar icon on the screen. The myriad of optional activities, from yoga to a starship-launch watch party, come off as ridiculous with our futures hanging in the balance. How am I supposed to savasana when I, too, could leave SKI in handcuffs five days from now?

I pace the floor between the window and my door, eventually slumping on the rigid couch and tapping the frosted window until it turns clear. Across the wide avenue, the Advertitude Hotel rises almost two dozen stories, partially blocking the sun. Unlike SKI's granite exterior, the hotel's walls are top-to-bottom screens. Companies and family members have rented out custom-size sections to display advertisements and well wishes to SKI's residents.

Melchers University. Career and alumni support in this life and the next.

See you on the other side, Gwennifer!

No soulmate? Join Culi Connections to locate your past loves. Hearts rain down through the other ads before dissolving.

The largest section of wall space reads, *Calling all adventurers! The Interplanetary Space Agency seeks volunteers of all skills and trades to colonize Thessaly in the Centauri system. Sign up today and receive 5,000 valuts in hazard pay!*

Five thousand? That's it? You'd have to pay me five billion to travel to that frozen hellscape.

In the top corner, a smaller video shows a girl with crimson hair dancing around a kitchen and waving a rolling pin in the air. *We love you, Ziva!* is emblazoned on top in bouncing red letters.

Oh gosh, if Vivi and Corah post videos of me on that wall, I'll never leave this room. . . which would present a problem since I'll need to eat at some point, assuming my appetite ever returns.

I curl toward the window and rest my elbows on the back of the couch. With each home movie that pops up, I speculate who the person was in their past life, deflecting the focus from my own uncertain fate.

Before I know it, the screen behind me beeps. Time for my first group meeting.

SEIK

SEIK—(seek) abbr. Acronym representing the Sanchez–Esteban Index of Kirlings, the database of every kirling since 1 A.K.

"Camera activating in ten, nine..."

I look across the room to the sweater-clad painting. A flush creeps over my cheeks. Will everyone in my group see that and wonder why I covered it up?

Beep. I rush over, pull the cardigan free, and launch it on top of my bag.

"Camera activating in five, four..."

Pulse pounding, I shuffle in front of the screen. Should I stand or sit? Why didn't I brush my hair or go to the bathroom when I had the chance? I awkwardly lean against the bed and run my hands over my heat-frizzed waves. *Damn this humidity!*

Beep. The screen fills with twelve faces, including mine and Windrose's. *Relax, Sivon.*

I massage my palms while examining the group. Half of us are perched on beds while the others sit at desks, eleven strangers who share the same birthday.

Our faces range from narrow to wide with markedly different features—eye colors and shapes, nose widths and lengths, forehead prominence, and lip fullness. Strange to think my soul could've easily ended up in any of their bodies, and vice versa. For the most part, we're an array of bronze skin tones, resulting from centuries of international peace and merging cultures. On either end of the spectrum are Rory, a boy with peach skin, red hair, and freckles, and Dikela, a girl with rich ebony skin and close-cropped black curls.

Windrose turns her specs translucent to address us, revealing hooded brown eyes. "Welcome again to the Semyon Kirlian Institute." Her lips press into a polite smile.

"Throughout your eighteen years, you've no doubt discussed your possible kirling outcomes with friends and family. However, the *vast* majority of souls receive nothing more than a confirmation of *existing* talents, interests, and personalities."

Not exactly comforting for those of us without notable talents or interests. I like to think I have a good personality, but can I be an honest judge of that?

"That being said, we recognize the inevitable anxiety this process creates. After kirling billions of souls over hundreds of years, we've crafted this orientation program to reduce stress and ease your transition back into the real world. Most who come through these doors share the same concerns, and based on your survey responses this week, the eleven of you are no different."

If Windrose could see auras, she'd realize how wrong she is.

"Let's get started, shall we? Today, our discussion will focus on folies of most concern. For those of you coming in from Fringe communities, 'folies' is short for 'former lives.'"

A guy in tinted glasses—plain old sunglasses, considering SKI's no-specs rule—snorts and lowers his head to the desk in front of him.

Do kids from the Fringe really not know what folies are? I search everyone's faces for signs they grew up on the outskirts of society. No one stands out as being particularly clueless about kirling.

"Allow me a second to pull up your survey responses." Windrose swipes at the air.

My mouth goes dry. I stared at the questionnaire for an hour last night before entering my kirling fears. After hitting submit, I closed my eyes and tried to sleep. The circles under my eyes speak to my lack of success.

"Here we are. Yes, most of you worry you were criminals in your folies. However, only about 7.5 percent of souls were ever incarcerated. Far fewer, around 0.8 percent, still owe time from unfulfilled sentences or postmortem trials."

I'm still stuck on the 7.5 percent. That feels incredibly high. Scary high. If someone said I had a 7.5 percent chance of winning the lottery, I'd be thrilled. Not so much when my freedom is on the line. My hands grow clammy.

"Let's think about those numbers more tangibly," Windrose continues. "Of the thousand souls here at the CD institute, 925 will not have a criminal record, and only eight have outstanding warrants."

What? I squint at the screen. Eight of us might go to jail this week? I thought the boy led from the building this morning was a rarity, not a daily occurrence. My fingers curl into the bedspread.

"How exactly is that supposed to calm our nerves?" Dikela asks, as if reading my mind.

"The better informed we are, the more easily we adapt to change. A criminal past does not define you or prevent you from becoming a productive member of society."

Mom would stand and applaud that statement, and Janus often

says the same in his interviews. I agree the sentiment is nice, but we all know the truth. Once branded a criminal, you're always thought of as one. Schools won't recruit you, and companies won't hire you. Kirling results are publicly searchable. We can't escape the mistakes of our past lives.

So who among us will be that unfortunate soul, the 7.5 percent? Rory? Dikela? Me? I swallow the doomsday thoughts that have plagued me all day. I have no control over what my kirling will reveal, so I need to focus. The better informed I am, the more easily I'll adapt. In theory.

"North America offers excellent course-correction programs for those entering the judicial system," Windrose says. "Inmates receive counseling services and career training to help their souls prepare for this and future lives."

"But aren't souls with a criminal past more likely to commit future crimes?" a girl named Norine with shoulder-length purple hair asks.

"Current figures suggest a twenty-nine percent recidivism rate. That may seem high, but it's down from forty-five percent only a hundred years ago."

"Just to clarify," Dikela breaks in, "nearly a *third* of people who've served time previously will commit crimes in future lives as well?"

"Yes, that's correct. But if you receive bad news this week, I hope you'll choose to move forward instead of looking back."

"Bullshit," whispers Norine.

"Yes, Norine?" Windrose quirks a brow. "You have something you'd like to share?"

"I said this is *bullshit*! The whole damn kirling process. If people didn't find out they were criminals before, they'd pursue a different path altogether."

Sunglass guy, Bardou, lifts his head.

"Exactly!" Dikela says.

Is Norine suggesting we should stop kirlings? Then what would happen to our inheritances? How would people like me know what they're supposed to do for a living? I'm nervous for my kirling, to put it mildly, but part of me *needs* it all the same.

Windrose sighs. "I understand your concern, but let's consider this scenario: A terrorist opens fire in a supermarket, murdering dozens, then kills themself to avoid capture. Should they escape justice simply by being reborn following such a heinous crime?"

Norine narrows her eyes. "We haven't had a terrorist attack since the Pulsar investigation was published 125 years ago."

She's right. That research demonstrated how closely souls are linked, that our future lives will carry the burden of any harm we've inflicted.

Two hundred years ago, a soul named Pulsar detonated a bomb, and himself, in New Union Times Square. But the study published seventy-five years later is what curbed all future attacks. It compared the bombing victims to Pulsar's friends and family in their following two lives. Turns out the bombing killed their future best friend, mother, two cousins, and a host of others Pulsar loved. The stranger you hurt in this life could be your spouse in the next.

"Yes, we are all familiar with the investigation, and Pulsar is an excellent example of how the system works," says Windrose. "She's completing her fourth life sentence and has *accepted responsibility* for her soul's crime. By holding souls accountable, we've decreased criminal activity by sixteen percent. We have much to be grateful for. Let's move on, shall we?"

"Ugh!" Norine sweeps her hand in front of her face, and her window disappears.

Windrose plasters on a smile. "Please take a few minutes to stretch. I'll return shortly." Her window also vanishes.

We stare at one another for an uncomfortable minute. I scoot back and pull my knees to my chest. How is it possible Vivi and Corah actually *enjoyed* their time at SKI?

Bardou runs a hand over his shiny black hair, groans loudly, then scratches his stomach, not-so-subtly showing off his sculpted abs. "Fucking waste of time," he mumbles.

Ah, the I'm-too-good-for-this type. Bet he ends up with a job in finance . . . or sports journalism. No, wait, club promotion.

"No one's forcing you to come to these meetings," Dikela says.

"What else am I gonna do? Join a Chessfield tournament like some nerd?"

"Of course not," I cut in. "Chessfield requires a modicum of intelligence. Sorry, you don't qualify."

Several people in the group chuckle.

Bardou's smirks. "Ooh, a *modicum*. Using big words to prove you're better than everyone?"

I purse my lips. "Not everyone. Just you."

Another round of laughter follows. Bardou huffs. "Nice. Well, if any of you ladies are interested in a *modicum* of fun tonight, I'm in room 417."

"Only a *modicum*?" Dikela pouts. "However will we resist?"

"Ha! Nice one, Dikela." I bounce my brows.

Bardou rolls his eyes, leans back in his chair, and looks out the window.

Just when the residual chuckles die down, Norine's and Windrose's faces reappear on my screen. Norine sullenly crosses her arms and chews on her cheek.

Windrose clears her throat. "I do sympathize with the stress you're under. Our topics of discussion may stir up long-repressed thoughts and emotions, which we'll further explore during our one-on-one meetings. SKI brought you here early to alleviate anxiety, not add to it.

"Let's go through more of your submissions." Windrose scrolls through the air. "Some of you expressed concern that you may be Flavinsky."

I curl my toes. That was one of mine. Flavinsky is the notorious soul who's taken their life after every kirling. While I can understand their shame for failing to protect General Molemo during World War III, that might explain one or two of their suicides, not all eleven. And yet, every investigation into their deaths has ruled out foul play.

Couple Flavinsky's numerous deaths with their incredibly short deathspans—only a day between each life—and their soul has become synonymous with tragedy and failure. I simply can't imagine finding out I'm Flavinsky. I hope I never will.

Windrose sighs. "Though Flavinsky's soul is indeed overdue for kirling, I'll repeat what I tell all my charges. Flavinsky is only one soul of over *fifteen billion*. You have better odds of winning the Vast Valuts lottery. Twice."

Finally something to ease my worries. My posture relaxes.

"My uncle won Vast Valuts two lifetimes ago!" Rory says. "But he spent it all in the last one." His hands lift into a whatcha-gonna-do expression.

"Thank you, Rory." Windrose smiles kindly.

Bardou flicks his gaze upward before dropping his head to his desk.

"We're almost out of time, so I'll briefly mention this last topic. Twenty-four hours after your kirling, SEIK will release your results to the public.

"We have no way of knowing whether another soul harbors ill will toward yours. Being of adult age, with autonomy from your families, you're presumed to be mature enough to accept your results and strong enough to defend yourselves against those who wish you harm."

Silence falls over the group. I rub the base of my neck, willing my thundering heart to settle down. Could I protect myself if someone confronts me outside? Vivi and Corah taught me some self-defense moves last summer, but I'm a bit rusty. Maybe SKI offers refresher classes. I should check the schedule.

A thunderous snore erupts from Bardou's open mouth, causing half of us to jump and the rest to giggle.

Windrose ignores him. "Any last questions before we disperse?"

"Yeah," says Norine. "Why are we meeting virtually when we're all in the same building?"

"This format works best with the counselors' busy schedules, but I recommend participating in some of our organized activities. If nothing else, they'll help pass the time and keep you in a better headspace. Have a nice evening. I'll see you in the morning."

Bardou snores once more before their faces vanish, leaving only my reflection in the slick, white surface.

I rub my eyes. *So, that was terrifying.* Criminals, Flavinsky, and vengeful assailants. Sounds like a recipe for another restless night.

Surely tomorrow's discussion will be better. I pull up the calendar to check the topic. Best-case scenarios. Perfect.

I heave a sigh and run a hand through my hair. So how should I spend the rest of my day? I scan the list of activities for a self-defense class.

Ha. There really is a Chessfield tournament about to start. But is it weird to play games only days before my kirling? I tap my lips. What else is there to do? Pace my room? Stare at the Advertitude hotel?

I glance out the window just as every advertisement disappears, and the wall turns solid white. One by one, black block-letter words pop up, each two stories tall.

STOP

MOPING.

GO

MEET

FRIENDS.

Who would take out a full-building message like that? Probably cost a gazillion valuts. The words disappear and are replaced by *xo, V&C.*

I gasp. *No.* They *wouldn't.* Must be two other people with the same initials. Not Vivi and . . . Two lifelike holo foxes run up the building and jump from window to window. My eyes tear up. Foxes! Kitsune and Raposa! Delighted giggles escape as I watch them cavort, then wink at SKI and disappear. A second later, the cacophony of videos returns to the hotel walls.

Never in a million years did I think I'd be giggling today. Leave it to Vivi and Corah . . . and their substantial inheritance. I check the schedule again for the location of the Chessfield tournament and dart out the door. A second later, I run back inside, whip the yellow T-shirt over my head, and find a blue one to take its place. Best not to take any chances.

Chessfield

> Chessfield—n. A holo adaptation of the classic game of chess. Though the pieces remain the same—pawns, bishops, knights, rooks, queens, and kings—their possible movements depend on the terrain and modes of transportation selected by the players.

I expect the SKI Lounge to resemble the ski lodge Mom and I visited a few years ago, with deep colors, cozy chairs, and a crackling fireplace. But like everything else at SKI, it's stark white. Missed opportunity, if you ask me. Speaking of which, why aren't the counselors called SKI Instructors? At least they got their security force right—SKI Patrols. Clever.

But no, I'm not vacationing in the mountains. And despite being called a lounge, the bright lights and cushionless chairs won't allow anyone to get too comfortable.

My footsteps echo off the far wall, interrupting the hushed quiet. I got lost on my way here and missed registration but decided to watch the matches anyway. Five couples sit at Chessfield boards in the center of the room, the tables arranged in a semicircle. Another two-dozen people hover around the competitors.

I recognize only one player, Norine, the purple-haired girl from my group. She moves her knight via airplane toward the opposing king's mountain. A pawn will certainly bring down her knight, but her strategy is clear. With the pawn out of the way, she can corner the king with her queen. It's a brilliant move.

I head to the next table. Oh, this poor girl is doomed. She chose a cyclo as her vehicle. Paired with the cave system, she has no path to success. What was she thinking?

The couple at the next table is better suited, but as soon as the bishop shuttles to the moon, it's over. Rook for the win in three moves if the guy has any sense.

I'm about to shuffle to the next board when the girl with crimson hair beside me catches my eye. She resembles the girl from the Advertitude video, the one dancing around with a rolling pin. I break into a smile and lean over to whisper, "Aren't you the dancing baker?"

A blush warms her light brown cheeks. "You saw that too? I haven't had the pleasure, but sure seems like everyone else has. Guess we all get our fifteen minutes of fame, huh?"

"If that's true, you're welcome to my share."

The person next to us glares our way, so we raise our brows and seal our mouths shut before turning back to the games.

The first three matches end as I predicted, but the last two continue for another fifteen minutes. I circle the boards to study the terrain from all angles, working out a strategy for each player to win. But soon enough, someone chooses the wrong path, and the winner has a straight shot to victory.

The tournament recesses for lunch.

The dancing baker comes over and holds out her hand. "I'm Ziva. At least, for the next forty-eight hours."

"Sivon. Yeah, strange to think we'll introduce ourselves differently after our kirlings. Forty-eight hours? That means you arrived yesterday?"

Ziva nods slowly. "Cannot think of a worse way to spend a birthday. When did you get here?"

"A few hours ago."

She makes a face. "A happy horrible birthday to you."

We share commiserating smiles.

Ziva motions behind her with her thumb. "I'm about to meet a friend for lunch who arrived today too. Wanna join us?"

Would I rather eat with a group this week instead of sitting alone with my doomsday thoughts? *Absofreakinglutely.* "Oh, sure, thanks. I'd probably get lost again trying to find the dining hall. This place is a maze."

"I suspect they're purposely hiding the exits." She nods toward the doors, and we set off. "I was watching you during those last two games. You knew who would win, didn't you?"

"After a while, yeah. One by one, the possible moves whittle down, and you either win by outsmarting your opponent or waiting for them to make a mistake."

Ziva chuckles. "You say that like it's nothing, but it sounds to me like you can predict the future."

"I wish." I wave a hand toward the white hallway. "This would be a hell of a lot easier if I already knew who my soul was."

"Tell me about it. But once you learn your folies, I bet your future path will be clear as day."

I puff out a breath. "That's my hope."

We enter the atrium, which—surprise, surprise—is just as sterile white as every other room in the institute. The only exceptions are the glass ceiling ten stories above and the dozens of colorful holo butterflies flitting over the hundreds of us sitting and standing around.

We pass one group near the elevators, and I overhear them discussing their kirling results.

"A nurse! It's so perfect, I started jumping up and down in the middle of Leeward's office. Has anyone heard from Gwennifer?"

I cheer internally for the guy and slow my steps, curious about the mysterious Gwennifer too.

"She won't come out of her room," replies a girl at the table. "Told Merris she was in jail a couple lives back."

"Oh no." The guy presses a hand to his lips.

"Yeah, she served the sentence and paid the fines, but she didn't get much inheritance."

"Could be worse. At least she's not Flavinsky."

A lump forms in my throat, and I catch Ziva's shiver as she leads me toward an empty table.

As soon as we're seated, a waist-high RAID—robotic artificial intelligence domestic—sets down trays of our preselected meals. "Enjoy your lunches, Ziva and Sivon."

"It's sih-*VAHN*," I snap at its retreating form. I sure hope my soulname is easy to pronounce.

Ziva spears a piece of broccoli in her pasta primavera. I don't want to bring up Gwennifer or our own kirlings, so I shift back to our first topic of conversation.

"Nice of your parents to do that for you. The Advertitude video, I mean." I take a bite of my caprese sandwich. Not bad.

She squints one eye. "If I had to guess, I'd bet my older brother was behind it. He's done everything he can lately to make me laugh. And he took that video when we were up late baking cookies a few weeks back." She cackles. "Woke up everyone singing at the top of our lungs. Wasn't long before the whole fam was out of bed and dancing around the kitchen."

Her laughter is contagious. "Aw, he sounds fun. I always wanted a big brother. Do you live nearby?"

"Atomdale," Ziva says around a mouthful of pasta.

"Really? My dad grew up in Atomdale, near the Ravensworth Museum. Mom and I are in Ashburn."

"We're not far from the museum. Your parents divorced?" Ziva raises her water glass.

"No, my dad died in a hover accident before I was born. Never even knew my mom was pregnant."

Her glass freezes mid-trajectory. "A hover accident? I didn't know people could die like that."

"Yeah, the safety system shorted out." I take another bite and glance around the sea of teenagers. "I guess there's a chance he's here for his kirling too." His deathspan would be awfully short. And souls rarely end up in the same location as their past lives, but you never know. "Wouldn't that be strange? Maybe he's you!"

Ziva coughs a laugh while swallowing her water. "Mm-hmm. I knew I liked you." She pats my hand. "Good to see you again, sweetheart."

I snicker. "Hi, *Dad*."

"Ziva!" Dikela, one of the girls from my orientation group, sits down to my right. "Oh hey! You were in my group this morning. Sivon, right? I'm Dikela."

"Yep! Nice to meet you in the flesh. Ziva and I just met a bit ago. How do you two know each other?"

"We go way back. To second grade, right?" Dikela asks Ziva.

"And we've celebrated our birthdays together ever since. Happy eighteenth to us." Ziva twirls a finger in the air. *"Yay."*

I shimmy my palms in unenthusiastic jazz hands. I swear, this roller coaster of emotions will break me far before I get to my kirling. New topic.

"Did you see Ziva's video?" I ask Dikela.

"No. What video?"

Ziva rolls her eyes. "Donovan posted a video to the Advertitude of me dancing around the kitchen. Everyone keeps coming up and asking me about it."

I wince. "Guilty."

"Aw, he meant well. Donovan doesn't have a mean bone in his body," Dikela says as a RAID sets down her lunch.

"Enjoy your lunch, Dickella."

Dikela closes her eyes and inhales. At least I'm not the only one dealing with mispronunciations.

"Dickella. Holy shit. I'm gonna call you that from now on." Bardou, still wearing his sunglasses, sits beside Ziva and across from Dikela. He nods to acknowledge me. "Oh great, my two favorite people."

"No one said you had to sit here," says Dikela.

Bardou quirks a brow. "Have you seen the other schmucks in this room? Might as well sit with the hot girls."

Ziva barks out a laugh, but Dikela narrows her eyes.

"Do you already know him too?" I ask Dikela.

"She wishes." Bardou crams a forkful of pasta into his mouth.

"Not until our group meeting." Dikela turns to him. "What's with the shades? Cataracts?"

"Nah. They make me look mysterious." Bardou turns to Ziva. "Name's Bardou. What's your story, Red?"

"*Ziva*," Dikela corrects, "was just telling us about her sexy older brother, Donovan."

The corners of my lips twist up. "Sexy, huh? You didn't mention that before."

"Ew. Do not call my brother sexy."

Dikela points her bread at Ziva. "He is sexy, and he's not exactly your brother. Donovan's adopted."

Ziva grimaces. "Same difference. And straitlaced and uptight is *not* sexy. Give me wild and free any day."

"Mm. I knew we were gonna get along. Come here, Red." Bardou pulls Ziva's chair closer and slings an arm behind it.

She drops her head into her hand but doesn't move away.

"Not me. I *love* a man in uniform." Dikela's brows dance up and down.

"Same." We clink our glasses together.

"Too bad Donovan treats me like a little sister."

Ziva flips a baby carrot at Dikela. "*Stop!* You're not allowed to crush on my brother."

Dikela tosses the carrot back. "Doesn't matter if I do or don't. He's got a soulmate." She runs a finger down her cheek, tracing the path of a nonexistent tear.

Oh, that's too bad. The conversation was just getting good. I'd much rather talk about guys than the reason we're here.

"Soulmate or not, if he wears a uniform, he's a prick." Bardou swipes a french fry from Dikela's tray, who growls in return.

Ziva scrunches up her nose. "No, he's not. He's Shepherd."

Shepherd. The soulname rings a bell, but I can't place it.

"Who's Shepherd?" Bardou and I ask simultaneously.

"Donovan is Shepherd," Dikela says.

Ziva beams with pride. "And Shepherd is, like, one of the best souls in the world. Their last deathspan was over *fifty years*."

Whoa, that's impressive. Most people are gone eight or nine years before they're reborn.

"Shepherd was a detective in Uruguay in foli 1. In foli 2, they were the Commissioner of Community Protection in New Zealand, and that's it. Only two folies."

Bardou raises his hand from the table. "Like I *said*. Total prick."

Ziva bursts into giggles and shoves her shoulder into his side.

Now I remember hearing about Shepherd's kirling. It must've been over a year ago now. Vivi, Corah, and I drooled over his photo in SEIK, all claiming to be his soulmate.

Since soulmates share similar life and deathspans, their kirlings usually happen within days or weeks of each other. As of that announcement, Shepherd's hadn't been identified in this life.

"Has your brother met his soulmate?" I ask.

Ziva and Bardou are now flirting on the other side of the table, so Dikela answers, "Not yet. Shepherd's soulmate hasn't been kirled in this life. And almost two years have passed since Donovan was matched to Shepherd's soul. Should be any day now."

"So it could be you after all."

"I doubt it." Dikela picks at her roll. "As much as I love looking at him—the boy is *beautiful*—he would've noticed me if we were meant to be."

Then maybe sixteen-year-old me was right, and he'll be mine. A good soul with a fascinating history and beautiful to boot? Sign me up! Ziva could end up my sister-in-law someday. Wouldn't that be wild?

Snapping out of my daydream, I redirect the conversation to

Dikela, asking her about her family. She's telling me about her parents when Ziva and Bardou stand.

"I'm heading up." Ziva's grin stretches into a check mark. "See you tomorrow?"

Bardou winks before sauntering away with both trays in hand, Ziva casually following behind. Dikela and I turn to each other, eyebrows arching high.

"Can't say I agree with that choice," she says, "but my girl sees what she wants and goes for it. I'll give her that."

A tinge of jealousy hits. Not because of Bardou—*gross*—but because Ziva so easily left her worries behind for a "modicum" of carefree fun.

With my kirling approaching, I've been too anxious to think about romance, not even a casual fling. Besides, after several regrettable *"He's my soulmate!"* proclamations over the years, I learned not to trust my foolish heart.

But my unintentional celibacy is for the best. A part of me always worried the person I gave my heart to would find out they have a soulmate, a soulmate who wasn't me. I didn't have to imagine that heartbreak. I'd witnessed it firsthand.

Coulomb's law

Coulomb's law—n. A law of physics stating, in part, that when the distance between two electrical charges is doubled, the attraction decreases to one-fourth of its original value.

Sunday, July 27, 228 A.K.—eight years ago—Ashburn, VA

Eyes brimming with mischief, Vivi and Corah grab my arms and pull me into their bedroom. I drop my red duffel bag and climb onto their huge bed, wondering what the heck they're up to now. Vivi checks the hallway before slamming the door. As soon as she spins around, they whisper, "Justice came home today!"

I blink. "Already?" Seems like yesterday their brother's girlfriend left for her kirling.

"Yes!" Corah leaps onto the bed. "Kopar said she's calling him at eight, and we *cannot* disturb him."

"That's why Mom and Dad let you sleep over," says Vivi. "So we'll stay out of his hair."

Corah snorts. "As if he's so fun to hang out with."

I snicker in agreement. Kopar's nose is always glued to his screen, finishing his college-prep work. He literally shuts the door on his ten-year-old sisters' attempts to grab his attention.

"He's barely come out of his room today," says Corah.

"Why? Is he nervous? It's not like Justice would've fallen out of love with him in the five days they were apart. They're *so cute* together." I hug the stuffed fox toy on their bed.

Justice first started coming over last year for physics tutoring, and we couldn't resist spying on them. She'd graze his hand when asking a question, or he'd tuck her hair behind her ear while explaining Coulomb's law.

Vivi and Corah gag at those exchanges, and I always go along. But deep down, I hope someday someone will look at me the same way. "I still can't believe Kopar and Justice aren't soulmates." I pick up the stuffed Giuseppe Giraffe and press its mouth to the fox's. "Mom knew they weren't the second she saw them together. Their auras don't merge like yours. She felt bad for not warning him after he returned from SKI so upset."

"He was so *annoying*." Corah chucks the fox at the wall between their rooms. "He got a *full ride* to *MIT*! You'd think he'd be over the moon."

"Seriously. His kirling results could've been far worse." Vivi rolls her eyes. "Sivon, your mom and dad weren't soulmates, and they loved each other."

"Totally in love. She still talks about him all the time."

"Kopar calmed down after Justice reassured him nothing had changed," Corah says. "They sat on the porch the night he got back, and she promised *they'd always be together*." She singsongs the last part, fluttering her lashes.

"That cheered him up. He didn't even yell at us when he spotted the bug we planted on the windowsill," Vivi adds.

I lift my hand to my forehead. "You hid *a bug* on your front porch?"

Corah smirks. "We have bugs all over the house."

"*Seriously?* Do your parents know?"

They shrug.

"Bathrooms are off-limits, of course. And the bedrooms *were* . . . until today." Corah temples her fingers and bounces her eyebrows.

Vivi bobs her head, biting her bottom lip.

"No way!" I whisper. "You're gonna spy on Kopar's call with Justice tonight?"

"No," says Corah. "*We're* gonna spy on Kopar's call with Justice tonight."

"Where did you hide the bug?" I ask as Corah logs into the sensor.

She plays with the focus and checks the audio, ensuring Kopar won't hear his own voice echoing through the adjoining wall. "On his bookshelf." Corah points to the blurry area at the top of their handheld screen. "That's the ledge of his antique microscope. We hid it behind that."

"How did you get all these bugs, anyway?" I inspect one of the little discs and drop it back into the repurposed jewelry box on their nightstand.

"Nana's deposits on our birthdays and holidays are *very* generous."

Vivi startles. "Shh! It's time!" She bounces on the bed.

Corah places her hand on her twin's leg, Vivi settles, and we lean in.

Justice lets out a happy sigh when her beautiful face lights up Kopar's screen. He sits cross-legged on his bed, surrounded by digital posters hung years ago of famous spacecraft—ancient ones, like *Apollo 11*, and the more recent *Survival*.

"It's so good to see your face," coos Justice. "You have no idea."

My posture relaxes at the same time as Kopar's. See? Still in love.

"So?" He tucks a swoop of dark brown hair behind his ear.

"You didn't look?" She bites her bottom lip.

"Of course not. We promised not to check each other's results." He bends forward. "Wait, did you check mine?"

Justice waves a hand. "Psh. No, baby. Remember how shocked I was when you told me?"

Kopar chuckles and nods. I hold my breath.

Justice tugs one of the natural brown curls haloing her face before blurting out, "Abernathy." She covers her mouth and laughs. "Can you believe it? I'm still in shock."

My jaw drops. Justice is Abernathy? The famous movie star?

"Wow!" Kopar leans forward. "Abernathy? Wow."

"I know!" Justice does a little dance. "I've been fielding calls from Dos Angeles all day."

"Holy shit, Justice. I . . . don't know what to say. It's great, though. Wonderful!"

Only a second later, his smile slips away. Viv, Cor, and I exchange anguished looks, already knowing what he just registered. Corah zooms in. I thread my fingers together and rub circles into my palms, crossing each with an X.

"Abernathy, huh?"

Justice's lips slowly turn down. "Kopar . . ." A tear appears in the well of her eye. "We knew this could happen."

He scratches the back of his neck. "Have you met?"

The guilt swelling my throat urges me not to intrude on this private moment, but I also can't look away. Abernathy has a soulmate, an equally famous one. Cadence.

"We met this morning at Two Lovers Point. SKI arranged

everything for us." She blinks rapidly. "He lives in Indostralia. Can you believe how far apart we were? But I've always dreamt of visiting Indostralia, so I'm sure that's how we would've eventually met.

"Oh, and I got to use the translation software in my earplant. Absolutely amazing technology! You would've loved—"

"Don't change the subject." Kopar clutches his stomach, a movement only the three of us can see. He nods a few times. "So you and Cadence, huh? How did that meeting go?"

A tear spills onto Justice's cheek. She bats it away, using the movement to turn her head to the side. "It was . . . everything I expected. I'm so sorry, Kopar. I didn't *want* to believe it at first. I *do* love you. I really do."

Cadence and Abernathy are perhaps the most famous soulmates in the world—lovestruck actors with posh lifestyles who always die young. But Justice loves Kopar, not Cadence. She just said so.

Justice's chin trembles. "But it was like electricity running over my body when we met. My soul *knew* him." She looks down and lets out an embarrassed chuckle. "We started laughing before we even said hello, and we sort of fell into each other. He kissed me, and it was like I'd never been kissed. . . ." Her words fall off.

Since SKI arranged Cadence and Abernathy's reunion, the show will broadcast soon. In fact, soul debuts usually air at eight p.m., so it's probably on right now. I can already imagine the swelling music as they share their first kiss in front of the iconic statue at Two Lovers Point.

Justice must've scheduled this call so Kopar wouldn't see it, but with famous actors like Cadence and Abernathy, he won't be able to escape it. They'll rerun it at all hours. *Poor Kopar.* I press a hand to my heart, unable to imagine myself in his shoes.

"So that's it? You're mine one day, and his the next?" Kopar's voice breaks.

Justice drops her head into her hands. "I'm so sorry! I didn't have any idea this feeling was even possible."

"*Dammit, Justice! Stop saying* my love isn't good enough!"

"I'm not! Try to understand." She breaks into sobs.

I climb off the bed and pace back and forth, keeping my eyes on the screen.

Another minute passes and Justice sniffles. "I was worried about this."

"About what?" Kopar presses the corner of his eye.

"That you'd be . . . jealous."

"Isn't jealousy a *completely rational* reaction? I just found out my *girlfriend* has a soulmate." He raises an open hand. "How am I supposed to feel?"

"It's not that. Of course you can—you *should*—feel however you feel." Justice tucks her chin. "But . . . we're *concerned* this might trigger you, like before."

Kopar's mouth falls open. "Justice, that was *three lifetimes ago*! You think MIT would give me a full ride if they thought I was a threat to anyone?" Betrayal clouds his eyes. "Wait. How did you know about that?"

I stop in my tracks. Vivi and Corah told me about Kopar's misdemeanor but said it was just an unruly conduct charge. He didn't hurt anybody. Justice, on the other hand . . .

She tugs at a curl. "You know I'm not good with surprises."

"You looked me up! What the fuck, Justice? We promised each other!"

"No, *you* asked *me* not to look in SEIK. Then you were gone for five days, and I started to wonder why you didn't want me to search for you. Like"—she wipes a tear—"maybe your *soul* was hiding something from me."

Kopar barks out a humorless laugh.

"So, I thought it was safer to look, to get a heads-up in case I needed to be careful about anything in your past." She leans in. "And *see*, I was right to check!"

"We've dated almost a year, Justice. If I was going to hurt you, don't you think you would've seen a sign of that already?" Kopar's mouth clamps shut, and he sits taller. "Is that why you insisted on a call instead of coming over?"

"Can you *blame* me?" Justice takes a calming breath. "Considering your history, Cadence and I thought it best if you and I didn't see each other for a while. Until, you know, things calm down."

"You just met Cadence this *morning*, and you're already talking to him about me?"

"I didn't just meet him. We've shared *six lives*! I trust him more than anybody."

Kopar gasps in pain. How can she be so cruel? I climb back on the bed and wrap my arms around Vivi and Corah, who are silently crying. The tears filling my own eyes make it hard to focus.

Kopar huffs. "Wow. Ya know, I always thought you were an amazing actor. I just didn't realize how much acting you were doing. Well, have a fucking fantastic life with your soulmate, Abernathy, and do me a favor..." He looks directly into the camera. "Keep your soul away from mine, in this life, and the next, and the next. I hope I never see you again."

He ends the call, but not before we hear Justice's sorrowful wail. I croak in disbelief before slapping a hand over my mouth. What just happened? How could their seemingly perfect relationship spiral down the drain so fast? My stomach roils. If love can be this painful, I don't want it. Not before my kirling. Maybe not ever.

Kopar whimpers and wipes his nose with the heel of his hand, then rushes from his room. The front door slams.

Vivi, her face blotchy and wet, clambers off the bed and darts into the hallway. On the screen, we watch her enter Kopar's room. She grabs at the bug, and the picture goes black. A second later, the toilet flushes.

Kopar doesn't come home all night.

Soulmates

Soulmates—n. Two souls with a 99 percent (or greater) match in their souls' light patterns.

Saturday, August 25, 236 A.K.—Day Two at SKI

"Despite centuries of research, many phenomena still escape scientific explanation," Windrose begins the next morning. "First, the large variance in deathspans. Some souls are reborn immediately, while a rare few go decades between lives. Evidence suggests souls with criminal records are reborn sooner than others, but that's not always true."

I take a sip of hot tea and bulge my eyes wide, trying to hold them open after another restless night.

"We have no way of knowing where souls go during their deathspans," she continues. "The religions of centuries past provided various speculations. But religions fell apart once humanity came to terms with our souls' inevitable rebirths and the confusion from practicing, for example, the Christian faith in one life and Buddhism in the next.

"We do know that souls interact with the same ones in every life, creating inexplicable networks of intertwined souls. However, souls can integrate with other networks. Picture a cluster of nerves with ends reaching toward other clusters."

Bardou, who's propping up his face with his hands, mumbles, "I don't understand anything you're saying."

He isn't wearing sunglasses today, and his eyes are crystal-clear blue, a striking contrast with his amber skin. If he wasn't such an ass, I might describe him as gorgeous, but nope.

He drops his hands. "Can someone explain this in English?"

I huff. "She's basically saying no one has any idea where we go when we die or why some souls take longer than others to come back."

"And if you're a jerk to someone in this life, they could make your next one miserable," says Dikela.

"Uh-huh, thanks, Dickella."

Her eyes narrow. "Off to a good start, then. Karma's a bitch."

"So is your mom." Bardou slides on his sunglasses and leans back in his chair.

I open my mouth to snap back, but Windrose raises her voice. "There's one more rarity, which is our first topic of discussion today—soulmates."

I sit straighter, Bardou forgotten.

"Soulmates have near-identical soulids, but matching light patterns don't explain why they share similar life cycles. And we're not sure why they only come in pairs, not groups of three or more. While popular culture romanticizes intense love matches, soulmates are often finely tuned platonic relationships, a symbiotic partnership. How many of you know a pair of soulmates?"

I thrust my hand up, but no one else does.

"Lovely. Could you share a little about the couple, Sivon?"

"I actually know two sets of soulmates and half of another pair."

"My goodness, three couples!"

"Three couples!" Bardou echoes.

I stealthily push a lock of hair behind my ear with my middle finger. "Yes, they're all kinda related. My best friends are soulmates. They're identical twins, so that wasn't a surprise. Their parents are also soulmates. And the half is the ex-girlfriend of their son, the twins' brother. He's eight years older than me, so I only knew her a little before they broke up."

"What an intriguing network of souls! I wonder if there's a correlation between *being* soulmates and *giving birth* to soulmates." She types notes in the air.

"No one else has met soulmates?" I ask.

The group remains quiet.

"They aren't common," Windrose explains. "Around ten million soulmates are registered in SEIK, or five million couples. Out of fifteen billion souls, that's less than one-tenth of a percent. So, I'm sorry to say, it's unlikely any of you have one. You can still form loving, healthy, and passionate relationships with others, but you aren't often with the same soul again, as a couple, in your next lives, or nelies."

"That's depressing," says purple-haired Norine.

"It depends how you look at it. Remember the soul networks I explained earlier? You will see your loved ones again, but your life spans probably won't match the way they do in this life."

Exactly why I haven't gotten serious with anyone. Who can I trust with my heart if they'll eventually abandon me in this life or the next?

Perhaps sensing we're no longer interested in talking about soulmates, she changes topics. "Let's discuss inheritances."

Dikela claps. "*Yes.* That's why I'm here."

Her excitement is contagious. We all break into smiles.

"Most of you will receive savings from your folies this week. The average inheritance is fifty thousand valuts, but one of my recent charges inherited seventy-five million."

I raise my brows, having a good idea of who she means. I'm still amazed that Vivi and Corah came out of SKI with their dream jobs, confirmation they're soulmates, and enough money to last two dozen lifetimes. If I get only one of the three, I'll be happy.

"We recommend consulting a financial adviser upon your release to create a budget and investment strategy for your inheritance. Per regulations, SKI provides a future-life estate attorney to update your next will and testament. Regardless of your results, you'll meet that attorney on Tuesday, the day after your kirling.

"And with that, our group is adjourned. Please check your schedules for your one-on-one consultation time later today. I'll see you soon."

"Anyone else feel like hurling when Windrose started talking about passionate relationships?" Bardou kisses Ziva's cheek and sits beside her on one of the lounge's pill-shaped rockers. "It was like picturing my gramps and granny hooking up." He shudders dramatically.

"You've been waiting hours to bring that up, haven't you?" I snark.

"Any excuse to talk about sex," Dikela says.

"It *is* my favorite pastime." He winks at Ziva. She returns a playful smile.

Dikela makes a disgusted face. "Uh, no. We don't wanna hear about any of that."

"*Sorry.*" Ziva bites her bottom lip.

Dikela runs a hand over her tight-cropped curls. "Don't get me wrong. I'm glad you're in a good mood. Tomorrow's your big day and all. What did you talk about in *your* group today?"

"Our talents and turnoffs, stuff like that." Ziva takes a sip of water. "They say whatever we're good at today is likely what we excelled at in our folies too."

Bardou smirks. He opens his mouth to say something, gets a stare-down from Dikela, and clamps it shut.

Ziva palms her forehead. "Shit. I walked right into that one."

"So, what *are* your interests?" I ask her.

"Gosh, so many things. I love baking and dancing, and I'm a *huge* fan of Cadence and Abernathy. I know I can't be one of them since they just died last year, but maybe I was in one of their movies, or the director of *When We Meet Again*, which is my all-time favorite."

"Oh, I love that one too," I say. "How does the line go? 'This isn't the beginning, nor is it the end. This life is merely...'"

Ziva and I stretch our hands toward each other, chorusing, "'A page in the story of our souls.'"

Dikela fake swoons, and we break into laughter.

Bardou scratches his head, looking completely clueless.

I don't mention that I knew Abernathy before she was Abernathy. Only eight years ago, she sat in this same lounge, probably telling her friends about Kopar. A few days later, she discovered what true love really is. It was heartbreaking to read about Cadence's and Abernathy's recent deaths, but at least they'll be together again soon.

"Dikela, any clue who you were before, based on your talents?"

Bardou raises a hand.

Ziva tugs it down. "Her folies don't matter. She's already a professional model."

"Seriously?" It makes sense, though, given her high cheekbones, long neck, and enviable curves.

"What? You didn't recognize me from the Culi Collection runway show?" She touches her fingertips to her cheeks and bats her lashes before swatting my shoulder.

Ziva sets down her water glass. "She's already got contracts lined up all year."

Dikela waves her off. "All that will mean nothing if I get shipped off to prison."

"You won't," Bardou says. "I know a criminal when I see one."

"Takes one to know one," Dikela murmurs.

Bardou leans forward. "My bet is on that redhead, Rory. It's always the nice ones you gotta look out for."

I quirk a brow.

Ziva studies me. "I bet Sivon was raking in valuts in Baja Vegas."

"Ew, I hope not." I lift a hand. "Nothing against a career as a professional gambler, but at minimum I hope to do something that makes a difference. Just clueless as to what." I rock my chair. "Did you do that creative writing assignment in eighth grade, when we guessed our folies and put them in a time capsule?"

"Oh yeah!" Ziva grins. "I think I wrote about being a ballerina."

"I said I was a doctor." Dikela huffs. "Which is impossible because I can't stand the sight of blood."

Bardou frowns. "What the fuck is a time capsule?"

"My point is, I could never imagine who my soul was. I wrote about my soulmate's past lives instead."

"*Ooh*. You think you have a soulmate?" Ziva tips forward.

"I grew up with soulmate best friends who have soulmate parents. It was hard to imagine anything *but* having one of my own."

"And maybe you will. What about you, Bardou?" Ziva asks. "Who do you think you were?"

He shrugs. "I already know."

Dikela, being mid-sip, spits her water at him. "What did you say?"

"I *said* I already know who I was." Bardou wipes his face with the bottom of his tee.

I squint. "Are you bullshitting us?"

"Why would I bullshit you?"

I cross my arms. "Your kirling is two days away. How the hell do you *know* who you were in your folies?"

Bardou takes a long sip of water, soaking up the attention. He swallows and smiles. "Because I live in the Fringe."

"Stop it." Ziva whacks his arm. "Why didn't you tell me that last night?"

"Well, Red, I don't remember doing much talking last night."

Dikela holds a hand in his face. "Okay, okay. So you live in the Fringe. *How*, exactly, did you get your kirling results early?"

"You've never been?" Bardou asks.

Dikela silently checks with me and Ziva before responding. "*Why* would we go to the Fringe?"

"Because it's fucking awesome."

"*Bardou*, tell us!" begs Ziva.

"Okay, Red, settle down." He checks over his shoulder to make sure no one is listening. "Gather round, children, and I'll tell you a bedtime story."

Dikela and I trade skeptical glances, then shift our rockers toward the two of them.

Bardou leans forward, resting his foot on the opposite knee. "Once upon a time, a *beautiful, brilliant* boy was born in the Fringe."

I burst out laughing. Ziva and Dikela join in.

Bardou brushes his shoulder. "When he was ten years old, such a spitfire he was, his mother took him to see the *Hidden One*." His voice lowers ominously. "The *Hidden One* took a good look at the boy and proclaimed, 'You, son, are a bad soul!' Bwa-ha-ha-ha-ha!"

Dikela scratches her neck. "I can't."

With a seated bow, Bardou adds, "The end."

Dikela, Ziva, and I trade confused looks.

"Someone in the Fringe did a kirling for you? When you were *ten*?" I ask. He can't be serious. "That's illegal. And downright horrible. Who would do that to a *kid*?"

Bardou shrugs. "Everywhere you go in the Fringe, someone is offering to do a kirling. They all claim they can access SEIK, but most are charlatans scamming parents out of money. This one guy can really do it, though. Real scum-of-the-earth type. Goes by the soulname Yinbi." Bardou's lips pull down.

He shifts his rocker back to focus on the ceiling. "I was this asshole kid, and my parents were worried about me. Took me to Yinbi, he did the thing . . ." Bardou clicks his tongue a few times. "Found out I was a girl in my last life and have three years to serve for stealing a hover." He sits upright. "My parents were *so* relieved."

I squint at him. "Your parents were *relieved* you're a criminal?"

"Yeah, I mean, just a little grand larceny. At least they knew I wasn't gonna kill them in their sleep. Harmless."

"*Harmless?*" Dikela asks.

"Yeah, Dickella. Harmless."

"You *stole* a hover vehicle."

He raises one shoulder. "Could be worse. And maybe I had a good reason. What if I needed the hover to get someone I loved to the hospital? Or sold it to feed my kids? Maybe I used it to escape from a husband who was beating me."

Ziva wakes from her stunned silence. "When do you have to serve your sentence? Will you go to jail after your kirling?"

"You really don't know anything about the Fringe, do you? Look, if you're born in the Fringe, you're still required to do your kirling, but that's it. The North American Peace Accord guarantees our right to a separate judicial system, and we don't serve time for crimes in past lives. Our kirling results are stored in SEIK, but they aren't published until our next lives . . . or if we decide to leave the Fringe for some reason. So, I'm off the hook, in this life, at least."

Dikela slumps into her rocker. "Whoa."

I can't imagine passing along a prison sentence to my neli, to have that hanging over me every day. Shouldn't he just get it over with?

"So you can't leave the Fringe?" Ziva asks.

"Not in this life, but I'd rather live there than out here, anyway." Bardou runs a thumb across her cheek. "You're welcome to visit anytime, Red."

Ziva scrunches her nose and takes his hand. "My family would never let me, especially Donovan. Was a time my sister, Golds, would've happily punted me into the Fringe." She rolls her eyes. "But we've gotten closer this year. She even slept in my bed the night before I left for SKI, like when we were kids."

"Aw, that's so sweet. How old is she?" I ask.

"Sixteen."

"So you have two siblings?"

"Four, actually. Donovan is the oldest, about to turn twenty. He was five and I was three when my parents adopted him. Golds is my only biological sibling. Three years ago, my parents also adopted Edin—he's twelve—and Linzy—she's nine. They're biological siblings too."

"I can't imagine that many brothers and sisters." Mom would never get anything done with five children running around the studio.

"This may sound rude—" Bardou says.

"How out of character." Dikela takes a sip of water.

He ignores her, asking Ziva, "Are your parents souldiggers?"

I press my lips together, unwilling to admit that I thought the same thing. A shocking number of parents create large families in hopes of "striking it rich" with their children's inheritances.

"Oh, no, my mom is a pediatric nurse at the children's hospital," Ziva says. "Kids are dropped off all the time, like left there."

My jaw drops. "Wait, parents just *abandon* their children at the hospital?"

"It happens. More than you can imagine."

"*Seriously?* Those poor kids!" My stomach tightens imagining how terrified, confused, and dejected they must feel.

"Yeah. Mom gets so distraught when it happens, she cries all night. Edin was nine years old, and Linzy was six at the time, so it's something they'll always remember."

Bardou bears a serious expression for once. "Parents do that a lot in the Fringe too. I consider myself lucky, acting the way I did back then...."

"I don't get it," I say. "Who could just ditch their own flesh and blood?"

"Maybe they're doing what they think is best for them." Ziva takes Bardou's hand in hers. "I'd do anything to protect my family. Even if that means leaving them behind. Wouldn't you?"

Bardou and Dikela nod, but I remain silent. I could never do that to a loved one, no matter the reason. I'd fight for them until my very last breath.

"Good evening, Sivon. I apologize for the late hour." Windrose looks exhausted.

"It's okay." I can't imagine doing her job, dealing with stressed out teens day after day. "How long have you worked at SKI?"

"Coming up on my thirty-eighth anniversary," she states humbly while flitting through data on her specs.

"Thirty-eight years doing the same thing every day?" My face flushes at the unintentional insult.

"It's more interesting than you might expect." She stops scrolling. "That's enough about me. We only have fifteen minutes, so I'd like to discuss your survey responses. You wrote that you're worried you won't like your soul."

Ugh, more talk about our fears? Can't we go back to soulmates or inheritances? I heave a sigh. "Yeah, I mean, what if I was a criminal, or Flavinsky, or, I don't know, a dog groomer?"

She chuckles. "Not a fan of pets?"

I shrug. "My neighbor keeps a boxer chained in her yard. It acts like it wants to rip my head off every time I jog by."

Windrose tilts her head. "That poor dog is acting out of fear.

Most animals can run if they're attacked, but the boxer's only defense is to prevent attacks in the first place. He's a product of his environment, not his nature." She waits for me to make the connection.

"So, you're saying if I *was* a criminal, it's because I was born into bad circumstances, not that my soul is bad?"

She smiles.

After more reflection, I add, "But your analogy doesn't explain Flavinsky. They were born into bad circumstances ten consecutive times?"

Windrose pinches the skin at her throat. "Remember Flavinsky is only one soul in fifteen *billion*."

"But what if I am Flavinsky?"

She clasps her hands. "In the unlikely event you are Flavinsky, you'll break the cycle. Like the terrorist Pulsar, you'll accept your sentence and make the best of it. You may lose your freedom in this life, but you'll do your neli a favor instead of propagating the myth that you're fated to repeat your tragic death in every life."

She leans back on her couch. "But Flavinsky isn't the only soul who has or will take their life. Despite anti-suicide laws, plenty of souls can't come to terms with their kirling results. Others fear their family's reaction or retribution. My chief concern for you, then—"

I wave a hand. "Stop, Windrose, stop. I'd never take my life, wouldn't even consider it. And my mom will love me no matter what—good, bad, or Flavinsky."

She purses her lips. "Well, that's reassuring. But we'll revisit this discussion after your kirling. SKI does provide life-preserving resources when needed, which can be implemented at either your or my discretion."

I clamp my mouth shut. If I say anything else, she'll probably overanalyze my every word.

"That's the end of our time. We'll have our next one-on-one after your kirling, but I'll see you for the next group discussion tomorrow at . . . three thirty p.m. Sweet dreams."

Yeah, fat chance. I'd have to actually sleep to have dreams, sweet or otherwise.

SKI Patrol

SKI Patrol—n. A member of the Semyon Kirlian Institute security and protection force.

Sunday, August 26, 236 A.K.—Day Three at SKI

I check the clock on my screen for the third time this hour: 4:49 a.m. I've tried blackening my window, following a guided meditation module, and turning on white noise. Nothing works. My mind spins with speculations about my kirling. Less than thirty hours from now, my past will be known, my future decided.

The one time I started to nod off, a nightmare of children crying for their parents startled me awake. Do I even want to sleep if dreams like that await me? *Screw it.* I rip off the covers, plod over to my duffel bag, and rummage through it until I find a sports bra and black running shorts. If I can't get rid of this restless energy, I'll put it to use instead.

I expect the gym to be empty, but at least two dozen others are working out inside. The room is roughly the same size as the lounge, and scattered throughout, holo personal trainers model a variety of exercises. In one corner, a guy skis downhill, near vertical in the simulator. Beside him, someone races a cyclo at breakneck speed over virtual mountains.

I search for open machines and spot an older model treadmill.

It won't have the ability to switch terrain from road to grass or sand, but at least it has variable gravity settings. And even better, Ziva is running on the one beside it.

"Hey. Couldn't sleep either?"

She shakes her head, issuing a winded "No." Sweat coats her face and shirt.

"What time is your kirling today?"

"Not . . . until . . . four."

"Damn, that sucks."

Ziva slows the pace. "Hoping to exhaust my body enough to"—big inhale—"take a nap later to"—deep breath—"sleep away some of the hours."

"Pretty sure that'll be my plan tomorrow." I start a warm-up jog.

After another minute of cooldown, Ziva says, "This would be *so* much easier if SKI didn't cut us off from everyone. I've never wanted to talk to Mom or Golds so badly." She yanks her towel off the railing and wipes her face with shaky hands. "I'd even take one of Donovan's bear hugs about now. Can't fucking breathe when he does it, but they always make me laugh."

"He seems pretty great." My heart twinges with homesickness.

"He has his moments." Ziva slows her treadmill to a walk and resets the gravity. "Know how I said I'd do anything for my family? Multiply that tenfold for Donovan. He'll probably be waiting outside when I'm released in case someone has it in for my soul. They wouldn't stand a chance."

"Can you send him back the next day to protect me too?" I never did find a self-defense class on the schedule.

"You've got it," she says, but I can tell her mind is elsewhere. She steps off the treadmill and bends over, hands on her knees.

"Are you all right?" I turn off my machine, slowly coming to a stop.

"I'll be okay." She rises back up, wincing. "Won't I?"

"Of course you'll be okay." I step down and squeeze her shoulder. "You're gonna go in there, figure out who you were, get a ginormous inheritance, learn Bardou is your soulmate, and live happily ever after."

She snorts. "I was with you till Bardou. He's been a much-needed distraction, but we both know it's just a fling. Besides, he would've bragged about a soulmate if he had one."

I chuckle. "You're probably right."

Her lips bunch to one side. "I guess I'll try to get some rest, but I'm glad I ran into you."

"Same. And I can't wait to hear your results tonight." I step back onto the tread. "Good luck, Ziva!"

"Thanks." She wipes her forehead. "Whew! I cannot wait for this to be over."

When I approach our dinner table, Dikela is mid-argument with Bardou.

"Why can't you be nice? No, *screw nice*, why can't you just be quiet?"

"He's annoying. I can't help myself." Bardou chomps on a sweet potato chip, unrepentant.

I guess they're talking about Rory, the poor guy.

In our meeting with Windrose this afternoon, we explored our talents and interests and how they could match our results. Rory said he enjoys his summer job, donning holo costumes for kids' birthday parties. Windrose suggested that perhaps Rory was an actor or a teacher in his former lives, but Bardou snapped his fingers and said, "That's it! You used to be Giuseppe Giraffe."

Giuseppe Giraffe, the cartoon character.

"*C'mon.* He looks just like Giuseppe. Back me up, Sivon." Bardou crunches another chip.

"Sorry, I'm with Dikela on this one. Windrose was right to mute you."

Dikela crosses her arms and tilts her head.

Bardou pushes away his tray. "*Man*, none of you have a sense of humor out here. My friends back home would've pissed themselves laughing."

"Yet another reason I'll never go to the Fringe. Sounds like a *whole town* of dumbasses." Dikela rubs her head. "I don't know what Ziva sees in you. If she was in our group, she wouldn't have given you a second look."

"I'll take my luck where I can get it."

"Where is Ziva, anyway?" I search the atrium. "I'm excited to hear her results. Have either of you spoken with her?"

Bardou scratches his neck. "Left her room around midnight. Haven't seen her today."

Dikela turns to scan the room. "We had lunch together. She was so nervous, her hands were shaking. But she said she had three espressos this morning, so I figured she just overcaffeinated. We even laughed about it."

"I'm sure she's just running late." I stand to get a better view, realizing most people are hunched over their tables, whispering in groups. When did it get so quiet in here?

In the distance, a girl scampers from one huddle to another. Goose bumps rise on my arms.

Bardou stands and turns in a slow circle. A girl walks behind him, and he stops her by the crook of her arm. "Hey," he whispers. "What's going on?"

Her eyes bulge. "Didn't you hear? Flavinsky was kirled today."

I squint in disbelief. "That wouldn't be public yet."

She shrugs. "It's what everyone is saying. Flavinsky is *here*! At *this SKI*. Can you believe it? *So* relieved I don't need to worry about *that* anymore." She flits away to another group.

I inspect the room for Ziva again. *Where the hell is she?*

"You don't think—?" Dikela starts.

"No," I interrupt. "There's no way."

"No fucking way," says Bardou.

I train my eyes on the elevator, willing the doors to open and for Ziva to step out. "It's someone from her group, is all. She didn't come to dinner because she was upset about it."

"We should check on her." Dikela rises.

"I'm not on her floor." Bardou's face has drained of color. "My fingerprint won't allow me access."

"I'm not either. What floor are you, Sivon?"

"Five. What's hers?"

"Seven," they reply.

Remain calm. Flavinsky is one soul of fifteen billion. Even if the news is true, even if Flavinsky is here, they'd be one soul out of a thousand. Today alone, almost two hundred people were kirled. One in two hundred are impossible odds. She's fine.

I weigh our options. "Okay, no big deal. We just need to find someone on the seventh floor to take us up."

"Purple hair!" Bardou scans the atrium. "What's her name? Doreen?"

"Norine?"

"She got off the elevator with us last night." He takes off toward the frizzy purple hair in the far corner.

Dikela and I abandon our trays to chase after him.

"Norine?" He taps her shoulder.

She spins around and narrows her eyes. "What do you want?"

"Hey, um, I . . . I mean we"—he gestures at us—"need a favor."

Dikela steps forward. "Can you get us onto the seventh floor? We need to check on a friend."

"Please." I press my hands together in front of my lips.

Norine's face blanches, and her entire table stares at us in horror. She wipes her mouth with a napkin. "I guess we can try. A bunch of patrols got off the elevator when I was heading down here."

My heart sinks. That's not a good sign.

"No wonder everyone knows," Bardou whispers as we rush across the atrium toward the elevators. "Like no one would notice a herd of assholes storming through the building."

"Shut up!" Dikela hisses, whisking away a tear.

I jog forward and grab her hand. "Don't worry. Ziva probably couldn't get downstairs because of the patrols."

How many of the two hundred people kirled today are staying on the seventh floor? One in twenty-five? Those are still good odds, but I liked them a whole hell of a lot better when they were one in fifteen billion.

We step onto the elevator with Norine, and she presses her finger to the sensor before selecting the number seven. Bardou shifts his weight back and forth. I squeeze Dikela's hand and count the floors in my head as the numbers light up. *Four, five, six . . .*

When the doors finally open, a bellowing voice echoes down the hallway. Dikela and I exchange fearful glances and lean out the elevator.

"... know who I am? Open the door!" shouts a man in a community protector uniform.

He's screaming at an emotionless SKI Patrol stationed outside a room halfway down the hallway. I count six red-lit doorknobs between us.

"You are Shepherd, soul ID 6HEPR0D."

Shepherd. Donovan's soulname. Ziva's brother is here? I cover my mouth with my free hand, refusing to acknowledge what that means.

"Your profession grants you no jurisdiction here," the patrol continues. "Please exit the building in an orderly manner."

It's a RAID. Why would they station a robot outside Ziva's room? We're not allowed to see her? This feels so *wrong*. Did I fall into another nightmare? With all the talk of kirlings and Flavinsky and Ziva's family, my mind must've conjured this incredibly vivid and terrifying dream. Ziva *cannot* be Flavinsky. I would've known if the girl I hung out with the past few days was one of the most tragic souls in history.

Donovan squeezes his eyes shut. "I'm her brother. Doesn't that mean anything?"

"Family members are twenty-five percent more likely than others to harm recently kirled criminals."

Donovan's hands form fists. "She's not a criminal, you fucking RAID!" He visibly trembles while tamping down his rage.

How do I fix this? Maybe sending someone who knows both

Donovan and Ziva would help? Dikela quakes beside me. I drop her hand and give her a nudge.

She stumbles out of the elevator, then breaks into a sprint. "Donovan!"

Bardou steps up beside me. We watch as stunned observers as Donovan hugs Dikela. She's tall, but he seems to tower over her.

"Is it true? Is Ziva Flavinsky?" she asks.

He rubs his eyes. "It must be a mistake."

"Shepherd, your building access has been revoked," the patrol says to his back. "Leave now, or you'll be forcibly removed."

"Kiss my ass," Donovan hurls over his shoulder.

The elevator dings, and the doors begin closing on me and Bardou. We push them back open but keep our safe distance. I pinch my arm, hoping to wake up any minute now.

Donovan sneers at us. "What the hell are you staring at?"

His animosity crushes my thundering heart. This isn't real. *Wake up. Wake up. Wake up.*

Dikela grabs his lapels. "Donovan, what's going on?"

"Ziva's on suicide watch. They put a *fucking stranger* in there but won't let in her own brother."

The patrol advances by a step. "Backup is on the way."

"Dammit." Donovan releases Dikela. "Ziva! Don't you dare give up! We'll figure this out. *Do you hear me?"* His voice cracks on the last word, shattering any remaining crystals of hope.

This isn't a dream. Ziva is Flavinsky. And Flavinsky kills themself after every kirling. And Shepherd is Donovan, and Donovan is Ziva's brother, and I'm just standing here, doing nothing to help them. What can I do? I don't know what to do.

The patrol reaches toward Donovan's arm.

"Don't touch me!" Donovan shrugs out of its grip and begins retreating. He brings his joined hands to his heart. "Please, don't leave her, Dikela."

"I won't. I promise I won't." She turns and shouts "Ziva!" before crumpling to the floor.

Donovan pushes his way into the elevator as Norine, Bardou, and I stumble out. My heart clenches at the agony and frustration on his face. I take an involuntary step toward him. *Do something, Sivon. Say something.*

My lips part, breaths coming faster. *This is your chance. Help him, before it's too late.* Panicking, my mind offers up a myriad of nonsensical moves. I can't just hug a stranger or attack a SKI Patrol.

The doors begin closing. At the last second, Donovan lifts his head, looking directly into my eyes with nothing but pure, searing hatred. The doors shut.

I stumble backward, tears of embarrassment and shame stinging my eyes. How could I just stand here doing nothing? I eye the staircase door and consider running after him, but what would that solve? We need to save Ziva.

I jog over to Dikela, who's slumped over on the white marble floor. I fall to my knees and wrap my arms around her.

"Ziva. Ziva. Ziva," she whispers, as if saying the name will make her appear.

Bardou saunters up to the patrol and clears his throat. "Hello, sir. We're Ziva's friends. Could you let us in to see her . . . please?"

Dikela stops crying, and we look up at Bardou in confusion. Did he just use *manners*?

The patrol peers down at Bardou. "You're not authorized for entry."

I heard private security companies were using RAIDs, but not our government. He... It... looks so human, except for the soulless eyes.

"What about Dikela?" Bardou points to her. "They've been friends for ten years. Don't you have some statistics proving that friends can help prevent suicides?"

"Ziva is safe in her room, and no visitors are allowed. I have orders to keep people from congregating in the hallway. Please disperse."

"*No*," Dikela cries. "I promised I wouldn't leave. I won't leave her!"

This is bullshit. We're not hurting anyone out here. And if I was Flavinsky, I'd want to know my friends and family were here for me. "Can you give her a message?"

"Only from select individuals."

I hold back a groan of frustration. "Who are the select individuals?"

"I'm not at liberty to say. Please disperse."

Would I get kicked out for slapping a SKI Patrol?

Norine bends down. "You can come to my room, Dikela. I'm right next door. Maybe we can talk to Ziva through the wall."

Dikela cries a few more seconds before nodding. Bardou and Norine each take an arm to help her stand, and I scramble up after them, eager to try something different.

Norine ushers us into her room, and Dikela rushes to the wall separating us from Ziva. She crouches and knocks. "Ziva? Ziva! Can you hear me?"

"I don't think she'll hear you," Bardou mutters.

"Fuck you!" Dikela shouts.

"No, listen." He squats down, holding out his hands. "Think about it. Have you heard anyone else in their rooms? Playing music? Walking around?"

He's right. I haven't even heard anyone in the hallway. The walls are soundproof.

"See what I mean?"

Dikela slumps against the wall and starts sobbing again. I groan with frustration. Why would SKI sequester people on suicide watch away from their friends and loved ones? It makes no sense. Any one of us would gladly sit with Ziva all night. I lay my hand against the wall. *We're right here, Ziva. We're right beside you.*

"What if we try to call her?" I sit beside Dikela and pull her to me.

Norine activates her screen and scrolls through the directory. "Her name is grayed out."

"Try Windrose?"

"Hers is grayed out too. All the counselors are."

I roll my eyes. *Great, just when we need them most.* "What about the Advertitude? Can we place an ad from inside SKI?"

Norine shakes her head. "We're cut off in here. Besides, we're on the opposite side of the building. She wouldn't see the message from her window."

I pound my forehead with my free hand. *Think, Sivon. You have to save Ziva.* The ceiling? It's smooth from wall to wall. No way to climb up and over. Slipping a note under her door? Maybe if we distract the patrol, but where would we find something to write on or with? I haven't held a piece of paper since Mom gave me five sheets for my eighth birthday with a set of homemade crayons.

Ugh, this is impossible!

I turn to Bardou. "Will you ask the patrol when we can see her?"

He nods and exits the room, leaving the door ajar. He returns a minute later and crouches in front of Dikela. "The suicide watch lasts twenty-four hours. They may allow visitors after that. So hopefully, we'll see her tomorrow afternoon. Okay?"

Dikela nods through her tears, biting her top lip.

"It's just one day. If I know Ziva like I think I do, she's strong enough to make it through one day. And once she's through the first, she'll make it through the next and so on. You know I'm right." He takes Dikela's chin between his thumb and index finger, encouraging her to look at him.

She complies, tears spilling from her eyes. When I asked Windrose what would happen if I was Flavinsky, she said, *You'll break the cycle.*

Ziva said she'd protect her family no matter what, even if it meant abandoning them. But taking her life would only hurt her family. She must know that. Right? I run my hands through my hair.

"You're welcome to stay here tonight, Dikela," says Norine. "I didn't want to be alone the night before my kirling, anyway. You'd be doing me a favor."

She holds out a hand to Dikela, who shakily accepts it. Norine turns down the covers of the bed, and Dikela slips in with punctuated gasps of air.

I stand and squeeze Dikela's hand. "You'll be okay?"

She closes her eyes and whimpers. Fresh tears cover her face.

"I'll take care of her," Norine says.

She follows Bardou and me to the door, but just as she begins shutting it behind us, Dikela croaks, "Can we leave it cracked?"

Norine nods and disappears from our line of sight.

Smart. With the patrol stationed next door, they'll hear if anyone comes or goes from Ziva's room.

I take another weary look at the disaffected patrol before shuffling toward the elevators, utterly helpless.

SKI is doing more for Ziva than just assigning a couple of patrols, right? Windrose mentioned life-preserving measures during our call last night. Maybe Ziva is talking with a counselor at this very minute, getting whatever support and medication she needs to help her process her results. That's literally why they keep us here an extra day.

I knead circles and Xs into my hands, reassuring myself Ziva will get through this. I'll see her tomorrow, right after my own kirling.

My stomach tightens. My kirling is *tomorrow*. I inhale sharply, fighting off the fear. I can't think about my kirling right now.

We reach the elevator. Bardou grabs his hands behind his head and whimpers.

"Are *you* okay?" I ask.

His arms flop by his side. "Yeah. I mean, I knew I wouldn't see Ziva after tomorrow. But she's *so fucking awesome*, Sivon." He shakes his head. "It's just not right."

The elevator doors part, ripping the bronze butterfly in half. SKI is nothing like Vivi and Corah described. How could they have enjoyed this place that I hate with every fiber of my being?

"It's not right," Bardou repeats as we step inside. The doors close behind us, and we begin our descent.

Soulid

soulid—(SOE-lid) Single word created by combining *soul* and *ID*. 1. n. The unique light pattern issuing from a person's soul. 2. n. The randomly generated seven-digit alphanumeric ID assigned to a soul.

Monday, June 26, 236 A.K.—TWO MONTHS AGO—Ashburn, VA

Before I ring the doorbell, Vivi throws open the door to their sprawling one-story home. She and Corah rush out, squealing, and embrace me in a "Sivon sandwich." We jump in a circle, laughing. They called to tell me their results as soon as they left SKI today, but I'd already looked them up in SEIK.

"Are they gone?" I ask, referring to the North American Intelligence agents who were on their front porch when they got home.

"Yes!" they shout, still jumping.

"Why was NAIA here?" I ask, giggling because they're obviously excited about whatever it was. If intelligence agents had been standing on my front porch when I returned from SKI, I doubt I'd be smiling about it.

"They want us to work for them!" Vivi says.

"Are you *shitting* me?" I shout and slap my hand over my mouth. We burst out laughing.

They haul me into their house, and I call a greeting to their parents before we shut ourselves into Corah's room. She claimed Kopar's bedroom after he graduated from MIT four years ago.

A holoshield now occupies a significant portion of the adjoining bedroom wall. The electronic partition has four possible transparency and sound settings, allowing Vivi and Corah to control their privacy. But as usual, the holoshield isn't on today, leaving an open window.

We climb onto Corah's bed, and I tuck a pillow into my lap. "Okay, okay. Start from the beginning. Were you roommates at SKI?" We took a field trip to the institute in seventh grade, and I still remember how the massive building made me feel so insignificant and powerless. Pretty sure that's when the nightmares started.

Corah snarls. "No, different floors *and* orientation groups."

"Oh man." I wrinkle my nose.

"Did you like your counselors?"

"Meh," says Corah. "Mine was *obviously* still in training. He kept repeating, 'Hope for the best, prepare for the worst.' I would've stopped attending the group meetings if he wasn't so damn hot."

I squeal and push her over.

Eyes twinkling, Corah rights herself and separates her black hair like a curtain. "Tell Sivon about your counselor, Viv."

"Oh, I *loved* her! In our one-on-one discussions, we talked about my connection with Corah, what I want out of life, and how my results could change that."

"That sounds perfect, actually. So, was your kirling scary?"

"More weird than scary," Vivi says. "I thought the kirling chamber would be white, like an operating room, but it was all black."

Corah narrows her eyes. "More like a dark gray."

"Okay, dark gray, whatever. So they attach these diodes to your neck and shoulders, little *dark gray* circles." She nudges Corah's leg, who rolls her eyes. "I can't remember how many. Like, over thirty. And they make you wear a rubber cap with diodes built in. Kinda like a swim cap. Then they activate them, but they do it two by two."

"It would be overwhelming to turn them on at once," Corah says. "They buzz. It's not painful, but it's a little overwhelming, especially when they're all on."

Vivi places her hand on my shoulder. "A girl we met this week fainted during her kirling."

"What? That's *awful*!"

Corah nods. "I know! She hit her head on the concrete floor and went to the emergency room. She's okay now. But imagine you're about to find out who you were, and you wake up in the hospital instead. I'd be pissed."

I press my thumb into my palm. *Circle X*. "That'll happen to me too. Something shitty like that. I know it."

Corah pats my knee. "Deep breaths, Sivon. Viv, tell her the rest."

"Okay, well . . . that's about it, though." Vivi shrugs one shoulder. "It's all tingly, you hear a handful of clicks, and it's over."

"There's no flash? Does it hurt?" I always imagined kirling as sitting in one of those barbaric electric chairs, having wires attached to my head, being dealt shock after shock until my soul finally revealed itself.

"No pain. I promise." Corah tugs my hands apart and squeezes them reassuringly. "The only light came from the small window in the door, but they play peaceful music to keep you relaxed. You'll be fine! It's over so fast."

Vivi nods. "So easy."

I can't imagine any part of the kirling process feeling easy. "How long did it take to get your results?"

They exchange glances and reply in unison, "Minutes."

"Dammit, stop *doing that*! You know it freaks me out."

They exchange a smirk, then lean toward me and rasp in their creepiest voices, "What's wrong, Sivon?"

I scramble from the bed. "I'm serious! I won't stay tonight if you start up with that shit again."

They fall into each other, laughing. I stomp my foot.

Corah stands, hooks her arm around mine, and swings me back onto her bed. "You can't leave. We leave for college on Saturday."

My heart sinks. So soon? They just got back! How will I survive the long summer without them? It's hard to hold my smile, but today isn't about me. Their dreams are finally coming true.

I pull them into a hug, soaking in the moment. "So, your SEIK profiles just said you were government workers in your past lives. How did intelligence agents come calling?"

"They only make certain parts of your results public," Vivi says. "Other things remain private, like how much you inherit, your will, your Last Letter, and specific details about your folies. You can even keep your soulmate private if you want, but intelligence agencies can access things the public can't."

"Makes sense. It was wild seeing your faces in SEIK, though. I can't believe you only have two folies."

"I know!" they chorus.

"And our birth and death dates are always exact matches. It's so weird," says Vivi.

"More like incredible. So, let's have it. Tell me all about your souls."

"If we tell you, we'll have to kill you," Corah says.

Vivi snickers and pushes her over. "Our soulnames are Kitsune and Raposa, which is what our soulids resemble. Mine is 7IT5UNE."

"And mine is R9P059," Corah says. "Get this: Kitsune is *Japanese* for fox, and Raposa is *Portuguese* for fox."

"No way! I have chills." I show them the raised hairs on my arm.

Of the dozens of languages we could study in high school, Vivi and Corah elected to learn both Japanese and Portuguese.

"You should've seen us when we told each other our results." Corah elbows Vivi.

"I was so happy, I couldn't stop crying." Vivi rests her head on Corah's shoulder.

"Aww!" I wrap them in a hug. "Were you always sisters?"

"No, but always friends. In foli 1, we grew up across the street from one another in Japan. I was a girl, and Vivi was a boy. We were private investigators but coordinated with the government on lots of cases. And we died in a fire when we were seventy-eight."

My eyes bug out. "*Seventy-eight?* That's so *old*."

"I heard people used to live till they were, like, one hundred," Corah says.

"I can't imagine why someone would wanna live that long. What about foli 2? Your deathspan was epic, yeah?"

"*Thirty-nine years.*" Corah raises her fist, and I bump mine to hers.

"We were born the same day to best friends in Brazil," Vivi says. "This time, I was the girl, and Corah was the boy. We worked for the South American Intelligence Agency and croaked at a much more respectable age."

"Sixty-seven." Corah leans forward. "But apparently we died in a *suspicious* plane crash."

"Dun-dun-*DUH*," Vivi sings.

"Whoa."

"Yeah, we looked up articles about it." Corah bends her leg to sit on her ankle. "Something about a fuselage leak, which is ridiculous because even *back then*, airplanes could self-repair in a hot second."

"Shady," I say.

"As a maple tree." Vivi narrows her eyes.

"So, come clean. Are you billionaires like I always suspected?"

They look at each other and laugh.

"*Let's just say* we have enough to keep us comfortable," Vivi says.

"For a few millennia." Corah winks.

I squeal and bounce on the bed. "Holy shit! Then why are you *leaving* me?"

"Aw, it's not about the money," Vivi says. "We want adventure! And to do something great for humanity."

"And if we hate it, we can just quit." Corah lifts her hands.

"But you won't hate it. You're gonna *love* it."

They nod in unison.

I raise my arms to block them from view. *"Stop."*

Chuckling, I lower my hands and give theirs a squeeze. "I'll miss you so much, but your results couldn't have been more perfect." And perhaps they're a good indicator for my kirling in a couple months. I can't be so bad if I'm friends with such wonderful souls.

"Oh, Sivon, you'll love your results too. Just wait." Vivi holds out her hand. "I'll even bet you on it."

Corah smacks it away. "Uh, no you won't. Sivon never loses a bet."

"Right. Good point." Vivi pulls a strand of hair across her lips, then her eyes light up, and she rises to her knees. "How about this? I bet your kirling will be terrible, and you'll end up miserable and alone." She extends her hand again, one brow raised in a dare.

I grab her hand, and we shake on it.

SCAR

SCAR—abbr. To halt the Global Suicide Crisis (5–35 A.K.), when an estimated one billion lives were lost, the Global Coalition of Governments (GCG) passed the Suicide Curtailment and Reformation (SCAR) Act, establishing a penalty of five years in jail plus a fine of ten thousand valuts per suicide, which pass to subsequent lives. Offenders also forfeit all accrued inheritances.

Monday, August 27, 236 A.K.—Day Four at SKI

By two thirty in the morning, the video of Ziva dancing in her kitchen has played on the Advertitude three times. *"We love you, Ziva."*

How very unfair that she can't see them. How very helpless I feel sitting on my bed, staring at a flashing wall.

The addition of red and blue emergency lights from the street below only emphasizes my futility. They can only mean one thing. I lost. And not a bet or a game, but Ziva.

Ziva is Flavinsky. And Flavinsky dies by suicide after every kirling.

How could this happen? How could it happen *here* of all places? Tears slip down my cheeks as I lie down with my back to the window, curl into a ball, and stare at Mom's painting. Amplified by the darkness and oscillating flashers, the indigo aura dances and glows, offering a comforting embrace that's impossible to accept. I cry for hours, lonely and despondent, until eventually, I succumb to exhaustion.

When I wake again, the sun is beating on my face. I press on my chest to soothe the ache and check the time. It's already 9:15 a.m. Three hours till my kirling. My body argues against my half-hearted attempts to sit up.

Stay here. You're safe here. You have no control out there.

But the sight outside prompts me to slide my feet to the cold tiles and gradually shift my weight to stand. After two steps, I perch against the couch's armrest, my chin trembling. Across the street, the Advertitude building is solid black from top to bottom. No words. No videos.

I swallow hard and cast my gaze to the sidewalk below. It's empty except for a man and someone I expect is his son. After sparing a few seconds to glance at the hotel, they share a quick one-armed embrace, and the boy walks through the doors of SKI, guiding his small suitcase behind him.

Don't think about Ziva. Don't think about her brother shouting at the patrol or the video of her dancing. Don't think.

I turn away from the window and slowly get dressed. After nanorizing my teeth and throwing my hair into a messy bun, I enter the hallway, count sixty-eight steps to the elevator, and keep my eyes on my feet during the descent.

The doors open. I step out, take a yogurt from a table in the hallway, and finally look up as I enter the atrium. Instead of the usual hubbub of activity, I'm met with only whispers and stunned silence. I can't be here. Conversation requires thinking, and thinking leads to remembering. I refuse to do either.

I return to my room. Seventy-one steps this time. I leave my breakfast on the table, sit on the bed, and stare at the black Advertitude wall.

A butterfly flits around my window, gray and black with orange, almost-red-tipped wings. Red. I cover my eyes. "Go away!"

I met Ziva only four days ago. What right do I have to mourn her? None. That honor belongs to her family, and Dikela, who's known her for . . . *Dikela!*

I cross to my screen, access the directory, and find Norine. My finger hovers over her name for several heartbeats. After touching it, I count the beeps—*four, five, eight, fifteen*. She answers.

"Hey, Sivon." Norine attempts a smile, but her lips don't cooperate.

"How's Dikela?" My voice quivers.

"She's at her kirling."

A tear slips from my eye. I let it run down my cheek and drop onto my shirt. "What happened?"

Norine slumps onto her bed and stares vacantly at the floor before answering. "It was awful. . . . We woke around two to the hallway patrol trying to enter Ziva's room." She pushes the heels of her hands into her bloodshot eyes and takes a shaky breath.

"It wouldn't answer any questions, just kept knocking and trying the doorknob, but the light stayed red. A few minutes later, the RAID inside finally opened the door, and we rushed in." She lowers her hands. "They had to break down the bathroom door. After a few kicks, it finally burst open, but it hit . . . her . . . as it swung."

She chokes on a sob. "Her face was purple, Sivon. *Purple!*"

I bring a fist to my lips and try to focus on Norine through the watery veil covering my eyes. Why didn't the patrol stop her? Did her counselor even *try* to provide real help, something other than a couple *robots*? And why does this feel like my fault, like I was personally responsible for stopping this? I forgot . . . I forgot, I don't know, something. Something that would've helped Ziva.

"Dikela kept screaming at the patrols who were trying to revive Ziva." Norine runs the heel of her hand under her nose. "More ran into the room, and a couple of them carried us back in here. After that, Dikela fell into an unresponsive trance."

I stretch the skin of my palms, digging in circles and Xs until the ache of my flesh echoes that of my soul.

Norine sniffs twice. "She was still curled up on the couch when I returned from my kirling this morning. At eleven, I reminded her that her kirling was in fifteen minutes. She went into the bathroom, washed her face, and left without saying a word.

"I doubt she'll come back to my room. Will you let me know how she is when you talk to her?"

"Yeah, of course." I wipe my cheeks. "Thank you, Norine. We barely know each other, but what you did last night . . ." Another tear escapes. I look directly into the camera. "You're a good soul."

"Thanks, Sivon." She smiles warily. "It appears I'm going into politics, so hopefully that won't change."

"Well"—my chin trembles as I try to return her smile—"you've got my vote."

An hour later and after many unsuccessful attempts to reach Dikela or Bardou, I enter the Kirling Center and take a seat in the waiting room. Two strangers sit among the ten chairs, bouncing their knees and biting their nails. But the sharp ache in my chest has supplanted the worries that accompanied me to SKI.

"Come on in, Sivon." Windrose stands in the doorway, her specs tinted to hide her eyes. She's taller than I expected. "Are you ready?"

"Yeah, sure."

"First door on the right," she says as I pass.

When I reach the door with a plaque reading KIRLING CHAMBER 1, I turn and catch her wiping away a tear with her pinkie finger.

I pull my brows together. "Are you all right?"

"Of course," she says unconvincingly. She pushes her specs higher. "It's just been a trying couple of days."

I hadn't thought about how the counselors would feel about Ziva's death, but I guess they're in shock too. Will Ziva's counselor get reprimanded for failing to give her the resources she needed? Did Ziva have the newbie Corah did? I usually find other's tears contagious but can't muster up compassion for Windrose and her colleagues at the moment. I open the door and enter the room.

My heartbeat ticks up, and an unexpected smile flickers over my lips. It *is* dark gray. My eyes sting with a sudden, visceral yearning to see Vivi and Corah. If they were here last night, they would've found a way to save Ziva. I'm sure I missed something.

The room is small, about three meters wide and deep. A large holoshield on the left wall blocks my view into the adjacent room.

"Where's the camera?"

"In the walls. See?" Windrose points to a black dot over her shoulder.

Then I notice more of them, each a centimeter in diameter,

punctuating the chamber walls. They're about twenty centimeters apart, arranged in a grid from floor to ceiling.

Windrose blows out a lungful of air. "Let's get started. Your kirling will link your body with your soul. First, I'll swab your cheek to collect a DNA sample. After that, we'll apply electronic diodes to enhance your soulid and take five portraits. SEIK will locate your soulid match and add your DNA and birthdate, recording the match for this life. The whole process takes only a few minutes."

I nod and fight to collect air as the walls press in. *Not a bad soul.*

Windrose dons surgical gloves from a tray of kirling supplies and opens a thin metal cylinder with a cotton swab attached to the lid. She instructs me to open my mouth, rubs the swab inside my cheek, and seals the sample in the tube. It lights up with my name and birthdate. I confirm my information, and she discards her gloves.

I picture Ziva standing here yesterday. She was as nervous as I am, the only one who truly shared my fears. What was it like hearing she was Flavinsky, finding out how many Suicide Curtailment and Reformation penalties she owed? SCARs—inescapable reminders of her past mistakes.

Am I about to receive similar news? I shuffle my feet. *Breathe, Sivon. You can't control your results, but if you pass out, you'll have to wait even longer to hear them.*

Windrose peels small diodes from a clear plastic sheet and moves my collar in various directions to apply them to my neck and shoulders. We don't talk, though I imagine we're both thinking about Ziva. If I could've talked to Windrose last night, maybe we would've found a way....

She opens a package, removes a rubber cap, and instructs me

to pull it onto my head, allowing my hair to fall straight out the bottom. Within seconds, my scalp protests the lack of airflow, sweat beading on my forehead.

"After leaving the room, I'll activate the diodes two by two, starting on your shoulders, working in toward your neck, up the back of your head, and toward your forehead. Expect some discomfort, but no pain."

"Okay." *Where were you last night?*

"Please step into this circle and face the door. Once all the diodes are buzzing, you'll hear five clicks, each a second apart. The equipment will then deactivate, and I'll come back to remove the diodes. We'll retire to my office to discuss your results."

I suck in a lungful of cool air, forcing myself into the present. It's finally my turn. The questions that have plagued me for years will be answered in mere minutes. Who was I? Why is my aura indecipherable? What should I do with my life? What's with the pervasive symbol that even now I'm worrying into my palms? How can I be undefeated at games of strategy but an utter failure when it matters most?

I'm fully awake now, my earlier lethargy replaced by nervous energy tingling into my fingers and toes. "Do I, um—should I smile?" My cheeks burn with embarrassment.

"No need." Windrose leaves the room. Before the door shuts, she leans back in. "Personally, though, I feel we should never pass up an opportunity to smile." She sniffles and closes the door.

Peaceful piano music fills the room when the buzzing starts, and I can't keep my lips from turning up. I must be losing my mind. *Why am I smiling?*

My grin grows wider as the diodes on my shoulders and neck activate. A tear spills from my left eye, and I keep beaming. When the buzzing encompasses my entire head, I let out a small laugh, and a second tear falls.

This is it. I'm about to learn everything I've ever wanted to know about myself. Despite my heartache, I'm about to burst with incandescent joy.

Click... Click... Click... Click... Click...

Holoshield

holoshield—(HAH-loe-sheeld) n. A harmless, soundproof electronic projection, providing customizable visual and auditory access.

The buzzing ceases, but the piano music continues. I wait a few minutes. Then another few minutes. Something is wrong. Where's Windrose? Did she forget about me?

"Hello?" I ask the holoshield just as she opens the kirling chamber door.

My instant relief turns to confusion at the pale bald man peering over her shoulder, looking me up and down.

"Sivon, would you come with me, please?" Windrose holds out a hand.

"Is everything okay?" Vivi and Corah didn't say anything about an extra person coming to *their* kirlings. Is he here to take me away? Does this mean I'm a bad soul? I edge toward the back of the room.

"Everything's fine." Windrose turns her specs translucent. "Nothing to worry about. Your results were a bit . . . abnormal. To confirm our findings, protocol requires we repeat the kirling in a different chamber and with witnesses."

"Abnormal?" My voice wobbles. Of course they're abnormal. I've known my whole life I'm different from everyone else. "What does that mean?"

"I can't answer that until we repeat the test."

My scalp burns hot under the cap. "Can I take this off?" I lift my arm to pull it up.

The man raises a hand. Windrose steps forward, gently taking hold of my arm.

"Yes, we'll remove everything in the other room." She guides me toward the door as I try to process what's happening. How often do people get abnormal kirling results? Why didn't she cover this possibility in our group?

As we exit, the man leading the way, I scan the room in confusion. I brought nothing with me but can't shake the feeling I'm leaving something behind, much like when I was packing for SKI. What am I forgetting?

We pass a door on the right and enter the next room. This kirling chamber resembles the last one, but it's a full meter longer and wider, with holoshields on both sides.

The bald man approaches, pulling on surgical gloves. "Hello, Sivon. My name is Marshall. I'll adjudicate your second kirling today. We've also gathered four additional witnesses"—he nods toward one of the holoshields—"to record and validate your results."

I stare at the partition, trying in vain to see the other side. Who is watching me? Do they already know who I am? Or did the equipment just glitch?

Marshall steps closer. Despite his commanding presence, he's about my height. "Please incline your head so I may inspect the placement of your cap."

I do as he requests, fighting the instinct to push him away and run. He slides his hands over my scalp and along the edges of the cap, making my skin crawl. I jump when he loudly proclaims, "I,

Marshall, certify the kirling cap is properly placed." Quietly, he adds, "You may remove the cap."

I peel it away, nearly sighing in relief as cool air rushes in. Using a pair of surgical pliers, Windrose takes the cap and seals it in a baggie. I shake out my hair to cool off.

"May I please inspect your shoulders?" Marshall asks. "I'll need to adjust the neckline of your shirt."

"Um, sure." Do I have a choice?

I cringe inwardly as his gloved fingers tug my T-shirt collar to expose the diodes one by one. While his touch is clinical, and he only reveals my collarbone and upper back, bile rises in my throat at the violation. He steps in and out as he circles, allowing others to check and record the disks' placement before inspecting them himself. We seem to have entered a bizarre, choreographed dance with only one moving partner.

Though I know it's coming, I still jolt when Marshall booms, "I, Marshall, certify the diodes are properly placed on the shoulders, back, and neck." Then, to me: "Sorry for startling you."

I dip my chin and shudder, relieved when he steps away.

"You may remove the diodes, Windrose."

"We have to repeat the whole thing from scratch?" I ask.

"Yes." Windrose peels the disks from my skin.

"You said my results were abnormal. What does that mean?"

Abnormal can be good, right? Maybe I'm a quirky artist like my mother. Though I never found the nerve to discuss her folies, I know for a fact Mom's past would've been difficult to interpret. Nevertheless, she's made a success of herself.

"Don't read too much into it. We already have someone performing diagnostic testing to rule out an equipment malfunction.

I'm sure this second test will provide us with something more typical."

I gasp. "Was I in the same kirling chamber as Ziva? Were her results abnormal too?"

What if Ziva wasn't really Flavinsky? *What if they got it wrong?* As tragic as that would be, it would make more sense. While I only have limited knowledge of Ziva and Flavinsky, from what I do know, their souls don't seem to align, at least not in the way Vivi's and Corah's did. *Flavinsky, the dancer?*

Windrose stops what she's doing to examine me with pained eyes. "Did you know Ziva?"

"We just met this week, but yeah." I bite the inside of my cheek to keep tears at bay.

She touches my shoulder. "I'm so sorry, Sivon. I'm so sorry about your friend."

Was Ziva my friend? I guess so. I can picture myself reaching out to her after we got home, chatting about our future careers, meeting each other's families. Oh, gosh, Donovan must be in so much pain right now. I nod as the ache returns to my throat.

Windrose inhales sharply, flutters her eyelids, and refocuses on her task. "But no, Ziva's kirling was in a different chamber, and we followed this same protocol for her yesterday." She dumps the disks into a clear bag.

Marshall seals and sets it on the tray. He inspects a fresh sheet of diodes and hands it to Windrose. She places them exactly where they were before, then hands me a fresh cap from a sealed bag. My head begins sweating again at the very sight.

Well, the sooner it's on, the sooner it's off. I work the cap over my hair until my ears are covered. Finally, Marshall repeats his waltz, complete with the shouting, then he and Windrose exit the room.

On wobbly legs, I step into the circle on the floor. The music and buzzing begin, but this time I don't smile. This time, my hands form fists, and I focus on the floor to abate my sudden dizziness. *Don't pass out. Don't pass out.*

Before I know it, the diodes turn off. I didn't even hear the clicks, probably drowned out by the whooshing of blood in my ears. I'm left standing in the dark for an eternity, peering into the static of the holoshields while sweat pools under the cap.

The door finally swings open. Someone rushes past in the hallway, saying something like "Alert the production department," but with the cap covering my ears, I can't be sure. Windrose reenters, alone this time, and instructs me to remove the cap. Her face bears no emotion as she begins to remove the diodes. What is she hiding? Her trembling hands and glistening eyes only amplify my anxiety.

Holy shit, I'm a bad soul. Despair weakens my knees and sends bile up my throat. What will Mom think? And Vivi and Corah? Was I a murderer or some sort of criminal mastermind? Will I go to jail today? "Windrose, who am I?"

"We'll cover your results in my office. I'm almost done." A bead of sweat appears on her forehead.

I shift my stance and fixate on a holoshield, imagining patrols flooding the opposite room to keep an eye on me. My hands knot together. *Circle. X. Circle. X.*

"Okay." She exhales in relief. "Let's go."

We turn down a long hallway and pass two women standing with their backs to the wall, brazenly staring at me. Ashamed of my very soul, I drop my gaze and follow Windrose's footsteps.

We finally reach a door displaying WINDROSE on a digital plaque, but the decor inside mimics a living room instead of an office. I recognize the painting from my calls with her and step closer to examine the entire piece for the first time—pink flowers growing out of dark water.

"Do you know anything about lotus flowers?" Windrose leans against the door frame, her calm demeanor restored.

I purse my lips, uninterested in her small talk, and sit on her brown couch.

She crosses to a navy blue high-back chair. "They're considered living fossils. Archaeologists have dated some species back to the Cretaceous period, 145 million years ago. Their seeds can lie dormant for a thousand years but will germinate and bloom when reintroduced to their habitat."

I shift my weight to show my impatience.

"I'd love to tell you all about them, but since we have much to cover, I'll just share one more thing." She eases herself into the chair. "At night, lotus flowers submerge into murky water but rise and bloom again the next day, clean of any residue. Pretty amazing, right?"

Is this another analogy? Am I the lotus, returning from a life of crime?

She settles her hands on her lap and smiles. A comforting smile? A reassuring smile? A you're-about-to-go-to-jail-so-please-don't-hurt-me smile?

"Windrose." My voice quivers. "Who am I?"

She lifts one shoulder. "You can be whoever you want."

I furrow my brows. She probably says that to all the bad souls. "You're beating around the bush. Just say it."

Her head tilts as she tries to work out how to break the news. I cannot take the delay a second longer. Today, this week, this summer, my whole life, I've waited for the next words from her mouth. Haven't I suffered long enough? Why won't she just come out with it? "*Please!*"

She adjusts her specs. "You're a new soul."

My heart stutters. A new soul? What the hell is a new soul? A tear drops from my jaw onto my shirt. "What do you mean? What does that mean?"

Windrose comes to sit beside me on the couch. "SEIK couldn't find a match for your soulid. It's a *good* thing."

"How is that good?" Two more tears fall. I bat at them with trembling hands. "I don't have a soul?"

She huffs. "*Of course* you have a soul. We just don't have a record of your soulid in SEIK."

How can I not be in SEIK? *No one* said that was a possibility. They can't throw out the rules the second I sit down to play. "You're wrong. It has to be wrong. We need to repeat the test, Windrose. The system is broken or something. First Ziva and now me. It's *wrong*! Can't you see?"

She removes her specs and sets them on the end table. "We verified everything, Sivon. After both kirlings, we ran your five portraits through SEIK three times. That's thirty total system checks. You saw for yourself how the equipment was inspected, replaced, and examined with witnesses. We've kirled over a hundred souls since Ziva. Those were all normal."

I fold my arms across my stomach. "What are you saying? I was never born before?"

"Possibly. Or you may have died before your kirling in your

past lives. It's also possible your deathspan is so long, your last life predates SEIK."

No. This isn't right. She's supposed to give me answers. "I *can't* be a new soul. That makes no sense." I lift my watery eyes to hers. "Please, you need to fix this."

I never thought I'd be jealous of Bardou, but at least today he'll walk out of here knowing who he is, even if he doesn't use that knowledge in this lifetime.

My back straightens. "Windrose, can you give me the soul of someone in the Fringe? They won't need it this life anyway. I promise no one will ever know."

A tear drips from Windrose's eye. "No, Sivon. I can't." She swipes it away. "You've received a beautiful gift."

I hang my head, hopeless. Even if she did what I asked, Marshall and the other counselors would know she lied. Manipulating my soulid would surely leave traces in SEIK. SKI probably has people to identify anomalies in the database. I'm pretty sure that was one of Dad's job duties when he worked here. We'd never get away with it.

Windrose sniffs and collects herself. "Do you know how rare new souls are?"

I stare vacantly at the floor.

"Our last one was forty years ago. Have you heard of Primus, the former leader of the Global Coalition of Governments?"

I blink once. "He was a new soul?"

"He was! And look how successful he was."

"But didn't he get ousted from office?"

She winces. "Yes, well, without knowing a soul's history, *some* people may question a new soul's motives."

My eyes go wide.

"But most people, I think you'll find, will be in awe of you . . . even jealous."

I scoff. "Why would they be jealous? I have no inheritance, no soulmate, *no direction*!"

Windrose sets her jaw. "You have every direction. Don't you see? You get to choose."

"I don't want to choose." I stand. "Someone is supposed to tell me. Otherwise, why did you make me come here? I have no idea who I am."

"Yes, you do."

I shake my head, pacing the room. This is absurd. They've cheated me out of a future, left me scrambling for purchase while everyone else gets a lifeline and safety net.

"You may not know how you'll make a living, but you know who you *are*, and those are two different things."

I slump into the corner of the couch. Today sucks. SKI sucks. *Everything sucks.* "Just tell me what to do, *please*. I don't know what to do."

"Take it day by day." Windrose swings her knees toward me. "You'll figure things out. We have a way of moving in the direction we're meant to go. Yes, kirling sets most people on their proper path sooner than figuring it out on their own, but remember, only two hundred years ago, people didn't know *their* former lives either."

I run a hand under my nose. "How did they figure out what to do with their lives?"

"They followed their hearts and chased their passions. They answered the call of duty. Explored, created, made bad decisions, and good ones too. They succeeded, and they failed, and all of it—*all of it*—was normal."

The only thing I feel called to do is get as far away from this place as possible. My mind spins with the questions left unanswered while new ones pop up left and right. "What if I make a move that leads me in the wrong direction?"

"If you find yourself going in the wrong direction, turn around."

"But what if it's too late? I might only have this one life." *Holy shit.* Fear seizes my insides. "Windrose, *I might have only one life*!" My fingers push into the damp hair on my scalp.

"Shh." She edges toward me. "Two hundred years ago, half the population didn't believe in reincarnation. They thought they only had one life too."

My fingers twine together, starting up with my nervous habit again. "But that's not enough time. I need more time!"

"Time for what?"

"Everything! Time to figure things out. Time to live!"

"Then you'd better get started." She pats my hand and settles back, allowing me a few minutes of quiet to process the news.

But the more I repeat "new soul," the more foreign it feels, and soon my thumbs are cramping from drawing circles and Xs across my palms. "Are you sure, Windrose? Is there even the slightest possibility you're wrong? That SEIK is malfunctioning?"

She looks me in the eye. "I'm certain. If you were in SEIK, we would've found you."

Not found. A lost soul. I'm lost.

I lost. Twice in one day. I groan, pressing my temples to ease the throbbing pain.

Windrose picks up a screen from the coffee table, unfolds it, and hands it to me. "Let's review a few details for the rest of your stay, and I'll walk you to your room. You look exhausted."

As soon as she says it, I feel it too. My muscles twitch under the unrelenting tension.

With a few taps, my kirling results appear:

> Semyon Kirlian Institute—Washington, CD
> 27 August 236 A.K. 13:11 UTC—Successful Kirling
> Sivon—DOB 24 August 218 A.K.—NAN 6#4-78-090&
> Soul ID match—[null]
> Witnesses—Windrose (3I2DR5E), Marshall (M9RS44L), Leeward (13E34R0), Northstar (NOR544R), Journey (2UR28YY), and Pilot (9I11O04).
> New Soul ID assigned—KRE44UR

"Please press your index finger to the screen to confirm delivery of your results."

I do so with a trembling hand. If I were anyone else, we'd have more to review—my past lives, potential careers, how much inheritance I'd receive or jail time to serve. But I'm not anyone else. I'm not anyone at all.

Windrose lays the screen on the table. "SKI would like to offer you a public debut."

"A what?" I couldn't have heard that right.

"A public debut. Like they do with soulmate reunions and celebrity reincarnations."

Is she serious? Does it *look* like I'm remotely interested in telling the world I'm soulless? "I . . . No. Just no."

"The Institute will pay you ten thousand valuts to do the show. Since you have no inheritance, those funds could help you begin your new life, doing whatever you decide to do."

My brows dip. Ten thousand valuts is a tonne of money. I could buy a used hover, not one that self-repairs, but definitely one that drives me from point A to B. But my chest tightens at the thought of a bunch of cameras pointed my way and Kureshtar, the famous SKI reporter, firing off questions. "I can't do it."

"I understand. You have until tomorrow evening to decide. If you change your mind, let me know."

I nod, positive I won't.

She takes a deep breath. "Okay, you won't like this part."

"I haven't liked any part."

She squeezes my hand. "As wonderful as I believe your results to be, I can tell you're disappointed. With the added tragedy of your friend taking her life this morning"—she heaves a sigh—"well, frankly, I'm concerned about your mental stability. I'm assigning a patrol to your room tonight. I feel it's best considering everything you're dealing with."

I wrap my arms around myself, squeezing my elbows. "No."

"We're talking about only"—she looks at her screen—"eighteen hours or so. And I won't station anyone outside your room, only a guard on the inside."

My chin wobbles. "Please . . . don't." I couldn't bear being locked in my room with a stranger, not after last night.

She places her hand on my shoulder. "I can't lose another soul, Sivon. Put yourself in my shoes."

What good were the guards for Ziva? None. Windrose can't seriously expect me to be okay with this. "I don't trust them, Windrose." I look her in the eye. "No RAIDs."

She wraps an arm around me. "Of course. I'll request Raphaela. She's my favorite."

Good Soul

Good soul—n. A person embodying one or more of the following characteristics: kind, genuine, trustworthy, thoughtful, benevolent, helpful, respectful, or just.

Exiting the elevator onto my floor, Windrose and I pass a group of whispering girls, and we turn the corner to find a woman in a SKI Patrol uniform looming outside my room. Great. Now I'm also the subject of SKI gossip.

The patrol is as tall as Dikela but must weigh another twenty-five kilos, consisting solely of muscle. The outlines of her quads show through her black pants, and thick biceps press against her fitted shirt as she raises a hand to wave. Despite her intimidating size, she offers a wide, friendly smile that tugs at the auburn hair in her tight bun.

Windrose breaks into a smile as well. "Raphaela, this is Sivon. Thank you for keeping her company today."

"Happy to help." She gives Windrose a professional nod and follows me into my room.

"You're in good hands, Sivon. I'll check in with you tomorrow morning for our one-on-one follow-up." Windrose closes the door behind us.

Soothing piano music begins playing. I shuffle my feet, searching for the right words to assure this total stranger I won't take my life tonight . . . or ever. Raphaela folds her arms to study me, no doubt prepared to tackle me if I do anything suspicious. Unable to bear her scrutiny, I study the tile floor and fiddle with the hem of my tee. Does she know who I am? Or, rather, who I'm not? Does she consider new souls untrustworthy?

Raphaela relaxes her stance and lets out a sigh. "Can I give you a hug?"

I raise my head. "What?"

"A hug. Sweetie, you look like someone dragged you through hell and back. Only three things are gonna help right now." She counts them on her fingers. "A warm meal, a hot shower, and a hug.

"In my opinion, keeping you young souls locked in here without family or friends is tantamount to a crime. Everyone could use a hug after their kirling. If I had a say, I'd make it a requirement. Fix a lot of stupid shit I see, that's for damn sure. So whaddya say?" She opens her arms wide. "Bring it in."

My breath catches. Never have I wanted a hug more, but from a stranger? I don't know. I wait for Raphaela to drop her arms, but she holds them open, her eyes only growing more compassionate. Fine. I lope toward her and accept the embrace.

The second she wraps around me, the fear and tension I've held for nearly a decade releases. I close my eyes and imagine myself in my mother's arms. In my delusion, I can even smell the tang of kinetic paint and Mom's rose-scented shampoo. Just when I expect Raphaela to let go, she begins to sway, knocking free the last of my restraint.

Tears course over my cheeks as the horrific events of the past twenty-four hours replay in my mind. Hearing the news about

Flavinsky, begging Norine to bring us to the seventh floor, the shouting, Donovan's anguish, Dikela's despair, and the black Advertitude wall. I squeeze Raphaela tighter as I relive my kirling—the diodes, the clicking, Marshall, Windrose's tears, and the judgment pouring off the holoshields. I cry and cry and cry.

"You're safe now. That's right. Let it go."

A few minutes later, I decrescendo into silent hiccups and sniffles.

Raphaela waits for me to pull back first. "Better?"

I release a shaky breath, jerking my head up and down, determined not to be embarrassed by my outburst.

"Good. Next step is a hot shower. While you're in there, I'll ask the kitchen to send up some food. I didn't eat anything the day of my kirling, and I see that unopened yogurt on your table, so I bet you haven't either. Did you pack pajamas?"

"Mm-hmm." I shuffle over to my bag and pull out soft-knit pink pants and a matching T-shirt.

"Excellent. We'll just pretend we're having a long-ass slumber party today. Sound good?"

I can't help but smile a little as I turn toward the bathroom.

"Just leave the door cracked a hair, will you?"

My grin vanishes, remembering how they found Ziva. Did Windrose assign Dikela a patrol as well? I hope so.

I stand frozen in the shower for the first five minutes, allowing the hot water to soothe my rigid muscles. *Don't think about the past. Push forward, to when you'll leave SKI, the relief you'll feel returning home.*

Mom will probably do backflips over my new soul.

See, I told you you weren't a bad soul. I know my own daughter.

Vivi and Corah will sympathize, though. They were as curious as me about my past lives.

My time capsule assignment comes to mind, and I marvel at my sixth sense. No wonder thirteen-year-old me couldn't imagine who my folies were. I didn't *have any*. So much for my imaginary soulmate, though. *See, Mom?* I've no one to calm my aura after all. I'm forever destined to be indecipherable and abnormal.

Huh. I guess this means Vivi won the bet.

I bet your kirling will be terrible, and you'll end up miserable and alone. Check, check, and check. For someone who's used to winning every game, I sure am racking up the losses.

Raphaela taps the door. "You okay in there?"

"Mm-hmm," I lie, but her question prompts me to stop standing here and actually wash myself.

A few minutes later, I shut off the shower and put on the pajamas, grateful I packed my favorite pair. I hold the collar to my nose and breathe in the lavender detergent. What I wouldn't give to sleep in my own bed tonight.

Back in the room, the aroma emanating from a tray of food makes my stomach growl.

Raphaela removes the lid. "Ordered my favorite, chicken tacos. You like tacos?"

"Who doesn't like tacos?"

"That's right. I knew I liked you."

We eat a couple each and feast on chips and salsa for dessert.

I sit back and pat my stomach. "Delicious. Thank you."

"I'll pass your compliment to the chef." She wipes her mouth while studying me, and I stack the dishes to avoid her discerning gaze.

"Wanna talk about your kirling?"

"Not really." I just want to relish my taco-induced nirvana for a minute. Is that too much to ask?

She bobs her head and places one hand over the other on her abdomen. Her gaze falls on Mom's painting and continues the circuit of the room until she's looking out the window.

The Advertitude hotel across the street is still fully black. Surprising, since they're probably losing a tonne of valuts to honor Ziva that way. Unless someone paid them to turn it black.

I sigh. So now I'm a cynic? If I can really choose to be anyone, will it be a hopeless pessimist? No, of course not. I'm just scared of what people will think of my results. So why not start small, with an audience of one?

"I'm a new soul." I hold my breath for Raphaela's reaction.

She meets my eyes and considers my announcement for a good five seconds while her brows slowly rise. "My, my." Her lips pull down at the corners while she bobs her head.

"But I was hoping for more . . . for some direction."

Raphaela bends toward me. "I don't know what Windrose told you, and I'm sure she gave you some great advice. But don't sit there thinking your new soul doesn't give you direction. The second your results go public, your life will never be the same. Pretty soon you're not gonna remember who the hell you *used* to be because everyone is gonna tell you who the hell you *should* be."

My knee bounces in rhythm with my accelerating heart.

"You wanted *more*? Well, you couldn't get any more. This is the *most* more that's out there." She taps the table twice, punctuating her words.

I wrap my arms around my middle. "You're not making sense."

"Oh, just wait. The day you leave here, people will be lining the sidewalks outside. They'll have to bring in community protectors to keep 'em back. Everyone will wanna get a look at you or touch you or meet you. You'll probably need security for the *rest of your life*."

Nervous laughter escapes my mouth. "Are you serious?"

"Do I *look* like I'm joking?" Raphael levels me with a gaze.

I sit taller and shake my head.

"Half the world is gonna believe you were never born before, that you're some sort of miracle child. The other half is gonna assume you last died before SEIK existed, meaning you have the longest deathspan ever recorded, at least two-hundred-and-thirty-six years."

I swallow hard. Part of me wants to stop her right there, the part that's still in denial. My hands knot together. *Circle. X. Circle. X.*

"You know how everyone believes the longer your deathspan, the better your soul is?"

Her words press against my chest as reality sinks in. *Oh shit.*

"Well, people are about to say you're the motherfuckin' messiah."

Primus

Primus—Soulid: 09R13U2. Kirled as a new soul in 196 A.K., the first since 172. He quickly rose to power, becoming Secretary General of the Global Coalition of Governments (GCG) in 225, only to be ousted three years later.

"A messiah? You mean, like a prophet?"

Raphaela opens her hands in confirmation, leaning back in her chair.

My restless feet force me to stand. "That's ridiculous. I'm not even sure I believe in God. How could I be a prophet?"

"I'm not saying you *are* a prophet, only that people will *say* you are."

"Why, though? Religions don't exist anymore. No one believes in prophets."

"You don't know that, and I'm not talking about religion. Lots of people want to believe in something bigger than themselves. They want to know why they're reborn over and over. They want someone to tell them where their souls go during their deathspans."

"How would I know any of that?" I pace in front of the couch.

"Doesn't matter. People will expect you to. They're gonna ask what you think. *All* the time."

I sit on the bed, my back to Raphaela, then flop onto my side.

How is this my life? Was a normal kirling too much to ask? The thought of public scrutiny churns my stomach. All eyes on me, and for what? I have nothing to offer—no talents or words of wisdom. I'm destined to disappoint them, a failure through and through. "I don't want to be famous."

She clears her throat. "I don't mean this to be hurtful, but your friend Ziva, she didn't want to be Flavinsky. And near a dozen kids are walking through the doors of SKI this week who'll leave in handcuffs. They don't want that either. It could be worse."

I didn't think I had any tears left to shed, but one rolls from my right eye onto the comforter. She's right, of course. I should be grateful, but this new soul doesn't sound like the gift Windrose promised.

"I'm not saying your life will be easy," Raphaela says. "You have a heavy burden to bear. Everybody is gonna be up in your business, and you'll always wonder who your true friends are. You can't trust anyone, ya hear? *Protect your heart.*"

I gather a handful of my shirt over my chest, wishing I could rip out the offensive organ underneath. How can I ever be sure someone isn't just pretending to care about me to take advantage of my new soul? *You must never fall in love, Sivon.*

Raphaela weaves around the couch to sit beside my head. "And don't be surprised if others don't trust you in return."

Her comments remind me of Primus. I was only ten when he was ousted from office but remember Mom watching it on the news, shaking her head in disbelief.

"What if I refuse to answer everyone's questions about life and death? What if I move to a remote location, never to be seen again? Then they can't say I'm good *or* bad, and they'll leave me alone."

"Yeah, you could do that. But when people are left to make up their minds about someone they're already suspicious of, they often think the worst. That could put you in more danger."

I tremble.

"Shh. You're gonna be okay. Look, you need to think big. What do you want? Because now you can get it. If you wanna be prime minister someday, you can be that. If you want to"—she waves a hand—"form a religion that worships cats, you'd probably get a good following.

"What I'm saying is you have a lot of power. More than you could've ever imagined. More than anyone in this world. And if you don't seize it, people will do it for you."

"But I don't want that kind of power. I just wanna be comfortable in my own skin for once." I cover my eyes and groan. "I have no clue what to do with my life."

"And why should you? You've only lived eighteen years and don't know what's worked for your soul before. I wish I could tell you which way to go, but you're gonna have to figure it out for yourself."

I slap my thigh in frustration. "But how?"

"Here's my last piece of advice, take it or leave it: *Trust your instincts.*"

I wait for her to say more, but she leaves it at that. I roll onto my back and tilt my chin up to look at her. "Trust my instincts? That's it?"

"No, that's not it. You haven't been paying attention. Protect your heart. Seize your power. *And also* trust your instincts."

"Oh, wonderful. Thank you for the very specific and helpful advice."

"You're welcome," she says without matching my sarcasm.

Raphaela stands to walk away, but I grab her hand. "I'm sorry. I know you mean well."

A corner of her mouth lifts. "I have seen my share of troubled souls come through this building. Wasn't long ago I was one of them myself."

My brows rise, and I sit up.

She nods. "Those of us who struggle with our kirlings usually expected too much from them. You did get answers today, just not the ones you wanted. Which means you have a lot in common with a bunch of us in here." She nods to the window. "And out there."

I open my mouth to argue, but she levels me with a gaze. "Like them, like me, you'll find a way. You *will*."

I quirk a brow. "By trusting my instincts."

She raises one finger. "Mm-hmm. And guarding your heart." She adds another.

"And seizing my power," I say.

She lifts the third. "That's right. Smartest new soul I've ever met."

Soulname

Soulname—n. The nickname a soul uses across every life, typically by reworking the SEIK-assigned alphanumerical Soul ID (soulid) into a word or words.

Tuesday, August 28, 236 A.K.—Day Five at SKI

I wake facing the window, but no light permeates the blacked-out pane. I roll onto my back, tangling with the SKI-provided bathrobe draped over me as a blanket.

The time on the screen reads 7:48. I drop my head to the pillow, consider for a second, and look again: 7:48 *a.m.* I sit up. It's morning already?

Raphaela observes me from the couch.

Last I remember, she called down for more tacos around seven thirty p.m., and I decided to lie down until the food arrived. "I slept for . . . twelve hours?"

"You certainly fought it for a while, but you finally settled down around one thirty."

You'd think I'd feel refreshed, but I want nothing more than to dream away the rest of my stay. Twenty-four hours to go, the requisite "adjustment" period. I sigh and rise to go about my morning routine in the bathroom. When I emerge, Raphaela has pulled up my schedule.

"Windrose is gonna call at nine. That's when I'll take off." She orders us breakfast through her com. "All right, I have an idea." She slides her hands together. "Something fun."

I face her with flattened lips.

"You should figure out your soulname. If *you* don't do it, someone else will."

Her advice about seizing my power echoes through my head. "Yeah, okay."

I tap the new Kirling Results menu, and we examine my soulid.

KRE44UR

I say the first thing that comes to mind. "Creature." My eyes go soggy again.

She bumps my shoulder with hers. "Nope, we're having none of that today. Look again. This is exactly why we need to figure this out. You don't want people running around calling you Creature."

She focuses back on the screen and winces.

I groan. See? No matter what soulname I choose, the most obvious one is, and will always be, Creature. I've dealt with the same problem my entire life. When people first see my birth name, they automatically rhyme it with Simon. They'll do the same with KRE44UR. And what better soulname for an untrustworthy new soul than Creature?

With mounting hopelessness, I stare at the letters and numbers, trying to work out hidden words. I keep picturing the *4*s as an *A* and *T*. "Creator? But I don't like that either. It'll make me seem better than I am, like the prophet you mentioned."

Raphaela side-eyes me and continues her silent perusal. I bite my thumbnail, repeating the word *creature* over and over. For someone who's long enjoyed puzzling out multiple soulnames from others' soulids, why can't I do the same for my own? Frustrated, I yank my hand down and thread my fingers together, switching to my other nervous habit.

A minute later, Raphaela breaks into a smile. "Care eh for."

"Carry what?"

"Care eh for," she repeats. "You know, the French word? *C-A-R-R-E-F-O-U-R*. Carrefour."

I tilt my head. "What does it mean? I studied Belarussian."

"My grandparents are from Quebec, and we speak French with them. Look, *KR* for *Care*, *E* for *Eh*, and *44UR* for *Four*. *Carrefour* means *crossroads*."

Chills spread across my body. I examine my palms, the crossroads symbol recently kneaded into them. And here I am, standing at a crossroads, looking for the way to go. The name fits like a missing piece of a puzzle. I love it. "That's perfect, Raphaela."

Carrefour. My soulname is Carrefour. I hold out a hand to Raphaela. "Hello, my name is Carrefour. It's nice to meet you."

She accepts my handshake, inclining her head. "The pleasure is all mine."

An hour later, we've finished breakfast, and Raphaela has told me all about her grandparents' fascinating journey from the war-ravaged Quebec through New Union to Washington, CD. She stands when Windrose appears on the screen.

"Good morning. How are you both today?"

"Doing well," Raphaela replies. "We had an uneventful evening. Sivon has eaten breakfast and is ready to begin her day. With your permission, I'll take my leave."

"Thank you, Raphaela. Your time is much appreciated. I hope you enjoy your days off."

With Raphaela headed home, I might never see her again. Though I'm still struggling with my kirling results, I'm in a much better place than yesterday. I owe that to her.

"Thank you for everything." I open my arms to Raphaela this time. She chuckles and accepts the hug.

"It was nice meeting you." She pats my back. "And I look forward to seeing what you do with that new soul of yours. Don't forget what I said." She turns her back to the screen and whispers, "Seize your power," while shaking a fist.

I nod, pointing to my head, then my heart. *Trust your instincts. Protect your heart.* She winks and pops a grape into her mouth on her way out the door.

I reluctantly face the screen, not at all interested in discussing my new soul and nonexistent career options.

"Good to see you looking more like yourself."

With her red puffy eyes, Windrose does not, but I keep that to myself. "Doing a little better. Doubt I'll ever be myself again. Raphaela was a big help, though."

"She's a gift to SKI and the souls who come through here."

I perch on the end of my bed.

"How do you feel about your results today?"

My first instinct is to say *Terrible*, but that answer wouldn't earn me any favors. Last thing I want is for Windrose to extend my suicide watch. "I'm still processing everything. Worried what people will think of me."

"Those feelings are normal. It'll take time, but I believe you'll come to appreciate your new soul."

I try to keep the skepticism from my face.

Windrose removes her specs. "The Institute hopes you've reconsidered the soul debut show."

My nose wrinkles. "I'm really not int—"

"They've increased the offer to fifteen thousand valuts."

Fifteen thousand? Restless butterflies flit around my stomach. Am I being too rash by walking away from that much money?

"It would only be a ten-minute thing. Over before you know it."

Ten minutes of my life that will replay over and over, like the Cadence and Abernathy reunion. Poor Kopar could barely walk into a room without being reminded of the girl who broke his heart.

He did eventually move on. Vivi and Corah told me about the people he dated in college. He now owns a research vessel in the Pacific Ocean, but I'll never forget the betrayal and heartbreak on Kopar's face that night eight years ago.

But I'm not Cadence or Abernathy. I'm a nobody with a new soul. People might tune in once, quickly realize I'm boring as hell, then forget about me. And fifteen thousand valuts is fifteen thousand valuts.

"I, um—please let them know I'll think it over."

She rubs her temples like she's fighting a headache. "I'm sorry. I know this is a lot, but Prime Minister Mirovnik asked to speak with you at nine thirty."

"I'm sorry, who?" I couldn't have heard that right.

"The prime minister. He'd like to speak with you this morning."

Words are coming out of her mouth, but they don't make sense. "The prime minister . . . wants to—"

"Speak with you, yes."

The sudden onset of nausea makes me instantly regret eating breakfast. "W-why? Are my results public already?"

"No, those will post to SEIK at twelve thirty, but they're disseminated to our intelligence community after each kirling. Mirovnik wanted to meet you last night, but we convinced him to wait until morning."

I have no clue what I could say of interest to the prime minister, but I'm not *against* speaking with him. "Sure. Okay."

Windrose taps the air, no doubt shooting off a message. "Finally, you'll meet with your future-life estate attorney later this morning. You'd typically update your will, but you'll build yours from scratch instead. Start thinking about what you'd like to bequeath your neli and write in your Last Letter. We recommend jotting down something before leaving SKI."

I still don't have a handle on this life and already need to plan for the next? Will I even have a next? "What do people usually write in their Last Letters?"

"Oh, it varies. Some direct their neli to locate other souls for one reason or another." She scratches her cheek. "Others include a little about themselves to supplement their foli histories in SEIK.

"The Last Letter is a free service provided by the GCG, but you're limited to about five hundred words. You'll set up a login during your meeting, so you can update it whenever you'd like. Your neli will get access to it at their kirling."

Assuming I *have* a next life.

"If that isn't enough space, you could include a username and password to a Foli Journal account. Foli Journal allows subscribers to save videos, photos, and other media, but the annual fee varies based on storage sizes. If you don't make provisions to pay the subscription during your deathspan, your account is erased, so that service comes with a bit of risk, especially for someone like you."

Right. I could store a bunch of memories only to lose them two hundred years from now when my soul decides to show up again.

The time in the corner of the screen grabs my attention. Nine twenty? My video conference with the prime minister starts in only ten minutes. I look down at my pajamas and over to the rumpled bed. "Windrose, would it be okay if we ended our call? I need to straighten up."

Her eyes flit to the mess behind me. "Of course. We're not scheduled to speak before your departure tomorrow morning, but I may check in this afternoon."

Palms sweating, I say, "Okay," and press the option to sign off.

Not sure what to do with our breakfast dishes, I stack them on the table and slide it out of view. Quickly, I straighten the bedding, then rummage through my duffel bag, hoping to find something decent to wear. I only have gym clothes, a few T-shirts, the black cardigan, leggings, and a pair of jeans. Damn Vivi and Corah for telling me not to pack anything nice!

I pull out the jeans and a plain red T-shirt and run into the bathroom to change and brush my hair.

The prime minister's pink face pops onto my screen the second I open the door, and I fight the impulse to slam it again, shutting myself inside. My heart is already racing due to my mad rush around the room, but trepidation now mixes with my anxiety. This could just be a friendly call, but my intuition tells me to stay on high alert. Every move carries weight now, more than ever before. I've reached a new crossroads.

Crossroads

Crossroads—n. A place where two roads intersect.

"Well, hello!" the prime minister says in his deep, round voice. His trademark white hair rests against his black jacket in shiny ringlets. He raises a plump hand in a kind wave before settling it on his rotund belly.

My vision swims from the vertigo-like sensation of déjà vu. Weird. I quickly shake it off, clasp my hands together, and sit straight-backed on the edge of the bed. "Hello, Prime Minister."

"How do you do, Sivon? May I call you Sivon? Or would you prefer a soulname?" He pronounces my name correctly, which may be a first.

"Um, sure, Sivon is good. My soulname is Carrefour, but either works. Sivon's great." *What the hell? You sound like an idiot.*

"When I received the news that a new soul joined our community, I simply couldn't wait to speak with you." His beard bounces on his belly as he speaks. "Thank you for taking my call and *congratulations* for having the longest deathspan on record. Absolutely wonderful."

"No, thank *you*, Prime Minister. This is all so . . ." My brain serves up a list of descriptors that I dismiss one by one—*overwhelming, upsetting, terrifying, horrible.* "So very unexpected."

"Indeed! You'd be amazed how fast the rumors have spread. A segment about you aired on the morning news."

My eyes go wide. "The . . . national news?" What did they say about me? Are they sharing my Sociaty photos and videos? Oh gosh, why didn't I go through those before coming to SKI? "They already know about me?"

"I'm afraid this kind of scintillating gossip is hard to contain. Of course, they're only speculating until the official results go up. I expect you'll receive many interview requests once you leave SKI. Enjoy the peace while you have it." He chortles, his bulbous cheeks glowing red.

I try to smile, but I'm not sure one makes it out. *More* interviews? I haven't even decided if I want to do the first one.

"You know, we met years ago."

My lips pull down. Pretty sure I'd remember meeting the prime minister.

"Your mother painted my portrait. You were much younger then, maybe seven or eight. That was my second sitting, actually. She's quite talented."

The memory pulls free of the trunk I'd shut it inside. "Oh yeah! I forgot about that. When the motorcade pulled up to our house, I thought they were coming to arrest us."

He returns my smile, considering me for a few seconds. "How much do you know about my career, Sivon?"

Carrefour. Why didn't I ask him to call me Carrefour? Sivon feels too personal, a name reserved for my closest friends and family.

I adjust my position and focus on his question. "Um, let's see . . . You took office four years ago, as leader of the Advancement party, and you're up for reelection in a couple weeks. I heard Senator Fahari's Improvement Party is tough competition." *What am I doing?* The prime minister took the time to call me, and I'm bringing up his *competition*?

"Well, well, reports of your academic excellence are true! And you're familiar with my folies?"

I tug on the threads of that government lesson. If I knew I'd be quizzed on Mirovnik's folies by the man himself, I would've studied instead of brushing my hair.

"Yes, uh . . . you were chief executive of the Eastern Asian Alliance in foli 1." I dig into the depths of my brain but come up short on his second life. "I'm sorry, I can't recall foli 2."

"In foli 2, I was president of the European Council."

Dammit, I *knew* that!

"The Eastern Asian Alliance and European Council are the most successful and stable governments in the world. It's my goal to do the same here by incorporating Fringe communities into our nation's framework."

He and his nephew, Janus, often repeat this same goal in their political ads. *Free the Fringe.* I wait for him to make his point.

"Judging by my folies' accomplishments, we're practically guaranteed success. Wouldn't you agree?"

He's leading up to something, but I haven't figured out what. I choose my words carefully. "Your résumé is certainly impressive."

His eyes twinkle. "Thank you, Sivon."

I grind my teeth at the sound of my name coming from his lips. Would it be rude to correct him now?

"May I ask what careers you're considering? Are you at all interested in politics?"

Is he worried I'll try to take his job? Good thing my jaw is clamped shut to keep the laughter at bay. "Not at all. To be honest,

I haven't considered *any* career much. I was waiting for my kirling to get some direction."

He leans back. "And you got just what you wanted!"

"How do you mean?" If he knows what I'm supposed to do with my new soul, I'm all ears.

"You're one of the most influential people in the country. Maybe even the *world*."

Clearly, he hasn't seen my Sociaty videos. And if he suspects I'd use my "new soul" superpowers to steal his office, he's sorely mistaken. "I hardly think—"

"I'd like to offer you a position on my staff, Sivon. Given your exceptional school record and amiable personality, you'd fit in perfectly."

My lips part. Oh. *Ohhh*. This call, his questions. Everything makes sense now.

Of course Mirovnik wants me to work for him. Since people think souls with long deathspans are "better" than others, then it would be like "the best soul in the world" endorsing his party and candidacy.

But do I want to work for the prime minister? I've always admired Janus's charitable work but know very little about the world of politics. "As tempting as that sounds, Prime Minister, I'd like some time to research the Advancement and Improvement parties before accepting your offer."

"Smart, smart." He waves a finger at me. "See, one of the reasons you'd love working with me is I encourage outside-the-box thinking and constructive criticism. Senator Fahari, on the other hand, has amassed an echo chamber of sycophants to encourage her dangerous ideals."

"Dangerous?" I doubt she'd be so popular if that were true.

"Undoubtedly. After millennia of unrest, our world has known real peace for two centuries, all thanks to the internationally accepted kirling system. Every country has united to hold bad souls accountable for their crimes and reward good souls for their benevolence."

Ziva's welcoming smile flashes across my mind. "But bad souls aren't necessarily evil. Many poor decisions are the result of tragic circumstances. Why punish them further?"

"Completely agree, which is why we focus on reform versus punishment and why Janus so passionately encourages people to look past their prejudices when interacting with those souls and their families."

Mirovnik's eyes darken. "But Fahari's proposed changes to the kirling system would threaten our nation's stability, destroying everything we've worked so hard to build. By curtailing SCAR penalties, she could spark a nationwide suicide crisis. The GCG would roll out sanction after sanction. I can't let that happen, and with your help, I won't."

Every suicide is a tragedy. I couldn't save Ziva, but if my new soul could save others like her, I should. I must.

And Mirovnik's track record is undeniable. If I remember correctly, his soulname means something like *peace bringer* or *peacemaker* in one of Europe's obsolete languages. Why wouldn't I want to work for him?

But I haven't left SKI yet, and I'm not the least bit qualified for a role on his staff. Would it be wise to accept the first offer that comes my way? "I do agree with everything you're saying, but perhaps I should consider my options first."

He holds up a hand. "I hear you, and I've no doubt you'll have your pick of careers. But my nephew said— You've heard of Janus, yes?" He grins knowingly.

Shit. Mirovnik *has* seen my videos. Why didn't I ever delete my ridiculous preteen proclamations of love for Janus? My cheeks sear with embarrassment. It's everything I can do not to dissolve onto the floor and slither under the bed.

My head nods and shakes in every possible direction. "Yes, of course. Your nephew. Janus. He said what?" I scratch my neck, trying and failing to appear nonchalant.

"He said I'd be a fool not to bring you on board. And if you join my staff, he'd like to escort you to the opening of the Holusion Museum Thursday evening."

Every bit of moisture leaves my mouth. "Janus? Escort me?" My voice cracks.

Mirovnik fights a smile. "As part of your work duties, of course. Many of our donors will be at the event. We'd like you to join us on the campaign trail, meet the public, take photos with our supporters—nothing too strenuous. We'll provide a new wardrobe, of course, though I'm not suggesting you care about something so superficial." He takes in my rumpled tee.

I tug at the hem. "That sounds great, but you're right. I'm not sure an art show and new wardrobe are what I need right now."

Mirovnik leans toward the camera. "Understood. I assure you I only have your best interests at heart." He taps his lips. "You know, we're expecting a large gathering at SKI tomorrow for your release. You'd be surprised how unruly crowds become when excited."

I recall the hoverball match last year where spectators were trampled while storming the field. Could that happen to me when leaving SKI? My rusty self-defense moves wouldn't stand a chance.

"I'm unauthorized to spend taxpayer dollars on security for private citizens. Surely you understand. But should you choose to accept my offer, that would change things considerably."

I break into a cold sweat. "Wouldn't SKI Patrols help me get out of here?"

"They'd assist you to your vehicle, sure, but afterward, you'd be on your own. Your home would be swarmed." His lips bunch up. "Is your mother alone at the house?"

Mom? Black spots enter my vision as I imagine rabid fans attacking her. "You can protect my mother too? Even if she doesn't work for you?"

"As long as you are in my employment, I'll do everything in my power to ensure the safety of you and your dear mother. Otherwise, she might use up her inheritance paying for round-the-clock protection."

I'd never allow that. Mom is living her best life, and I won't destroy all her hard work. "What could you do for us?"

"Well, to start, I'd send a Secret Service agent to coordinate your SKI departure and shadow you twenty-four seven. And I can supplement your salary with the funds necessary to pay for your mother's private security, send out a team first thing tomorrow."

My thumbs massage my namesake into my palms, wishing I had more time to weigh the pros and cons. I need to give Mirovnik a decision, and soon, but perhaps not this second. "You've given me plenty of reasons to say yes, but I don't want to make an impulsive decision. Would it be okay if I get back to you later today?"

He smiles brightly. "Of course. How about I send you the employment contract to review? As long as you agree to the terms by, say, ten o'clock tonight, we should have time to get everything squared away by your departure."

My next breath comes more easily. "Thank you. I really appreciate this. Your call, the offer, all of it."

"And I appreciate your diligence. I look forward to hearing your decision." He signs off.

I scrub a hand down my face and flop back onto the mattress, immediately regretting my request. I should've said yes, but something keeps tugging me in the opposite direction. I picture myself on Mirovnik's staff, and my legs jerk in fear. But fear of what? Publicly embarrassing myself? Meeting Janus? Meeting Janus *and* embarrassing myself? Yes to both.

As soon as I decide not to accept the offer, crushing shame presses against my chest. Declining would make me a coward. And foolish. How else will I protect myself and Mom?

It's a no-win situation. The only way forward is to figure out what I'm least willing to sacrifice.

Deathspan

deathspan—n. The length of time between a soul's lives. The average deathspan is 8.4 years.

The estate attorney never says more than necessary during our virtual meeting, but I feel her silent judgment as I sign a dozen documents with my fingerprint and create my Last Letter account. She ends our connection thirty minutes later, no doubt on her way to deliver a Sociaty exclusive about me.

Shortly after, the employment contract pops onto my screen. I read each clause twice, barely understanding the legalese. Best I can tell, the contract is standard, outlining both my rights and my employer's.

Raphaela said to trust my instincts. But my instincts are at war with each other. I guess I'll take that as a sign to wait.

Speaking of signs . . . I stretch my arms above my head and face the blackened window. I haven't worked up the courage to look outside today. If the Advertitude remains solid black, I don't want to see it. Ziva's loss is still too fresh, yesterday too hard to process. But if the Advertitude isn't black anymore, I don't want to see that either. And I'm sure it won't be, not if news outlets are already talking about me.

Did those same news outlets even mention Ziva? I avoid the window and stare at the clock until it reads twelve thirty p.m. This time yesterday, Windrose called me back for my kirling, and now the world will gain access to my results.

With crossed arms, I rock back and forth, finally mustering the courage to pull up SEIK. I don't have to search for myself. An announcement at the top of the home page displays my photo, name, and soulid.

DEATHSPAN RECORD SHATTERED, reads the headline, with the subtitle, *First New Soul in Forty Years*.

But I select the announcement underneath mine instead.

> FLAVINSKY KIRLED AT WASHINGTON, CD SKI—Meets Another Tragic End
> Foli 1—18–36 A.K. (COD: War injury)
> Foli 2—36–54 A.K. (COD: Suicide)
> Foli 3—54–72 A.K. (COD: Suicide)
> Foli 4—72–90 A.K. (COD: Suicide)
> Foli 5—90–108 A.K. (COD: Suicide)
> Foli 6—108–126 A.K. (COD: Suicide)
> Foli 7—126–144 A.K. (COD: Suicide)
> Foli 8—144–162 A.K. (COD: Suicide)
> Foli 9—162–180 A.K. (COD: Suicide)
> Foli 10—180–198 A.K. (COD: Suicide)
> Foli 11—198–216 A.K. (COD: Suicide)
> Foli 12—218–236 A.K. (COD: Suicide)
> Flavinsky's first recorded death followed injuries sustained while unsuccessfully protecting General Molemo, the beloved leader of the Coalition Forces during World War III. Historians believe Flavinsky's neglectful actions and decisions pre-

cipitated Molemo's murder. Some say they caused it. Flavinsky was either tricked by the traitorous Ladiron or, though never proven, participated in the unsuccessful coup himself. Due to Flavinsky's subsequent and repeated suicides, as well as their abnormally short deathspans, they have become a worldwide source of derision and symbol of inescapable tragedy.

Flavinsky's soul now carries an estimated fifty-five-year sentence and owes 110,000 v in SCAR penalties, plus interest.

To curb the Global Suicide Crisis, the Global Council of Governments (GCG) passed the Suicide Curtailment and Reformation (SCAR) Act, establishing a penalty of five years and 10,000 v per suicide in 36 A.K., shortly before the end of World War III.

Twelve lives. Flavinsky's long list of dates astounds me. I hate that Ziva's were stuck at the bottom without mention of the person she truly was. Could the article be more coldhearted? Did they even try to interview her family or friends?

I try again but still can't contact Dikela. She's either under suicide watch or has deactivated incoming calls.

I search for her by name in SEIK, hoping her folies aren't adding to her stress. Her photo pops up right away. Looks like she was a model, spokesperson, and talk-show host in her former lives. Perfect fit, then. That's one worry I can cross off my list.

Avoiding the ominous window to my right, I search for others in our orientation group. Bardou's results will remain private, so I skip him and look up redhead Rory. He wasn't a criminal like Bardou suspected but a teacher in all three of his folies, even winning national recognition in his last one. Good for him.

Norine already told me about her political background, so I just skim her résumé. In foli 1, she was the political editor at a newspaper in Venezuela and ended up a North American Senator in foli 3. *Impressive.*

I try calling Dikela again. No luck.

The dark windowpane taunts me. *Couldn't you use a little sunshine? Don't you want to see what's on the other side?* Nope.

The stack of breakfast dishes need cleaning. I could return them to the atrium but don't want to risk everyone's stares and whispers. Left without a safe alternative, I carry the plates and cutlery into my bathroom and wash them in the sink with hand soap. Once that chore is done, I stack the plates neatly on my table and stare down the window.

How much longer are you gonna put this off?

I can't ignore the outside world forever. I'm going home tomorrow morning. Shouldn't I know what I'm walking into?

I trudge over to the couch, sit in the corner, and hug my knees to my chest. With my eyes shut, I rest my hand against the cold pane of glass. *Go on. You can do this.* I lift my index finger and tap once to turn the window clear. The back of my eyelids glow orange from the bright afternoon sunshine. I squint one eye open, then the other.

Welcome, New Soul! The cursive script stretches across the white backdrop of the entire Advertitude facade. Holo fireworks burst from the building, showering down a few stories before dissolving. I heave a sigh of relief. Worried for nothing.

The message disappears. In its place, a whole slew of photos and videos from my Sociaty account pop up.

Oh no.

Taken out of context and slowed down to exaggerate my expressions, I appear wild and freakish. *New soul = no soul.*

My heart sinks. *No soul?* I rub my shoulders, desperately hoping whoever paid for this ad doesn't have enough disposable income to post it elsewhere. Anxiety constricts my lungs, making it impossible to breathe.

A solid black wall replaces the collage. I sit up straighter. Ziva! Someone remembered Ziva! Thank you, whoever you are.

But a crescent scratches into the blackness above the top-floor windows, revealing glowing embers underneath. To the right of the crescent, another scorch appears, a straight one this time. No, not a single line, a letter. *R.* One by one, more letters appear on the surface, glowing like evil clawing out of the depths of hell.

C-R-E-A-T-U-R-E

Hairs rise on the back of my neck as the word appears again and again. *CREATURE, CREATURE, CREATURE, CREATURE, CREATURE.*

My teeth chatter. I reach over to darken my window, but the building across the street goes white again. In huge block letters, the same font Vivi and Corah used before, the words *BE CAREFUL* appear.

I wait for the foxes, for reassurance this message is a warning from Vivi and Corah, not a threat. But the words remain as is on the building, not signed, not even necessarily directed at me. Maybe they're warning people *about* me instead of the other way around.

Movement below catches my eye. A few dozen people have congregated by SKI's entrance. Some hold up holo signs, but I can't read them from five stories up. Will they yell at me when I leave SKI?

I turn the window black again and rest my chin on my knees. *What should I do?* How can I defend myself, prove I'm not a creature?

Raphaela said I have the power, but I'm stuck in here until tomorrow morning. Silenced.

The answer hits like a slap to the cheek. My heart pounds in violent revolt against my decision. I don't see another way, though.

I cross to the screen, pull up Mirovnik's contract, initial the clauses, and seal it with my fingerprint. Done. My jaw clenches with doubt, but I remind myself I'm not signing my life away, just accepting a job offer—an incredible one at that. Now Mom and I will get the security we need. Besides, if I don't like working for Mirovnik, I can quit.

But my next move isn't one I can reverse later. To release some tension, I shake out my hands while jogging in place. *Face your fears. Be brave. Just do it.* With a final puff of air, I pull up the directory and make the call.

After only two rings, Windrose picks up. "Sivon? Are you okay?"

"I'm fine. Um, sorry to interrupt."

She waves off the apology. "What can I do for you?"

I have the power. "I'll do the debut show . . . for fifty thousand valuts."

Her eyes narrow. Then she breaks into a smile and relaxes back on her couch. "Wonderful. I'll sort out the details and post your new schedule in a few minutes." My screen goes blank.

Damn. I should've asked for more valuts.

Chromix

chromix—(KROE-mihks) n. Color-shifting nanoparticles, used commonly in cosmetics and hair products.

A new schedule lights up my screen ten minutes later. My interview will be at six o'clock tonight. I have a wardrobe fitting in thirty minutes, then makeup and hair at three thirty. *Is this really happening?*

I hurriedly shower, pull on the SKI bathrobe, and start a quick blowout. The doorbell resonates over the sound of the evaporator. I turn it off and activate the peephole. The sight of the slender, dark-skinned man makes me gasp. *Whoa.* It's Stiletto, the famous fashion designer. Beaming, I throw open the door, and he steers in a clothes rack covered by a large vinyl bag.

"I'm Stiletto." He holds out a manicured hand. "And you, my dear, are a sight for sore eyes. Just lovely."

He is, in fact, wearing red stiletto heels along with a white, perfectly cut three-piece suit. Just like in his Sociaty videos, he's in full makeup with his hair styled to perfection. Red-framed specs encircle his smiling eyes.

Suddenly self-conscious in my ill-fitting bathrobe, I smooth down the bulky fabric. "Thank you, but no need for false compliments." I can pull off lovely on a good day but not after days of crying and months of restless nights. I accept his handshake, praying he doesn't notice my chewed-up cuticles.

He tsks. "You don't see what I do—a beautiful canvas waiting for the perfect frame, and it's my honor to build that for you. What name shall I call you, sweetie?"

"Oh, I'm Si—" I stop midsentence. Gotta get used to using my soulname. "Carrefour. I'm Carrefour."

He takes a step back, his eyes sparkling with delight. "But of course, the Carrefour Diamond!"

One of my brows quirks. I have no idea what he's talking about, but he seems to like my soulname. I'll count that as a win.

His face drains of color. "Oh, I wish I'd known. I would've reached out to the Smithsonian." He waves a hand. "Never mind, we have five hours before the interview. I'll figure it out." He touches the side of his specs and frantically types a message midair.

"What's a carrefour *diamond*?"

He sends his message. "Don't you know? It's *your* soulname, after all."

"Doesn't *carrefour* mean *crossroads*?"

He waves a hand. "That might be what it *used* to mean, but now *everybody knows* it's a four-pointed star-cut diamond. One of a kind, just like you." He taps the tip of my nose.

A diamond? I worry it feels pretentious. Ugh, why couldn't I have just inherited a soulname like everyone else?

"Okay, let's get down to business." Stiletto shields the clothes rack with his body as he unzips the cover. "I already stalked your Sociaty profile for your complexion and size to pull together some pieces." He whips away the vinyl, revealing the garments within.

Every single one is white. I roll my eyes. "White? Really?

Don't you think the pure new soul angle is a little obvious?"

He settles his hands on his waist. "If you think about it, there's no other viable option . . . well, except one."

Wearing a devious grin, he unzips a black bag, revealing a host of accessories, all red. "In Western cultures, the color white symbolizes new beginnings. But in Eastern cultures, red depicts the same. So we shall marry the two. How does that sound?"

I tilt my head back and forth. Mixing in a bit of red could be fun.

Stiletto attaches a full-length retractable mirror to the wall, then presents a dozen different outfits—tops and skirts, dresses, a pantsuit, and an elaborate ball gown. He talks me into trying on the latter after promising he won't make me wear it for my interview. It *is* stunning, but not the impression I want to make. I agreed to the interview to prove I'm a normal teenage girl, not some highbrow celebrity.

The longer we chat, the more at ease I become. Stiletto points out why each item works with my figure, boosting my confidence. By the last outfit, I'm fully enjoying myself, something I thought impossible after recent circumstances.

We settle on a simple A-line dress with spaghetti straps. Stiletto likes how it shows off my strong shoulders, and I'm drawn to the wrinkle-free material. We experiment with a few ruby-red belts before deciding on a dainty one with a small bow in front. I agree to matching kitten heels after warning him I'd fall over in anything higher, and he assures me jewelry will arrive shortly to complete the ensemble.

I'm admiring my reflection when the doorbell chimes. Stiletto opens the door to a petite woman with long black hair that's so shiny, it practically sparkles. I look again. Nope, her hair is actually sparkling.

"Carrefour, this is my dear friend Lepota. She'll be doing your hair and makeup."

Lepota drops the items in her arms—a duffel bag, a satin purse half her size, and another bag emanating a delicious aroma. She grabs my hands, and sinks into a low curtsy. "I—I'm beyond honored, Your Grace."

I swallow hard, unable to find words.

"Lepota, darling, you're scaring her," Stiletto says out of the corner of his mouth. He tugs her shoulders until she's standing upright again. "Let's take it down a notch, okay?"

I manage to free my hands from her grip. "Nice to meet you."

Lepota winces. "I'm sorry, so sorry. I've never met a new soul before, and I kept telling myself to play it cool, but now here you are, so unbelievably perfectly beautiful and just so very . . . new." She turns to Stiletto. "Can't you just feel the virtuous energy coming off her?" She bends over. "Oh gosh, I think I need to sit down."

Stiletto slides one of the dinette chairs behind her just as her legs give way. He begins fanning her face, so I help out as well, my gaze ping-ponging between them. I'd hoped Raphaela was exaggerating about how people would treat me, but if Lepota is any indication, she was spot-on. This is so surreal.

"She just needs a minute," Stiletto says. "Did the same thing when she met Lavonne last month."

But Lavonne is a world-famous singer with actual talent. I'm just me. After another few wafts of air, Lepota's eyes reopen.

"Oh gosh. I did it again, didn't I?" She groans. "So much for my calming affirmations. Sorry for embarrassing you, Stiletto."

He pats her shoulder. "You did no such thing. We are who we are." He winks at me. "She's the best cosmetologist you'll ever meet."

Lepota pats his hand and sighs. "My one redeeming grace." She rises to stand in front of me. "Sorry about that."

Still in a state of shock, I scratch my jaw. "You know I'm not, like, a saint or anything. Right?"

Her eyes flick to Stiletto, who barely perceptively nods. "Sure, of course. Just a run-of-the-mill, everyday new soul, then. Got it."

Fuck. Proving I'm normal will be harder than I thought. "So for my hair and makeup, let's downplay the innocent vibe. Okay?"

She nods about three dozen times in quick succession. "Got it. But I don't think smoky and sultry—"

"Fresh, Lepota." Stiletto clasps his hands at his waist. "Let's go with fresh."

Her shoulders relax, triggering mine to drop as well. Fresh it is.

Lepota opens the fragrant bag and hands me a sandwich, which I devour in six bites. After nanorizing my teeth, she wets my hair, applies a heat-activated chromix gloss, and wraps it on top of my head. Next, she brushes clear chromix makeup in programmable layers onto my skin, eyelids, and lips. By sliding her finger across her screen, she changes the hue, saturation, and luminance. We play with a few combinations, settling on bright eyes, dark lashes, rosy cheeks, and glistening crimson lips.

Stiletto leaves us to answer the doorbell while Lepota starts on my hair. Her nonstop chitchat keeps my mind off the impending interview, but she has to repeatedly remind me to stop shaking my foot. I veto an updo or wild hair colors, so she subtly shifts the shade to a warmer brown and styles my locks into large, sleek curls that flirt with my shoulders. Who knew my hair could do that?

Lepota finally sets down the evaporator, and we admire her handiwork. I still look like myself, but a more sophisticated version. We exit the bathroom to light applause from Stiletto and a polite nod from a uniformed man holding a small parcel.

The screen's clock reads 5:02 p.m. How did the time pass so quickly? My interview is only an hour away, and I still have no clue what I'll say or how to act.

If I'm too humble, people will think they can walk all over me. But if I'm too confident, they might find me haughty. Too innocent, and they'll glorify me. Too conniving, and I'm a creature. *Crap.* This is impossible!

If I took the elevator to the first floor and ran out the front doors, would anyone stop me? My kirling is over, after all. They keep us here an extra day to give us and our loved ones time to digest our results. But the additional hours aren't working in my favor. If anything, they're encouraging a crowd to gather. A crowd I'll need security to escape.

Lepota dabs sweat from my forehead. "Are you okay?"

Not at all, but I have to go through with this. My eyes longingly flit to the door, then the purple velvet case Stiletto accepts from the guard, which he opens to reveal the most stunning jewels I've ever laid eyes on. Well, if I'm about to embarrass myself, at least I'll look my best.

Stiletto first hands me two stud earrings, simple red gems in the shape of Xs. I face the mirror to thread them into my ears. My hair will mostly cover them from view, a shame since they're so understatedly beautiful.

He steps behind me and clasps a necklace around my neck. The X-shaped scarlet stone encircled by platinum rests perfectly below the dip in my collarbone. The jewelry matches my lips, belt, and shoes, creating a cohesive picture of elegance. At least I look confident, despite my stomach's ballooning population of butterflies.

"The Carrefour Diamond," Stiletto whispers, staring at the necklace.

The stone feels warm against my skin, as if it's already a piece of me. For a brief instant, wooziness shifts my vision, as it had earlier with the prime minister. What's with all the déjà vu today?

Mesmerized, I reach up to touch the gem but decide against leaving fingerprints. "This is a diamond? Not a ruby?"

"A red diamond, the rarest color of diamonds, in a one-of-a-kind carrefour cut and setting. It couldn't be more perfect for you." He fluffs the bottom of my hair to frame the necklace.

"It must be worth a million valuts."

"It's priceless. But after some persuasion, the Smithsonian agreed to loan it for the occasion. It *is* your namesake, after all." Stiletto nods to the newcomer. "This guard will follow you until the interview is complete, when the jewels will be transported back to their exhibit."

So much for making a run for it.

On the elevator up to the tenth floor, shaking with nerves and flanked by the security guard, Stiletto, Lepota, and a SKI Patrol, I wonder again if I'm doing the right thing. Then I remember the group of people gathered out front, the disgusting and intimidating ads playing across Advertitude, and Lepota's reverent behavior.

I *have* to do this. Besides, I've watched debut interviews a million times. Kureshtar is a pro, always making his guests look good. I have nothing to worry about.

Except as it turns out, Kureshtar isn't the one interviewing me.

New soul

new soul—n. A unique soulid never before indexed by SEIK. By 100 A.K., the number of new souls decreased exponentially. Weeks, months, then years began separating them.

"Ujjwala?" I ask when we step off the elevator. What is my former schoolmate doing inside the SKI studio?

"Hey, sweetie!" She rushes over and gives me air kisses.

Ujjwala was a senior when I was a junior, though she went by a different name at the time. Despite running with the "in crowd," she was always nice to everyone. Since her kirling, she's amassed millions of followers and dozens of sponsors on Sociaty as a professional influencer, adopting the same persona as her uber-successful past life.

"Wh-what are you doing here?"

She takes my elbow, leading me across the busy set to plush yellow chairs on a royal blue platform. "SKI chose me to interview you!"

Unease stirs my gut. "I thought Kureshtar did the SKI interviews."

"He has appendicitis. When my agent got wind of it, she threw my hat in the ring. She's *amazing*, by the way, if you need someone. Since I already knew you and have the most Sociaty followers, I was a shoo-in. Well, *had* the most followers. You've gained like fifteen million in the past six hours."

Fifteen million? I blow out a burst of air and focus on the first part of her speech. "Kureshtar has appendicitis?"

"Yeah, rumor is he's not treating it. Said he's ready for his neli."

"Seriously? Isn't he only in his forties?"

She shrugs and waves at someone I don't recognize.

A pang of foreboding halts me in my tracks. My interview is now in the hands of a Sociaty star. "I'm not ready for this. I don't think I can—" I step toward the elevator.

Ujjwala hooks her arm with mine. "Don't be silly. You're gonna do great. Trust me."

Calm down, Sivon. Working yourself up will only make this worse. SKI wouldn't have chosen just anyone to interview a new soul, right? They would've wanted the best, so if they trust Ujjwala, I should too.

"I heard your soulname is Carrefour?" She points to my necklace. "Nice touch."

I gesture toward Stiletto, who's talking with someone on the crew. "It was all him."

She gasps. "Is that Stiletto? Oh, I've been *pleading* with my agent to connect us. Will you introduce us later?"

"Yeah, of course."

As she tries to catch his attention, I take a moment to look her over. Her emerald-green hair is a striking change from her natural brunette, but it somehow suits the copper undertones of her skin. She wears a cropped black jacket over a shimmery top and colorful pants that taper to her ankles. Her strappy heels emphasize the jewelry on her toes. I always did envy her wardrobe.

Golf-ball-size drones lift from the ground and zoom around

the room. I resist the urge to bat one away as it approaches.

"Don't mind the cameras," Ujjwala says. "They're synchronizing color and lighting data."

I duck as the swarm hovers closer. "Do you, um, have any tips you can share?"

"Oh, just be yourself! Pretend we're just two old friends catching up."

Ouch. I mean, sure, we weren't *actually* friends at school. Ujjwala was more someone I knew *of* than truly knew, but she didn't need to throw the "pretend" in there.

Whatever. Let's just get this over with. "Will the interview be aired live?"

"No, it'll broadcast at eight p.m. like usual. Your exit from SKI tomorrow will stream in real time, though."

"*Great,*" I mumble, wondering what wrinkled top I should wear for that momentous occasion.

Stiletto and Lepota weave around staffers to the stage. I introduce them to Ujjwala, who exudes confidence as they strike up a brief conversation. Stiletto adjusts my skirt, and Lepota applies a microphone chip to my temple and dabs a dot of chromix over it. "Stop sweating, or your makeup will melt."

Not helping. I clasp my hands, imagining I'm on frozen Thessaly instead of this stuffy studio under scorching lights. *Circle X. Circle X.* A conversation between old friends. *You can do this.*

Stiletto and Lepota disappear, and Ujjwala throws out a few more tips, ending with "No matter what the cameras do, keep looking at me." I nod and rub my clammy palms against my skirt before clasping them again.

A countdown clock flashes across the center camera, resembling a hovering eyeball. My heart skips a beat.

Five... Oh gosh.

Four... I take it back.

Three... Why me?

Ujjwala tilts her head, displaying her perfect white teeth. "Hello and thank you for joining us today at the Washington, CD, Semyon Kirlian Institute for a special *Kirling Debut Show*. This program is sponsored by Purity Body Wash, making you feel as clean as a new soul."

Ha. Ha.

"I'm Ujjwala, standing in for Kureshtar, who has sadly taken ill. We're all thinking of you, Kureshtar, and wish you the very best."

Thinking about stealing your job is more like it. She turns to a second camera behind my shoulder. "I'm honored to introduce our guest today. She just shattered the longest deathspan record by *forty years*. May I present one of my dear friends, Carrefour."

I sit in shock with a smile affixed to my face. *Dear friend?*

Okay, sure, I'll play along. I need this interview to accomplish one thing, to make me seem human, not divine or diabolical. With renewed determination, I say, "I'm so grateful they chose you to interview me, Ujjwala. Feels like fate."

"Aw!" She gives my hand a quick squeeze before sitting up straight. "Carrefour, you're the first new soul in decades. What was it like hearing your results?"

Be honest. "Well, I was surprised . . . and overwhelmed. I expected to hear all about my past lives and didn't have any." A nervous chuckle escapes. "I was sure the results were wrong, but they performed the test twice, and here we are." I shrug.

"Oh, I assure you, the news shocked us all!"

Is she mocking me? Before I can overanalyze her word choice, she jumps into the next question.

"So tell me, what did you expect your results to be? Were you hoping for something this special?"

Hell no. "Um, well, I didn't really have any expectations, just hoped for a little direction. Truth be told, I'm still uncomfortable with my results. Between my kirling and Flavinsky..." I swallow hard. "I'll probably feel better after talking with my mom and friends."

"Well, isn't it wonderful that SKI brought the two of us together today?"

I somehow hold a smile. "Yes, so wonderful."

"Our viewers may not know your mother is the world-renowned Artifex." She faces the camera over my shoulder. "Artifex has the unique gift of visualizing people's auras, which she paints for celebrities and influential personalities. I've been on her waitlist eight months myself." She turns back to me. "Carrefour, did your mother predict your new soul?"

I shake my head. "She doesn't see soulids, only colors, which reflect people's personalities and emotions. That's not the same as a kirling. Soulids can be photographed. Auras cannot."

"Do you see auras as well?"

I genuinely laugh. "No, but I've always wanted to. I used to get headaches squinting at people, trying to see their colors. It does seem like a useful gift, getting a read on people that way. I'm lucky to have such a gifted mother."

"I bet she feels the same about you." She pats my hand. "What do you suppose your mom thinks about your results?"

I huff a laugh. "I bet she's absolutely elated. She'll say I was given a blank canvas, so to speak. She always says kirlings can't tell us who we really are."

Ujjwala's eye twitches. "How controversial! Is she a member of the Improvement Party?"

We're talking about my mother's political affiliations now?

"I wouldn't know. She doesn't discuss politics with me."

Ujjwala shifts her knees away. "Well, how about art? Did you inherit your mother's artistic talent?"

"I've picked up some of her techniques but not her incredible talent. While she couldn't predict I'd be a new soul, we both knew I wouldn't be an artist."

Ujjwala laughs. I made a joke! And it was even a little funny. My posture relaxes. *See? You're really doing this.*

"I know our audience is curious about that new soul of yours. Tell us who you are at heart, Carrefour. Would you say you're a spiritual person?"

Here goes. A camera approaches from my right, but I ignore the looming eyeball and focus on Ujjwala. "No, not really. People may think because I'm a new soul, I have answers to the meaning of life. They want me to say things like 'I think you're in heaven during your deathspan' or 'Souls who are reborn quickly need to atone for past sins.' But I'm as clueless as everyone else."

"Are you suggesting you're *disappointed* with your results?" Ujjwala's fingers curl.

"Honestly, yes. Like everyone else, I dreamed of receiving an inheritance, job offers, maybe even a soulmate, and well, I got nothing." The ache in my throat returns. *Don't you dare cry on camera. Pull it together.*

"No job offers? That can't be true."

Does she know about Mirovnik's offer? Am I allowed to talk about that? I signed the contract, and he recruited me to help his campaign, so he'd probably want me to mention it. But would discussing it help prove I'm normal? Well, it's certainly not helping my image to sit here blank-faced instead of answering her question.

"Actually, yes, I've already received one offer. The, uh, prime minister asked me to join his staff, and I accepted."

Ujjwala's eyes widen, as if saying, *Was that so hard?* But the actual words out of her mouth are "How very kind of him! Isn't he the lucky one?"

"Thank you, but the honor is mine."

"Sounds like a match made in heaven. Speaking of which, you mentioned soulmates. Do you have someone special waiting at home?"

I adjust my posture. Do we have to discuss my relationships, or lack thereof? "No. I mean, I've gone on some dates, but no one really clicked. Yeah, like most people, I hoped for a soulmate.... This would be a different show, if so."

"Indeed!" She lifts a hand, cocking her head. "Then again, why share the spotlight when you can have it all to yourself?"

She and I couldn't be more different. "Well, I've never wanted fame, so a little moral support would be nice. I have no idea what I'm doing."

"Don't sell yourself short, Carrefour. You're doing great!"

"Thank you, Ujjwala. Must be because we're such dear friends." I manage to say it without sarcasm.

She holds a hand to her heart. "That means so much to me. It feels like old times, doesn't it?"

"Sure does." I should win an award for not rolling my eyes.

"Thank you so much for joining me this evening, Carrefour. I wish you the very best for tomorrow and the future."

As she says good-bye to the viewers, I beam in satisfaction. Except for the job-offer part, the interview went pretty well! Maybe that stumble will play to my advantage. Normal people freeze up on camera all the time. No way could anyone watch this show and still believe I'm shady or special. Check and mate.

NASS

NASS—(nass) abbr. An acronym representing the North American Secret Service.

Wednesday, August 29, 236 A.K.—Final Morning at SKI

The doorbell's relentless chiming startles me awake the next morning. I lurch into a seated position, brushing the hair from my eyes to check the screen: 6:45 a.m. *Who the hell is here this early?*

After extricating myself from the twisted sheets, I carefully approach the door, wary it will burst open. I activate the peephole and stand on my tiptoes to peer through. It's a community protector. With his head tipped down, bearing only the top of his hat, he taps the buzzer with his right hand while the other hammers away.

Has something happened to Mom? Did someone break into our home? Is she hurt? I release the lock and throw open the door.

"Finally! What took you so long?" The protector rushes in and slams the door on a jostling herd attempting to peer into my room.

My heart, already thumping wildly, picks up the pace. It's . . . him. He carries the same judgmental glare and commanding presence as before, but now he's burdened by the weight of profound loss, so painfully tangible it nearly brings me to my knees.

It's Ziva's brother, Donovan, the one who yelled at me for

gawking from the elevator. *Why is he in my room?*

His dark eyes hold even more venom than before. Adrenaline surges through my veins, putting me on high alert. What did Ziva say about him? That if someone wanted to hurt her, he'd take them down before they had the chance. Does he hold me responsible for that night? Or blame me for not doing more?

Neither of those reasons seem rational. But would a grieving brother, an overly protective one, be thinking rationally? Absolutely not.

Be careful. The Advertitude threat screams through my head, transposing the bold black letters over his features. Did Donovan write that message? A warning of his inevitable return?

His square jaw flexes as he eyes me up and down. "Ready?" he growls.

Ready for what? To *die*? I cautiously backstep toward the bathroom. "I'm *so sorry* about Ziva. I met her my first day here, and she was . . . very kind to me."

He furrows his brows. Shit, he doesn't believe me . . . or doesn't remember me at all. Maybe he's just going room to room, exacting vengeance for his sister's death. Should I jog his memory of that night, or will that make things worse?

"Dikela wasn't allowed to stay in the hallway, but we got her into the room next door. She tried to talk to Ziva through the wall, but they're soundproof." I take another step away. *Fuck! The walls are soundproof!* A crowd of people right outside the door, and they'd never hear me scream. "Ziva w-was my friend."

His lips turn down as he leans toward me. "Stop talking about my sister. I don't want to hear her name from your lips ever again. Got it?"

My pulse quickens. Was that a *threat?* The hatred in his eyes shreds my soul into pieces, threatening my very sense of being. How did we get here? "L-look, I don't know what you want"—I continue edging back, raising my hands—"but I'm asking you, respectfully, to please leave."

He glances at my hands and squints like a lion studying his prey. *Get out of here, Sivon! Run!*

I dart into the bathroom, slam the door, and fumble with the lock until it latches. I slide down the door until I'm crouched on the floor. My hands shake so violently, I have to sit on them to hold them still. *What should I do?* I can't contact anyone from here.

Muffled laughter filters through the door. The bathroom isn't soundproof! Maybe I can talk him down somehow?

"We don't have time for your drama, Carrefour."

Drama? "What, are you on some sort of revenge timeline? Too many people to kill today? Sorry for slowing you down, buddy."

Donovan laughs again. "Oh, you're a riot. This will be more fun than I thought." Sarcasm drips from every word. He really does hate me.

"Please," I whimper. "I'm sorry, I'm *so sorry* about Z—your sister. Please don't hurt me." I release my hands to hug myself into a ball.

He bangs the door. "Will you stop fooling around? I'm not here to hurt you. I'm your security escort."

I raise my head and wipe a tear from my cheek. "W-what?"

"I was sent to protect you." He mutters something like "New soul is a moron."

Moron? He's the one storming into my room, acting like I'm personally responsible for Ziva's death. If he's here to protect me, shouldn't he be a little nicer? "You're lying so I'll open the door."

"Anyone with a brain would know they don't allow just anyone into the building. This place is on lockdown."

I take a stabilizing breath. *Ignore the insults, Sivon.* He's Ziva's brother and obviously going through hell. "Oh yeah? Then how'd you get in the other night? And Mirovnik said he was sending the Secret Service, not a community protector."

"*I am Secret Service!*" he shouts, then mumbles, "Unbelievable."

"I can hear you, you know."

He snorts. "Good."

Smart-ass. "Prove it!"

"Excuse me?"

"Prove you're Secret Service. I want to see your, uh, your credentials."

He lets a few seconds pass before responding. "Okay, Your *Majesty*."

After a bit of rustling, a thin electronic card slides under the door. I pick it up.

A photo of Ziva's brother appears on the small screen with the name *Shepherd* underneath. I study the sharp angles of his face, his full lips, copper skin, and perceptive eyes. My heart skips a beat. Out of fear, of course, not because he's attractive. A few seconds later, an official seal replaces his photo, stating, *North American Secret Service—Uniformed Services Division*.

I pass the card under the door. "How do I know that's real?"

He laughs again. I'm getting irritated by how funny he thinks I am.

"Let me get this straight. You think I'm on some vendetta to avenge my sister's death, so I somehow procure a NASS uniform *and* credentials, find out which room you're staying in, and work my way here, during lockdown, with hundreds of cameras pointed at the building and patrols on duty. And I did all that to kill *you*, some random spectator in the hallway the night Ziva died?"

So he *does* remember me! Ha!

But as Donovan's logic sinks in, shame and embarrassment flush my cheeks. He wouldn't be allowed in this building, much less shown my room if he wasn't directed to do so. I keep forgetting I'm not a nobody soul anymore. I swallow and sit on my heels. "Well, when you put it that way . . ."

"I'll tell you what, I'm gonna cross to the other side of your bed to stand by the window. When you open the bathroom door, you can reach the exit faster than I could get to you. Would that make you feel better?"

"Um, yeah, okay." I stand and startle at my reflection. The chromix shifted overnight, warping my features. Whatever. Who cares what this jerk thinks of my appearance?

My first instinct is to run straight to my bedroom door, but that would only provide him with more fodder for ridicule. We've already established he's here as my guard, not to hurt me. So I will exit this bathroom calmly and rationally, with my head held high.

As soon as I open the door, he raises his hands. "Hey, see. You're good. I'm not moving."

I don't miss the amusement in his features. My body betrays my intelligence by walking directly to the door, positioning me within arm's reach of the handle. I try to regain some dignity by casually leaning against the wall.

"Okay if I put my hands down?" He raises his expressive brows.

I huff at his teasing. "The prime minister said to meet you in the lobby."

"The prime minister didn't consider that, along with the horde of people outside, a thousand souls inside SKI also want a look at you."

He removes his hat, sets it on the bed, and scratches his short black curls. "The NASS director thought it best if I escorted you down."

A horde of people outside? I head over to the window, brace myself for more bullying ads, and turn it translucent again. I gasp. Foxes! Hooray, the foxes are back!

"We love you, Carrefour!" The *O* in *Carrefour* resembles a crossroads symbol, with a red *X* through it. Two adorable foxes climb the artful letters, occasionally stopping to wave and blow kisses. Better yet, the message doesn't change, remaining steadfast to the wall. Of course Vivi and Corah would find a way to stop the haters.

A smile works itself out of my war-torn heart. How do I deserve their friendship? I'll have to pay them back for this kindness.

Movement on top of the hotel draws my attention. Security guards line the rooftop, holding incaps—targeted incapacitators. Thankfully, the protective devices are tucked against their chests, not aimed at the street.

I gasp at the transformation below, not at all resembling the quiet avenue I stepped onto five days ago. Barricades cordon off the sidewalk, stretching from the SKI entrance to a guarded black hover vehicle. Waist-high fences line the street, condensing four lanes into one, void of all traffic.

The sidewalks are crammed with thousands of people packed tightly together. Dozens of drones float above them like a sea of eyeballs. The crowd chants under the rolling waves, but no sounds breach the window. From up here, they seem cheerful, celebratory, even, not an angry mob. I sag in relief, my hip settling onto the armrest. I'll take cheers over jeers any day, but didn't they see my interview? Surely they wouldn't have come out in droves like this if so. Maybe SKI hasn't aired it yet?

I glance at Donovan, who's studying me through narrowed eyes. Was he watching me this whole time?

"Ready to meet your adoring fans?"

Is he serious? He thinks I *want* this? I'm just relieved I won't be *harassed* on my way out. "You don't know me." I lift my chin, grab the garment bag Stiletto left on the couch, and march back into the bathroom, taking pleasure in slamming and locking the door.

After showering, I unzip the bag and sigh at the white silky tank top and matching slacks. More white, but at least they're casual, and loads better than my gym clothes and T-shirts.

I get dressed and go through the bag's other pockets. The shoe compartment holds red espadrilles, and the accessory pouch contains a matching belt, choker necklace, and chunky sunglasses. The choker consists of two thin red cords tied to a silver ring. They cross in the center, making an X inside the circle, a crossroads symbol. I hook it around my neck and slide on the belt and shoes, saving the glasses for later.

Now dressed, I open the door to release steam while I dry my hair. Expecting the summer heat to be in full force when we get outside, I sweep my thick mane into a low ponytail. Finally, I bend down to gather my belongings from the floor. When I stand again, Donovan steps out of view.

Was he watching me again? "What are you doing?" I ask, calling him out.

"Checking if the hallway is clear. I sent up some patrols while you were showering."

"Oh." Did I think he would watch me *dry my hair*? Clearly, I'm on edge.

I stuff my pj's and toiletries into the garment bag and grab the sunglasses from the counter.

Donovan, with his hat back on, stands at the end of the bed, blocking the way to my duffel bag. As I approach, he sucks in a breath but doesn't move. I take a half step closer, hoping he'll get the hint. He doesn't, just peers down his nose at me, raising the hairs on my arms. What's his problem?

"Excuse me?" I motion toward my bag.

"Oh, right." Clearing his throat, he steps aside.

I drop the garment bag onto the bed, set my duffel beside it, and move my items into the latter. I roll the now-empty garment bag into as tight a ball as I can. Worried I'd look like a movie star, I drop the red sunglasses into my duffel as well.

"Wear the glasses."

"What? Why?"

Donovan sighs with annoyance. "I don't care *who* you are. When you get outside, and people are clambering over themselves to get to you, it'll be scary. If you hide your eyes, they won't see your fear."

Oh, he's giving advice now? "Maybe I *want* them to know I'm scared. Maybe then they'll leave me alone."

"Never, *never* let people know you're afraid. You don't want to appear vulnerable." He fishes the glasses out of my bag and hands them over.

Guess it couldn't hurt to wear them. Movie star it is, then. I unfold the sunglasses but pause before sliding them on. "Oh, shoot. I need to make a quick call."

But Dikela's name is still grayed out in the SKI directory. I chew the side of my mouth. So much for saying good-bye.

"She left last night," Donovan says, "for the funeral."

My heart sinks. *Ziva.* "That's today? Why aren't *you* there?"

He shifts his weight, his eyes again burning with fiery rage. He *hates* me. And no wonder; I'm the one keeping him from his sister's funeral.

But this isn't my fault. I didn't know who Mirovnik would assign as my bodyguard, nor did I know when Ziva's funeral would be. Why was Dikela allowed to leave for it but not me?

Because no one knew Ziva and I were friends. Because I just met her five days ago. Because I didn't help her one bit, not when it really mattered. Perhaps Donovan's ire is deserved, after all. "I didn't know. I'm *so sorry*, Donovan."

His jaw flexes. "My *name* is Shepherd."

The words hit like a gut punch, knocking a breath from my parted lips. The breach of etiquette was my faux pas, of course. Just because Dikela and Ziva called him by his birth name doesn't give me permission to take the same liberty.

"Of course." Blinking rapidly, I put on the sunglasses, tuck the garment bag under my arm, and shoulder the duffel bag. "I'm ready."

He turns his back to me and presses his earlobe. "Moving out." After checking the peephole, he unlocks and opens the door, gesturing me through with a dramatic sweep of his arm.

NASShole. I jut out my chin as I pass by.

In the hallway, SKI Patrols are positioned at each door. I avert my eyes from the runway of red-lit doorknobs, focusing on the marble floor as I walk toward the elevator, unnerved by the creepy silence in a corridor full of people. Unless they're RAIDs that look like people. That thought is even more unsettling.

Are the robots assigned to protect Ziva still at SKI? Or were they decommissioned for their categorical failure to do their only job? I study the faces of the two patrols who join me and Shepherd in the elevator. Neither resembles the bot outside Ziva's room, and they both appear to be breathing. But maybe they're programmed to do that. I shudder. Stuff of nightmares.

The doors open. This is the same lobby I passed through five days ago, but it couldn't look or feel more different. Instead of bustling with dozens of teenagers and staffers, a single receptionist stands behind the counter. Two patrols are stationed beside the elevator, and two more by the exit. Outside the floor-to-ceiling windows, people press against the glass, banging and shouting. The only sound inside is the hum of air conditioning blowing through the vents.

I gather my wits before starting toward the doors. *Here we go.* I'm halfway across the lobby when the receptionist clears her throat.

"Excuse me, uh, Carrefour. We need to complete your release documentation."

I hesitate, then change directions to approach the counter, followed by Shepherd and the two patrols from the elevator.

"I hope you enjoyed your stay at SKI," she says in a small but cheerful voice.

"Sure, thank you." She probably doesn't want the truth.

After I confirm the gym and food charges for my stay, the receptionist slides my specs over the counter. *My specs!* I can't believe I almost left them behind. I'm tempted to switch out the red sunglasses but need total focus over the next few minutes. I shove the specs into the outside pocket of my duffel instead.

I face the entrance. How should I do this? Do I interact with the crowd? Shake people's hands? Smile and wave? This is so surreal.

As we approach the doors, Shepherd gives orders into his earplant, then turns to me. "No matter what happens, keep moving toward the hover. *Do not stop.*"

The hint of concern in his eyes squelches my inclination to dismiss his command. "Got it."

I adjust the garment bag under my right arm, rub my hands on my pants, and take hold of the duffel's strap with my left hand. Suddenly lightheaded, I'm tempted to drop my head between my knees, but some unknown signal sets everyone in motion.

Shepherd steps behind me. The patrols from the elevator move ahead of us, and the two stationed by the doors push them open. Once we walk through the first set of doors, the patrols holding them follow us.

The muffled roar of the crowd reaches us now, and their energy amplifies as if sensing my approach. "Care eh four! Care eh four!"

They're chanting my name! And cheerfully so. Behind the doors, the sound warps to "Carry forth!"—like a squadron marching into battle. I quickly adopt the mantra. *Car-ry forth. Car-ry forth.*

They're not yelling at you, they're encouraging you. Hold your head high. Seize your power.

I peer around a patrol's shoulder and out the doors to the hover, only fifteen meters away. SKI Patrols line the barricades, each a meter apart. *Car-ry forth.*

Shepherd acknowledges a report through his com, then shouts in a booming voice, "We're moving!" *Car-ry forth.*

The exterior doors open, and the sound is immediately deafening and disorienting. The chant dissolves, as does my confidence. I don't have the time or inclination to smile, shake hands, or wave. My innate reaction is to protect myself. I duck my head and tuck in, adjusting the grip on my duffel until my knuckles turn white.

Patrols stationed by the doors join our group. We move quickly, a tight circle of seven with me in the center.

Only a handful of steps in, a man leaps over the barrier to my right. He crashes onto the patrol beside me, pulling him down. Taking advantage of the opening, the crowd claws for me, tugging at my hair, scratching my skin. I shout and lunge to the left. Someone pulls the empty garment bag from under my arm, lifting it away.

"Shepherd!" I clutch my duffel against my chest.

Another man attempts to grab my shoulder, but Shepherd leaps over the downed patrol to push him away. Shepherd wraps his arm around my waist, half carrying me to the hover, lifts me through the open door, and pulls it down behind us. I tremble uncontrollably as he tugs the restraint across my chest and secures it by my hip.

I look past his shoulders to the crowd trying to break through the blockade. The man who jumped over the barrier now lies face down in handcuffs.

Shepherd commands the navigator to go while securing his own seatbelt. "Fucking SKI Patrols." He looks at me, then does a double take. "Whoa. Hey, you're okay. Yeah?"

I'm shivering too much to reply. That was so, *so* much worse than I expected. I press a clammy hand to the bright red scratch running down my right forearm. No blood seeps through, but it sears like a fresh burn. My chin trembles and tears fill my eyes.

"Shit." Shepherd unbuckles, takes off his jacket, and lays it over me before strapping in again. "Listen, Carrefour, you need to pull yourself together. If you go into shock, and we go to a hospital, we'll have to do this all over again. Catch my drift?"

I nod, still unable to speak.

"Okay, take some deep breaths."

I try, but all I can muster is a jagged, staccato rhythm. We crawl down Massachusetts Avenue, still passing thousands upon thousands of people crowded together, waving and screaming.

He taps an overhead screen to turn the windows black.

"Hey, look at me." He takes hold of my jaw and turns my face toward his, pushing the sunglasses onto my head. "You're all right. We're going to breathe together, okay?"

I hiccup a sob and meet his eyes. His warm hazel eyes. A kaleidoscope of sea green, honey brown, and prismatic gold. Had I really thought they were cold and black before?

He drops his hand to his lap. I resist the urge to pick it up and place it back on my jaw.

"In." He inhales deeply.

I mirror him, drawing in the scent of fresh pine and river water.

"And out." He exhales.

I copy him, hypnotized.

"In." He repeats. "Out."

He does this a few more times until my heartbeat returns to a semi-normal tempo. We stare into each other's eyes for another synchronized breath, the corners of my lips lifting in gratitude. He gives me a tight smile and leans back to talk into his com.

I force myself to look away. It's not without effort.

Hover

hover—n. A vehicle with undercarriage magnets that repel magnetized roads, allowing it to float and move without resistance.

Buzzing at my feet breaks me out of my stupor. My duffel bag rests against my ankles, and it's vibrating.

I bend over, unzip the side pocket, and take out my specs. When I put them on, the name *Mom* dances over a photo of her making a silly face. I've never accepted a call faster. *"Mom?"*

I pass Shepherd his jacket. He taps another option overhead, and a holoshield activates between us and the navigator.

"Sivon! Oh, thank goodness."

"Mom . . . I—I . . ." Where do I even begin?

"Oh, sweetie, I know all about it. I just watched you leave SKI on the news. Are you okay?"

I want to say no but don't want to worry her. "I'm all right, just . . . overwhelmed. I miss you so much!"

She's in our living room, the light from the front window illuminating her face. Multicolored framed photograms of my childhood decorate the wall behind her. How I wish I could go back to those simpler days.

"I miss you too, but what a relief to see your smiling face during the interview last night. I'm so happy for you. A *new soul*!"

Ugh, I knew she'd say that. "But the institute was *awful*, Mom. My kirling, the horrible ads on the hotel next door . . . and one of my friends d-died."

Shepherd shifts away and taps his foot. I gulp, instantly regretting bringing up Ziva. How selfish I must sound when he's missing her funeral today.

"Oh, my sweet Indigo. I'm so sorry. You've been through so much."

Her comforting words wash over my soul like a warm bath. "Are you okay, Mom? What's it like at home?"

Her eyes shift from the camera to the window, her lips twisting with apprehension. "Probably best to just show you."

She flips to the front-facing camera. At first, the lens only focuses on the windowpane. Then it adjusts, revealing a throng of people at the end of our driveway. Hundreds, maybe thousands, are gathered in the street with a cloud of drones floating over them. "A security team arrived a few hours ago and moved them off the lawn."

I cover my mouth. Off the *lawn*? "I'm so sorry, Mom. I'll be home in about thirty minutes, and we'll figure this out."

Shepherd shifts to face me, his brows drawn. He opens his mouth, but Mom speaks first.

"No. You cannot come here, Indigo." Her voice trembles. "It's not safe right now. Not for you."

"But I need to see y—!"

Shepherd taps the side of my specs to mute the call. "Absolutely not."

What the heck? "Since when do you dictate where I—"

"If you go anywhere near that place, you're begging for a repeat of this morning. The best way to keep your mother safe is to stay far away."

This is bullshit. How can I be the most powerful person in the world if I can't even go home? But as much as I want to hug Mom and sleep in my bed again, I can't put her life at risk.

I unmute my glasses, blinking away frustrated tears. "You're right. I'll give it a few days, until your security clears out the crowd."

She wipes the dampness from under her eyes. "Do you have someone to watch out for you? Someplace safe to go?"

If we weren't headed to my house, then where was Shepherd taking me? And why wasn't I told? I eye him, wondering if I could exchange him for a different model. "Sure do. I'll call you tomorrow, okay? Fill you in on everything."

As soon as we say our good-byes, Shepherd presses his earlobe to ask for a status update. He relaxes and reaches up to turn the exterior windows translucent again before answering another call.

The streets of CD now appear normal, with tourists milling about and regular morning traffic. We're turning onto Coalition Avenue, heading in the direction of the White House.

"She's fine. No injuries."

Liar. I hold my scratched arm in his face, but he turns away.

"You already knew I wouldn't be going home today. Didn't you?"

Shepherd holds up one finger and plugs his ear with the other. "Yes, sir. Thank you, sir."

He presses his earlobe and leans into the seatback, focusing on the road ahead. "What are you griping about now?"

"Why didn't you tell me I wasn't going home?"

"Why did you think you would be?"

I clench my jaw. "*Because* that's where I live? I agreed to *work* for the prime minister, not move in with him."

Shepherd guffaws. "You're not moving into the White House. At least, not yet."

I narrow my eyes. "What's that supposed to mean?"

"*Oh, Janus!*" Shepherd says in a falsetto. "You're so handsome and intelligent. I just *know* we're made for each other." He flutters his lashes.

My nostrils flare. How dare he? "That's not fair. I was *thirteen* when I made that video."

"Imagine that—a new soul *and* a Nostradamus. Can you also predict Vast Valuts numbers?"

I growl with annoyance. "You know what? I *am* looking forward to meeting Janus. People with manners are in short supply these days."

"Well, I'm sure he's gonna *love* you and your delightful personality. I can already hear the wedding bells tolling."

"Ringing," I correct. "Wedding bells ring. Death bells toll."

He smirks. "I meant what I said."

I clench my jaw. He's a NASShole, plain and simple. Are the rest of them like this too? I'm definitely requesting a different one at the first opportunity. "If we're not going to the White House, and we're not going to my house, then where the hell are you taking me?"

"To your fancy new penthouse suite at the Kismet. Surprised you didn't foretell that too."

Penthouse? The prime minister mentioned a new wardrobe, not a suite at the most upscale apartment building in CD. But I'm glad *someone* had the forethought. I'm not about to look a gift horse in the mouth, especially a thoroughbred one, so I ignore Shepherd's jibe. He'll be out of my life in no time. "What then?"

His brows furrow. "Hmm?"

"After the apartment. Am I meeting the prime minister? Do I have any events this afternoon? Tonight?"

"Mirovnik is campaigning in Dakota. Janus won't return from his mission trip until tomorrow afternoon. *You* will be safely tucked in your apartment until the Holusion gala tomorrow night."

I cross my arms. "You seriously expect me to sit around all day in an empty apartment, twiddling my thumbs? No freaking way. I just got out of one prison cell. I won't let you throw me in another."

"Not sure if you noticed, but you can't just walk around the city—"

"Take me to the funeral."

Shepherd slowly turns to meet my eyes, disgust shadowing his features. "No."

"Why not? I only knew Z—" I check my tone, remembering he's mourning her loss. "I only knew your sister for a few days, but we *were* friends. You said I don't have anything else on my schedule today. We should go."

"It's not happening," he says with steadfast determination. "You think you're the only big news today? Ziva may not have the throng of worshipers you do, but hundreds are gathering to pay their respects. And what? You want to parade in, wearing white and red like a bride on her wedding day?" He rubs his jaw. "No fucking way. I won't let you steal the spotlight."

Wow, he really doesn't know me at all. "That's not what I'm trying to do! I wouldn't wear *this* to a funeral." I sweep my hand past my outfit.

He jerkily shakes his head. "Not on your life. You think my

family wants to hear you spewing bullshit about Ziva having to atone for past sins?"

I try and fail to assemble his words into something coherent. "*What* are you *talking* about?"

He laughs mirthlessly. "Don't bullshit me, Carrefour. You said that exact thing in your debut show."

"I said nothing of the sort!"

"Do you think I'm stupid?" He withdraws a screen from the seatback pocket, taps a few options, and throws it into my lap.

A video plays. I'm sitting in a yellow chair, wearing the dress I was in last night. Ujjwala asks, "What was it like to hear your results?"

"Well, I was surprised, absolutely elated. I was given a blank canvas, so to speak."

"What the fuck?" That was my answer to a different question, what *my mom* would say, not me.

Instead of the actual Q&A, the program cuts to a reporter. "When asked for her thoughts on deathspans, Carrefour had this to say...."

I again appear on set with Ujjwala. *"I think you're in heaven during your deathspan. Souls who are reborn quickly need to atone for past sins."*

My back goes rigid. I check the source of the video. It looks legitimate, but it can't be. They wouldn't just change my answers like that. "Is this a joke? That's not what I said."

"Don't try to pull that shit on me. You clearly said those exact words."

The distaste in his eyes, his blatant lack of sympathy, the cold animosity from the moment he stormed into my room. This video did that. This horrible, disgusting, heavily edited video.

My stomach tightens as the full extent of deception sinks in. SKI, Windrose, Ujjwala. Did they *plan* this? Is this what everyone thinks of me now? How do I begin to fix this?

I shift in my seat, turning toward Shepherd. "No, I *didn't* say those words. I mean, I said them, but not that way. That wasn't what I meant."

He scoffs. "Too late to take it back."

"But I didn't say that! Ujjwala asked if I was spiritual, and I said no, and something like people *expected* me to say those things. But that's not what I believe. Not at all." I grab his hands, noting their warmth, and hold them between mine. "I promise you. That wasn't my real answer. I don't believe those things. I *promise*."

He looks at our hands, and for a split-second, the ever-present furrow in his brow disappears. Then he pulls free of my grip. "How can I trust a new soul?"

I swallow hard. "Let me show you. *Please*. If I do anything at the funeral that pisses you off, I'll . . . I'll ask Mirovnik to assign someone else. You can go back to doing whatever you do for the Service." I bet Shepherd will find any reason to cede his position, but at least we'll have made it to the funeral.

"Now you're *threatening* me?"

"*What?*"

"You will *not* take this assignment from me. The assholes at work already think I'm a little shit for skipping years of training. They're searching for reasons to kick me out. *You* won't be it. Do you hear me?"

He *wants* to be my bodyguard? Could've fooled me. But at least now I have some leverage. "You know what? I'm *this* close to calling

Mirovnik and asking for a replacement." I hold my pinched thumb and forefinger in his face. "You've been nothing but hateful since the second you burst into my room. And I get that your sister just died, and you thought I dishonored her memory. But I've told you the truth and given you no reason to distrust me. On the other hand, I have plenty of reasons to distrust you."

Shepherd's face blanches.

"If this assignment of yours is gonna work, if I will *allow* it to work, you need to treat me with respect. And we need to trust each other. It's gotta go both ways. So we're starting today, at *Ziva's* funeral." I say her name with all the reverence it deserves.

Shepherd's eyes grow wet. He leans forward, propping his elbows on his thighs to shield his face from view. The hover comes to a stop outside the Kismet, but neither of us moves to open the doors.

"I'm supposed to keep you safe. How can I do that in a crowd of hundreds without time to prepare?" He says the words to the floor.

"No one expects me to show up at Ziva's funeral today. Only Dikela and one or two others even knew we were friends." I contrive a plan. "Look, we'll change clothes, switch to a different hover, and arrive like regular guests. Your family has a separate room for the service, right? Won't they already have security if they're expecting hundreds of people? It'll be *fine*."

Shepherd sits up, tipping his head back to stare out the roof. I can practically read the thoughts in his head. He's worried I might say something terrible to his family, or I'll be attacked, and he'll lose his job. He's also tempted to be there for Ziva. "If the prime minister or my director hears I brought Carrefour to my sister's funeral, I'll be dismissed."

Without hesitation, I initiate a call on my specs. The prime minister's assistant, Pono, answers on the first ring. *Whoa.* At some point I'll come to terms with the power I now yield, but I'm nothing but grateful in this moment.

"Good morning, Carrefour." Pono's brassy voice doesn't at all match his bald, hulking form. "The prime minister will be delighted to hear from you. May I ask why you're calling?"

"Could you just pass along a message, please? I'll be attending Flavinsky's funeral today. She and I became friends at SKI, and I'd like to pay my respects. However, it's come to my attention that the Secret Service officer assigned to me is related to her, and his motives for attending may be questioned. Please assure the NASS director and prime minister that we're going *only* at my insistence."

Pono opens his mouth to reply, but I end the call and raise a brow to Shepherd. "Are we doing this or not?"

His Adam's apple bobs, then he reaches up to deactivate the holoshield, and says, "Change of plans. We're heading to Atomdale."

Shepherd

shepherd—v. To guide in a particular direction.

Wednesday, August 29, 236 A.K.—Atomdale, VA

During the thirty-minute ride, I rewatch the entirety of my debut show, pinching my lips between my fingers and seething over the way SKI rephrased my answers. What did I say that was so awful? Nothing.

But clearly they didn't like my answers. I shift perspective, coming at it from their side. SKI's entire purpose is to tell people who they are, and that only works if they have 100 percent participation. Every other debut show or soulmate reunion highlights the advantages of kirling—fame, wealth, love. But I talked about how my results felt wrong, how uncomfortable I am, and that I wished for a soulmate I didn't get.

I huff at my naïveté. Ujjwala's questions and her responses to my answers were attempts to shift our conversation to the positives—the job from Mirovnik, my newfound celebrity, not having to share the spotlight. While I was focused on appearing "normal," she wanted me to portray joy and gratitude. She failed. So they changed the narrative.

I was only playing offense, never in a million years expecting a counterattack. How can I be mad at SKI if I'm the one to blame for losing? I need to think strategically from now on, as if I'm playing a game of Chessfield.

We pull into the driveway of a charming gold-brick house, probably three hundred years old given its pre-kirling architecture.

The navigator glances over his shoulder as we climb out. "What's the plan, Shep? Want me to stick around?"

Shepherd looks back and forth on the quiet street. "Nah. Thanks, man." The door closes, and he taps the roof.

Worried about being spotted, I hold my duffel by my face and rush past pots of impatiens to the porch steps. "Is this your house?"

"My parents'."

Oh gosh, I'm about to meet his family. Nerves tingle my body. I hope beyond hope they didn't watch the interview too.

Shepherd slides open the door, and I lower my bag while stepping inside. No lights are on, and the house is silent. Six steps down to my immediate right lead to a belowground den.

"My room is down there," Shepherd says while walking past.

He still lives at home? I crane my neck, curious to see his room, but he gestures to another handful of steps leading up. "My siblings share a couple rooms up there."

Ziva told me their names once. What were they? Golds, who's a year or two younger, and the adopted pair—Linzy and Edin.

To our left, a small table extends from the windowsill into the quaint kitchen, but I follow Shepherd into a spacious living room, which has a bay window overlooking the yard. The tall privacy fence helps me relax. Neighbors can't spy on me back here.

Shepherd indicates a short hallway to the right with a bedroom at the end. "You can change in my parents' room."

"When's the service?"

"Soon. We'll be a little late."

I nod and hustle into the bedroom, dropping my bag onto their cornflower-blue comforter. Determined not to make Shepherd wait for me, I dig through my clothes, hoping to miraculously find something suitable for Ziva's service. Alas, since my bag holds no magical powers, I extract the black cardigan to go over my silky white tank and switch out my pants for black leggings. It'll have to do.

In the bathroom, I frown at my reflection. At some point during the scuffle from SKI to the hover, pieces of hair were tugged free of my ponytail, jutting out in loops and unkempt strands. My eyes are swollen and skin blotchy. Gross.

After blotting cold water on my cheeks. I work up a disguise, quickly making two braids and then using the chromix app to change my hair color from rich brown to blond. Not bad.

I'm relieved to finish changing before Shepherd does. He emerges from the basement in a dark suit, tucking in his white shirt and clasping a belt buckle. Not sure which I preferred more, the uniform or this, but he'd probably look good in a potato sack.

He looks me over with no discernable facial expression. "Ready?"

"Mm-hmm. Should I leave my bag?"

"Yeah, we'll come back for it." He leads me through the kitchen to the attached garage and an older-model hover. Once seated, he taps the option to raise the garage door, says the address, and we're off.

Shepherd talks into his com the entire ride over, coordinating with security to get us inside without drawing attention. I fidget with my braids, wishing he didn't need to go through so much effort to attend his sister's funeral.

We use the building's rear entrance, and a couple of guards

escort us to the back of a private room. A large holoshield and a door to the assembly hall encompass the opposite wall. Four rows of chairs line our room, but only the first two are occupied. The shoulders of their inhabitants shake with sobs. I wish I thought to bring a handkerchief.

"He's lost it," Shepherd mumbles and gestures to the two closest seats.

Confused, I step over to the second chair, but as I sit, the man inside the hall draws my attention. He's standing onstage wearing a tutu over his pants and a feather boa across his shoulders. And he's tap-dancing. The people in the front rows aren't crying, they're *laughing*.

The man stops tapping. "Then she yelled, 'Daddy, you're doing it wrong! It's shuffle, hop, step, flap, step,' and I said, 'Ziva, that's exactly what I did!' She put her hands on her hips and gave me this look."

He demonstrates, scrunching up his nose and pulling down his brows. "If you knew her, you've seen *the look*."

Yes! I'm pretty sure she made that face at Bardou when she met him.

"And she said, 'No, Daddy, you did shuffle, hop, step, *shuffle*, step. Sit down and leave it to the professionals!'"

Laughter erupts from the audience.

"So I tried the steps again, and she threw her little eight-year-old hands into the air and stormed away, shouting, 'I can't work like this!'" He cracks up laughing with the audience.

The large screen behind him begins playing a father-daughter recital. Tears stream down his cheeks as he watches the dance. Even at eight years old, she danced circles around the other children. Has

Flavinsky always shared that talent? If they didn't have such a tragic past and so many accumulated SCAR penalties, would Ziva have ended up at a dance academy instead?

When the video ends, her dad aims a kiss into the air. "Love you, baby girl."

I blink away tears. In my peripheral vision, Shepherd raises his right hand and wipes the corner of his eye. He sniffs, sitting taller in his chair.

A teenage girl steps up next to Ziva's dad. Golds? They hug and share a private laugh, then she comedically kicks him off the stage in a move that makes us chuckle, Shepherd included.

When their dad enters our room, still in the boa and tutu, a woman in front embraces him. With delight, he notices Shepherd sitting in the back row and turns her in his direction. She throws a hand to her chest, a fresh tear spilling down her cheek. I slouch into my chair as she begins to move our way. But Shepherd shakes his head and points to the stage. The woman nods, and they take their seats.

"... hard act to follow, Dad!" the girl in the assembly hall shouts in our direction. "For those of you who don't know me, I'm Golds, one of Ziva's sisters." Though they're biological siblings, Golds is a head shorter than Ziva, more muscular, and her hair is platinum blond instead of red. But they share the same light brown skin and checkmark grin.

"So, my mom is a nurse, and she works a lot of nights. Growing up, whenever Mom wasn't there to tuck us in, Ziva sang me a lullaby. My older brother did, too, but he'd never admit to it."

Shepherd's lips quirk. I'm so glad I made him come. I'm so very honored to be here.

"They'd sing it to the same tune Mom always used. I think it was Brahms's 'Lullaby,' but Ziva changed the words, and, well, I guess you should know she loves to bake." She clears her throat. "Fair warning, I'm not the best singer, but this is for Ziva."

Golds closes her eyes. She opens her mouth to sing, then clamps it shut again and whimpers. Her mother quietly rises from her chair and joins Golds onstage. My eyes ache with unspent tears as they join hands and sing.

"Lullaby, pumpkin pie,

Apple pie, cherry pie.

Lots of butter, warm loaf bread,

Danish pastries we're fed.

May your brownies be the best.

May your pound cake have zest.

When the biscuits have been pressed,

Only then will we rest."

Given the charming lyrics, the song was likely meant to bring levity to the occasion, but not a dry eye remains in the house.

"As you can imagine," Golds says, clinging to her mom's hand with both of hers, "more nights than not, we'd sneak out of bed to get a late-night snack. Brings another meaning to the phrase 'sweet dreams,' doesn't it?" She laughs through her tears, earning a chuckle from the audience.

"Sweet dreams, Ziva." Golds chokes out the words and hurries down the steps. When she enters our room, she immediately spots Shepherd and runs to him. He stands and hugs her, whispering into her ear. Golds breaks into sobs and squeezes him tightly while he cradles her head to his chest.

I use my sleeves to dab the tears from my cheeks, doing my best not to invade their private moment but feeling like an interloper all the same.

A man in the assembly hall thanks everyone for coming, ending with "Our pain is lessened by the knowledge that someday, somehow, we'll see you again, Ziva."

The video from the Advertitude of her dancing in the kitchen plays behind him. My heart breaks. Ziva was so loved. How could she leave them without even a goodbye?

The family stands to hug and talk, but I remain seated to keep from intruding. Shepherd greets his relatives, giving each a warm embrace. This is the version of Ziva's brother I imagined after hearing her talk about him, the version I wish I'd met earlier today.

From the corner of my eye, I see Dikela nervously step into the room. I stand to get her attention.

"Sivon!" She makes her way to me, stopping on the way to hug Golds, a tall boy, and a young girl—probably Ziva's other siblings Edin and Linzy.

When she approaches, I greet her with open arms. "How are you?"

She wipes away tears. "Ugh. What a shitty week."

"I tried to call you a few times but couldn't get through."

"I ended up leaving yesterday. Didn't want to miss this." She waves a hand. "And my agency intervened when they got wind of the chaos coming this morning."

I wince with guilt.

Dikela rubs my arm. "So . . . new soul, huh? That's unreal. I bet *you've* had a wild couple days."

"I'm still in shock."

"That debut show, though. That was *something*."

"That was *not* me. They switched my words around for the broadcast. I sounded like—"

"You sounded like a stereotypical new soul. Exactly what the public wanted to hear."

"That's not me, though." I grab onto my elbows.

She pats my arm. "My mother always says, 'Words don't make us. Our actions do.'"

"I sure hope she's right." I search the crowd in the assembly hall, wondering if Bardou made it here as well. "That saying could apply to Bardou too."

She chuckles. "Truth. That boy was all bark and no bite."

"Is he here?"

"No, he had to return to the Fringe, or they'd arrest him."

"Oh, right. That's too bad."

"Yeah. He wasn't my favorite, but I do think he cared about Ziva. Maybe I'll check on him in a few days." Dikela waves at someone trying to get her attention.

"I bet he'd appreciate that."

We exchange another hug.

"Take care of yourself, okay?" I say into her shoulder. "I've been so worried."

"I'll be all right. You're the one who needs to be careful." She quirks a brow before walking away.

Be careful. There's that Advertitude warning again. But Dikela couldn't have placed the ad from inside SKI. She's right, though. My skewed interview proved I can't trust anyone.

I scan the room, my gaze settling on Shepherd just as he steps out of an embrace. His focus shifts from the elderly woman to me, and his open smile flattens into hard-set professionalism. He nods briefly before bending down to lift his youngest sister, Linzy, into his arms. She hugs his neck and settles her head against his shoulder. Warmth suffuses my chest.

Whoa. Apparently, I can't even trust myself. *Yes, Sivon, be careful.*

Lost Soul

lost soul—n. 1. A soul who doesn't reappear in SEIK in the expected time frame based on their average deathspan. 2. A soul with an unexpected or tragic death.

Neither Shepherd nor I speak on the drive to his home. I use the quiet to reflect on Ziva, trying to comprehend why she took her life and how the guard on duty couldn't stop her. I'm fully aware that people in a mental health crisis can hide it from their loved ones. And I barely knew Ziva, certainly not enough to determine what was and wasn't out of character for her. But something about her death doesn't sit right with me. It could be the sudden nature of it, or maybe I'm just creeped out by the RAIDs they sent to guard her.

A shiver runs through me. Okay, it's definitely the RAIDs. Why would SKI put robots on *Flavinsky's* suicide watch? Not one counselor volunteered to sit with her? Had they already resigned themselves to her fate? And if so, doesn't that defeat their entire purpose? Why do we even report to SKI early if not to save lives?

The hover pulls into Shepherd's garage, and the bay door closes behind us, encasing us in darkness. I focus on the sound of his shallow breaths, wishing I knew the right words to say. This must feel to him how it would if I lost Vivi or Corah, and I cannot even fathom that agony. How did he even get out of bed today?

After an audible swallow, he taps the door release and mumbles, "Makes no sense."

Fully agree, but before I can ask him to elaborate, the sounds of laughter and conversation filter through the kitchen door. I place my foot on the concrete floor and hesitate. "Do you know the people inside? Is it safe?"

"We only invited family and close friends." He places his hand on the knob. "But stay in sight, okay?"

Not very reassuring.

Shepherd receives a round of hugs when we enter the kitchen, but all chatter ends as everyone's eyes settle on me.

"Who's this?" his mom asks. Her light brown skin and smiling eyes remind me of Ziva's.

Shepherd flings a hand in my direction. "This is Carrefour. I'm assigned to protect her."

I grit my teeth. Whispers of "new soul" dot the room. Drawn by the silence in the kitchen, a few heads peer around the corner. They'll all be wondering why I'm here, assuming I believe Ziva must "atone for her sins."

"Thanks, Shepherd," I murmur, then focus on his mother. "Ziva and I met at SKI last week and were becoming friends. I wanted to offer my condolences . . . and thought Shepherd should be here too."

He rolls his eyes.

I wring my hands together, outlining the crossroads symbol. "And, well, if you watched my interview, I wanted to explain that they edited my responses to mean the opposite of what I intended. So . . ."

Shepherd's jaw flexes. Does he still not believe me? His mom shoos Shepherd away, then guides me by the elbow to a table of food in the dining room.

"I'm Lisabet, and my husband is Barnelege, and any friend of Ziva's is welcome here. Please, make yourself at home." She hands me a biscuit. "These are Ziva's recipe. Do you like biscuits?"

I nod, taking a bite of buttery heaven. "*Wow*," I say, holding my hand over my mouth.

"Amazing, right?"

"Can I eat them all?" I joke.

Lisabet laughs. "Have at it. We have way too much food." She pats me on the shoulder and rejoins her guests in the kitchen.

Maybe I wasn't kidding after all. The spread of homemade food calls to my empty stomach. When did I last eat anything? The sandwich Lepota gave me? I grab a plate and make my way around the table, all the while feeling Shepherd's gaze on me. Claiming a chair against the wall, I stuff my face with the carbolicious foods.

Ziva's youngest sister, a girl with fair skin, ginger hair, blond eyebrows, and millions of freckles, spies on me from around the corner, evoking memories of Vivi and Corah. To make her reconnaissance more interesting, I make silly faces until we both break into giggles. I beckon her over, and she shyly tiptoes my way.

"Hey there! Are you Linzy?"

She nods.

"Nice to meet you. I'm Carrefour."

She lifts one of my braids. "Can you make a French braid?"

"Um, sure! You want me to braid your hair?"

She grabs my hand to lead me away.

"Why don't you get your brush and an elastic, and we'll do it here? I'm not supposed to leave Shepherd's sight, or he'll yell at me like a big meanie."

She breaks into laughter. "He wouldn't do that! He's never mean."

Now I'm the one to laugh, but she runs away and returns in less than a minute. I pull the chair away from the wall to stand behind it. She sits, and I start braiding. Once I've made it to the bottom, I notice Shepherd, his mom, and Golds watching from the kitchen with tears in their eyes.

What? I mouth at Shepherd.

He shakes his head and turns away. Golds and his mom return to their guests. Did I do something wrong?

"Okay, I'm done," I say to Linzy. "Wanna go look in the mirror?"

She hops up and dashes away.

I approach Shepherd and tell him I need to use the restroom, and he steps out of the kitchen to watch me head down the hallway. Finding that one occupied, I backtrack. He's now talking with someone but notes my reversal and points down, so I descend the basement stairs.

The den has three doorways to the left, and standing in the first is Windrose.

"Windrose?"

She whirls around, a hand to her chest. "Oh, goodness, you startled me!"

"W-what are you doing here?" I never thought I'd see her again, much less in Ziva's basement.

Windrose presses a handkerchief to her cheeks and gestures to the open bedroom door. "I still can't believe she's gone." She covers her mouth with the cloth, shaking her head. "Only a few months ago we were chatting at Golds's birthday party, and now . . ."

"I didn't know you were friends with Ziva's family."

She nods and sniffles.

Her tears at my kirling were more than sympathy for a lost soul. And she had to listen to me complain about my results when Ziva would've given anything... "I'm so sorry, Windrose."

She focuses on her feet. "I never thought she'd do this. I just... thought she was stronger. That night—" She trembles. "They wouldn't let me intervene. If only she'd been in my group...."

"I'm sure you did everything you could."

"But that's just it." She twists the cloth. "I could've done so much more.... My hands were tied."

I cock my head. Is she suggesting someone intentionally kept Ziva from getting proper care? "Who—?"

Windrose inhales sharply and blinks rapidly. "I'm sorry. What am I doing? You don't need to listen to my blubbering." She backs toward the steps. "I was about to head out anyway. Stopped down here to use the bathroom and got lost in my memories.

"Lovely seeing you again, Carrefour." She bobs her head and darts upstairs.

Okay, that was weird. Maybe I'm reading too much into Windrose's words, but it seems she shares my doubts about Ziva's suicide watch. Is this more than simple negligence? Was Ziva somehow *encouraged* to take her life? That would explain why the bot in the hallway couldn't get in and why the other allowed her to lock herself in the bathroom.

I take Windrose's place in Ziva's bedroom doorway. It's barely big enough for her bed, desk, and closet, but her vibrant personality shines through nonetheless. A twirling ballerina hologram sits high on a shelf, surrounded by old dance shoes, costume pieces, and photograms of her performing. Like me, she probably left home expecting to return five days later. And like me, she was completely and utterly wrong.

I wish, as Ziva suggested, I could've seen into the future and predicted what would happen. If I knew what awaited either of us, I would've dragged her out of SKI with me.

A small hand takes hold of mine, nearly scaring the soul from my body.

Linzy holds out a brush to me, her hair wholly undone.

I press a hand over my racing heart. "What happened?"

"Make it tighter."

I smile down at her, grateful to have some small way of making myself useful. "As you wish."

Once the guests leave and the two youngest are in bed, the rest of us sit around the table and share memories of Ziva. Most of the stories are humorous, making me wish I'd met her sooner. But eventually their laughter dies down, and Barnelege settles his hand over Lisabet's, giving it a comforting squeeze.

He clears his throat. "Carrefour, my wife and I were wondering if you might share a little about Ziva at SKI. Did she seem . . . depressed or anxious?"

I slide my arms around my waist. "Um . . . anxious, of course. We all were." Barnelege, Lisabet, Donovan, and Golds stare at me with hopeful eyes, waiting for answers I don't have.

"But she had Dikela there, who I'm sure was a huge comfort, and she made friends with me and . . . others." Not about to tell them about Bardou. "When we were all together, she seemed happy, talked a lot about you all. How you adopted Linzy and Edin . . . that

Golds slept in her bed the night before she went to SKI . . . and how much she wanted one of Shepherd's bear hugs."

Golds bursts into tears. Shepherd pounds his fist on the table, then scoots back his chair. He gathers up the dishes and heads into the kitchen, clanging them onto the counter. The faucet turns on.

Can't I do one thing right? "I'm so sorry," I say to the three of them.

Lisabet rubs Golds's back. "Donovan is having trouble coming to terms with this. We all are." She heaves a sigh. "Barnelege is a pediatrician; I work in intensive care. We're trained to look for signs of . . ." She purses her lips. "Maybe we were just too close to notice."

Barnelege rises from the table and heads into the kitchen. So Ziva's death really was out of the blue. I guess the burden of Flavinsky's past could've caused her to spiral, but I'm beginning to wonder if she killed herself at all. Without facts to substantiate my theory, I'm unwilling to voice it. Nor do I wish to pour salt in their wounds.

"She loved you all *so* much." My voice breaks. "I wish I could help."

Lisabet pats my hand. "When Linzy found out about Ziva, you know the first thing she said?"

I shake my head.

"She said, 'Who'll braid my hair now?'"

I press my fingers to my lips, my eyes welling with tears.

"I promised I would learn but haven't found time with all the arrangements," Lisabet says.

"I'll teach you, if you want."

"Me too?" Golds asks.

I nod.

Barnelege pops his head around the corner. "Me three?"

"Of course." I chuckle. "We can do it right now."

Golds agrees to be my model, and by the time they've got the hang of it, it's near midnight. I sink into one of the dining room chairs, exhausted. Shepherd emerged from the kitchen thirty minutes ago, but he hasn't engaged with any of us since.

Lisabet pats his hand. "Why don't you two stay here tonight? You've both had a long day."

A long *week*, I think. Slogging back to the city to sleep in some unfamiliar apartment sounds like sheer torture.

Shepherd looks at me through half-mast eyes and raises a shoulder. "It's your call."

The tension leaves my body. "I'd love that, Lisabet."

"Good, it's settled. I'll change the sheets." She heads toward the basement stairs.

I lurch to my feet. "Oh, thank you, but it doesn't feel right to sleep in Ziva's bed. Seriously, the couch is perfect."

"Don't be ridiculous. Our guests don't sleep on the couch."

"I'll take Ziva's bed." Shepherd stands. "Carrefour can have mine. It's fine."

Seventeen hours we've spent together today. He's yelled at me, mocked me, argued with me. And yes, he also protected me and offered advice, but this is the one and only time he's done something kind. Considering where we started, it feels monumental, even though he walks downstairs without a backward glance.

I roll my neck and follow him downstairs with my duffel bag. We take turns in the bathroom. When I exit, his mom comes out of the far room, holding a bundle of sheets.

"All set. Good night."

"Thanks so much." I turn to say good night to Shepherd only to find Ziva's door closed.

He's grieving. Cut him some slack.

I enter his small bedroom and inhale the warm, earthy scents of pine, sea salt, and mint. *Mmm.* My eyes skip over the twin-size bed on the right and settle on the three images hung on the left wall, commemorating his kindergarten graduation, high school graduation, and some sort of Secret Service ceremony. Adorable, sweet, and impressive.

A tall, wooden dresser and coordinating desk fill the remaining space. The desk showcases a handful of antique books with actual paper pages, including ones on police reform, military strategy, and a true-crime story about the Belarussian mafia at the turn of the first century.

I thumb through the last one before pivoting toward the dresser and examining the two framed photograms on top. The first is of his whole family, only a couple of years old, going by his siblings' ages. They look so happy. Ziva looks so happy.

What happened that night, Ziva? Will we ever know?

I frown and move to the next one of Shepherd, Ziva, and Golds. He looks about fifteen and is laughing at the camera with his sisters wrapped in his arms. They're cracking up, squeezing him tightly in return.

I pick up the frame and hold it closer, trying to reconcile this carefree version of Shepherd with the hostile one I met today. He seems to smile for everyone but me. I set it back down, grateful the doorway is still empty when I turn around.

No longer able to resist the siren call of his bed, I turn down the coffee-colored comforter and climb between the freshly laundered sheets. I fall asleep before the sensors turn off the lights.

Sociaty

Sociaty—(soh-SAI-uh-tee) n. A centuries-old social network platform that curates news and commentary, as well as personal photos and videos.

Thursday, August 30, 236 A.K.—Atomdale, VA

I wake hugging Shepherd's pillow, feeling fully rested for once. Not surprising. His room is practically an aromatherapy spa. If this is what it takes to sleep well, maybe I should smuggle out his pillow when we leave today. I peek down at my overstuffed duffel bag, wondering what I could sacrifice to make room.

Oh noo. Oh no, oh no, oh no. They're gonna *kill* me. I hop out of bed and dig the specs from my bag, where they've hidden since my call with Mom after leaving SKI. Wincing with guilt, I slide them on and dismiss the hundreds of missed messages. I pull up my contacts and stare at their names, wondering which to call first. The decision is made for me.

"Where the hell are you?" Corah demands the second I answer.

Vivi hits her sister's arm. Corah winces and rubs the spot. "Are you okay, Sivon?"

"I'm fine but so very sorry. My specs were in my bag all day yesterday. I went to Flavinsky's funeral, and my bodyguard is her brother, and we stayed at his parents' house last night, and—"

"Whoa. It's okay," Vivi says. "We were just worried."

"*And* pissed off." Corah's lips pull flat.

I flop back onto Shepherd's pillow. "Understandable. I'd be angry, too, after everything you did for me at SKI. Thank you for the Advertitude messages. They really helped."

"What Advertitude messages?" Corah looks at Vivi. "Know anything about Advertitude messages?"

Vivi raises her hands. "Got me." But their mischievous smiles give them away.

I roll my eyes. "Uh-huh, yeah. The foxes? And that 'be careful' one, which, to be honest, kinda messed with my head."

"Be careful?" Corah frowns. "We only did the two—an early one to nudge you out of your room and the one yesterday for your exit."

Unease settles into my bones. "A full-building message popped up the day after my kirling that said 'Be Careful.' It resembled your first one, so I thought you made it. Honestly, it could've been meant for anyone. Maybe another parent was worried about their kid's kirling, considering mine and Flavinsky's happened back-to-back in the same location."

Vivi leans her head into her hand. "It must've been hard being there with Flavinsky."

I take a stabilizing breath and fill them in on my past week—Ziva, Windrose, the kirling, Mirovnik, the debacle of the debut interview, and finally, Shepherd and the funeral. While I manage not to cry, my voice quivers a few times. "So yeah, it's safe to say I lost our bet, Vivi. My kirling was indeed terrible, and I'm both miserable and alone."

Vivi and Corah are both holding a hand to their mouths.

"No wonder you didn't call us back yesterday," Corah says through her fingers.

Vivi leans in. "I'm so sorry, Sivon. Can we do anything to help?"

I scratch my brows. "Can you dig up a past life for me? Wouldn't mind some Last Letter advice about now. I bet yours was chock-full of helpful information, wasn't it?"

Vivi and Corah share a silent conversation before turning back, wearing matching grins.

"So, our Last Letters weren't really typical," Vivi finally replies.

"What do you mean?"

"*Well*," begins Corah. Vivi nudges her to continue. "They're written in code."

I bark out a laugh. "*Of course* they're in code."

"But we can't figure them *out*!" Vivi whines.

"Ha! Seriously? That's awesome."

Corah rubs her forehead. "It's annoying! We *have* determined they go together. Like, Vivi's and mine intertwine. And they use a huge combination of ciphers and a bunch of foreign characters, symbols, numbers, and, *fuck*, it's hard! We've tried the usuals—the binary cipher, the digraph, the Rosicrucian . . . Nothing fits!"

I snap my fingers. "Shucks. I was about to suggest the Rosicrucian."

Vivi snorts. "We're pretty sure part of it is computer code but don't want to risk running it through AI and raising flags. So we need to find someone trustworthy who understands code from, like, fifty years ago."

"I wish my dad were still alive. Mom said he was a programming whiz." An idea strikes. "Hey, what about Ensio? Isn't he a computer genius?"

Ensio dated Corah during sophomore and junior years.

Vivi knocks Corah with her shoulder. "See? I told you!"

"Yeah, I know, but we haven't talked since he moved away last summer."

"Really? Not once?"

"It was my idea. I told him the long-distance thing never works. He was about to be kirled anyway. I didn't want him to feel guilty if he had a soulmate. And, you know, I didn't want to go through what Kopar did. It was an opportunity for a clean break."

The Abernathy thing did a number on us all. But Corah and Ensio had great chemistry. "*Does* he have a soulmate?"

"He does not." Vivi taps her fingertips together.

Corah whacks Vivi on the head. "*Stop!* Fine, I'll give him a call, but *only* for help with that part of our letter, no other reason. So, quit it, you two."

"Uh-huh." Vivi and I wink at each other.

Corah rubs her forehead, her blush growing brighter.

After they sign off, the toilet flushes next door. Shepherd must be awake, which means we'll be heading to my new apartment soon. I reluctantly extricate myself from his sheets, make the bed, and dress in workout clothes, my last clean outfit. The other rooms are empty when I emerge, so I take advantage of the bathroom and head upstairs to the kitchen, duffel in hand.

Also dressed in athletic clothes, Shepherd sits at the table, flipping through his screen and sipping from a coffee mug. He doesn't acknowledge my entrance.

"Good morning, Shepherd."

He grunts in reply. *The guy is in mourning. Cut him a break.*

I glance around the kitchen. "Do you have any tea?"

"Coffee." He waves a hand toward the coffee dispenser.

I scrunch up my nose. It'll have to do. "Okay, where are the mugs?" I tap the wall console to open cabinet doors.

Shepherd stands, still looking at his screen, and reaches in front of my face to open the cabinet over the sink. I scowl at his back before pouring a cup of coffee, grateful when I spot a canister of sugar on the counter. Luckily, the silverware is in the first drawer I try.

"Can I have a banana?" I point to the bunch on the counter.

He shrugs.

I choose a ripe one and claim a seat at the table. After stirring in the sugar, I take a sip of the coffee and grimace. *So bitter.*

He chuckles. Okay, now he's just being rude. *NASShole.*

I hold the warm mug with both hands and lean into the chair, unabashedly examining him. He scratches the scruff on his jaw that wasn't there yesterday. Didn't think he could get cuter, and yet... Dikela's crush makes perfect sense. I feel sorry for his soulmate, though. Hopefully he'll treat them better than he does me.

I take another sip, forcing myself to swallow. "So you still live with your parents?"

Shepherd keeps his eyes trained on his screen. "Not that it's any of your business, but I didn't receive an inheritance. I'm saving up to buy a place."

"No inheritance at all? That's unusual." Especially for someone with such a good soul.

"Don't you have friends to call or something?"

"Nope." I lean forward, planting my elbows on the table. "What's on the itinerary today?"

He finally looks at me. "That's not how this works. I'm not your *tour guide.* Maybe instead of posting to Sociaty and chatting up your pals, you could take the time to check your schedule."

What's he worked up about now? "I didn't post anything to Sociaty."

He clicks his tongue. "I can't decide if you're a pathological liar or just completely oblivious. Not a good look either way." He slides his screen in front of me, then storms into the backyard.

I pull his screen closer, already knowing I'll hate what I see, given his reaction to it. The Sociaty post belongs to the username Carrefour, though I haven't made an account with my soulname. It shows one image of me entering the back entrance of the funeral home yesterday and another of me leaving, wiping tears from my eyes.

The caption reads, *Paying my respects to Flavinsky's family. I hope we can all learn from her tragic death—to value each life and make the best of each day we're given.*

While the language seems innocuous enough, the undertone insinuates Ziva did neither, which couldn't be farther from the truth. My lips curl back. Who did this? Who is using me, putting words in my mouth? I'd never insult Ziva or her family by posting this.

But Shepherd doesn't know that. He probably thinks I used her funeral to bolster my own image. I drop his screen to the table and press my hands to the cool surface to ground myself. What did he call me? Oblivious? Well, he's not wrong. Raphaela *warned* me about this, and even still, I keep falling for it.

This wasn't SKI, though. I told only one person I was attending the funeral—Pono, the prime minister's assistant. A random drone could've captured the photos, but paparazzi wouldn't put those words in my mouth. Whoever posted this wants to control my image, and the only person interested in my image, besides me, is Mirovnik.

Lisabet enters the kitchen, pulls out a coffee mug, walks over to the pantry door, and takes out a tin of tea. Tea? So much for Shepherd's kindness last night.

She extracts a teapot from a cabinet and puts on water to boil before finally noticing me. "Oh, Carrefour! Sorry, I didn't see you there. Can I get you something?"

I shake my head. "That Sociaty post. I—I didn't write that. I had no idea someone would take my photo yesterday or . . ." How am I again apologizing to Ziva's mother for something I didn't say?

"What's this you're talking about?" She sits in the chair Shepherd vacated.

I show her the screen. "This wasn't me, but I'll get to the bottom of it. I'd never say Ziva didn't value her life. Like you said last night, she never once gave the impression she'd do something like this."

Lisabet pushes the screen away.

I soften my tone. "What caused her death? Did she have an autopsy?"

She frowns. "They said she ingested oleander seeds, causing a heart attack. We grow an ornamental variety in the flower bed out back. I didn't even know they were poisonous."

The kettle whistles, and she rises to pour the water into her mug. Ziva brought poison with her to SKI? I can't imagine why. She showed no signs of depression and had no way of knowing she'd be Flavinsky. Then again, the RAIDs wouldn't know about her family's oleander bushes. Are they commonly grown in this area? Could that be a coincidence?

Tea in hand, Lisabet returns to her chair. "Carrefour, if nursing has taught me anything, it's that death never makes sense. No matter when or how it happens. Those of us left behind always wonder if we should've done or said something while we had the chance. So whoever wrote this is right." She points to Shepherd's screen. "We have to go on living, making the best of each day. Ziva would want that for us." Her eyes well with tears.

I wish I could do something to take away her pain. "I can see why she admired you so much."

A tear slides down her cheek as she takes her first sip of tea. Before long, she's staring vacantly out the window.

I leave her to her thoughts, washing my mug in the sink and returning it to the cabinet. In the living room, I approach the bay window and spot Shepherd in the back corner of the flower bed. He's digging up a shrub brush bearing beautiful pink blooms. The oleander.

My heart swells with compassion, but as much as I want to help, he deserves time alone to grieve. He'd probably spit another insult at me the second I stepped outside anyway.

But maybe I *can* help. I'm the new soul, after all. I work for the prime minister now. Surely I can ask him to make an inquiry into Flavinsky's death. How and when did Ziva ingest the oleander? Wouldn't the bot have recorded its time alone with her?

I turn from the window to find my specs and nearly run into Shepherd's younger brother. Where did he come from? "Hey! You're Edin, right?"

With his millions of freckles and blond eyebrows, he's identical to Linzy except for his added height and short, floppy hair.

"Yes, and you're Carrefour. Is it true you know where we go when we die?"

I cough. "No! Who told you that?"

"A few of my friends."

That's it. It's time to make some public statements I actually agree with. "Well, tell them you heard from Carrefour herself that's not the case. Okay?"

He lifts one shoulder then focuses out the window. "You're lucky Donovan's your bodyguard."

Luck isn't the word I would choose. "Ya think? Why's that?"

"He promised if my parents ever tried to take me and Linzy back, he'd fight them for us."

I doubt a Secret Service officer would ever betray the rule of law. Then again, Ziva said something to the same effect—how protective Shepherd is of family. "You don't want your parents to come back for you?"

"They suck."

My brows shoot up. "Why do they suck?"

"They used up their inheritances on drugs, didn't care if we went to school. I spent most days babysitting Linzy and begging strangers for food."

I shudder. No wonder Shepherd agreed to fight them off. "Do they know where you are now?"

"Oh, sure. They don't care."

Shit, I'm ready to punch them myself. Wouldn't Ziva consider how a suicide would affect her younger siblings, who were abandoned once before?

Outside, Shepherd sinks his shovel into the mulch again, wrenching it down until the roots finally pull free. His accompanying shout filters through the window. He stumbles back a step before falling to his knees and running the back of his arm across his sweaty brow.

The sight of the bush lying on its side brings me relief as well. Would it be too much to set it on fire?

"I hope Crosier is never kirled," Edin says.

The shift in topic throws me. "Crosier?"

"Shepherd's soulmate."

Ah. I start building a picture of them in my head, piecing together who would make the perfect soulmate for Shepherd. They'll have to put up with his moodiness, balance out his tempestuous spirit, and bring out the best in him. Basically my opposite on all counts.

"I bet they'll be horrible."

I snort. "*Edin!* They will not be horrible. You love Shepherd, right?"

He shrugs.

"Well, Crosier will be like his other half. You'll be *glad* to see them together because Shepherd will be so happy."

"Do *you* have a soulmate?"

I try to keep disappointment from my voice. "Nope, but my parents weren't soulmates, and they loved each other. Are Lisabet and Barnelege?"

"No, and I hope I don't have one either. Don't you think it's better to choose who you love?"

"Wow, this is pretty deep, Edin." I lean against the windowsill to gather my thoughts. "Um, well, love takes many forms. My best friends, they're soulmates and identical twins but not at all interested in each other *that way*."

Edin grimaces, and we share a laugh.

"And I've never seen two people more in sync. Their bond comes as naturally as breathing. The soulmate connection is beautiful and incredibly rare, and I have a lot of respect for it. Envy it, even."

The near-silent click of the back door signals Shepherd's return. He wipes his hands on a rag and eyes the two of us warily. "You okay, buddy?"

"Yeah, just discussing life and love with the guru here." Edin pats my shoulder.

I go slackjawed. Is that why he was speaking so openly with me? For some new soul advice? "That's not . . . I'm not . . ."

"Take it from me." Shepherd ruffles Edin's hair as he walks past. "You can't believe a word she says."

His words hit like a sucker punch. I shoot daggers at his back as he heads downstairs.

Shepherd pauses on the first stair. "The hover will be here soon. You ready?"

Ready to be dropped into a strange apartment with a man who hates my guts? Nope. "I've been ready. You're the one dripping in sweat." My throat clenches. Did I really chastise him for destroying the bush that could've killed his sister?

He huffs and jogs down the rest of the steps. The bathroom door slams shut.

Great, you just dug your hole even deeper. I run a hand through my hair and go to retrieve my bag from the kitchen. Time to see about repairing my public image before Shepherd starts tossing dirt on top, burying me along with my reputation.

Kismet

Kismet—(KIHZ-met) n. 1. Destiny, fate. 2. A luxury high-rise apartment building in central Washington, CD.

Shepherd sits up front with the navigator for the ride to my new apartment. Fine by me.

We don't have to be friends. He's my bodyguard, not my flipping soulmate. I couldn't care less what he thinks about me.

I *do* care that the statements attributed to me are actually mine, not SKI's or Mirovnik's. So I pull up Sociaty and log in to my profile, the one under my birth name, Sivon. This one holds all my personal photos and videos from the age of thirteen, when Mom finally allowed me to create an account.

After skimming through the comments, half mocking me and the other half remarking on how sweet and "pure" I am—which is creepy as hell—I decide not to let a bunch of strangers spoil my favorite memories. I make sure my videos and photos are backed up and delete my account.

My pulse begins racing, panic setting in. I check my files again to ensure the memories are safe and sound. Still there. Okay, settle down, heart.

Next step, claim the new account under my soulname. I navigate through a series of forums and help menus but come up empty.

The chatbot support only sends me in circles. I get that Sociaty needs profile protections, but who set up my soulname account in the first place? Most likely Mirovnik or someone on his staff. I initiate a call.

"Good morning, Carrefour," says Pono, the prime minister's assistant. "How may I assist you?"

"Hi, Pono. Sorry to bother you with this, but I'm trying to claim my soulname on Sociaty and getting nowhere. Could you put me in touch with whoever handles publicity?"

"She's meeting with Mirovnik at the moment."

I'm about to ask to leave a message when he adds, "But your contract granted the Advancement Party access to your soulname account. All high-profile employees have the same provision to ensure our communications are unified."

"*My* contract didn't." I read through it twice before signing. If it included language forfeiting control of my soulname account, I'd remember.

Pono frowns. "Let me check for you. One moment." His eyes dart about as he whips his finger through the air. His lips start moving as he silently reads to himself. "Yes, here it is. Section H, letter i. The undersigned employee hereby grants unfettered access to social networks in their soulname. If no such account exists, the employer may create one on the employee's behalf. The employee waives the right to preview or approve social media statements or posts."

I fight to control my temper, annoyed at his patronizing tone. "Yes, I'm sure that language is included in *some* employment contracts, but that wasn't in mine."

"You initialed it right here." He twists his hand, and the contract replaces his face.

I zoom into the highlighted section and compare my initials to the others. The language in the sections above and below I remember, but not this one. Did I skip over this clause both times? Unlikely.

That means the contract was modified. By whom? The why is clear as day. Mirovnik wants to use me and my new soul. I knew so the minute he offered me the position, but I had no idea he or someone on his staff would resort to something so underhanded.

What should I do? Quit? That's the obvious answer. I could find another way to make money, hire private security, and leave Shepherd behind. But quitting over a post about Flavinsky feels impulsive. And I'm determined to request an investigation into her death when I see him next.

Perhaps I could try renegotiating this clause first. I'm the one with the power here. They need me, not the other way around.

"Yes, I see. Would you please send me a copy of the signed contract?"

"Of course. You should've already received one, but I'm happy to send another."

His condescension irks me to no end. I went straight to a funeral after getting my specs back. I haven't had time to go through the 5,325 emails waiting for me, and he won't make me feel bad about it.

"I appreciate that. Thank you." On the off chance the two contracts don't match, I can use that as leverage.

His finger taps the air. "All set. Can I help with anything else?"

"Would you please ask the publicist to call me as soon as possible?" I'm sure she'll turn over my new Sociaty account after I ask. This is the prime minister's office, not a crime syndicate.

Pono's smile doesn't reach his eyes. "Unfortunately, she's in back-to-back meetings the next few days. Here, let me pull up her schedule, and you can select the best time to chat."

The calendar appears in front of me. Sure enough, her next four days are booked solid. I press my tongue into my cheek and choose the first available opening on Monday morning. "Thank you, Pono."

"Of course. Happy to assist." He ends the call.

Left alone in the silence of the hover, I growl and stomp my foot. Why was I so hasty to delete my old profile? I could've used that one to post whatever I wanted.

I flip back to Sociaty and try to resuscitate my former account, but no surprise, it's impossible. And now that I've both deleted an account and unsuccessfully attempted to access another, I can't create a new one for thirty days.

Frustrated beyond measure, I shout and punch the seat beside me.

"Everything okay back there?" Shepherd's voice permeates the holoshield.

"No! Nothing is okay. Not now, nor at any point in the past week. Not that you care." I flop my head against the headrest.

A few seconds of silence follow. "As long as you're not dying."

"Go away." I tap at the screen on the ceiling until I'm pretty sure our connection is once again muted.

The hover comes to a standstill in the morning traffic. I press my forehead against the window, calculating how much farther we have to go. At least two kilometers. I'm tempted to get out and walk it.

And why not? I've got workout clothes on. They can drop off my duffel bag later. And if I change my hair color again, like to . . . this hideous shade of dark grayish purple, who would recognize me?

This time I won't tell a soul. No photos or videos, complete obscurity.

I tap the door release. Nothing happens. I press it again. Still nothing. Muffled laughter comes from the two guys in front. Glad to know I'm so funny. Well, I'm not some prisoner they can hold hostage. I flip through the various options on the screen above until I find the one I'm looking for. With only a second's hesitation, I hit it. Emergency release.

Every single door and window on the hover opens. I chastise myself for not unbuckling first, but soon enough, I'm darting through the stationary hovers to the sidewalk, where I break into a sprint.

Shepherd is fast on my heels. Within seconds, I'm within arm's reach, but he doesn't grab or tackle me like I expect. Instead, he matches my pace, speeding up when I do and easing into a more sustainable clip once I realize he won't stop me.

We breeze past unsuspecting tourists and commuters as I take turn after turn. By following the map on my specs, I know our location in relation to the Kismet, but high on adrenaline from my escape, I'm in no rush to get there. The two kilometers turn into four, then six, until the insufferable heat and undeniable thirst bring me to the building's front doors.

Shepherd doesn't mutter a single word, not during our run and not when we enter the lobby. Stopping to speak with no one, we approach the gates, press our fingers to the sensors, and board the first available elevator. I scan my finger again and the elevator lifts.

Sure. This is normal. Direct access to a luxurious penthouse suite? Regular old Thursday.

On the ascent, Shepherd stands behind me, his right shoulder aligned with my left. I focus on my breaths, not the comfort his presence brings, my gratitude for being allowed to run, or his intoxicating scent. Who knew salty pine was my thing? Annoyance hits when I realize our breathing has synchronized again. He probably did that on purpose just to irk me.

The elevator doors open. I hesitate, taking in the otherworldly decor. The bone-white floor, ceiling, and walls are one and the same, not a seam or square angle in sight. The seating and shelving grow out of the floor and walls as if someone molded them from clay, pushed into existence. Crimson cushions, pillows, blankets, and sculptures contrast with the apparent snow drifts. It's one thing to wear red and white, another to be surrounded by it entirely. Would it hurt to throw in a few more colors? Or stick with a neutral palette?

The elevator buzzes, so I step into the foyer, bringing the kitchen into view on my left. Like the couches—if that's what you can call them—the island and four stools are pressed up from below, part of the floor and yet weirdly not. The sink, faucet, and doors to all three ovenwaves are crystal clear. Atop the cleaved-out shelves rests the likewise clear dishes. I take down two glasses, fill them with water from the sink, and pass one to Shepherd.

We silently chug them down. When we're done, he holds out a hand for my glass and refills them both. While I'm certain I'll find a refrigerator or pantry eventually, I can no longer resist the call of the window, which I would call floor-to-ceiling if the room had either.

Sipping on the water, I step closer and study the stop-and-go traffic twenty-five floors below. We're at least ten stories higher than any other building in sight. The White House, only two blocks away, appears minuscule in comparison.

A strange man exits the room to my left, wearing a red apron and holding a tray of food. I jump back, splattering water, which is quickly absorbed by the floor.

"Greetings, Carrefour. Might I interest you in a cucumber sandwich?"

"Who are you?" Shepherd gets the words out before I do. How did he leap in front of me so quickly?

"I'm Carrefour's personal RAID. It's nice to make your acquaintance, Shepherd."

Other than also appearing male, it looks nothing like the robot stationed outside Ziva's room, but it ignites the same instinctual terror. The remaining liquid sloshes against my now-trembling glass.

"No," I whisper to Shepherd. "I don't want it here. Send it away."

"You heard her," Shepherd says at full volume. "Get out."

The RAID takes no offense to the order. "As the lady wishes. I will let Janus know my presence was not appreciated."

Janus sent him? *Great*. He'll think I'm ungrateful when he arrives to escort me to the Holusion Museum tonight. I can only imagine how much a personal RAID costs. But I couldn't relax for a second with it here, not to mention sleep at night.

The bot sets its tray on the counter and crosses to the elevator. As soon as the doors shut behind it, Shepherd presses his earplant and barks orders, rescinding apartment access to everyone except the two of us.

"And Kitsune and Raposa," I whisper, but he waves me away. "And Artifex." He rolls his eyes but adds their names to the list before he signs off.

I like getting my way with him. I lift a cucumber sandwich from the tray, but Shepherd knocks it from my hand.

"Hey!"

"No prepared foods. You don't know what's in that."

I stare down at the tray of sandwiches, suddenly ravenous. "Why don't you eat one first? If you don't die, I'll have the rest."

Shepherd's lips twitch, but just when I think he might actually smile at my joke, they slip into their familiar sneer. "You'd love that wouldn't you?"

I lift a shoulder. "Wouldn't be the worst thing to happen this week."

"Oh, and what's that? Finding out you were a new soul? Oh, boo-hoo. Cry me a fucking river." Shepherd scoops the sandwich off the floor and sends them all down the compost disposal.

"For someone who claims they want to keep their job, you sure don't act like it."

"I'm beginning to think that wouldn't be so bad. Beats following your attention-seeking, entitled, ungrateful ass around." Shepherd tilts his head, challenging me to make the call to Mirovnik.

I step closer. "I'm not *any* of those things, and if you stopped jumping to conclusions and took a second to talk with me, you would've already figured that out."

He edges toward me. "Sure, okay, then explain the vanishing act earlier. You just thought you'd slip free, putting your life in danger and my career on the line? What if something had happened to you?"

"I never once thought I'd outrun you. That wasn't about vanishing or escaping. It was my first chance, and my last for who knows how long, to feel the sun on my face after being locked up for a week. It was a release of frustration after expecting to get answers about what to do with my life, maybe who I'll spend it with, and losing a friend and all hope within hours of each other." I force down my sorrow.

"And sure, my results could've been worse, but this?" I gesticulate toward the abhorrent decor. "This is *not* me. The crowds, the threats, the security, the fame? Deplorable words put in my mouth, photos posted of me crying at a funeral, my social accounts being hijacked? Never what I expected and not for a second what I wanted. I'm literally trying to survive right now."

Shepherd's eyes soften, but I'm not done yet. I take the last step toward him, until we're so close I feel the heat radiating from his skin.

"And then there's *you* with your condescending, self-righteous attitude." I punch a finger into his chest. "Calling me names, making me feel like an idiot at every turn. Well, I'm allowed to be scared and confused. If you were me, you'd also be frustrated to find yourself in a game where the rules keep changing. Where there aren't any rules at all."

Our chests rise and fall in synchronized rhythm. The newfound sympathy in his eyes makes it too difficult to retain my anger, so I focus on his chin instead.

"If you were me, you would've hit that emergency release too."

Shepherd swallows. I watch the dip and rise of his throat with fascination. The back of his hand briefly touches mine, sending a shock through it. I wince and rub my hand while he steps away, flexing his.

He purses his lips while studying my face, then nods to himself. "I appreciate your explanation and will modify my behavior accordingly." He says the words over my head. "Please accept my apology for contributing to your traumatic week."

My brows dip, and I back away. "Are you mocking me?"

Shepherd meets my eyes. "No, Carrefour, I mean that with all sincerity."

He's telling the truth, that I can tell, but an inscrutable undercurrent flows in tandem with his words. What is he hiding? Pain? Worry?

He retreats another step. "From now on, I'll conduct myself with the professionalism that befits my position."

"Professionalism?"

"You have my word." He scans the room, but it feels like an excuse to not look at me.

"I should sweep the apartment to ensure we don't have any other unwanted guests. Your schedule is clear until the museum opening at seven tonight. Why don't you order some staples for the kitchen? And let me know the next time you need a little sunshine. I'll make the necessary arrangements."

Instead of walking past me, he circumvents the couch-like protrusion and heads through the first of the two curved doorways behind me, neither of which has an actual door. I cradle my still-tingling hand to my chest, wondering which version of Shepherd I disliked more.

Colorier

colorier—(coh-LOR-ee-ay) adj. Color-changing, generally in reference to textiles.

After receiving the all clear, I claim the bedroom on the left, for no reason other than it's where my duffel bag ended up. The two rooms are mirror images of one another, each occupying a quarter of the circle, while the living area, kitchen, and foyer make up the other half.

My bathroom is to the right, sharing a wall with Shepherd's. The closets on the wall abutting the kitchen hold every imaginable article of red and white clothing, from undergarments to cocktail dresses. A doubled-over note card sits on the top shelf.

> My dearest Diamond,
> It is my sincere honor to provide your wardrobe for the season, each item carefully selected from my latest collection. May you feel as beautiful wearing them as they will surely look on you.
> Your friend, Stiletto

More enamored with the note than the clothes, I run my hand over the thick card stock, marveling at the rare luxury. Does he own an actual ink pen too? I open a random drawer and tuck the note under red polka dot pajamas.

One of the wardrobe doors hides a laundromatter, so I pull over my duffel bag, extract all the clothing, and dump them into the machine, deciding at the last minute to include the bag as well. Let's just wash that bad SKI mojo off everything, me included.

I take the longest shower of my life, relishing the citrus-scented cleansers and moisturizers. Thoroughly refreshed, I find the pajama drawer again and pull on a white satin set. The laundromatter finishes the same time the evaporator does, so I remove the folded pieces and sort my old clothes in with my new ones. The casual pieces look completely out of place, exactly how I will tonight if I don't start getting ready.

I head back into the bathroom and apply chromix makeup the way Lepota showed me, adjusting the levels to match hers. I'm not sure what to do with my hair, other than return it to dark, chestnut brown.

Janus sends me a message at five thirty p.m. **My apologies. I'm a bit delayed returning to town. I hoped to pick you up but will need to meet you at the Holusion Museum. Looking forward to it.**

I bite my lip. Janus, *the* Janus, sent me a personal message! My elation is quickly replaced by panic as I try on dress after dress, wondering which one will make the best first impression. I want to come off as both elegant and professional, especially considering he probably saw my embarrassing preteen videos proclaiming my undying love for him.

My hands cover my flaming cheeks. I wish I could time-travel back five years to beg younger me not to post those. What was I thinking?

Hopefully, he won't mention them. I can't imagine he would. He has more decorum than that.

I send pics of my dress options to Vivi and Corah, who choose a fitted, strapless dress with colorier sequins that alternate solid white or red every fifteen minutes. It's fun, and as Stiletto hoped, I feel pretty in it.

While I was showering, Shepherd went through every item in the pantry, composting over half of them. I bemoaned the waste, but it's not like we could donate possibly poisoned food. Fresh replacements arrived an hour ago, and he carefully inspected those items as well.

"You don't have to cook for me," I remind him as I step out of the room, drawn by the aroma of garlic, tomato, and onions. "I'm sure that's not part of your job description."

Shepherd wears a red apron over a white collared shirt, the sleeves of which are rolled to his elbows. Black-socked feet peek out from under his dress pants. "I know," he says to the pan. "But I like to cook. It relaxes me."

"Then by all means . . ."

He looks up and does a double take. "Your dress."

"Is it too much?" I pat the material. "It changes color." I couldn't have timed my words better. Sequin by sequin, red replaces the white. I raise my arms and twirl like a pinwheel, then freeze and hold out my arms. "Ta-da."

Shepherd is smiling, an honest-to-goodness smile. "Very impressive."

"My twirling skills are unparalleled."

"I meant the dress."

"I know." I saunter over, plant my elbows on the counter, and support my chin on my fists to stare at the pot of sauce. "How much longer?"

"A few minutes. Think you can make it?"

"Newp," I say with all honesty but manage to push myself away to round up dishes and cutlery.

As if he's also made of colorier sequins, he becomes his professional self while we eat. I probe him with questions about his friends and childhood, but he answers with only a few words each and doesn't ask me anything. Soon we're eating in uncomfortable silence. A homicidal RAID would've made better company.

It's not until we're seated in the hover—Shepherd in front again—that nerves begin to stir.

I've met celebrities before. The rich and famous entered our house on a weekly basis. But having them in our home isn't the same as entering their circle, especially now that I'm the "Carrefour Diamond."

Pangs of loneliness join my self-doubt, forming a jangly ball of anxiety in my gut. I take out my specs and call Mom, hoping the sound of her voice will calm me down.

"There you are," she says. "You almost forgot your promise to call, didn't you? Oh, don't you look lovely."

Our calls are the only times she gets me without my aura. Whatever colorful energy she sees around people doesn't translate to video transmissions.

"Thanks, lady. How was your day? What colors are the security people?"

"Uneventful. And gray and beige. Every last one of them." She chuckles.

"Good to hear. Dependable, protective, and serious. Just what you want in the team guarding your mother."

"Speaking of security, when can I meet this Shepherd of yours?"

"Mom, he's not *my* Shepherd."

"You know what I mean. He's with you, isn't he?"

I wince. "Yes, but—"

"I promise not to embarrass you, but I'll feel better after meeting the person in charge of protecting my little Indigo."

Grr. She won't let up now, and considering the events of the past week, I'd like to reassure her I'm safe. "Fine. Hang on a sec." I mute the call and switch off the hover's holoshield.

He and the navigator are sharing a laugh.

Are they making fun of me? Nope, doesn't matter. "Hey, Shepherd."

His smile vanishes. There one second, gone the next. "Yes?"

He's switched from hating me to tolerating me. Perhaps I should be grateful, but I'd feel better if the person I'm stuck with day and night would make *some* effort at civility.

"My mom wants to meet you. Would you mind talking with her?"

"Sure, no problem." He reaches back.

I hug the specs to my chest. "Could you be nice, please?"

The navigator snickers.

Shepherd waves his hand for the specs. "I'm always nice."

"Nicest person I know," says the navigator.

"Yeah, well, not the nicest person I know by far." I pass the specs through the opening. "She's the most important person in my life, so please—"

"Carrefour. I've got this." Shepherd slides on my specs but mutes the holoshield, so I can see him but can't hear what he's saying.

I tap the controls above, but his settings must trump mine

because nothing changes. I'm forced to watch the entire five-minute conversation instead. He starts serious and deferential, but minute by minute, his smile spreads until he's giggling uncontrollably with a hand over his eyes. What the hell is she *saying* to him?

Shepherd notices me glaring and turns off the visual access as well. A minute later, the specs shoot through the holoshield. I grab them from him and put them back on. The call has ended, but I have a new message from Mom.

Mom: I'm guessing gray and beige for him as well. Have a nice evening! I can't wait to hear about the holusions.

That's it? What did she tell him about me? I groan and sink into the seat.

The hover pulls up to the museum, but due to the line of vehicles, it takes another ten minutes to reach the red carpet. While we wait, I take in the spectators and floating drones near the entrance—their numbers only a fraction of those at SKI. A three-meter-high clear wall rises on either side of the walkway, holding back the crowd. I settle into my seat and fill my lungs. The red, puffy scratch from yesterday still mars my forearm, but this crowd won't be able to touch me.

The hover stops at the curb, and the passenger-side doors lift. I wait for a hand to help me out like everyone before me. But Shepherd isn't my date or escort. Guess I'll have to exit the hover myself, the way I have my entire life . . . hopefully with a little more grace. I swing my legs over and plaster on a smile while stepping out.

A drone swarms down, coming only centimeters from my face before Shepherd volleys it to the ground. The orb smashes into pieces near my feet, and I jump toward him to avoid the shards.

"Hey!" a woman shouts from at least fifty meters away.

"Keep your cameras back!" Shepherd calls over his shoulder. He steadies me by placing his hands on my waist—his strong, warm hands. "You okay?"

"Yep. Thanks."

We lock eyes, and I follow his silent suggestion to take a deep breath. I'm okay. He's got my back.

Just as I'm about to pivot toward the crowd, Shepherd whispers, "Wait." He moves a misplaced strand of hair back into place.

My body stiffens at his touch.

"Perfect. Go get 'em." He winks.

I nod jerkily, but bolstered by his marching orders, I pull back my shoulders and start toward the museum. My dress must hold some sort of thermal power because ten paces later, the calming heat from his hands remains.

Following the lead of the couple before me, I take measured steps toward the entrance, waving at whoever calls my name, mouthing *Thank you* to their compliments. But through the roars of "Carrefour," another name surfaces.

Relax, Sivon, it's just your overactive imagination. Everyone here seems genuinely excited to see me.

Nope, there it is again. I swivel right, looking for the source. That man with the mustache? The woman recording me with her screen? It comes from the left next time. I swear, I *swear* I heard it, but no way did it come from that little girl's mouth or her mother's. Is my mind deceiving me?

We reach the stairs, and I look over my shoulder at Shepherd. Did he hear them too?

He's studying the onlookers and muttering into his earplant. Over the shouts and banging on the walls, I manage to make out a few of his words, stoking my fear and quashing my self-doubt.

"... both sides. Creature."

Holusion

holusion—(huh-LOO-zhun) n. an optical illusion created with holograms.

Only two steps into the Holusion Museum, I forget about the taunts. *What is this magic?* I've seen holo art before—the butterflies at SKI, the foxes on Advertitude. I even had a couple holo teachers senior year—but this is like nothing I could've ever imagined.

The expansive room resembles a fish tank. While the four columns are probably simple white pillars, they instead appear as swaying algae. Brightly colored fish swim around, floating above our heads and darting between groups of decked out attendees. Bubbles slide up the walls, tossing and turning whenever a fish swims past.

I'm so entranced, Shepherd has to nudge me forward. I take three steps, and though the floor feels hard under my shoes, the mirage of pebbly sand leaves indents precisely where I step. "Unreal," I mumble.

I turn to Shepherd, curious about his reaction, but he's not looking at any of the projections. He's studying the living occupants of the room instead, completely stone-faced. Mom was right. Gray and beige all the way.

A RAID floats over, disguised as a catfish and bearing a tray of drinks. I reach for one, but Shepherd guides my wrist back to my side.

I drum my fingers against my thigh. "Surely these aren't all poisoned."

"Surely you're not thinking of drinking something you didn't see prepared," he says while scrutinizing the crowd.

"We're not at some college party. These are probably the richest people in North America." I motion to the nearby group of people sipping cocktails.

"Your point being?"

"I'm supposed to *mingle*."

"I never said you couldn't mingle."

My hands form fists. "But I have to fit in. All of *them* are drinking. Look, that woman just took one from the same tray."

"I'm not responsible for keeping all of *them* alive. Just you." At my growl of frustration, he says, "I can't stop you from drinking, Carrefour, but I strongly advise against it."

Ugh, I hate knowing he's right. "Killjoy."

I huff and search the room. My eyes land on a handsome young man leaning against the bar, holding a glass of water. Janus. My cheeks flush warm, and my hands join to trace circles and Xs on my palms.

He doesn't notice me, fully engrossed in conversation with an older couple I don't recognize. Probably donors. How is he so effortlessly cool, especially around this intimidating crowd?

My eyes are pulled from Janus's calm demeanor when a group approaches me. Time to prove to both of us I belong here. *You can do this!* They introduce themselves—daughter of Senator So-and-So, chairwoman of such-and-such board, president of XYZ Bank. Their names and titles enter and exit through the revolving door of my mind. I deflect questions about my kirling, affirm my appointment to Mirovnik's staff, and ask them about themselves. While I find the small talk tedious, I enjoy the challenge of directing the conversation, much like Ujjwala did during my interview.

Speaking of whom ... despite keeping my back to her from the moment she entered, Ujjwala makes a beeline straight for me and takes my elbow. "Carrefour, hey!" She nods at the group I'm with. "Okay if I steal her for a minute?"

She tugs me away, not waiting for their reply. Her rudeness curls my toes, but why would she care what they think? She's probably wealthier than all of them combined. Shepherd's sneer matches my own as she leads me into the corner of the room. Guess he remembers her from my interview as well.

"Hey, listen." Ujjwala sets her hands on my shoulders, then redirects her focus to Shepherd.

Unlike with the earlier group, when he politely stayed a few meters away, Shepherd hovers behind me now. If I reached back a few centimeters, I'd probably hit his leg.

"Do you mind?" she asks him, further stirring my ire.

I remove her hands from my shoulders. "I don't care how you talk to me, but this is an agent of the North American Secret Service."

Her brow crinkles. "Sorry, of course. My apologies, sir."

Shepherd doesn't move; if anything, he steps closer. Ujjwala looks at me, then him, then back to me. But if she's waiting for me to dismiss him, she'll be sorely disappointed. I want Shepherd to hear our conversation. "What is it, Ujjwala?"

She scratches her cheek. "I didn't know they would do that. To you." Her eyes dart about, and she lowers her voice. "The producer asked me to keep things light and to bring up your position with

Mirovnik, but I had no clue they would…" Her gaze flicks to Shepherd. "Change things."

While I hate the reminder of that dreadful interview, sweet vindication courses through my veins. *See, Shepherd, I'm not a pathological liar.*

Ujjwala squeezes my hand. "It's weighed on me ever since. I'm so sorry."

"Carrefour, there you are!"

I freeze at the familiar voice, though it's the first time I've heard it in person. My head swivels to take in the man I've admired for a good third of my life.

My world suddenly shifts into focus, like I've surfaced from a lifetime underwater. My senses begin rapid firing at once, so overwhelming that I sway on my feet. I home in on Janus's confident gait, his thumb casually tucked into a pocket. As he approaches, the white noise discussions of the crowd and the pulsing bass of background music amplify. Shepherd edges even closer, and the undercurrent of salt water in the air—did the artist pipe that in?—mingles with his pine scent, the warmth of which I grab onto and stuff into my pores.

Janus nods to both Shepherd and a starstruck Ujjwala, then lifts my hand from her grip. "I've been looking for you everywhere." He holds my gaze while brushing his full lips over my knuckles in a gesture both electrifying and oddly familiar. His dimples emerge, and my inner thirteen-year-old squeals in disbelief. Janus just kissed my hand!

I groan internally, wishing he'd found me five minutes ago, while I was entertaining the political elite. He probably thinks I've been hiding in the corner all night. My stomach tumbles like it did earlier in the hover, twinging the back corners of my mouth. Where'd that tray of drinks go?

"It's wonderful to meet you, Janus." Despite the turmoil inside, my voice emerges cool and collected. As it should. I'm an adult, not some hormonal adolescent, and Janus is more than his good looks.

"The pleasure is mine." Janus places my hand on his forearm and leads me away from the corner.

I turn to wave goodbye to Ujjwala, but she's already joined a group of chittering Sociaty stars. Shepherd falls back, making me feel too exposed. How can someone be so irritating and comforting at the same time? No, stop focusing on Shepherd. Think of something interesting to ask Janus.

"How was your mission trip?" I ask at the same time he says, "How are you settling into your new soul?"

We chuckle.

"You go first," I say.

"No, please. I insist." Janus nods at a couple passing by.

But now I'm confused. Should I answer his question or restate mine? *Oh, just pick one. The point is conversation.* "My new soul . . . Can I be honest?"

Janus's brows peak. "I'd expect nothing less. And promise the same in return."

I fill my lungs, relieved. "It kind of sucks."

Janus laughs heartily.

"I don't mean to sound ungrateful. I'm so immensely appreciative to your uncle for the job, apartment, clothes, and security. But I'd gladly exchange them for a night in my own bed."

Janus comes to a stop in the middle of the room, facing me. "I know how you feel."

I place my hands on my hips. "You promised honesty."

He chuckles. "No, truly. I may not know what it's like to suddenly be thrown into the spotlight, but when I'm traveling, believe me, there's nothing more I want than to get back home again." He leans closer. "And I know how much it *sucks* to be incessantly scrutinized by the entire world." His gaze flits left, then right. A prompt.

My lips part as I take in the wide circle of onlookers, whispering to one another.

Janus lifts my hand from his arm and directs me through a slow spin. "Our new soul, ladies and gentlemen."

I graciously nod at their applause as my stomach twinges painfully. *This is why you're here, Sivon—to lend your celebrity to a good cause. You have to get comfortable with this.*

As I'm completing my turn, my eyes land on Shepherd, whose look of disgust twists my gut even more. Oh gosh, I'm gonna throw up.

Ladiron

Ladiron—Soulid: 1VD1R0N, primarily known for shooting and killing General Molemo and Flavinsky in World War III. Currently serves as the head of the Global Civil Liberties Union.

I'm so sorry. Would you excuse me for a minute?" Without waiting for a reply, I head toward the doors in the back, where I hope to find a restroom. But the second I push through them, I regret it. The long corridor is checkered black and green, but the pattern moves, warping the floor and walls. As much as I try to walk straight, the optical illusion throws me off-balance, making me stumble.

Shepherd seizes my upper arm. "Close your eyes."

Sighing with gratitude, I follow his advice while he escorts me to the other end.

I hear him knock on a wooden door. "Anyone in here?"

When he gets no response, he pulls me inside and shuts the door. "All clear. You can open your eyes."

But when I do, the walls of the bathroom bend like I'm stuck in the last hallway. I burst into the first stall and vomit up what remains of our pasta dinner.

Behind me, water splashes against the sink basin, and Shepherd presses a cool, wet towel to my forehead. I take it from him and manage to cough out "Thank you" before my stomach seizes once more.

A minute later, I flush the toilet and sit on my haunches, the vertigo and nausea having now passed.

Shepherd chuckles. "I imagined you reacting a million different ways to meeting your childhood crush, but that was not one."

I shoot daggers at him over my shoulder. "Quit it."

"Can I please be the one to tell Janus he made you sick to your stomach?"

I push to my feet. "Don't you dare. That was probably more your cooking than anything."

I lumber to the sink to wash my hands and take advantage of the nanorizing kits inside the mirror well. When I look back up, Shepherd's face has drained of color.

"What's wrong?"

"Do you really think it was dinner? What if someone sabotaged our groceries?"

I lean against the basin. "Do you feel sick too?"

He considers for a minute. "No, I feel pretty great, actually."

"Then it wasn't the food."

"Good, I can go back to blaming Janus."

I roll my eyes. "What do you have against Janus?"

Shepherd purses his lips. "Bit conceited."

"Ha. You should talk." I walk toward the exit but pause before pushing open the door. Still weak, I'm not ready to rejoin Janus but also don't want to leave early. "Can I ask a favor?"

"Anytime."

Shepherd's quick affirmative takes me by surprise. He could've said *of course*, but *anytime* means he's open to multiple favors. Maybe he doesn't hate me so much anymore. Or he just feels bad for the girl who threw up at her first swanky event.

"Could you lead me into another room, one that's not so . . . wobbly?"

He dips his chin. "We could just leave."

"No, I only need a minute. I'll be all right."

Shepherd chews his cheek, studying me with obvious concern. "Okay, close your eyes and hold my hand." He reaches out, palm up.

I settle my fingers in his grip and close my eyes. Left without my sight, my other senses come to life. The coarse pad of his thumb skirts over my hand, sending tingles up my arm. He exhales a waft of sweet mint my way. Mint. I bet I could taste it if we . . .

He pushes open the door and leads me into the corridor. Cool air douses my skin like a bucket of ice water. Whoa, did I really just imagine kissing Shepherd? My bodyguard? Who has a freaking soulmate? The nausea must've addled my brain.

After Shepherd tries one door, only to mumble a quick "Nope," he leads me inside another room. Or are we outside? The chirp of crickets greets my ears, accompanied by the gentle trickle of a stream and the rustle of leaves from a breeze that doesn't exist.

"You can open your eyes now."

I do so and gasp in delight. We're in a forest at dusk. If I squint, I can make out the corners of the ceiling, but otherwise, the massive trees stretching into the evening sky look shockingly lifelike.

I take a step along the leaf-strewn path, and one audibly crunches under my foot. My amazement emerges in the form of delighted laughter. "Incredible."

No longer do I wish to rejoin the party, not when this heavenly respite exists. A lightning bug sparks near my chest, and when

I reach out to capture it, only then do I realize I'm still holding Shepherd's hand. He loosens his hold, and our fingers gently slide apart.

I curl my fist, fighting the impulse to take it back. "Have you ever seen anything more intoxicating?"

"Never."

I lift my eyes to his, noting how quickly he shifts his gaze to the doors. Shepherd's posture suddenly goes rigid.

Mine does the same when I turn to find Janus approaching. "Carrefour, you're quite the enigma. Not a party person, then?"

Great. First he finds me in the corner. Then I complain about being a new soul and run away the moment he introduces me to the crowd. He can only assume I'm hiding away again. Some spokesperson I am. "Just needed some fresh air." I wave a hand to the room. "But we can get back—"

My sentence falls off as someone steps up next to Janus. Is that who I think it is?

"Don't blame you one bit. But Holusion's resident artist asked to meet you." Janus gestures to the newcomer. "This is Trevin. Trevin, meet Carrefour."

Trevin? Oh gosh, Mom is gonna be so jealous. We've long obsessed over their many lifetimes of groundbreaking art. When we heard the news of Trevin's kirling last summer, Mom and I vowed to go to their next show together. I had no idea they'd be here tonight!

Trevin wears an aqua-blue tuxedo, perfectly matching their hair, which is shaved on one side, chin-length on the other. "Glad you found your way to my favorite room."

I pump their hand a bit too enthusiastically. "It's stunning, Trevin. I'm such a fan of your work."

They incline their head. "I've heard great things about you as well."

I smile at Janus. Was he talking me up? He nods to a couple entering the room, then excuses himself to chat with them.

After he walks away, Trevin leans closer. "We have a mutual friend. I was under strict orders to tell you, 'The bet's not over.'"

My eyes bulge. Vivi! "You know Kitsune?"

Trevin's cheeks flush. "*Getting* to know."

Oh. My. Gosh. Vivi and *Trevin*? It takes all my willpower to not squeal and jump up and down. "Vivi and I did a project about your mother senior year. Did she tell you about it?" Gosh, how was that only a few months ago? So much has changed since then.

Trevin's mother is the infamous Ladiron, the soul responsible for killing General Molemo and Flavinsky in their foli 1. Today, she's the leader of the Global Civil Liberties Union. The transition from despised criminal to upstanding leader inspired our Foli Studies senior thesis.

In foli 1, Ladiron was a he, a captain fighting for the North American alliance, until he turned traitor and murdered General Molemo and Flavinsky. At the time, Flavinsky and Ladiron were close friends, so Ladiron either fooled Flavinsky into abandoning his post or together they planned to kill the beloved World War III general. After General Molemo was murdered, Ladiron and Flavinsky shot and killed each other.

Ladiron was kirled seven years later, a girl this time and only seven years old, before it was illegal to kirl children. She disappeared shortly thereafter but likely lived to a ripe old age due to the length of time between that kirling and the next.

When foli 3's kirling rolled around, Ladiron was arrested to fulfill the life sentence for Molemo's murder. He served thirty-one years until his death, but while imprisoned, he earned a law degree and helped many of his fellow inmates overturn their convictions or reduce their sentences. His speeches about character, perseverance, and hope were so inspiring, they were live-streamed around the world.

Now, Ladiron is Trevin's mom, and the leader of the Global Civil Liberties Union. If Ladiron can turn their soul around, anyone can. Even Flavinsky. My doubts about Ziva's death surface again, but I push them down to focus on the celebrity artist I've long wanted to meet.

Trevin smiles warmly. "Kitsune did not mention that."

"Make her show it to you. We earned full marks."

"I absolutely will."

A man taps Trevin on the shoulder and whispers in their ear. They nod. "I need to run, but please, let's all get together soon."

"I'd love that."

As they walk away, I pinch my wrist to make sure this isn't all a dream. I can't believe I just met Trevin, and that Vivi didn't tell me she was talking with them!

Janus returns to my side. "Wow, right?"

"I'm a bit awestruck."

"Understandable. My uncle and I are huge fans. Especially of their mother's work." He looks after Trevin and sighs. "Ladiron's endorsement could mean a lot to my uncle's reelection. She personifies everything we stand for. Don't you think?"

"Oh, yes. She'd be perfect." My mind begins whirring with ideas. Perhaps I could arrange an evening to bring everyone together—

Vivi and Trevin, Ladiron and Prime Minister Mirovnik. "I might be able to help with that."

Janus's brows rise. "Really? That would be extraordinary, Carrefour."

Considering the lackluster impression I've made, this could be my saving grace. And an opportunity to prove I'm worth more than just my new soul. "I promise to try."

"What more can we ask?" Janus takes my hand and places it back on his arm. "Now, tell me. Is there anything I can do to help you?" He escorts me toward the doors.

"You mean besides the job, apartment, clothes, and security? I wouldn't dream of—" I pull to a stop, my thoughts again racing, reorganizing my strategy. "Actually, there is something." *Say it, Sivon. Trust your instincts.* "I was planning to bring this up with your uncle, but perhaps you can advise the best way to proceed."

Janus studies me with intense gray eyes. "I'd be happy to. What is it?"

I lick my lips. "I'd like to request an investigation into Flavinsky's recent death."

Shepherd coughs from a meter away, but I keep my gaze on Janus, studying his reaction.

He blinks several times. "Sorry, that wasn't at all what I expected you to say. It's my understanding that Flavinsky's suicides are always reviewed. Did they do an autopsy?"

The heat of Shepherd's stare calls to me, but I don't want it to look like I'm doing this for him. I shuffle to the right, and Janus turns to face me. Now that Janus can't see him, he might not make the connection. "Yes, but they should do more than determine the cause of death, like check the footage recorded by the RAIDs on duty and investigate why bots were placed there in the first place."

In the periphery of my vision, I notice Shepherd's jaw flex. *Don't look at him, Sivon.*

Janus tilts his head. "Where is this coming from? Do you have reason to believe Flavinsky didn't take her life?"

"Just some unresolved questions. I was there that night, and—" This is a lot to throw on him five minutes after we met. "Sorry, I didn't plan to discuss this in the middle of a gala."

"No, *I'm* sorry." Janus rubs my wrist. "The first thing out of my mouth should've been 'of course.' Yes, I'll absolutely ensure the authorities conduct a full investigation. Don't worry about it a second more, okay?"

I inhale his scent of sweet linen, relieved to find he's as wonderful as I always expected him to be. "Thank you, Janus. That means a lot to me."

Janus pulls open one of the double doors, and I wince. How the heck am I gonna make it back through the corridor of horrors? But as we're exiting the room, Shepherd speaks into his com, and by the time we turn into the offending hallway, the holos are off.

I turn back and mouth *Thank you* to Shepherd. He dips his chin as his lips form the same words. My soul glows with pride. Maybe, just maybe, I've fully redeemed myself tonight with both Janus and Shepherd.

The crowd in the expansive foyer ballooned in the twenty minutes or so since I left. After speaking with the first group Janus introduces me to, I turn and come face-to-face with Norine, the purple-haired girl from SKI.

"Oh my gosh! Norine!" I envelop her in a hug.

"Sivon!" She squeezes me back.

"It's so good to see you. What brings you here tonight?"

"You're looking at the newly minted Chief of Staff for Senator Fahari." Norine points across the room to her new boss.

The senator, her mahogany complexion perfectly complemented by a magenta-and-gold gown, is speaking animatedly with a transfixed Trevin. Crap. Of course Mirovnik's competition would want to mingle with Washington's elite tonight as well. And naturally, Fahari would seek out Trevin, whose mother's endorsement could tip the election. I'll have to move fast to arrange that meeting between Ladiron and the prime minister.

"Congrats, Norine! Not surprised one bit, but I guess that makes us sworn enemies now." I wink.

She wraps an arm around my waist. "Never. This town needs people willing to compromise."

"Count me in," I say, though my competitive nature wants nothing more than to interrupt the senator's and Trevin's conversation.

It's fine, I tell myself as Norine makes her way toward them. *You've only just entered this match. Give yourself time to learn the rules, who the key players are.* But instinctually, I know, as if staring down at the pieces on a Chessfield board, Ladiron is important. Perhaps even more than my new soul. Mirovnik can't win without Ladiron. Which means neither can I.

Hoverball

hoverball—n. A popular team sport wherein a levitating melon-size ball is kicked, kneed, head-butted, or spiked through ten roaming circular goalposts scattered throughout a 60 x 100-meter field.

The rest of the evening flies by in a whirlwind of introductions, Janus remaining steadfastly by my side. I'm unsure whether he does so out of inclination, obligation, or concern that I'll sneak away at the first opportunity.

The temptation to do so is strong. Though my stomach settles down, my brain does not. I don't know if it's the holusions, the socialites, or simply Janus's company, but I feel as if I've been breathing pure oxygen for hours. Alert and overstimulated.

I handle it by emulating everything Janus does, taking cues on when to shake hands or exchange air kisses, who I can speak with casually and who prefers deferential treatment. By the time he escorts me to the hover, I'm sure I couldn't utter another word, both from exhaustion and hoarseness from talking for hours.

Janus reaches into his jacket pocket and peeks at his screen. "One a.m. Can you believe it?"

"So late? I had no idea." I left my specs and clutch behind in the hover.

"And to think we hit the road in five hours."

I try to keep the confusion from my face. Where are we going in five hours?

He scratches his forehead. "Tomorrow morning will be brutal, but my uncle can't wait to have you join him on the campaign trail."

I nod as if I already know this information, certain a trip wasn't on my schedule the last time I checked. But I'm not going to bail on my first official event. "It's almost better to stay awake at this point." My voice cracks on the last word. Hopefully, the prime minister doesn't expect me to give any rousing speeches tomorrow.

"You've got a point." Janus ducks his chin. "Are you sure you're up for it? I'm used to this lifestyle, but you admitted it's been a difficult adjustment. Maybe we should wait a week or two, ease you into things." He frowns. "Or we could find something else on my uncle's staff. Something less . . . public. If that's what you want."

Embarrassment floods my cheeks. Why did I whine about my new soul earlier? Now he's lost faith in my abilities. I thought I'd come back from that, but . . . "Did I do something wrong?"

"No, no." He takes my hand, cupping it between his. "I didn't mean to imply that at all. You were exquisite tonight. Did you enjoy yourself?"

"I did!" The lie comes out effortlessly, as if I was used to spewing falsehoods instead of shamefully confessing even the smallest of infractions while growing up. No harm, no foul. I'm protecting my job, my livelihood, perhaps even my life.

"Glad to hear it." He sweeps his thumbs over the back of my hand, a surprisingly intimate gesture after an evening of professional decorum.

Don't read into it, Sivon. It was meant as a comfort, a kindness.

"But if at any point you get tired of the spotlight, let me know, okay? I'm on your side." Janus raises my hand to his lips, but he doesn't close his eyes like when we met. This time, he holds my gaze and lingers a split second longer. His eyes darken, sending a thrill down my spine.

"Thank you, Janus," I say breathily. "I guess I'll see you in five hours." I climb into the hover.

"I'll be counting the minutes." He nods to his NASS agent and heads back up the red carpet.

Shepherd ducks into the front seat and activates the holoshield between us. The doors lower, sealing us into our separate worlds. I look out the window, focusing first on Janus's back, then the window itself.

Did someone...? Are those...? I tilt my head, reversing the backward letters, so faint in the thin layer of pollen, I nearly missed them.

CREATURE

The sun still hasn't risen when we depart the Kismet at six a.m. I barely slept, but Shepherd fared far worse, staying up to ensure the graffiti would get processed for fingerprints. We were too bleary-eyed to attempt conversation as we stumbled around getting ready this morning. And I definitely don't have the energy for whomever is calling from the White House at this hour.

"Good morning, Carrefour. I'm the prime minister's publicist. I only have a minute, so let's get straight to it."

I sit upright in the hover's back seat, snapping into alertness. The publicist! This is the person who can grant me access to my Sociaty profile, the one who attributed that heartless Flavinsky quote to me. "Yes, thanks for calling. I wanted to ask you ab—"

"You have three stops today—Philharmonica, Wilmington, and the Delmarva Fringe community of Federalsburn."

Okay, rude. "Yes, but can we—"

"For the first two, you'll stand onstage, focus on whoever is speaking, and clap when appropriate. Take cues from the audience."

Does she think I'm daft? I knew Mirovnik hired me as his show pony, but she doesn't have to be so condescending. "That's fine, but—"

"Janus has another commitment during the Federalsburn event, so you'll make a few brief comments. We're crafting a speech and will send it over shortly." She disconnects.

What the fuck? I growl and call her back, but she declines it on the first ring. I try again. Same thing. I send a message to the same number. **Please call me back. We need to discuss Sociaty posts.**

The immediate response reads, **We're sorry, this account does not accept incoming messages from unapproved sources.**

Unapproved sources? I'm the *freaking new soul*!

That's the second person on Mirovnik's staff to be rude to me. I guess I can understand Pono's contempt. I wasn't exactly friendly when I told him I was going to Ziva's funeral. He must've told the publicist I was a little brat, so now she won't hear me out.

So how do I fix this? I'm not about to complain to Janus again. I'd sound entitled. No, if I want respect, I need to earn it. And that starts with doing my job and helping Mirovnik win this election. If I can secure Ladiron's endorsement, that will be a game changer.

I start to draft a new message to Vivi, then delete it. Am I really going to take advantage of my best friend's crush to keep my job? What if Vivi doesn't have feelings for Trevin? She might feel obligated to date them just to help me out. I couldn't do that to her. First, I'll suss out her feelings, then explain my predicament, openly and honestly. If the Ladiron endorsement doesn't work out, it doesn't work out. I won't sacrifice our friendship for that.

I check over my schedule and, after resigning myself to the fact a heart-to-heart won't be possible today, draft a new message.

Me: Viv, got time to chat tomorrow?

Me: PS. Trevin is 100% smitten with you.

My stomach bottoms out when we pull up to the Philharmonica hoverball stadium. I thought we'd be in a theater or school gymnasium, not in front of fifty thousand people. The doors lift and the roar of the crowd assaults my eardrums, setting me on edge. Fighting my instinct to duck and cover, I plaster on a smile and accept Janus's hand.

"Good morning, Carrefour."

How does he look so well rested? "Good morning. Nice to see you again so soon."

He's traded his tuxedo for a navy suit, his white collar sitting open at the neck. Between Shepherd and Janus, I'm now surrounded by handsome men. Not a bad thing.

I hazarded a guess on appropriate attire and selected a confidence-boosting red pantsuit. Just in case, I tossed a scarlet dress in my bag as a backup. Seems like I chose perfectly, though.

Janus points to his temple, a subtle reminder I'm wearing my specs. Shoot, I forgot I had them on. I toss them on top of my duffel. Once I'm on my feet, he turns me to face the crowd, placing his hand on the small of my back. My muscles there snap taut, engaging my core.

Like last night, I take a cue from Janus and wave at the crowd, all the while searching for signs of detractors. Are any of them shouting *Creature*? Threatened by my new soul? I see only smiles.

"Get any sleep?" Janus asks.

"Not much." The little I did get was plagued by nightmares of demons crawling out of the depths of hell. "You?"

"A little. Uncle Mirovnik invited me to share his copter, so that gave me an extra hour."

Not that I expected them to include me, but also, *why didn't they include me*? My smile wavers. *No, don't pout. You're just cranky from sleep deprivation.* They would've offered if they had room.

"Ready for this?" Janus motions toward the staff entrance.

I take his offered elbow. Shepherd follows behind as we walk up the long pathway.

"That suit looks stunning on you, by the way." Janus waves to the right.

I blow a kiss to the left. "Thank you, Janus."

"So if my uncle asks you to change, think nothing of it. He's just very particular, tries to control every little detail."

I smooth down a lapel, suddenly doubting my choice. "Oh, I thought this looked professional. I have a red dress, too, but it's back in the hover. Should we go back for it?" I point over my shoulder.

Janus waves off my concerns. "Not necessary. We have a whole team of stylists here. I've found it's best to let them do their thing and not take any of it personally."

A guard pulls open the door, and the rush of cool air dries up the dredges of my confidence.

Janus grins down at me. "But if I were prime minister, I wouldn't change a thing."

A spontaneous round of applause from the hallway drowns out

his last few words, but his intent was hard to miss. Is Janus *flirting* with me? And if so, how do I feel about that?

I wish I knew, but it's hard to focus on Janus when dozens of hands are now reaching toward me, begging for my attention. Who are these people? Constituents? Stadium employees? Fellow staff members?

I shake their hands and attempt to respond to their comments, most along the lines of "You're such an inspiration" and "We're so happy to have you with us." But either my lack of sleep, Janus's compliment, or Shepherd's uncomfortable distance throws me off-kilter.

Why has Shepherd fallen a full ten meters behind? Any one of these strangers could attack me long before he could do something about it. I slow down, hoping he'll catch up, but he maintains our measured separation.

Calm down, Sivon. If Shepherd's not concerned, you shouldn't be either. He wouldn't put me in danger. I know it. These people probably went through weapon detectors to get inside. I take the next offered hand, pushing down my anxiety. I can do this. I *am* doing this.

We finally make it down the hallway, and Janus guides me into a bustling locker room smelling of sweaty feet. He makes a handful of introductions but soon gets pulled away to answer questions and give orders. I linger in the corner for a few minutes, eventually settling on one of the benches.

Someone hands me a cup of water. I lift it to my lips, catch Shepherd's eye, and set it beside me instead. The slight lift of his lips fills me with foolish pride. *See, Shepherd, I'm not totally oblivious.*

The buzz dies down when Mirovnik enters. Without speaking to another soul, he heads straight to me. I rise and respectfully bow my head. "Prime Minister."

"Sivon, what a delight! So lovely to meet you in person." He makes air kisses on either side of my face.

Unaccustomed to the gesture, I awkwardly mimic him while practicing saying *Actually, I go by Carrefour now*, but can't force out the words.

"Janus sang your praises the whole way here. I knew I made the right choice in hiring you. How are you today? Can I get you anything?"

Four to five hours of sleep would be nice. "I'm okay. Thank you."

"Wonderful. I love this red on you, but . . ." Mirovnik turns to someone standing nearby. "Could we find her something in white, please? And perhaps someone to do her hair?" He turns back to me. "The updo is stunning, truly stunning, but let's keep your hair down for these events. Looks more . . . new-soul-like. Don't you think?"

Across the room, Janus winks as if to say *I told you so*.

I suppress a commiserating eye roll and simply reply, "Of course." I can play up the new soul part if that's what Mirovnik wants. That's why I'm here, after all.

"Thank you, Sivon. If there's anything you need, just ask. Anyone in this room will happily get it for you. Isn't that right?" He raises his chin and smiles at the chorus of *yes, sir*s.

Their half-lidded glares warn me not to do any such thing. The second Mirovnik turns to talk to someone else, a woman takes me by the elbow and leads me into an adjacent room. The makeshift dressing room has three racks of garment bags and a retractable mirror attached lengthwise to one wall. Without saying a word, she pushes me onto a stool near the mirror, yanks apart my bun, and starts brushing my hair.

I curl my fingers, holding back a scream as she jerks my head about. Shepherd and I make eye contact through the mirror. He's trying to tell me something, but what?

"Ow!" I hiss and press fingers to my burning scalp. Pretty sure she pulled out a lock of hair.

Shepherd steps forward as if he's about to intervene, but I hold up my hand. "Give me the brush. I'll do it."

The woman slaps it into my palm and goes over to the racks, shoving bag after bag aside until she finds the one she's looking for. Shepherd turns his back while I undress. She helps me into a frothy white gown with long translucent sleeves and a high collar that splits in the back. It's hideous.

I clear my throat. "Do you have something a little more understated?"

Instead of responding, she wheels out a rack of clothes, leaving me alone with Shepherd.

I turn side to side, frowning at my reflection. Sweat prickles my brow. "I cannot go out there like this." I face Shepherd, smushing down the voluminous ruffles.

He crosses his arms, his eyes trailing from my worried expression to my meter-wide skirt. "Why didn't you speak up for yourself?"

"She was so *mean*."

"And you went along with it."

"What was I supposed to do?" I flop into the chair, my skirts bouncing in protest.

"Anything but that." Shepherd takes a step toward me. "Where's the Carrefour who yelled at me yesterday for treating you like shit? Why didn't you call her out too?"

"Because I don't know her. And she's just doing her job."

Shepherd lifts a hand. "Same."

"Well, you're . . . you're different."

He quirks a brow.

Studying my reflection, I realize the collar is meant to resemble wings. I look like a fucking angel. I huff and go over to the remaining racks of clothes, hoping to find something better. I unzip bag after bag of men's suits before finally finding one white dress. The heavy material feels like pure silk under my fingers. *Ooh, this one might work.*

With renewed hope, I remove the clear straps from the hanger and reach around to unzip the abomination I'm wearing. The wings block my access, and just when I'm about to tear the dress itself apart, warm fingertips brush my skin.

Tingles trail down my spine. I spin around. "What are you . . ."

"Looked like you were struggling." He clears his throat and averts his eyes. "Sorry, I shouldn't have—"

"No." I swallow at his pained expression. "I mean, yes, I'd appreciate some help. Thank you." I turn back around and hold my breath in anticipation of his touch.

Shepherd gently sweeps the hair from my back. Stars fill my vision, prompting me to inhale. How could such a simple gesture feel so incredibly sensual?

Centimeter by painful centimeter, Shepherd edges down the zipper, turning my insides to molten lava. I bite my lip, then remember he can see my reaction in the mirror and release it. When he reaches the bottom of my spine, he withdraws his hand quickly, as if caught doing something he shouldn't.

He turns as I step into the next dress, but I watch him in the mirror, the way he tucks his chin, flexes his jaw, and curls his fists. I'm not the only one who felt that. Whatever *that* was.

I secure the zipper at my side and release the top, allowing the dress to settle in place. The straight skirt hits perfectly on top of my feet. The corset-like middle is so snug, it holds the weight of the dress, allowing the silky fabric above to gently curl over my breasts and dip in the middle. "What do you think?"

Shepherd slowly pivots. His lips part while his eyes hungrily skim my body until they reach and hold mine in the mirror. Without saying a word, he conveys a million messages, chief among them reassurance and admiration. A part of me I didn't know I'd lost returns, but along with it, the sudden and excruciating fear of losing it again.

A knock on the door jerks us out of our trance. "You're on in five."

Shepherd steps away, his posture rigid, eyes drained of emotion. Good. Neither of us can afford to be distracted. I got so caught up in the moment, I nearly forgot why I was here, who I am, and what I must do. *Protect your heart.*

I slip into my newfound confidence like this formfitting dress and secure it in place with resolve and determination. Shepherd has a soulmate. The only right move is in the opposite direction. I'm certain of it. I pull back my shoulders and open the door.

Thunderous applause erupts as I walk onto the stage, but the crowd is less intimidating when the closest people are twenty meters away with dozens of security guards between us.

Janus raises his brows. "Goodness. You look incredible." He leads me to the front of the stage, beaming with pride and bolstering my courage.

At the podium behind us, Prime Minister Mirovnik announces, "Carrefour, ladies and gentlemen! Our immaculate *new soul*!"

The stadium goes wild, and chanting begins: "Care-eh-four, Care-eh-four."

Janus leans into my ear. "Take a little walk. Play the crowd."

To my utter surprise, I actually *want* to, not for them, but for myself.

Carry-forth. Carry-forth. I stride left, waving high and low, before crossing to the other side of the stage. Drones fly past, circle around, and float over my head, but I pay them no heed. This is my moment. Nothing and no one can bring me down.

When I reach the right side, a distant echo of "Creature!" transcends the shouting.

My heel wobbles, but I maintain my balance. *It's one person, Sivon. Don't let them fluster you.*

I hold my smile and return to Janus's side. Mirovnik resumes his speech. Janus and I nod and clap when the audience does, but amid the next round of applause, Janus murmurs, "Was I hearing things, or did someone call you 'Creature'?"

"It's nothing," I say and pretend to laugh along with the crowd.

Janus doesn't, maintaining his serious expression. "Just be careful, okay?"

My smile falters. *Be careful.* Like the message on Advertitude. But Janus's eyes hold concern, not malice.

"Of course. That's why I keep that guy around." I tip my head toward the back of the stage, where Shepherd stands at attention.

Janus flicks a glance his way, his brows drawing together. "How much do you know about Shepherd?"

I don't like his cautious tone. "What do you mean?"

The national anthem plays at the conclusion of Mirovnik's speech.

Janus leans closer to be heard over the music. "On the copter this morning, my uncle was debriefed about the incident with your hover last night. At first, I figured it was a stupid prank. But the report said an anonymous buyer posted something like that on Advertitude a few days ago, and just now, someone out there shouted 'Creature.'"

I clap for the prime minister while glancing over my shoulder at Shepherd. He's speaking into his com, but I can't hear what he's saying. I follow his gaze into the crowd but don't see anything suspicious. "Are you suggesting Shepherd had something to do with those threats?"

Janus guides me toward the front of the stage. My steps are more hesitant this time, but I manage to wave at the crowd. Shepherd was upset about my interview answers, but that didn't air until after the Advertitude ad.

Janus speaks through his smile. "I highly doubt it. But out of concern for your safety, I asked my NASS detail about him today."

I suck in my cheeks, suddenly defensive on Shepherd's behalf.

"And they said Shepherd hasn't finished training, but he's trying to edge them out for promotions. I worry he's not qualified to protect someone so incredibly valuable, that he might see this assignment as a stepping stone."

His fingertips caress my back. My cheeks flush with warmth. Valuable? To his uncle's reelection or to . . . ? No, surely Janus doesn't have feelings for me. We just met last night. But I don't miss the way he focuses on my lips, then licks his own before he waves at the crowd.

"Have you considered a robotic guard?" he asks. "They're far more capable and not as easily distracted."

Distracted? Shepherd is all business whenever we're in public. And I'm not about to trust a RAID, not after Ziva. "Shepherd has been nothing but professional since the moment we met."

Not exactly true. I was about to fire the guy yesterday, but now I feel compelled to stick up for him. "And he won't get promoted if I get hurt, so I'm safer with him than a RAID who couldn't care less if I lived or died. Literally."

"I hear you. Just be careful."

Be careful. My heel wobbles again, but this time I can't save myself. Janus tugs me up next to him, playing it off like a friendly side hug. The crowd goes wild.

Janus looks down at me, his lips spreading into a slow, satisfied grin that's much too seductive to be professional. "I think they like us."

This time I'm the one who licks their lips. What have I gotten myself into?

Fringe

Fringe—n. Established during World War III peace negotiations, thirty-one Fringe communities occupy a total of 3 percent of North American land. In exchange for the right to bear arms and self-govern, Fringe inhabitants agreed to report for kirlings and open port access but are ineligible for government aid or imports, including food, medicine, and technology.

The Wilmington venue is half the size of Philharmonica, but the crowd is just as enthusiastic. For this speech, Janus and I stand on either side of Mirovnik, preventing us from conversing. When Janus escorts me across the stage, his hand rests not on my back, but on my waist. The crowd eats it up. Janus practically radiates with contagious happiness.

At the back of my mind, a niggling thought has me wondering if it's me he's drawn to or my celebrity status. But that's silly. He's already a celebrity, and he's met thousands more. I allow the stirrings of my preteen crush to resurface, then quickly drown them again. His kirling is in two days. Janus could have a soulmate too.

I chuckle at the thought. Wouldn't that be my luck? Finding myself attracted to not one guy with a soulmate, but two.

As soon as we step offstage, I'm hustled to the exit so we'll make it to the next venue in time. No one thought that I should take the copter too?

When Shepherd pushes open the door, I shield the sun with one hand and wave at the crowd with the other. They're standing behind portable barriers, rounded and wider at the base. This group, more unruly than the last, begins pushing on the tops, making them sway. *Whoa.* That can't be safe. My leg muscles tighten, urging me to run.

"Shepherd," I say, somehow maintaining my smile.

"Yep, I see them. Let's hustle."

We begin our trek toward the hover at least a hundred meters away.

"Creature." The shout sails over the swinging barricades, designed to right themselves if pushed.

I increase my pace, but my tight dress restrains my strides.

Shepherd walks so close behind me, our legs nearly tangle. "Faster, Carrefour."

"You try walking in heels and a pencil skirt." I clip clap as fast as I can while trying to maintain a calm demeanor. *Don't amp them up. Don't show your fear.* A trickle of sweat slides down my cheek. *Keep walking. Halfway there.*

Shepherd steps between me and the crowd, taking my opposite elbow.

Another barricade swings low. This time, someone leaps on top, but they're no match for the momentum, which launches them back into the crowd. Shit. This isn't good. It won't be long until people team up to coordinate efforts.

My fingers go numb. The suffocating din is replaced by a high-pitched ringing in my ears. *"Shepherd."*

"Fuck this," he murmurs and scoops me into his arms to race toward the hover.

Seconds later, the dam bursts. Several people spill over a downed barrier, pinning it long enough for others to follow their lead. Soon it's an all-out stampede. Screams echo as people are shoved and trampled.

Why are they doing this? What do they want from me?

I desperately cling to Shepherd's neck, helplessly watching as they close the distance. If they reach us, it's over. We won't be able to push through that many people. "They're getting closer."

"So are we."

A man leads the pack, his face set with determination. What will he do when he catches up with us? Tear me out of Shepherd's arms? I dig my nails into his jacket, preparing to hold on for dear life.

"Ten meters!" I shout, as if Shepherd wouldn't hear the horde of footfalls.

"Duck!"

I tuck my chin as Shepherd tosses me into the hover. My hips hit the seat hard, but I surge toward the door and push away the reaching arms and hands so Shepherd can shut it without trapping anyone.

Wearing manic expressions, they shout and bang the windows, but we can no longer hear them. I curl my knees to my chest to escape their prying eyes.

This is too much. I don't want to live like this, constantly in fear of my life. Surely some other job can provide me and Mom with security without putting me among the very people I need protection from.

"Cover your ears." Shepherd flips through the screen menus and touches the phonox option.

My hands hit my ears a split second before a deep-bass frequency blasts from the undercarriage, making my chest rattle. The people surrounding us clamp their hands over their ears and stumble backward. Our navigator uses the opening to edge forward.

"Oh, *now* they show up?" Shepherd mumbles.

A least twenty community protection officers rush in and push the group onto the sidewalk. A few minutes later, we're turning onto Interprovince 1.

I unfold, taking a second to ensure my dress is covering the essentials, and stare out the windshield. My jaw clenches, but I'm too stunned, scared, and angry to speak. Why weren't the protectors around when we left the building?

Shepherd leans forward. "I don't know what happened back there, but I take full responsibility." He rubs his brow. "Protectors were supposed to be stationed along the barricades. I received confirmation they were in place right before we walked outside."

"Confirmation from who?"

"Only NASS can access this channel." He points to his earlobe.

"Great. Now someone in the Secret Service has it out for us too." My shaking hands belie my sarcasm. If that's true, I don't stand a chance.

But if Janus is right about Shepherd, perhaps it's not me but Shepherd they're sabotaging. He pissed off some of his fellow NASSholes, leaving us both to deal with the fallout.

"But I should've checked that report myself first. Or made you wait inside until backup arrived." He runs a hand over his face. "When we get to the Fringe, I'll ask to be reassigned."

My mouth drops open. "The hell you are." If Shepherd's colleagues care more about keeping him in his place than my safety, I can't trust them. "I could end up with the person who nearly got me killed back there."

"That was me." His jaw flexes. "You deserve better."

"No, I deserve the best. Which is why Mirovnik chose you for the job and why, despite your stubborn-headed and, quite frankly, aggravating personality, I didn't fire your ass yesterday."

Shepherd huffs and meets my eyes. "This isn't stubbornness, Carrefour. I messed up. And nearly got you—"

I lay a hand on his arm. "It's not your fault you were given faulty intelligence." I won't let him take the fall for this. And a not-so-small part of me worries my very survival hinges on convincing him to stay. So I'll do whatever it takes, even if that means begging. "Don't leave me, Shepherd. Please."

His eyes study mine, pulling me into their depths. For a second, we both stop breathing. Then he grunts and flops against the headrest. "That's not fair." A smirk lifts his lips. "You can't pull out the puppy dog eyes every time you want to get your way."

A bubble of hope rises in my chest. "Does that mean you'll stay?"

He wipes the smile from his mouth, replacing it with fear and doubt.

"Please." I rest my temple against the seat. "You're the only one I trust."

When did that happen? The words surprise me, but the sentiment is 100 percent true. Shepherd has saved me twice now.

He removes his hat and runs a hand through his black curls. "Yeah, well, we're gonna have to change that. I'm off every Sunday and Monday."

. . .

Ten minutes later, we cross onto the Delmarva peninsula and pull into an empty parking lot.

"Why are we stopping?"

The doors lift and Shepherd climbs out. "Come see for yourself."

I follow after him. The lot below the hover is the same silver magnetic surface of your everyday, ordinary road, but it changes to a different material in the Fringe, like rocks held together with black glue. In some places, the glue is cracked, and in others, chunks are missing. Hovers can't operate over glued rocks.

"How do we get to Federalsburn from here?"

Shepherd points up the road. "A car is coming to pick us up."

"A *car*? Like, with plastic wheels?"

Shepherd snickers. "Rubber tires, but yes, actual wheels."

Sure enough, a large black vehicle pulls up next to us, and the window lowers. "Hey, Shep." The woman driving is about ten years older than me, with dark brown skin and short black hair pulled into a low ponytail.

"Hey, Mudak." Shepherd shakes her hand. "Thanks for stepping in last minute."

"Of course, glad to hear they have a lead on your faulty intel."

A lead? I place my hands on my hips. *See, Shepherd? No one blames you.*

Mudak shifts her gaze to me. "Carrefour, I'm sorry to hear what happened today. The director asked me to pass along his apology and to assure you nothing like that will happen again. You have our word."

"Thank you, Mudak." Having studied Belarussian in high school, I can barely say her soulname without flinching.

I grab my duffel from the hover and climb into the car's back seat. Instead of a holoshield, an actual window separates the two rows. How old is this thing?

Shepherd hesitates by my door, then climbs in back, mumbling, "These old cars have shit safety features."

I was going to ask him to sit back here anyway. Based on what I've heard of the Fringe—from weapons hoarders to Bardou's tale about Yinbi, the child-kirling monster—I'd glue Shepherd to my hip if I could. He just has that calming, reassuring way about him.

"Did you know Mudak's name means 'asshole' in Belarussian?" I ask while buckling up.

"I do, and so does she. Though she insists it means 'NASShole.'"

Nice. I draw in a slow breath to catch what I can of Shepherd's warm pine scent and settle into the soft black leather, the adrenaline crash and lack of sleep catching up with me. Mmm. Someone bring me a pillow.

One stop to go. How does the prime minister have the stamina to do this while running the country?

As the car sets off, I tightly grasp the door handle, unaccustomed to the bumps and divots of the rocky road. The constant noise of the tires irritates me too. How do people think in these things?

But as we drive into the first town, the strange architecture diverts my attention from what's under me to what's ahead. The buildings are straight out of photos we studied in history classes. Red bricks, wood boards, vinyl siding. All fading, peeling, and derelict.

In our fourth or fifth town, I'm craning to look out Shepherd's window when I notice his back straighten. At a dangling yellow light fixture with the top of three circles glowing red, Mudak comes to a stop. Lips parted, Shepherd lowers the window, scanning the street.

A sinking in my gut reignites my earlier panic. Has he picked up on some threat? Are we about to get ambushed? "What's wrong?"

"I think I've been here before."

My muscles relax. "For work?"

"No. I'm pretty sure my parents lived a block up that way." He points out the window. "If I'm right, we'll see it in a second. White, with a front porch swing. Windows on either side of the front door and a light gray roof with three dormers."

"Lisabet and Barnelege lived in the Fringe?" As soon as I ask, I realize what he meant. "Oh, your *birth* parents?"

Mudak accelerates through the intersection. The buildings pass, revealing the house Shepherd described.

"Do you want to stop? Knock on the door?"

"Not even a little." He shivers.

I turn to watch the dreary house he grew up in disappear from view. "You don't want to meet your birth parents?"

Shepherd scoffs. "Do I want to meet the people who abandoned their five-year-old kid just because he was born on November eleventh? No, I don't."

My mouth goes dry. "You're an eleven-eleven baby?"

He scratches his cheek. "Mm-hmm. 11/11/216."

A cursed child. Now it's my turn to shiver. "Oh, Shepherd. I'm so sorry."

The reality of his circumstances hits me like a tonne of bricks. Shepherd was born the day after Flavinsky's last death—November 10, 216. Up until Ziva, Flavinsky's deathspans were always one day long, so the entire world expected them to be born again on November 11, 216. Flavinsky had lived eleven lives at that point, and Ziva's death was the eleventh suicide. The number eleven is considered extremely unlucky and everyone born on November 11, 216, cursed.

Shepherd's parents must've suspected he was Flavinsky. Shepherd himself probably assumed he was Flavinsky until his actual kirling. *Damn*, I thought *my* time at SKI was nerve-racking. I can only imagine what those 11/11 babies went through.

Ice shoots through my veins. Yinbi kirled Bardou eight years ago. Is it possible he was also kirling children fourteen years ago, when Shepherd was five? Is that why Shepherd's parents gave him up? Could Shepherd be Flavinsky?

I huff. Of course not. Ziva is Flavinsky. Windrose assured me they did all the system checks for her too. And Donovan couldn't end up with Shepherd's soul if he was actually Flavinsky. SEIK would've made not one, but two errors, and mix-ups to that extent wouldn't have gone unnoticed. Especially with a soul as famous as Flavinsky.

But for most of his life, Donovan expected to learn he was Flavinsky and found out he was an amazing soul like Shepherd, only to have his sister end up with the dreaded match. I can't imagine how hard that was, especially considering his protective instincts.

We've exited the small town, but Shepherd still stares out the window, massaging his neck. His free hand lies on his thigh between us, fingers curling and uncurling. I consider taking his hand to offer reassurance but just as quickly dismiss the idea. Too unprofessional.

But people in working relationships can offer comfort, right? We're human, after all, not robots.

Directing my eyes out my own window, I lift my right hand and gently lay it over his. My pulse pounds against my throat, waiting for his reaction. Will he nudge me away?

A second passes, then another without any sign he even noticed. Just when I'm about to withdraw my hand, Shepherd slowly exhales and relaxes his fist, straightening his fingers to grip mine between his. The tension in my muscles unfurls. We take our next breath together.

Creature

creature—n. 1. One who is a servile dependent of another. 2. A person viewed with pity, contempt, or possessiveness.

By the time we reach Federalsburn, my foot is tapping against the floorboard in uncontained annoyance. Where the hell is the speech the publicist promised? Does she expect me to wing it?

But all thoughts of speaking today, even getting out of this car, vanish when we come upon the crowd gathered around the three-story brick building with letters spelling OWN HALL adhered to the grimy marquis. The missing *T* is represented by a darker yellow than the rest of the once-white sign.

The people number far fewer than our other stops, but they're not cheering. Far from it. Their faces are contorted in anger—brows furrowed, cheeks blazing, sweat dripping, and spit spewing along with their hateful words.

"Go away!"

"Leave us alone!"

"Flee the Fringe!"

"Snake!"

My entire body begins quaking with fear. Do they really expect me to go out there? "I can't do this."

"The back entrance is secure," Mudak says over her shoulder.

"No." I shake my head. "I'm not going in." No wonder Janus backed out of this event. If he doesn't have to do it, neither do I.

Shepherd presses his earlobe. "Carrefour's out. We're rerouting to CD."

His brows furrow at the response. With apology in his eyes, he reaches down to my duffel bag, pulls out my specs, and hands them to me.

I mutter a silent *Fuck* before sliding them on.

"Sivon, my dear." It's Mirovnik. "I know this seems scary, but I assure you the people inside are the kindest, most supportive bunch you'll meet today. We've vetted each and every one."

My fingers curl into my skirt. "I'm sorry, Prime Minister, but I don't feel safe."

"I know, I know. I heard what happened in Wilmington, and we're already taking steps to prevent something like that again."

Our car turns right at the next intersection, and I breathe easier knowing we're turning away from the crowd.

"Thank you, but surely you don't need me there."

"On the contrary, you're exactly who I need by my side to show these beautiful people how wonderful the kirling system is. *You* are the very reason I planned this stop."

My chest tightens. "I just don't think—"

"We'll be in and out in fifteen minutes. Twenty, tops. I wouldn't insist if I thought it risky for either of us. And after today, I'll ensure you get some much-needed rest. I could use some myself." He chortles.

The car turns right again, heading north. No way would the Secret Service allow him to enter that building if they thought it was dangerous. But my instincts tell me to run, and my instincts are always right. How do I explain that without sounding like a coward?

"The thing is—"

Mirovnik's smile wavers, darkness sliding into his eyes. He clears his throat, and it disappears, concern returning full force. "I'm not sure if you've spoken with your mother today, and I don't mean to alarm you, but thousands of people are camped around your home, with more arriving by the hour. She can barely leave her house, the poor woman."

Mom? I squeeze my hands together and work the crossroads symbol into my palms.

"But don't worry. I've taken the liberty of hiring an additional security firm with my own personal funds until the fervor dies down." He tilts his head. "I have only your best interests at heart, Sivon. No one cares about your safety as much as me."

If I pull out of the event, he could retract Mom's added security. Could I get her more help before something happened? I'd never forgive myself if she got hurt.

"Thank you, Prime Minister. That's truly above and beyond." He's backed me into a corner. It's my safety or Mom's.

The car makes a third right, pulling up behind Own Hall. I tamp down a growl of frustration. Mudak was probably heading here the entire time.

A temporary chain-link fence surrounds the lot, two and a half meters high and covered in green vinyl. Community protectors are stationed around the perimeter and others stand on the roof of the building. We're ushered through the gate, which clanks shut behind us. Only a copter and three other vehicles sit inside.

"Ah, wonderful. I see you've arrived. I'll meet you at the door myself." The call disconnects.

I throw the specs into the bag and drop my head into my hands. Shepherd places a hand on my knee. "You don't have to do this."

"I think I do." I take a fortifying breath before meeting his gaze.

The tension in his features does nothing to calm my nerves, but I have no other choice. Shepherd sighs before directing Mudak to pull as close to the rear entrance as possible. My door nearly scrapes the building when Shepherd swings it open.

I zip my duffel bag closed, deciding to bring it with me. I haven't looked at my reflection since our mad dash to the hover, so I no doubt need a little refreshing. With Shepherd's help, it only takes a second to cross to the entrance, where Mirovnik holds out his hands for mine.

"See? Piece of cake." He wraps an arm around my bare shoulders for a side hug. "This is wonderful of you, just wonderful. I won't forget this, Sivon."

"Carrefour," I mutter.

"What's that, my dear?"

I shake it off. This isn't the time for soulname discussions. Just get through this last stop. "Nothing."

He leads me into a dressing room set up similarly to the one in Philharmonica. "We need you onstage in five minutes, but this crowd is a tad more conservative than the others. Would you mind changing into something less, uh, revealing?"

His eyes don't dip, but I get his meaning. No cleavage. "Sure. As long as I'm allowed to choose my dress." If I have to go out there against my better judgment, I'm sure as hell not wearing some frilly costume.

"Of course." He excuses himself, and Mudak enters the room, shutting the door behind him.

I drop my bag and start rifling through the racks of clothes. "Where's Shepherd?"

"He was called away."

My hand freezes. I must have heard her wrong. "What do you mean?"

"He's needed for questioning in regard to the Wilmington incident."

A knot forms in my stomach. I turn to face her. "Shepherd *left*?" My eyes sting with a mixture of fear and betrayal.

Mudak shifts her weight. "He had orders."

Yes, but he knew how scared I was to come here. Couldn't he answer their questions from here? Or was his plan always to abandon me in the Fringe, when I'm at my most vulnerable?

Janus's words come back to haunt me. *Shepherd hasn't finished training . . . he might see this assignment as a stepping stone.*

Is that all I am to him?

What else would you be? He has a soulmate. Crosier. You're just his job.

Stupid, stupid, stupid. Infuriated with both him and me, I jerk the zipper down on the next garment bag and yank out the white dress. Fitted bodice, long skirt, a turtleneck, and sleeves that open at the elbow and drape to the floor. Whatever.

I unzip my dress and yank the new one over my head, quickly becoming tangled in the fabric.

Mudak steps up and pulls it down for me. "For what it's worth, he asked to remain by your side until you returned to CD. His request was denied."

I blink away tears of relief as my rage resurges. "Great. Glad to know the Secret Service takes my safety so seriously." The dress is so stretchy, it requires no zipper at all. I settle the built-in cups into place and untuck the neckline.

"They didn't leave you stranded. I'm right here," Mudak says with forced patience.

But I'm still furious when I step onto the stage. How dare NASS take Shepherd away when I need him most? Can I trust Mudak? Why didn't Mom tell me she needed more help? Then I wouldn't have to put my life on the line to save hers. How could Mirovnik ask this of me? And where's my damn speech?

The audience claps politely at my entrance, remaining seated. I doubt they care one bit about my new soul. Mirovnik makes promises in exchange for their support—inheritance matches, commuting of sentences, federal aid, and representation.

To be honest, the offer sounds incredible for this decrepit town. Why are the people outside so incensed? They'd be fools not to accept it.

When Mirovnik beckons me to the podium, I still have no clue what I'm expected to say.

He claps and leans into my ear. "Just read the words on the teleprompter. Easy as pie." He motions to the clear pane attached to the podium.

I take his place and smile nervously at the assembly. "Good afternoon."

A few people applaud. I clear my throat, massage Xs and Os into my palms, and focus on the words flashing across the display.

"As our incredible prime minister said, I'm Carrefour, the world's first new soul in forty years. When I entered the Semyon

Kirlian Institute last week, I was lost, searching for direction, a purpose. I hoped for an inheritance and soulmate. I received none of that."

So far, so good. They're finally letting me speak my truth.

"What I got was something beyond my wildest dreams." Oh shit. I try to read ahead, but the words appear only a second before I have to say them. "I received a calling, to bring hope to the hopeless, love to the brokenhearted, forgiveness to sin—"

I stop reading, rage turning the words red, lighting them on fire. No wonder they didn't send me the speech ahead of time. Well, I'm not some brainless cow they can herd around and force to do their bidding. And I certainly won't let them make me out to be some sort of messiah. I'm the new soul, dammit.

I raise my eyes to the couple hundred people gathered. *Finish the speech; deal with NASS and Mirovnik later.* A man wearing a plaid shirt in the front row runs the pad of his thumb across his lower lip. A bitter taste fills my mouth.

I grip the sides of the podium and focus on the lights at the back of the auditorium. "And while I'd love to offer you those things, I'm only human. Just a simple girl with a shiny new soul who thinks this man"—I wave a hand at Mirovnik—"has a great plan to help your community. Please cast your vote for the Advancement Party on September twelfth."

I bow my head and step back. Before the audience can respond to my wreck of a speech, the lights go out, throwing us into sudden darkness.

What's happening? My balance wavers as I search the room for any source of light. Shouldn't emergency arrows light up the escape routes? Where are the exit signs? Does no one have a flashlight?

Cries of panic rise from the crowd.

"Creature." The whisper comes from the balcony.

I stumble back three steps. *No, you're imagining it.* They vetted every—

"Creature."

That one was closer, from where the man in plaid was sitting. Shit. I knew I shouldn't come in here. I *knew* it.

A rush of footsteps sound behind me, but the prime minister shakes off whoever came to get him. "We're fine. Power outages are a daily occurrence around here. The lights will come back on in a minute."

"Creeeature."

Well, I'm not waiting around a second longer. I run toward the wings, briefly entangling myself in the thick, velvet curtain before pushing through. "Mudak!"

"Carrefour?"

Fuck! She's on the other side of the stage! I'm not going back out there. I hold my arms in front of me, knocking into chairs and plastic bins as I search the backstage maze for the double doors I entered through. "Mudak!"

"Carrefour, stay where you are. Our equipment is compromised."

"Creature."

Someone is back here with me. I swing around, disoriented. The doors should be right here! I lunge to the side, and my shoulder slams into a wooden surface. My hands fumble around until they locate a metal bar. The door! I press the release three times before it finally gives way.

"Carrefour, don't leave!" Mudak calls.

Too late. I fall into the pitch-black hallway, and the door clangs shut behind me. I hold my breath, listening for movement or whispers, but it's as devoid of sound as light.

My heart thunders in my chest while I work out a plan. If I can get to my specs, I can call for help, assuming they still work.

I push to my feet and close my eyes, which somehow makes it easier to recall the turns I made from the dressing room to the stage doors. I reverse them in my head, running my hand along the wall until I reach the first intersection.

Turn left. I switch hands, moving to the opposite side of the hall. I follow the bumps and grooves until the painted concrete blocks end. *Now right.* The dressing room should be another meter ahead. *Keep going. Almost there.* My hand nudges against the cold metal of a door handle.

I exhale a sigh of relief. *Okay, get your bag and return to the parking lot. Once you're outside, you'll feel better.*

I swing open the door and feel around on the floor for my duffel. There! I pull it toward me and hug it close, inhaling the lingering scent of lavender detergent. My chin wobbles. I want to *go home*.

No. You will not cry. Keep your shit together and get out of this hellhole. Then you can worry about home.

"Creature."

I freeze. It wasn't a whisper this time. The nearby voice was male and gravelly but unrecognizable. He could be lurking around the last corner I turned.

Where the hell is Mudak? I don't dare call her name. The guy would find me in a heartbeat.

Thankful for the silent material of my dress, I step out of my shoes one by one and silently pad away from the man, toward the exit at the rear of the building. My measured breaths can't keep up with my jackhammering heart. Sparkling lights flash across my blanketed vision. But I'm so close now. Just a few more meters.

A hand clamps over my mouth. I jerk in surprise, then my instincts take over. *Fight, Sivon. Fight for your life.* I open my jaw and bite down as hard as I can, tasting blood. The man releases an anguished cry and yanks it back. I drop my bag and run.

"Come back here, you little bitch."

Hands grab for me, yanking my hair.

"MUDAK!"

His beefy palm covers my mouth again, smelling strongly of dirt and grease. He pulls my head tight against his chest, wrapping an arm across my torso. The moves Vivi and Corah taught me spring to the forefront of my mind. I bend at the waist, throwing him off-balance, then shove an elbow directly into his kidney.

He grunts but doesn't release me. I shout against his palm, "HELP!" and slump down, making him support the entirety of my weight.

He hoists me up as if I weigh nothing, dragging me toward the exit while I use what little leverage I have to punch his legs, aiming for his balls. "Shout all you want. I locked everyone inside the theater. No one's coming."

Cold, ferocious tears cascade down my face, but I don't give up, twisting and jerking, hoping to break free. Why is he doing this? Why me?

He shoves open the door with his backside, letting in the first light I've seen in five minutes. My vision takes seconds to adjust. Where's the Secret Service? Why aren't they guarding this exit? I wrench my head from his grip, releasing a full-throated scream.

Another man bursts out the exit, my duffel bag strapped diagonally across his plaid shirt. I narrow my eyes in recognition and curse myself for not trusting my instincts.

"It's about fucking time," says the guy holding me. "Grab her legs."

I go feral, kicking and scratching, biting and screaming, recalling Vivi and Corah's most important advice: *Never let them take you to a secondary location.*

"Fuck it! I didn't sign up for this," shouts the plaid-shirt guy. He runs away, climbing the chain-link fence and jumping to the other side.

I use the distraction to finally nail my captor between the legs. His hold releases, and I dart toward the gate. But the earlier crowd now waits on the other side. Their shouts of "Flee the Fringe!" overpower the thundering pulse of my heart. I'm cornered. Nowhere to go.

Sobbing, I cover my ears and slump into a crouch. *"Shepherd!"*

The Own Hall door bursts open. An astonished Janus exits first, followed by Mudak and a half-dozen Secret Service agents. Janus's jaw drops at the sight of the burly man curled up by the door.

I fall to my bottom, both infuriated and relieved. How dare they? How dare they show up now?

Janus approaches me slowly, his hands outstretched. I shake my head, first in short jerky movements, then wildly. *They* did this. They made me come. I said no. *I SAID NO, DAMMIT.* "No," I whimper.

But when Janus wraps his arms around me, I don't have the strength to push him away.

"Shh . . . you're okay now." He tucks his head beside mine. "I'm so sorry."

I tremble. "W-where were you?"

"Mirovnik asked me to meet with a group of constituents a town over. We didn't think I'd make it in time for the event, but I arrived minutes before the lights went out." He gently lifts my hands, turning them. "Is this your blood? Are you hurt?"

I ignore his questions and stop ignoring my doubts. "I can't do this, Janus."

He gulps, his eyes pleading with mine. "Please, Carrefour. My uncle played no part in this attack."

I push him away. "Mirovnik downplayed my concerns, assured me I'd be safe." I rise to my feet. "And that speech? The one I wasn't shown until I stood in front of the teleprompter? Reprehensible. I'm not a savior, Janus. And I won't let you exploit me like some brainless child."

Despite my declaration, Janus looks up at me with such reverence, I worry he really does believe I'm some sort of goddess. He rises to one knee and gingerly takes my hand.

"Carrefour, I swear to you with every fiber of my being. From now on, you'll be treated with nothing but respect. I will personally see to it that you get anything and everything you want."

A rush of déjà vu nearly sends me back into the dirt. I search the lot to regain my bearings. The man who attacked me now leans against the wall in handcuffs. Mudak stands only meters away, muttering urgently into her com.

Despite my inclination to run and never look back, some . . . hunch, the same part of me that knows exactly how to win, tells me to stay. To use this moment to my advantage.

Everything I want, huh?

I pull my hand free. "Okay, I want to leave now. On the copter."

"Of course. I was about to suggest th—"

"And I want the weekend off. I don't want to see or hear from you, Mirovnik, or anyone on his staff until Monday morning."

His lips quirk. "Easy. I report for my kirling tomorrow anyway."

"One more thing, and I don't care what it takes. Once we get back, I go nowhere without Shepherd."

Specs

specs—*n.* A voice- and gesture-controlled computer and communication device, resembling a pair of glasses.

Shepherd is waiting for me on the Kismet copterpad. After assuring Janus I don't need a hand, I step down and walk past Shepherd toward the elevator. His eyes briefly flit to me, and his jaw flexes before he resumes his stare down of Janus and the prime minister. After they lift off, he follows me into the waiting cabin.

We say nothing to each other for the one-flight descent, but as soon as we exit the elevator, he says, "Carrefour, I'm s—"

I whirl to face him. "You *left* me," I growl. "You knew I was scared and that I trusted only you to protect me. And you left anyway."

Shepherd covers his mouth with a fist, not even attempting to defend himself. He blinks back tears. I know my anger is misplaced. He would've stayed if he had a choice. But logic can't heal my wounds.

I examine my hands, covered in scratches, my fingernails caked in some other man's skin and grime. Tears well my eyes.

"You weren't there," I manage to whisper.

"I'm here now." He chews the side of his lip, then tentatively opens his arms.

My chin wobbles as I greedily accept his offering. He wraps his arms around me, cocooning me in his pine and soapy scent. My brain completely turns off, the inner turmoil silenced in an instant. As quickly as the tears started, they stop. For the first time in a long time, I know everything will be okay. As long as I have Shepherd, everything will be okay.

I begin to pull away, but he tightens his hold, moving his jaw to my shoulder to keep me close. It's my first honest-to-goodness bear hug. I can see why Ziva yearned for one before her kirling. It really does help.

But as the seconds tick on, I become mindful of the muscles in his arms and the strong back expanding and contracting under my hands. I revel in the sensation of my chest pressed against his, creating sparks of awareness in my core.

I step away, unwilling to meet his eyes. *He's your bodyguard. And he has a soulmate. A soulmate who is not you.*

Shepherd runs his thumbs under my eyes, drying my tears. "I'll stay as long as they let me, for as long as you want me."

I nod but keep my gaze on the floor, ashamed of how badly I want him. He belongs to Crosier, not me.

He backs away, giving me space to collect my thoughts, to protect my heart. "Why don't you hop in the shower? I'll make us some dinner."

"You don't have to make me dinner."

He huffs. "I *know*."

Arguing would be foolish. Food and a warm shower sound like heaven right now. I trudge toward my bedroom.

"Where's your duffel bag?"

"Stolen."

Shepherd inhales sharply. "And your specs?"

"Also stolen."

"Fuck," he whispers as I head into my bathroom.

I spend way too long in the shower, gingerly cleaning the streaks of blood on my arms and legs. I find a cut on my foot and a sore spot on my scalp, though that could've come from the woman brushing my hair this morning.

Halfway through the shower, peaceful music echoes through the bathroom. I close my eyes and allow the hot water to wash away the terror. If that man had a weapon, I wouldn't have escaped so easily. I won't think about what could've happened next.

No, let's focus on the why. This was a coordinated attack, to be sure. But they didn't go after the prime minister; they wanted me. They called me *Creature*. And to attack me in the dark without weapons, it's like they wanted to scare me more than hurt me.

But why me? Why go through all that effort to scare a new soul? If one Secret Service agent had stayed outside instead of running through the alley doors to protect the prime minister, they would've easily stopped the attack. A high-risk attack, but for what reward? Ransom? Maybe. Are the people in the Fringe so desperate?

I can't assume it was a resident of the Fringe, though. The Creature signs and chants have followed me since my time at SKI. Someone with resources would've had to purchase the Advertitude messages. I doubt Fringe residents could afford something like that, and they didn't know I'd be working for the prime minister.

Okay, that narrows down the suspects. Did the prime minister arrange the assaults? He's counting on me to help him beat Senator Fahari. What good would it do to scare me? The more confident I am, the more likely I'll win people over. Not Mirovnik, then.

Janus? He was at the same events where people called me *Creature*. But like Mirovnik, scaring me would be counterintuitive to helping his uncle win the reelection. Janus did remind me to be careful, which was weirdly coincidental. But that Advertitude message could be interpreted as a threat or warning.

No. I rub my eyes with prune-like fingers. It must be someone else. Janus thinks I walk on water. Senator Fahari, then? Trying to get rid of Mirovnik's advantage? Or perhaps someone who hates new souls in general, like that woman who brushed my hair.

I've gotten nowhere. I tap the console to stop the water. When I'm toweling off, the aroma of maple syrup makes my stomach growl.

"Are those pancakes?" I step out of the bathroom dressed in my pink pajamas.

"Pink." Shepherd says when I walk into the kitchen. "Don't think I've seen you in anything but red or white."

I don't remind him what I was wearing the night Ziva died. "I needed a change."

"The color suits you."

"Thanks." I feel my cheeks flush.

I shovel every morsel into my mouth, grabbing one more pancake from the stack to sop up the remaining syrup on my plate. "Delish."

Shepherd watches me carefully. "Glad you like 'em."

"*Love.*"

He sighs. "Good, because we need to have a difficult conversation."

My stomach clenches with dread. I get up, pile the dishes into the sink, and begin washing them. The last thing I want to do after my hellish day is have a serious discussion. What I do want are my mom, twelve hours of uninterrupted sleep, and to never think about today ever again.

I reach for the faucet, but Shepherd grabs my wrist. "Leave the dishes. Let's talk."

"What did I do?" I don't intend to pout, but my bottom lip has a mind of its own.

"You didn't do anything, but I'm worried someone else will." He lets go of my hand and gestures to the couch-like lump.

I plod over to the amorphous sofa and sit next to him.

"What model are your specs?"

My specs? "Mom gave me the X1s for graduation."

"Good. Those are practically impossible to hack."

"Practically?"

He runs a hand through his curls. "I'm afraid so. We have a little time, but not much."

He pulls a screen from his pocket and taps different options, bringing up the login page for my model's security access. "Log in. Let's see if we can find them."

Energized with hope, I do so, but deflate to find they're powered off.

Shepherd scoots back, rubbing his mouth. "You need to wipe them clean."

"What?"

"Execute the kill switch for your specs. Delete your cloud storage too. Best to play it safe."

He can't be serious. "But I deleted my Sociaty page. If I do that, I'll lose every photo and video from my entire life."

"I'm so sorry, but we have to assume that whoever is after you will do whatever it takes to hack into your specs and access your accounts. Would you be comfortable giving the world open access to your every memory?"

Then it hits me. My entire cloud storage as well? My every homework assignment, messages and voicemails from loved ones—most of whom are no longer with us—six years of journal entries. Oh fuck. The journals! My every tortured thought about boys, friends, kirling, and more. On display for everyone to see?

"Shepherd, please. There must be some other way—changing passwords? Copying the data to another account? I'm not the first person to have their specs stolen."

"It would take weeks to transfer that much data. Time we don't have. Once they find where your data is stored, they'll hack the password. That's the easy part." Shepherd clasps his hands. "And you may not be the first person to go through this, but you're probably the most famous. They won't stop till they get it all."

I push my fingers against my eyelids, a hard lump forming in my throat. This is so unfair. I hate my new soul. *Hate* it.

I have no more fight left in me. Not after today. Not after this week. A tear slides down my cheek as I take the screen from him. My shoulders shake with silent sobs as I navigate through multiple menus, initiating the system restore and deleting every memory of my childhood. Gone.

I sag into the foam-like cushion, staring vacantly out the window. "I'm so tired, Shepherd. This new soul has taken everything from me. My freedom, my family, my safety, even my memories. I have nothing left to give."

He hesitates for a second, then lays his hand over mine, offering the same comfort I did for him earlier today. Like Shepherd did, I entwine my fingers with his, appreciating their reassuring warmth.

He doesn't point out that I still have my health, my actual memories, a job, a swanky apartment, and fancy clothes. I know all that, but my sacrifices dwarf those things.

"I just feel so lost."

Shepherd stands, pulling me up as well. "C'mon. Let's call it a day. The dishes will wait till morning."

He leads me into my bedroom and waits for me to climb under the sheets before waving at the sensor to turn out the lights. In the darkness, a million hands reach for me.

I bolt upright, catching his arm before he steps away. "Wait."

He turns to face me.

"Would you . . . ?" I rub my forehead. "It's the dark. Could you perhaps stay until I fall asleep?"

His muscles tense underneath my grasp. "Yeah, of course."

Shepherd circles to the other side and lies on top of the bedding. He brings his hands to his stomach and crosses his ankles.

I curl onto my side to face him.

"You okay?" he asks.

"I think so." I study his profile, memorizing the curves of his brow, nose, lips, and jaw.

Shepherd turns to look at me, but I feel his concern more than I see it. "You were brave today. You know that? From the moment we reached Philharmonica this morning—walking across that stage, pushing away the people reaching into the hover, and saving yourself from the son of a bitch who attacked you."

A tear slips out of my eye. "I don't feel brave, Shepherd. Not like this . . . scared of the dark."

He pats the comforter until he finds my hand. "We're all scared of something."

We lie in silence for long, peaceful minutes, his thumb sweeping across mine in rhythm to our breaths.

My eyelids begin drooping. "What are you afraid of, Shepherd?"

He takes so long to answer that I can't be sure I didn't dream it.

"Crosier."

Valuts

valuts—(VAL-uhts) n. Globally accepted currency, as established by the Global Coalition of Governments (GCG) in 34 A.K.

Saturday, September 1, 236 A.K.—Washington, CD

I wake alone in my bed, the comforter still bearing the impression of Shepherd's body. I run my hand along the indent, then tug it back. *No doors, Sivon. He can see you.*

I tuck my hand under the covers and caress my thumb, replaying the memory of last night and marveling at Shepherd's uncanny ability to make everything seem okay. Even when it's not.

I flip onto my other side to gaze through the archway, looking for signs of him. How long did he stay by my side? And why do I wish so badly he was still there?

"Shepherd?" I whisper, not wanting to wake him if he's still asleep.

He rounds the corner, holding a steaming mug. "Good morning."

He's wearing a white V-neck T-shirt and blue pajama pants with tiny whales spurting water. I've seen him in his uniform, a suit, and workout clothes, but this might be my favorite look yet.

I open my mouth to say good morning, but he holds up a finger. "One sec."

Shepherd presses his earplant. "Yeah, okay. Send 'em up."

I sit up. "Who's here?"

"You have visitors." He takes a sip of coffee.

"*No.*" I flop onto my pillow. "I can't deal with people today."

Shepherd crosses to the elevator. "I think you'll want to see these people."

"Nope."

The elevator doors ping. I groan, lifting my head to see who it is. Vivi and Corah burst into my apartment, drop bags on the floor, and rush over to climb in bed with me. I break into sobs and pull them to me.

"How are you here?" I choke out. They're crying, too, so they take a minute to reply.

"Shepherd messaged us last night," Vivi says.

"He did?"

Corah nods into my shoulder. Shepherd beams at me while sipping coffee.

Thank you, I mouth, tears streaming down my face.

Vivi and Corah are here! I start giggling, which makes them giggle too. Shepherd retreats into his bedroom, and his shower starts.

After we collect ourselves, Vivi and Corah pull me into a seated position.

"Shepherd contacted you?"

"Yeah, around midnight," Vivi says. "He told us about the attack, and your stuff getting stolen. Frankly, we were shocked. Nothing was mentioned on the news, neither Wilmington nor the Fringe attack."

"If we'd known earlier, we would've come last night." Corah slowly spins, taking in my strange apartment. She heads over to the console and turns the window clear.

Vivi takes my hand, frowning at the scratches. "He said you could use some new specs, a new bag, and, well, friends."

My eyes refill with grateful tears. Shepherd did all that? For me?

She drops her head to my shoulder, hugging me to her side. "So, as luck would have it, our summer term just ended, and we have a couple of weeks off school."

"You *do*? Are you staying the whole time?" I rise onto my knees in hopeful anticipation.

"I wish! Gosh, we have so much to catch you up on." Vivi motions to Corah, who jumps onto the bed, landing on her side with her head propped on her hand.

They fill me in on their Last Letters, which they finally deciphered with Ensio's help.

"Cor, what did Ensio say when you called him?"

"Oh, it was epic," Vivi replies. "He said"—she switches to a low baritone and shimmies her shoulders—"'What took you so long?'"

Corah rolls face down to hide her embarrassment.

"Is he as cute as he was in high school?"

"Cuter," she says into the comforter, making Vivi and I laugh.

Once Ensio helped unravel their clues, they located a standalone Foli Journal on a private server.

"Why all the secrecy? What did you find?"

"Another cipher, of course," Vivi replies.

"Seriously?"

"I know." Corah sits up. "I wish I could meet our past selves and give them a little talking to." She slams her fist into her palm.

"So, what's your progress with that one?"

"Oh, we solved that too." Vivi waggles her brows.

"You're *killing* me. What did it say?"

Vivi bites her lip and glances at Corah. "It was a set of coordinates." She focuses intently on me. "And a symbol."

"Coordinates to what?" My vision swims as she replies, as if I already know the answer.

"The Mariana Trench." Corah stands and lifts the choker Stiletto gave me from the bedside table.

"In the Pacific Ocean?" My pulse pumps against my eyeballs. "You think your former selves left a secret treasure for you?"

"Something like that." Corah holds the necklace toward Vivi, who nods and presses her lips together.

They slowly turn to face me, their synchronization straight out of a horror film. But I don't joke about it this time. Whatever this is, it's no laughing matter. A stabbing pain seizes my gut. I drag my hands together and work the circle and X into my palm.

"What was the symbol? The one in your cipher?" I don't know why I ask. The answer is clear as day. My heart pounds as if it's trying to push my soul free of my body.

Vivi takes my wrist and pulls one of my hands toward her, then takes the choker from Corah. She sets it on my open palm, the crossroads symbol centered in the middle. She dips her chin, confirming my prediction.

I stare at the necklace in my trembling hand. "It's just a coincidence."

"Maybe." Corah leans against the bed. "Maybe not."

I drop the choker onto the comforter. "Let's be reasonable. How would Kitsune and Raposa know their future best friend would have a soulname that means crossroads?"

Vivi draws the circle and X onto my palm. "This symbol

predates your soulname, Sivon. You've done this as long as we've known you."

I swallow hard. "But I'm a new soul."

"Yes, but maybe your new soul found us for a reason. What if our buried treasure holds some sort of prophecy?"

I huff. "You don't really believe that, do you? I'm not some holy being. You of all people would know. The revenge plot against the girl who bullied Corah freshman year? That was *my* idea. I cuss, I'm competitive—"

"We're not saying you're some chosen one." Vivi nervously licks her lips. "But we can't ignore the fact that our past lives left us this symbol that represents someone we love."

Corah moves to sit beside Vivi. "We leave Tuesday, and lucky us, Kopar is working near the Mariana Trench. He agreed to take us down."

Their brother—space enthusiast turned deep-sea explorer— just so happens to have a ship stationed where Kitsune and Raposa hid their spoils? Windrose told us about soul networks, but wow, that's . . . another unexplained coincidence.

"Do you want to come with us?" asks Vivi.

"Yes," I say without hesitation, surprising even myself. "I *highly* doubt what you buried has anything to do with me, but my curiosity is piqued."

"Yay!" Vivi claps.

"I *want* to go, but I'm not sure I can. The election is only eleven days away. I'll have to convince Mirovnik—" I break off. Janus said I could have anything I wanted. But I have to be strategic about this. I still have a job to do, after all.

I scratch my jaw. Perhaps I can sugarcoat my request by

stopping for a campaign event in Guam, one of North America's Pacific islands. Small population, though. Not a significant number of votes. Hmm. What else?

Ladiron. If I could win her support... I wince, knowing as soon as I ask for her help, Vivi will agree.

She raises a brow. "What is it?"

I scrunch my nose and spill my predicament—meeting Trevin at the gala, Janus mentioning they could use Ladiron's support, and wishing I could do more than just prance around a stage. "But I don't want to use you and don't want Trevin to think you're using them. You know?"

"You're making a bigger deal out of it than it needs to be. If we're honest with Trevin, I'm sure they'll be happy to help. We can ask them tonight."

I sit up straight. "Tonight?"

Vivi's eyes twinkle. "Mm-hmm. Trevin's having a party at their art studio. Asked us all to come." She glances at my scratched-up arms. "Only if you're up for it, of course."

Never in a million years would I say no. Not because of some political agenda, but because I can tell Vivi is as enamored with Trevin as they are with her. None of us have had an easy time with relationships, not after the Kopar and Justice thing, so I'm determined to support Vivi and Corah with their new crushes. "A party at Trevin's studio? I wouldn't dream of missing it."

Vivi squeals and jumps off the bed, running toward the bags they dropped earlier. She returns in a flash. One of the duffels in her grasp resembles my stolen red and white one. She puts it on my lap. "I know it's not the same, but it's the closest we could find on short notice."

My eyes pool with tears. "So thoughtful, thank you."

Vivi unzips it. "And voilà! Mom and Dad helped smuggle out your clothes." She wraps her arms around me. "Your mom asked me to give you a hug. She says she misses you and to please call her."

I pull out an armful of clothes and hold them to my nose. They smell like home. "This means so much to me. Please tell your parents thank you!"

"Hopefully you can find something to wear tonight." Corah pulls out a tube of bruisey ointment and hands it over. "Nothing white or red. You're going incognito."

"We also got you this." She opens another bag and hands me a thin box. "Shepherd said to buy the best ones we could find."

I stare at the image of the specs printed on the lid. "*Omegas?* Holy shit! Aren't these, like, five thousand valuts?" I flip the box around in awe.

"We got 'em for three. We know people." She winks.

"Oh gosh, this is too much. I'm paying you back."

Corah begins sorting my clothes. "Pay Shepherd back. He sent us the money."

The water shuts off in the adjacent bathroom.

Shepherd paid for them? It better not be from some misplaced sense of guilt. I don't blame him for anything that happened yesterday, and these must've cost him months of savings. Savings for the house he plans to buy with his soulmate. Crosier.

My heart aches, spurred by a mixture of yearning and jealousy. "*Shepherd!* After you're dressed, can you come in here?"

He appears in my doorway only a minute later, bare-chested and wearing gym shorts. Droplets of water fall from his curls and run down his pecs. I swallow a mouthful of saliva.

"Everything okay?"

I clear my throat and hold up the specs. "Thank you for these. I'll have the money back in your account later today." I climb off the bed to approach him.

"That's unnec—"

"I *will*." I raise a hand, cutting off further arguments.

Shepherd huffs and adjusts his stance.

"And we're going to a party at Trevin's studio tonight."

He narrows his eyes. "A party?"

I nod. "Giving you a heads-up so you can make the necessary preparations, but the fewer people who know, the better. I don't trust anyone at NASS right now. Present company excluded."

His lips twitch. "And the party guests? How do you plan to keep them quiet about your whereabouts?"

I gesture to Vivi and Corah. "Meet my best friends, the queens of disguise."

They lift their chins in greeting, playing along.

Shepherd scratches his temple. "Carrefour, it's not safe."

"But that's why I have you." I take a step closer, raising my eyes to his. "Protect me, Shepherd. Keep me safe."

He swallows hard, then pivots and heads to his room. "Fine."

AIJay

AIJay—(AY-jay) n. An artificial-intelligence DJ.

Trevin's studio is located two dozen blocks northwest, in the heart of the art district. We take Vivi and Corah's hover, and Shepherd doesn't bother to report our destination. I suppose NASS can track him through his earplant, but if there's a mole, at least they won't get an early heads-up.

He's dressed in all black, and I'm wearing my black tank top with cascading rainbow lights and a black skirt. Vivi and Corah changed my locks to copper red and added smoky eyeshadow. I doubt anyone besides the four of us would recognize me. At least, I hope not.

The party is already in full swing when we step inside, with pounding music, laughter, and dancing. The surrounding holusions create an atmospheric trance. Dimly lit globes of varying colors float around, pulsing with the music. Most are out of reach, but occasionally one dips low enough to be tapped. It bounces back up and scrambles the others overhead.

The partygoers sparkle with silver light wherever they touch. The instant we step inside, mine and Corah's linked arms start twinkling. Nothing happens when I touch my own shoulder, but when I tap Vivi's, sparks erupt from my fingertips. From the number of light bursts peppering the room, people are taking full advantage of their new superpower.

Trevin spots us within seconds and darts over. They embrace Vivi, illuminating the entire room with the connection. "I'm so glad you made it."

"Me too. This is magical, Trevin." Vivi walks her fingers down Trevin's arm to take their hand.

Trevin beams with pride and greets Corah with a glimmering peck on the cheek. "Great to finally meet you!"

"Definitely!" Corah returns the gesture.

"This is our friend, Sivon." Vivi nudges me forward.

Trevin's mouth gapes open. "*That's* Sivon? Your Sivon?"

My smile grows wider. The disguise works! "One and the same. Let's just keep our earlier meeting a secret, okay?"

Trevin embraces me. "You don't have to tell me twice. I've done my share of hiding from the spotlight. You know who my mother is, right?"

"I do." They've given me an opening, but intrinsically, I know this isn't the time to mention a meetup. No politics, at least not yet. "I'm a huge fan of her accomplishments."

We pull away, and I point to Shepherd. "This is Sh—Donovan." We agreed to go by our birth names tonight, hoping no one would make the connection.

"Nice to see you again, Sh-Donovan." Trevin holds out a hand.

Shepherd chuckles. "Donovan is fine. Thanks for having us."

"Of course! Make yourselves at home. We have food and drinks in that corner." Trevin gestures to the far right. "And the AIJay is taking requests." They point to a golden retriever–resembling RAID that's meandering through the crowd, glowing when petted.

The next three hours are the most fun I've had ... probably ever. Vivi, Corah, Shepherd, and I meet Trevin's closest friends. They're all immediately smitten by Vivi because she's amazing like that. Corah and a new friend commandeer the retriever to request tunes, so Shepherd and I find a quiet corner, giving Vivi time alone with Trevin.

I lean my shoulder into the wall. "You look awfully suspicious scanning the crowd like that." A new song comes on, bluesy and sensual.

He continues to sweep the room. "I'm *doing my job*. The one you insisted I do tonight, remember?"

I chew the corner of my mouth. "Yeah, but you're drawing even more attention my way. No one else has a bodyguard following them around."

Shepherd's lips quirk. "Should I pretend to be your date instead?"

Is he serious? I will him to look at me, tempted to take him up on his suggestion. *No, Sivon. Don't.* "That would ... be safer."

His eyes snap to mine, burning fiery hot, setting my pulse racing. What have I done? My mother was wrong about him. This man's aura is not gray and beige. Not by the way he's looking at me right now.

He licks the inside of his cheek. "Sure. If that makes you more comfortable." He points to the floor in front of him. "Come here, then."

My breath hitches. I ignore my inner turmoil and step into his personal space. *What are you doing, Sivon?*

He turns me by the shoulder, bringing my back against his chest. One arm wraps around my waist. The other hand slides down my now scratch-free arm, creating iridescent trails that feel exactly how they look. "There. Now we can both be on the lookout for someone who might hurt you."

I close my eyes, knowing full well the person most likely to hurt me is already holding me in his arms. Nevertheless, I can't bring myself to step away. I skim my fingertips over his skin from wrist to elbow. His forearm twitches.

"I like seeing you this happy." His words tickle my ear.

Happy? Maybe ten minutes ago. But here in his arms, I feel every emotion at once, all contradicting each other. Happy but scared, nervous but hopeful, excited but relaxed. "Shepherd, I—"

"Donovan. Everyone I care about calls me Donovan."

My heart flips. Everyone *he* cares about. I settle against him and say, "Donovan," never before experiencing such pleasure from uttering a single word.

His huff of appreciation brushes past my ear, tickling my skin. Does he have any idea what he's doing to me? This can't be one-sided. Tell me I'm not imagining this magnetism between us, how perfectly we fit together.

Yes, he has a soulmate, but Crosier has kept him waiting almost two years. Am I really going to keep denying my feelings over someone who might never show up? No. I can't fight this any longer.

His caresses move up my arm, across my shoulders, and into my hair. I hum and tilt my head, encouraging his explorations. Our heaving breaths sync up, melding our bodies together with each rise and fall. He skirts his lips across my temple and traces my bottom lip with his thumb.

I shiver with anticipation as he guides my chin toward his. His eyes are no longer on the room. Maybe they haven't been this whole time. I hungrily watch his tongue sweep across his top lip.

He's about to kiss me, and I've never wanted anything more. Every single event in my past has led to this moment, and I'm grateful for each one. I am utterly, entirely, blissfully his.

The song changes, and Donovan pulls back. As if magnetically drawn, my head stretches toward his, but I somehow yank free. Something is wrong.

Donovan's face drains of color. He presses his earlobe. "Repeat that?"

The room around us begins buzzing with gossip. His arms fall slack, and I hug myself to fight off the bitter chill. *What is happening?*

"New soul," someone whispers nearby.

I whip around. Did someone recognize me? But no one is looking my way. I turn toward Donovan, hoping he'll have an explanation.

Corah takes my elbow. "Sivon, another new soul was kirled today."

My mouth falls open. "Are you serious?"

"It just hit the news."

That explains Donovan's call. Intelligence officials would've been notified immediately. "But if it happened today, news outlets would just be speculat—"

"It's Janus," says Corah.

"Janus?" I blink twice. "Janus is a new soul?"

"Yes. The prime minister just released an announcement."

I temple my hands and press them to my mouth, my brain spinning. Another new soul? Janus? Does that mean I'm out of a job? Are they pulling Donovan off duty already?

I step in front of him, but he turns away, covering one ear to drown out the excited conversations.

"Are you sure?" he asks.

I circle around to face him again. He sets a hand on my shoulder and closes his eyes, still listening to his com. I shift my weight, frustration building. Why won't he look at me?

"No, I'm not interested. Yes, I'm sure. I don't care how many valuts." He tugs me into his chest, wrapping an arm around my back. "Send me her contact info. I'll figure it out on my own."

Her contact info? Oh no. *No, no, no.* Donovan hugs me tighter and presses his earlobe, disconnecting the call.

"Crosier?" My voice cracks.

He nods, rubbing my back. "Yeah."

My muscles go rigid. Part of me hoped . . . Oh gosh, he's *consoling* me.

I push away from him. Donovan reluctantly lets me go, his remorseful eyes telling me everything I need to know. I press my lips together and nod repeatedly. His soulmate finally showed up.

He rubs the back of his neck. "She was kirled yesterday at the Annapolis SKI in Buryland."

Every part of me wants to burst into tears, to melt into the floor. But I won't. I can't. "That's . . . wonderful." Never have two words been harder to speak.

Donovan studies my expression. "Yeah."

I force a smile, though my legs threaten to give way at any moment.

"They asked me to do a reunion show." He scrubs a hand through his curls. "But you know how I feel about SKI interviews."

A rush of relief spreads through me. Watching the two of

them meet over and over, like Cadence and Abernathy, would be soul-crushing. I imagine the constant replay of Crosier jumping into Donovan's arms, falling over laughing, kissing each other with reckless abandon. How did Kopar endure it?

Donovan leans forward, his breath tickling my neck. "Can we go somewhere to talk?"

Talk? No. I couldn't bear to be alone with him right now. Besides, we have nothing to talk about. It's not his fault he has a soulmate. And now that Janus is a new soul, Donovan probably won't be my bodyguard much longer anyway.

Perhaps fate was only supposed to take us this far, to teach me a lesson. *Protect your heart.*

I force cheer through the knot in my throat. "We should be celebrating. This is good news, right? You've waited for Crosier for years. And when you meet her, you'll be so relieved and full and complete. I . . ." My voice falters, but I force myself to continue. "I'm so happy for you."

He flinches. My eyes sweep the room for Vivi and Corah, for an escape. I can't be here anymore. Not with him. Before I break down in the middle of Trevin's party, I push through the crowd toward the exit.

I don't make it far before I'm swallowed by the mass of revelers. When did it get this crowded? Blinding lights flash in all directions as people laugh, kiss, and sway to the music.

"To the new soul!" Someone holds up a drink.

They all chorus, "New soul!"

Get me out of here! I trip over an outstretched foot and reach for something, anyone to keep from falling.

And then he's there, pulling me into his steady arms, cupping my face. He looks at me like I'm the only person in the room, the only soul in the world. "Sivon," he whispers as he lowers his chin toward mine.

For one dazzling moment, I allow the kiss to play out in my mind, imagining the beauty of our two souls coming together, joining as one. I let that wondrous, impossible dream fill me with the strength and willpower to say what I must.

"Don't."

He stops. And the closeness of his lips to mine, our breaths mingling, nearly breaks my resolve. It would be so easy....

Donovan's eyes open. With a single blink, he pulls himself out of the moment. He knows as well as I do—kissing me would only create more hurt and regret for both of us. *Protect your heart.*

The step I take away requires more effort than any I've made before. So do the next words out of my mouth. "And my name is Carrefour."

Folies

folies—(FOE-lees) n. A soul's former lives.

Sunday, September 2, 236 A.K.—Washington, CD

My eyes spring open the next morning at the sound of the elevator doors shutting. I lurch into a seated position and stare through the archway. Who's here? Where's Donovan?

No one comes or goes, but I swear I heard something. Vivi and Corah are sound asleep on either side of me, so I crawl to the foot of the bed to stand. I cautiously approach the archway, keeping my eyes focused on the foyer in case someone pops out. Did I dream the sound?

I step out of my room and find Mudak sitting on the couch. My steps halt. No, I must be seeing things. I blink rapidly, hoping to clear my vision.

"Good morning, Carrefour. Didn't know you were up." Mudak sets her screen on the coffee-table lump and rises to stand, smoothing down her uniform.

"Where's Donovan?"

Her lips pull down on the sides. "He's off on Sundays and Mondays. Didn't he tell you?"

I walk into his bedroom, expecting to find him there. He

wouldn't leave without saying good-bye. Not after the Fringe. Not after last night. I backtrack, ignoring Mudak's questioning stare, and cross to the foyer.

The closed elevator doors taunt me. *"We tried to warn you."*

I slide a hand into my hair and tug at the roots. He's gone. He's gone to meet *her*.

My chin quivers as I turn back to Mudak, rush into my bedroom, and shut myself in the bathroom. I sit on the closed toilet lid and pull my knees to my chest. I knew this would happen if I opened my heart to Donovan. I fucking *knew it*. And I let myself anyway. Stupid, *foolish* heart. This is my own damn fault.

I rise and wash my face, but the sorrowful ache in my throat persists. Maybe I should stop wallowing and focus on yesterday's other big news. Janus's new soul.

Mudak's arrival this morning is a decent indicator I still have a job. For now. But that could change in a heartbeat. And what of two new souls appearing back-to-back like this? Another coincidence? Or could it mean more? Is this another prophecy soon to be answered by Vivi and Corah's underwater stash? And now that Janus is also a new soul, do I have enough leverage to ask for the trip to Guam with them?

"*Shit!*" I slap the counter. I forgot to talk to Trevin about their mom last night.

A knock sounds. "Sivon? You okay?" It's Vivi.

I tried to restrain my gasps and sniffles last night as I cried myself to sleep, but my friends were intuitive enough to put two and two together. They both edged closer in the bed until Vivi rested her head against my shoulder, and Corah entwined her pinkie with mine.

I knead my throbbing temples and open the door. "Not really."

Vivi rubs the back of my arm and hands over my specs. "They buzzed a couple times."

"Thanks." I lope toward my bed and sit with one foot tucked under me.

Two new messages pop up when I slide them on, sent only seconds apart. The first is from Donovan.

Sorry for leaving without saying good-bye. I didn't have the heart to wake you. I'm sure you have doubts about Mudak after the Fringe, but I specifically requested her because she's the best, and I trust her the most.

See you Tuesday.

I read through the message three times, analyzing his every word. At least it's something. I resolve not to reply and open the message from Janus.

Carrefour,

In light of recent developments, my uncle and I would love to host you and your mother for lunch tomorrow. We'd like to reaffirm our commitment to you and your safety and discuss how our new souls can best support the Prime Minister and each other.

Yours,

Janus

Perhaps I'm not being fired, then? Not if Mom is invited. I tap my finger against my lips and read it again. With its professional tone, I'd suspect the publicist wrote it if it weren't for the valediction—*yours*. As usual, I'm left wondering whether I'm reading too much or too little into his words.

I show Janus's message to Vivi, who then passes my specs to Corah.

"What do you think?" Corah hands them back.

I set them on the table. "I thought Mirovnik would drop me in a heartbeat, especially considering the added costs of protecting both me and Mom." My lips turn down as I reconsider his move. "But the only thing better than one new soul is two. If he lets me go, I could accept a job with Fahari. Mirovnik would lose his edge."

I scratch my cheek. "It's oddly coincidental, though. Don't you think? My new soul, then Janus's new soul."

"Maybe that *means* something," Vivi says. "You've admired him for years."

"He's not my soulmate, though. SKI would've matched our soulids at his kirling, and I would've received the same call Donovan did."

Corah motions toward my specs. "They're sure treating it like a soulmate match. Inviting your mother?"

Vivi lifts her hands. "Maybe your kirling wasn't as tragic as you first thought."

I scoff. "You're still trying to lose that bet, aren't you?"

"Being a new soul can't be so terrible when your childhood crush is also one. Perhaps you won't end up miserable and alone after all."

I roll my eyes. Too soon. "Janus's invitation could be equally benign. Mom has been trapped in her house for days, and Mirovnik paid to step up her security. They probably included her to prove she's safe. Which, honestly, I'm thrilled about.

"So that's good. And so is Janus being a new soul." I flop onto my pillow. "I won't have to bear that burden by myself anymore." A weight slips free from my chest. There's a new creature in town.

After breakfast, Mudak excuses herself to Donovan's room, claiming work. Vivi closes herself in the bathroom to talk to Trevin, and

Ensio calls Corah, so I let her have my room. I sink into the couch and eventually work up the courage to call Mom.

She's understandably shaken by Friday's events, but surprisingly unenthusiastic about the White House luncheon.

"What's the matter?" I don't need to read auras to pick up on her obvious concern.

"It's nothing. Of course I'll go with you."

What is she not telling me? "Mom?"

She sighs. "Well, you know how I've painted Mirovnik's portrait twice before?"

"Out with it."

"He's red and black." She grimaces at my hiss. "I know, but each color has both positive and negative interpretations. Red and black could easily mean power and love."

"Or dangerous and evil." Super. Maybe the prime minister arranged the Fringe attack after all.

Nope, the same argument still applies. Even *if* Mirovnik is evil, he wouldn't risk losing the election.

Mom presses her hands to her cheeks. "It's not just his colors, though. I've always felt uneasy around him. Mirovnik's first sitting was shortly after your father died, and he kept asking questions about his work at SKI."

My hackles rise. Why would Mirovnik care about my father?

"At his second sitting, he offered me a job, saying he could use someone with my talents. But my days of being used are behind me."

And now I'm letting him use my new soul.

Mom sighs. "I'm sorry. I should've said something sooner."

"Uh, yeah, you should have." Now I'm left wondering what to do with this information. Should I quit?

"But remember, people change, and with it their auras. Maybe he was just power hungry when we met. Now that he's prime minister, older and hopefully wiser, his colors could've shifted. We should give each other the grace to grow; otherwise, why are any of us here?"

I quirk a brow. "*You* may have changed and grown, but I'm pretty sure you're the exception."

"Is this an invitation to finally talk about my past lives?" She leans toward the camera.

I groan and fall onto my side. "Do we have to?" Years ago, I admitted to looking up Mom in SEIK, but I've denied her every attempt to discuss her folies.

"Of course not. Just let me know when you're mature enough—"

Oof. Right in the gut. "Okay, *okay*. I'm listening."

Mom scoots back on the kitchen chair. "Well, as you know, I've had three folies. When I was first kirled in 1 A.K., I was twenty-three years old, serving time for stealing from a john."

I wince at the idea of my *mother* as a sex worker.

"I'm not ashamed of my past, Sivon. Everything I went through molded me into who I am today."

"Ugh, fine. I'm listening."

"So, I'm in jail, and the people doing the kirling said their research proved reincarnation. Realizing my future self would be judged for my actions gave me the push I needed to reform my life. I created a charity to help women escape the sex trade. But you already know this, right?"

"Some of it." The SEIK details are vague memories.

"My first life is my favorite."

I tuck my chin. "Really?"

"Yes! Foli 1 taught my future lives I was capable of anything I aspired to. Imagine if I'd died in jail. What do you think I would've done in my next life?"

I plant my face in the foamy cushion, refusing to think about it.

"Don't you see? Kirling makes people think they're qualified for only one thing. What if *my* thing was a professional escort? What if I never found out I could evolve and grow?"

"Mom . . ." I shiver, imagining what our lives would look like now. Probably not too different from Linzy and Edin's childhood. Would Mom have left me at a hospital as well?

"In my second life, I became a social worker. But guess what else I did."

I push myself to a seated position, not sure I want to hear.

"I won a national photography competition. How fun is that?" She grins with pride. "In foli 3, I started as a social worker but quit three years later and traveled the world, writing articles and taking photos for *International Geographic*. You can still find my stories in their database if you search for my soulname."

My eyes bulge wide. Mom was a journalist? I must've been too disturbed by her first life to absorb the rest. But now I'm nothing but amazed. She's my own personal Ladiron. "Do you think you could see auras in every life?"

"I know I could. I wrote about them in my Last Letter. Back then, I used my skill to get a better read on people—who I could and couldn't trust. Whereas in this life, I fully embraced my unique gift and combined it with my love of art. Sometimes it takes several lives to find ourselves."

How I wish I had former lives to guide me. Mom was able to dissect her past moves, change the game. I'm left fumbling around in the dark.

"I'm glad to see you thriving, Mom. But it took you four lifetimes to get where you are. I'm barely surviving and might only have this one."

Mom leans forward. "I'm sure you've figured out by now that your name spelled backward is *novis*, a declension of the Latin word for 'new'?"

My mouth falls open. I figured that out years ago but didn't think anything of it at the time. Why would I? "Are you telling me you always suspected I was a new soul?"

She waves a hand. "Of course not. Auras don't work that way. But even at your birth, your aura was like nothing I'd seen before. You have an aura, just different from everyone else's. I eventually had to stop zooming in, searching for prevalent colors, and step back to admire the collective beauty of your rainbow."

She leans on her forearms. "Perhaps you're too close to understand what's right before your eyes. Take a step back. View everything from another angle. What if your *soul* knows you only need this one life?"

I tilt my head. Could my soul know what's best for me better than I do? If so, I hope the rest of me catches up before it's too late. "Thanks, Mom. That helps."

She blows me a kiss. "See you tomorrow, Indigo."

At eight p.m., we make a bowl of popcorn and settle in to watch Janus's soul-debut interview. Through Corah's curious inspections of my apartment, she discovered the living room window also doubles as a screen, and all the "furniture" in the room is modular. Two lumps resembling chairs now protrude from the floor on either side of the couch. Corah claims one, Mudak the other.

"You're kidding me," I say when the two figures appear on stage. Apparently, Kureshtar, the popular SKI reporter, did not succumb to appendicitis after all. I toss a kernel of popcorn at his face.

Not that Ujjwala is to blame for the way they changed my answers. In fact, who's to say they won't do the same with Janus?

Because, unlike me, Janus knows exactly what they want to hear.

Kureshtar releases Janus's handshake and settles into his chair. "First thing's first. What shall we call you now?"

Janus covers his face, chuckling. "Oh man, why do you have to embarrass me right from the start?" He rubs the back of his neck. "I tried. We even got staffers involved, but none of us could make anything of my soulid."

The letters and numbers flash on the screen—*XY9ZLZZ*. Ooh, tough one.

"So I'm sticking with Janus. Maybe Carrefour can help me brainstorm a soulname, since hers is so perfect."

I gasp. He said my name! We all expected Janus to mention me at some point, but knowing it was coming didn't prepare me for the reality of it. It's so surreal that someone I've admired for so long actually knows who I am, and that we share this one huge thing in common now.

"Since you brought her up, is it okay if I ask some questions about Carrefour?"

Janus beams. "Please do. I'd much rather talk about her than me."

I pass the bowl of popcorn to Vivi and lean in, both curious about and terrified of what he might say.

"She joined your uncle's staff last week, correct? Have you had the opportunity to meet?"

"Oh, absolutely. I escorted her to the Holusion Museum opening Thursday night." Janus drops his head, shaking it back and forth. "And I've gotta admit, the second I laid eyes on her, she took my breath away. I had watched her interview, of course, but something about seeing her in person..." He brings a hand to his chest. "Wow."

I stole his breath? He didn't seem that entranced when he walked up to me, but his years of meeting celebrities and dignitaries could've helped him mask his reaction. I feel Vivi's, Corah's, and Mudak's attention on me, but as with all of Janus's interviews, I can't peel my eyes away.

"I spent some time with her Friday as well. Not as much as I would've liked, but at risk of coming off as a starstruck teenager, I can one hundred percent attest that she's the most intelligent, witty, and brave woman I've ever met." He winces. "Sorry, Mom." He kisses his hand, then points it to the sky. His parents passed away seven years ago from a cold-like virus.

"*Someone has a cru-ush,*" Corah singsongs and pelts me with a popcorn kernel.

I scoff. "I do not."

"I was talking about Janus."

Ridiculous. Admiration does not equal attraction. I wave my hand to shush her.

"Sounds like you hit it off." Kureshtar edges toward Janus. "Excuse me for jumping to conclusions, but it's hard to ignore the fact that your birthdays are so close, and you're both new souls. Are you and Carrefour soulmates?"

Janus blushes but covers it by running a hand through his hair. "Not if you use the scientific definition of soulmates. Our soulids don't align in that way."

I draw circles and Xs on my palms and imagine what it would've been like to learn Janus was my soulmate last night. A relief, I'm guessing, to finally be able to trust someone with my heart. If only. . . .

Kureshtar frowns. "That's too b—"

"But maybe this is something new." Janus tugs the knees of his pants. "Something the world hasn't seen before."

My stomach flutters. A new kind of soulmate?

He bites his bottom lip and raises his brows. "What do I know? It's only been two days." His tips his head back and forth, dimples popping. "The first two of many, I hope."

The Sabine Women

Rape of the Sabine Women—n. Paintings created by Pablo Picasso during the Cuban Missile Crisis, depicting the abduction of Sabine women by Roman soldiers and intended to symbolize the threat of nuclear annihilation.

Monday, September 3, 236 A.K.—Washington, CD

Mom meets me in the driveway outside the White House. I cling to her for several long minutes, as if I haven't seen her in years instead of ten days. Why was I in such a hurry to leave for SKI? If I'd known what awaited me, they would've had to send a community protector to collect me.

"Hello, Carrefour, Artifex. We're delighted to have you with us today." Wearing a polite smile, Pono introduces himself to Mom and shakes our hands.

His earlier snark is gone. The same was true when I met with the publicist this morning. She couldn't have been any friendlier, sending over the login to the Carrefour Sociaty account and agreeing to give me at least eight hours to review speeches and posts before they go live.

Clearly Janus meant his promise in the Fringe, which has eased my concerns about staying on with the prime minister. But I'm so curious to hear what Mom sees today. If Mirovnik's aura hasn't changed, I need to reevaluate my position.

We're ushered through the double doors of the North Portico and into the family dining room. "The prime minister will be with you shortly."

Mudak pulls the doors closed behind us, remaining outside the room, but four other NASS agents are stationed in the corners. The walls are bright white and covered with monochromatic artwork. Mom approaches the centerpiece painting on the left wall, while I examine textured black plaster on the ceiling, a perfect hiding spot for bugs.

"What a delight to see you both again!" Mirovnik's booming voice startles me. He approaches from a door in the far-left corner. "Janus will be with us shortly."

"Is this a Picasso?" Mom points to the painting that has her transfixed.

"Why, yes—yes, it is!" Mirovnik beams with pride. "It's from his Rape of the Sabines series. Powerful, isn't it?"

The piece depicts a dark figure on a black horse attacking a nude woman with a dagger. A bit violent for my tastes, especially at a midday luncheon.

"He was unapologetically anti-war," Mom says.

"As am I, my dear. I'm his biggest fan . . . and yours as well. You recognize this one, I'm sure." Mirovnik gestures to the opposite wall. The portrait is undoubtedly one of Mom's, but I've never seen its equal. A crimson red aura singes to black along the edges, undulating on the canvas like a beating heart. It's the only object of color in the room.

"My goodness, I'm honored!" Her voice quivers.

"What a stunning portrait, Mom." I give her my best you-need-to-relax smile.

"Thank you. One of my finest representations, if I may say so."

When Mirovnik turns to sit at the table, she widens her eyes, confirming he hasn't changed one bit. I tip my chin to the ceiling, hoping she gets the point, and lead her to the table set for four.

The floral centerpiece contains white lilies, reeking of sweet satin. While they're supposed to represent purity and rebirth, they always remind me of funerals.

Mirovnik pulls out the chair for Mom, and she thanks him while sitting. When I grip the chair back next to hers, a gentle voice says, "Allow me."

I whip around so fast I knock my cheek into Janus's face. "Oh gosh, I'm so sorry! Are you okay?"

He laughs, rubbing his nose. "Never better. How was your weekend?" Janus's eyes sparkle with mirth. He wears gray slacks and a fitted white polo that accentuates his muscular biceps. Handsome as ever.

Actually, that's not true. He's brighter, more vivid than before. As his smile intensifies, I realize I've left him hanging. He asked me something.

"My weekend was . . ." *terrible*. I can't say that. "Not as exciting as yours. You had quite the whirlwind trip to SKI."

He chuckles. "To be sure. In Saturday, out Sunday. Guess there are advantages to being the prime minister's nephew."

I hold back a jealous retort. "I still can't believe you're a new soul."

"How do you feel about that? I've been worried that you're, I don't know, upset?" He grimaces.

I can't restrain my laugh. "*Upset?* No, not at all."

"So you were *happy*?" He shuffles his feet.

I nod several times. Not at that exact moment, of course, while simultaneously learning of Crosier's kirling. But am I happy about Janus being a new soul? "Yes, Janus. Once I realized your uncle wasn't about to *fire* me . . ." I tip my head to Mirovnik, who's engaging my mother in conversation. "I was incredibly relieved."

Janus releases a breath. "Whew. Glad to hear it." He pulls out my chair for me.

"Not sure what to make of the coincidence." I take my seat. "But it was a welcome one."

Janus sits to my right and raises his bubbling champagne flute. "To happy coincidences."

I hesitate, remembering Donovan's warning about eating or drinking something I haven't seen prepared. But I'm at the White House. Surely their staff has gone through background checks, and the dishes are examined for poisons. Still, as I clink my glass against Janus's I survey the contents, comparing the color of my liquid to his, checking for seeds.

Seeds. I want an update on Ziva's death investigation. But this isn't the right time. We'll need to see where the conversation takes us.

I turn to cheers Mom, but her face has gone pale, and the hand holding her glass is shaking. "Mom, are you okay?"

She sets down her glass, sloshing champagne over the side. "I don't feel so well. Could you escort me to the restroom, Sivon?"

Oh no. Was she poisoned? I jump up and take her by the elbow. "Should we call a doctor?"

She shakes her head, keeping her eyes downturned. "No, no. I'm sure I'll be fine in a few minutes."

Mirovnik rounds the table and directs us down a short hallway to the lavatory. Once inside the single-stall room, Mom locks the door and turns on the faucet full blast. My chest tightens as she grabs my arms with cold hands.

"Mom, what's wrong?"

"It's Janus," she whispers. "His aura."

I exhale and lean against the counter. "Good grief, I thought you were dying." What could be so important that she had to drag me in here?

"Is he red and black, too?" I shudder, envisioning Mirovnik's portrait of evil. Mom definitely wasn't giving him the benefit of the doubt when she painted that.

Her eyes fill with tears. "No, Indigo. His aura is unreadable too. He's your mirror image."

Auras

auras—n. Hypothetical colors indicative of traits and emotions that emanate from living beings. Their existence cannot be scientifically proven as all attempts to photograph auras have been debunked.

Mom taps cold water to her cheeks while I sit on the toilet lid in stunned silence.

"When you say 'mirror image'..."

"Exactly that. When you flash orange up in this corner, he flashes orange down here." She moves her hands around my head. "A swirl of blue here, a swirl of blue there."

"But our auras don't merge?" Soulmate auras always blend together.

"No, they're separate but equal opposites." She massages her temples. "I don't know what to make of it."

"Could our indecipherable auras indicate a new soul? We're the first in forty years, so it would make sense for us to match, right? Have you ever read Primus's aura?"

She shakes her head. "I haven't. Maybe you're right."

Janus shares my wholly unique aura? I knead the Carrefour symbol into my hand. What could it mean?

Well, one thing's for certain. I won't figure it out hiding in this bathroom.

"We should probably get back out there. Think you can make it through lunch?" I can only imagine how unsettling it would be staring down our three auras.

She nods. "I'll be all right."

I hug her. "Thanks, Mom. It means a lot that you're here."

She flushes the toilet for show, and we both wash our hands before opening the door.

Janus rises from the opposite windowsill. "Are you okay?" He wraps an arm around Mom's shoulders.

She dons a weak smile. "Yes, I knew it would pass. Sometimes I get lightheaded when meeting new people."

"Explains why you're such a homebody," I say, adding credibility to her excuse. I lean toward Janus. "Can't take her anywhere."

He chuckles, adopting our casual nature. "I'm glad to hear it. We had a physician on standby, just in case."

As he leads us back to the dining room, I reevaluate our current circumstances. Two new souls, born eight days apart, with equally inscrutable auras, working for the same man, and sharing mutual admiration for each other. How many more signs does the universe need to send before I admit Janus could be the one for me?

He's handsome, kind, captivating, intelligent. *Available.* Whereas with Donovan ... My heart plunges. Donovan is probably with his soulmate at this very moment, standing under the statues at Two Lovers Point.

My fingernails dig into my palms. *You have to stop thinking about Donovan.*

Janus settles Mom into her chair, then pulls out mine again.

"Where's the prime minister?" I ask while sitting.

"He received an urgent call, but I'm sure he'll return momentarily." Janus pulls his napkin onto his lap and winks. "Can't take him anywhere."

I huff a laugh and add *witty* to his list of attributes while sipping my water. Okay, so if I humor Janus's presumption that we're a new kind of soulmate match, how does that play into my decision to work with the prime minister? If I quit now, am I simultaneously cutting off ties with the person I'm meant to be with? I don't get how someone known the world over as a peacemaker could be evil. Could Mom's interpretation of Mirovnik be wrong?

Waiters set salads in front of us.

Janus lifts his fork. "I wanted to thank you for coming through on the Ladiron thing."

I break into a coughing fit. Mom pats me on the back while I take a larger gulp of water. Ladiron? Did Vivi bring it up with Trevin? Because I never did. Probably best not to mention that, though. "Oh, you heard from her already?"

Janus nods. "Yes, she finally accepted our invitation this morning. Agreed to a meeting tomorrow afternoon." He spears an olive and motions to our plates. "Please go ahead and eat. No telling how long my uncle will be."

"That's great news. Should I plan to be at the meeting?" Please say no. I was hoping to leave with Vivi and Corah tomorrow.

Janus shakes his head while swallowing his bite. "My uncle does his best work one-on-one. His persuasive abilities are unparalleled. He'll be fine without us."

I smile at Mom, impressed that she eluded Mirovnik's enticement to his staff. Clearly I wasn't as capable. Then again, I wouldn't have otherwise met Janus. And since I'm no longer the only new soul, perhaps the Creature attacks will be a thing of the past as well. I take a bite of salad, enjoying the tangy vinaigrette.

Mirovnik strides back into the room and sits across from me. "Sorry about that. Never a dull moment." He gulps down his champagne, then raises his glass to a passing waiter, signaling for more.

Mom grips my leg under the tablecloth. My eyes flit to hers, but she's smiling at the prime minister.

"Is everything okay? You seem a little out of sorts." Her hold tightens.

Mirovnik chuckles. "You would know, wouldn't you?" He winks at her. "Yes, yes. All in a day's work. We may live in peaceful times, but maintaining that is a daily battle." He shifts toward her, and she visibly flinches. "But how are you feeling? I was so worried for you; I could barely focus on that call."

"Much better, thank you."

Janus leans forward. "Any cause for concern, Uncle?"

"I'm afraid it's top secret." He nods as a waiter refills his champagne flute.

Janus's brow dips for a moment. "Of course. I'm sure we'll discuss it later."

Mirovnik waves him off. "It's no concern of yours. Let's enjoy our lunch, shall we? I feel like I barely know Carrefour at all."

His gaze settles on me, but the darkness in his eyes transforms him into a totally new man. This isn't the person who offered me a job, who gave speeches about hope and prosperity. I've never seen auras before, but Mom's red and black paint strokes seem to fuse themselves to his very being, twisting and taunting. I lay my hand over hers. *I understand. I'll be careful.*

I grin at the prime minister, picturing the table between us as a Chessfield board. All right, then. Let's play.

"What do you want to know?" I raise my fork to my mouth.

He cuts his salad into small pieces. "Tell me something I couldn't learn on paper. How do you spend time when you're not working?"

I swallow my bite and resolve to give him as little information as possible. "Probably the same as every other North American teenager. I exercise, scroll Sociaty, and worry about what I'm doing with my life." I wink at Janus, hoping that by inviting him into the game, I'll improve my odds.

Janus chuckles and pats my arm. "Sounds about right." Point me.

"No, really," Mirovnik says around a bite of food. "How do kids these days get to know one another?" He wipes his beard with his napkin. "Did you make any friends at SKI?"

My mouth goes dry. I take another sip of water, glad to see my hand isn't shaking.

Don't talk about Ziva. The thought comes out of nowhere, but instead of dismissing it, I remember Raphaela's advice. *Trust your instincts.*

"I did, yeah. But we haven't stayed in touch. It went by so fast." I wave a hand, making it seem like the friends I made there were of no consequence.

"It's my understanding you were at SKI when Flavinsky was kirled. Wasn't there a Sociaty post of you at her funeral?"

Why is he asking about Flavinsky? "Yeah, we met that week. She was really nice. Such a tragedy what happened."

Janus frowns, matching my own expression. "It truly was. I can't imagine what that would've been like for you."

Did Mirovnik learn something about Ziva's death just now? If the investigation mentioned foul play, Mirovnik's questions would make more sense. One thing's for sure, I'm not quitting this job until

I get my hands on those findings, and I'll probably have more success requesting them through Janus. So it's time for a subject change.

"Yes, but you asked about making friends. My closest two moved onto our street ten years ago. I'm pretty sure Mom had a hand in bringing us together. Probably wanted me to stop moping around her studio. Am I right?" I nudge her foot, hoping to break her out of her trance.

She gives me a tight smile before setting down her fork, having barely touched her salad.

"Kitsune and Raposa, I presume?" Mirovnik signals to the wait staff, who come to clear our plates.

I shift in my chair. His knowing their names shouldn't come as such a shock. NASS probably reported who my visitors were this weekend, but hearing their names from his lips puts me on the defensive. Point: Mirovnik.

"The very same. I'm not surprised you've heard of them, given their impressive folies." I lean into my chair. "I bet it was you who told NAIC to recruit them, wasn't it?"

Mirovnik's lips twitch. My flattery worked. Point: me.

"Of course." He takes another gulp of champagne.

A waiter sets a salmon dish in front of me. *Do not eat it.* I fold the napkin on my lap and tuck it beside the plate, signaling I'm done.

Mirovnik notices my gesture but doesn't react to it. He digs into his own meal.

Where's his counter move? Has he given up so easily? Or is he simply using this course to reconsider his options?

Well, if he won't seize the opportunity to make a move, I will. Just need a segue....

"Kitsune helped me secure the Ladiron meeting. Janus said

Ladiron's endorsement could be just what we need to win." I strategically use the word *we* to show I'm on his side and further drive home that point by placing my hand on top of Janus's.

His dimples emerge as he curls his fingers around mine. "We make a great team, don't we?"

As if waking up, my vision sharpens, my thoughts shift and organize. "Feels like fate."

"I was thinking the same thing." Janus beams at me, sending a thrill down my spine.

My reinforcements are in position. Ask now. I turn back to the prime minister. "Since you're meeting with Ladiron tomorrow, and my calendar is otherwise empty, I'd like to request a couple of days to accompany Kitsune and Raposa on a short trip. They're visiting their brother on his research vessel near the Mariana Trench."

Mom snaps out of her stupor. "Oh, how nice of them to invite you. Kopar was your brother as much as theirs." She turns to Mirovnik, wearing a smile that would make Abernathy proud. "Perhaps you could spare her for this quick getaway?"

Mirovnik chortles. "Of course! You should absolutely go." His jolly countenance returns full force, cheeks glowing red. "And take Janus with you. You're all welcome to stay at our vacation home in Guam. You remember the one, Janus."

"Of course." Janus's thumb sweeps over mine in a reassuring gesture. "That's a very generous offer, Uncle, but I wouldn't want to crash their reunion."

I'm not particularly keen on it either. Vivi and Corah were hesitant to share their Last Letter, and if it weren't for the crossroads symbol, I doubt they would've invited me. How would they feel if I brought along a near stranger?

Mirovnik twists a curl of beard in his fingers. "Consider it a work trip, then. We can't assume I'll secure Ladiron's endorsement, and if the two of you took some photos together at Two Lovers Point, the public would go wild."

I tug my hand out of Janus's grip. Is the prime minister suggesting Janus and I fake-date each other for votes? I'm one of his *employees*, not a paid escort. Mom scoots her chair back by a few centimeters, as if she's ready to bolt.

Janus chuckles nervously. "Uncle. That's absurd. You didn't hire Carrefour to date me, and I refuse to take advantage of her in that way. She's worth much more than—"

"No, I'll do it." My words come out so fast, I wonder if I'm the one who said them. It certainly wasn't the think-before-you-speak part of my brain that did so, and it takes a second to catch up with my purely instinctual response.

If Mirovnik's permission is conditional on doing a photoshoot with Janus, I'm game. I'll have to find a way to exclude Janus from Vivi and Corah's excursion, but I'm sure I'll think of something. And as for the trip to Two Lovers Point, well, I'm not convinced we're soulmates, but I'm certainly intrigued by Janus. Spending time alone with him in paradise might be just what I need. "It's just a few photos, right? I don't mind if you don't."

Janus glares at his uncle before turning to face me. "Of course I don't mind. Not even a little, but are you sure? I couldn't possibly ask this of—"

"I'm sure." I hoped to visit Guam with my soulmate someday, but perhaps, in a way, I am.

Mirovnik clasps his hands over his belly. "Wonderful. It's settled, then."

A satisfied smile crosses my lips. I did it. If I can beat Mirovnik at his own game, who cares what colors he is? And my sacrifice wasn't a sacrifice at all. I take Janus's hand in mine, curiosity taking root. His lips curl seductively, as if he's the victor instead of me. His desire only adds to my triumph, stitching the gashes in my self-esteem. I forgot how good it feels to win. Damn good.

I lift my champagne flute and congratulate myself before finishing every last drop.

Crosier

crosier—(CRO-zher) n. An ornate bishop's staff in the shape of a shepherd's crook, often bearing a cross.

Tuesday, September 4, 236 A.K.—Washington, CD, to Guam

Vivi and Corah agreed to stay at the prime minister's vacation home in Guam only seconds after I sent the photos. They were planning to bunk up on Kopar's ship, so the cliffside retreat with an infinity pool was quite the upgrade. In return, they offered to host us on their private jet since their flight was already scheduled.

The chips have fallen into place once again. Coincidence. Fate. These words keep spinning through my head, around and around until they take the shape of a circle with an X through it. Something big is about to happen. Another crossroads.

But first, I need to brace myself to see Donovan again. He's back on duty today, and a mix of dread and anticipation tightens my chest as the hover carrying him comes to a stop on the tarmac.

"It's not too late to change your mind," Corah whispers in my ear.

"No, it's fine. I'm fine." Despite my words, I reach for Vivi's hand. She squeezes it and exchanges a worried glance with Corah.

The doors rise, and I hope beyond hope I'll feel nothing when he steps out. If Janus and I have a soulmate-like connection, I should be able to walk away from Donovan the same way he did me. I reinforce the steel cage around my heart, willing it to stand firm.

Mudak approaches the hover's door and begins speaking with Donovan. I hold my breath, growing more anxious by the second. What's taking him so long?

Janus pops out of the jet and pushes his specs onto his head. "Oh good, they're here."

They? Did Mirovnik hire an extra NASS agent for me?

Donovan rises from the hover, but before I can fully take him in, he offers his hand to someone inside. Delicate fingers settle on top of his, and my knees nearly give out. No. He wouldn't. He *couldn't*!

Except he did.

Crosier rises gracefully from the hover, making my toes curl inside my sneakers. She's stunning. Of course she'd be stunning.

Her aqua-blue silk dress swishes and billows in the breeze. A silver-embroidered veil of the same fabric covers her ebony hair, which falls in graceful waves past her shoulders. I suddenly feel underdressed in my white tank top and shorts.

Crosier's porcelain face showcases heavily lined amber eyes, a long nose, and delicate lips. Donovan smiles at her with a gentleness he rarely showed me.

A dagger slides right between the bars of my useless cage, piercing my heart. *Ow.* I never even stood a chance.

Janus comes up beside me and wraps an arm around my waist. I lean into him, needing the extra support. Okay, so I'm not over Donovan. So what? That doesn't mean I *can't* get over him. In fact, seeing the two of them together sets my resolve to do just that.

Don't look at him. He'll have those apologetic eyes, and he has nothing to be sorry for. You're the one with the reckless heart.

"Crosier, this is Carrefour," Donovan says. "The new soul I was telling you about." He's not holding her hand, and for that small mercy, I'm grateful.

"I am honored, Carrefour." She takes my hand between her fragile ones, offering a genuine smile.

Against my better judgment, I look over her shoulder at Donovan. He wears an expression of such pride; I have to fill my lungs to hold my shattered heart in place. *You will not cry, dammit.*

"Shepherd has said such wonderful things about you," she says.

Ha. She's still calling him Shepherd. At least I get to use his birth name.

"And he was right on all counts." Janus pulls me into his side.

Donovan stiffens, homing in on Janus's hand on my hip.

I focus back on Crosier. "It was nice of you to see Shepherd off."

"Oh." She looks at Donovan in question.

Donovan looks between Janus and me, his face draining of color. "I thought—"

"Sorry, I should have mentioned sooner." Janus turns to me. "Whenever one of our staff or servicemembers meets their soulmate, they're given a few days leave to visit Two Lovers Point. But considering we were headed there already and your insistence at having Shepherd for your security, we agreed inviting Crosier would kill two birds with one stone."

You have *got* to be kidding me. Donovan's soulmate is coming with us? What the actual fuck?

Donovan meets my eyes, and I nearly growl at his remorseful gaze. Heartless. He's absolutely heartless.

I wrap an arm around Janus's back. "How very thoughtful."

He winks at me.

"But," I add, focusing on his dimples, "wouldn't that be a conflict of interest for Shepherd? How can he protect me while playing tour guide to his soulmate?"

Donovan's posture stiffens.

"She won't accompany him while he's working, of course." Janus sweeps a piece of hair from my shoulder. "You're my number one priority. I'd never be so cavalier with your safety. But if we're just hanging out at the house, I'll have my own security, and Vivi and Corah will be there. Shepherd and his girl would have plenty of time to get acquainted."

All eyes land on me. I keep mine on Janus, holding back my shout of *BUT HOW WILL I BEAR IT?* Instead, I huff appreciatively. "You always think of everything, don't you?"

Janus's chest swells with pride. "I certainly try."

Crosier clears her throat. "If you'd rather I stay behind . . ."

Yes, I think. "No," I say. None of this is her fault. And she's *Donovan's soulmate*, so she's destined to be amazing. I can't let my animosity toward him affect my opinion of her. "Are you kidding? I've wanted to meet you since Shepherd told me about you. And sounds like Janus has it all sorted out. So I guess we should stop standing around and get this show on the road. Yeah?" I turn to Vivi and Corah, pleading for help.

Vivi takes my elbow and escorts me to the jet. I eye the handful of steps warily. Am I really going through with this?

Yes. I must. I need to prove to myself that Donovan and Crosier are meant to be together, and what better way than spending a couple days with them?

Janus follows me up the stairs and into the jet. Two black

and tan couches face one another with a stationary coffee table in between. The sunroof is set to shade, dimming the bright sun but allowing plenty of natural light inside. Four single seats in the back face the cockpit. Janus's Secret Service officers occupy half of those, so I sit on a couch instead. Janus eases down on one side of me and Vivi on the other. Across from us, Corah sits opposite Vivi, and Crosier across from me. Donovan hesitates, eyeing his colleagues.

"Have a seat, Shepherd." Janus gestures across from him. "I'd love to hear more about you and your soulmate here."

Corah and I exchange glances. Vivi leans her shoulder into mine. I nod at Corah and pat Vivi's knee. I'm good. All good.

"Tell me about yourself, Crosier." Janus shifts back to sit taller. "Where did you grow up? What are you planning to do with your kirling results?"

Crosier smiles. "I'm from a small Fringe community on the Severed River, where I study religions."

My lips turn down. "I thought religions didn't exist anymore."

She nods. "Common misconception. But remnants remain throughout society—lighting candles the first days of winter, knocking on wood for luck."

Janus settles his arm behind me. "Come to think of it, my uncle grew out his beard and gained thirty kilos to resemble a magical Christian elf who delivered presents every winter. He believes people's subconscious will associate him with happy memories."

I hold back a laugh. A magical elf? Seems like a lot of effort to get people to like you.

Crosier smiles. "That lovable caricature evolved from a very real and generous bishop, but yes, that's another example. Our community hopes by studying religions' rich history and common threads, we can help others attain inner peace and understanding."

"Fascinating," Janus says. "But weren't there hundreds of religions? That must take years of study. How long is your program?"

"I've committed to a ten-year apprenticeship, after which I'll serve as a spiritual guide."

Donovan gives Crosier the devoted attention you'd expect from a soulmate. Will he move to the Fringe to be with her? That might be for the best, actually. Out of sight, out of mind.

In fact, I should find an opportunity to tell Janus he no longer has to adhere to my earlier employment stipulation. I was terrified for my life when I demanded Donovan remain my guard. But Mudak proved herself capable over the past couple days. She'd be a viable replacement.

"How long until you graduate?" I ask.

"Began the program when I was seventeen, so I have seven years remaining."

But if she's three years into a ten-year program, that would make her—

"You're twenty," Vivi states. "How did you just have your kirling this week?"

"A mostly obsolete GCG provision allows people to defer their kirling for religious reasons."

She's twenty. And Donovan turns twenty in November. That explains why he's waited for her so long. If she didn't postpone her kirling, they would've been together nearly two years now. And I never would've fallen for him.

I'm suddenly jealous of Crosier for a second reason, wishing

I, too, could've delayed my kirling. Two more years of normalcy would've been sheer bliss.

"Flight sequence initiating," a soothing female voice says. "Please buckle your harnesses."

After we do so, Janus points between Vivi and Corah. "So which one is which?"

Corah raises her hand. "I'm Raposa. She's Kitsune."

Janus grins. "I guess you get that a lot. Thanks for letting us hijack your trip to visit your brother. He works on a ship in the Pacific Ocean? How long since you've seen him?"

"That's right," Corah answers. "And it's been years, so now that we have this jet and a few days off school, we decided to pay him a courtesy call."

We lift from the ground.

"I bet he's excited to see you." Janus's thumb sweeps across my shoulder, but I can't be sure if it was intentional or from elevation change.

Donovan's gaze flits to Janus's hand, then the table in front of him. While his expression doesn't change, he noticeably swallows.

"What's his soulname?" Janus asks Corah. "What kind of work does he do?"

"His soulname is Forscher, but he never lets anyone call him that. He goes by Kopar. He runs a scientific research company in the Mariana Trench, the deepest part of the ocean."

"That still boggles my mind," I say. "Given his fascination with spacecraft, I thought he'd colonize Thessaly or explore another habitable world. Instead, he's sinking into the abyss every day."

"Just wait till you see his submarines," Vivi says to me. "They look like spaceships."

"I'd like to see that myself." Janus turns to Vivi and Corah. "Do you think Kopar would mind if I came out to his ship with you?"

Kopar wouldn't. But how would Vivi and Corah explain their treasure hunt to Janus? If they're about to discover something about my soul, I'm not sure I want him there either. My foot begins shaking.

With only a glance, my friends share a silent conversation.

Corah lifts her hands. "He'd love it."

Janus suggests we play a game to pass time on the four-hour flight.

Corah groans. "Clearly, you haven't challenged Carrefour before, or you'd know how futile that would be."

"What do you mean?"

"You can't beat her. No one has."

I scoff. How many times over the past couple of weeks have I felt the twinge of loss? So many, I nearly lost *myself*. But I'm turning a new leaf today, forgiving my scared, unsure, and irresponsible behavior. Old Sivon is back, the one who can face down any opponent and knows exactly how to win. "That's not true. It takes at least three rounds of rock-paper-scissors to hit my stride."

Corah gestures to me. "See what I mean?"

I roll my eyes. "You make it sound like I'm supernatural or something."

"Have you met your mother?" says Corah. "She has the ability to see people the way others cannot. I think you have the same gift, but it presents itself differently."

"Well, now we *have* to play a game." Janus rubs his hands together.

Donovan leans forward. "Yeah, I'm in. Let's test this out."

"You asked for it." Vivi touches the corner of the coffee table, and the wood grain dissolves into a screen. A few selections later, and the game menu appears. "Choose your poison."

Crosier leans over the coffee table, examining the options. "How about Scramble?"

"One of my favorites," I say.

We partner with the person seated across from us. Crosier and I win within fifteen minutes.

"Switch places," Janus says. "Let's go again."

Corah and Crosier switch spots. Twelve minutes this time. Corah's a solid partner.

Janus flips through the other game options, then narrows his eyes at me. "How are you with Corazon?"

"You're about to find out." Corah pulls up the holo card game.

"Switch with me first." Janus circles the table to take her place, sitting across from me.

His excitement is contagious, and I giddily return his determined smirk. This is fun. Janus is fun.

The cards are dealt, and we exchange several flirty looks over our hands. My confidence wavers when Donovan and Crosier throw down two hearts, but Janus and I pull out a win four moves later.

Donovan huffs and flicks through the games. "Sequences." He nudges Janus. "My turn."

They switch spots, and the new game board lights up the table. Donovan and I avoid each other's eyes as the cards are dealt, but once mine are organized, I take a stabilizing breath and glance up at him.

A shock resuscitates my heart, setting it racing. Time stops and multiplies, stretches and bends, breaks and rebuilds.

"Your turn, Carrefour." Corah says, yanking me out of my stupor.

How long was I staring at Donovan? Did Janus notice? I grit my teeth and focus on my cards, then the board. Only a few spots are claimed so far, so I quickly tap the one that best suits my hand.

Donovan checks my move against his cards and purses his lips. When it gets around to him, he selects the one I hoped he would, bringing us closer to making our first of two sequences. Okay, perfect. Let's see if he's as good a partner as he is a bodyguard.

From that moment on, every glance at the board bears clear meaning, and every meeting of our eyes sends precise instructions. My heart thrums wildly under his undivided attention. The first sequence comes easily, but the other two teams combine their efforts, playing only defense against us, trying to predict and thwart our moves. They don't stand a chance.

When Donovan claims his next spot, I cheer inside and signal victory with but a blink. It comes around to me, and I throw down a wild card, completing the second sequence and securing our win. I could probably *run* to Guam and back right now and still have the energy to climb Mount Everless, but I tamp down my excitement. Donovan and I exchange brief nods.

"What's next?" I ask. "Should we watch a movie?"

"Wait a sec." Janus taps the screen until he finds Chessfield. "Would you be up for a one-on-one challenge?"

I tip my head. "Those are my favorite."

Donovan's jaw clenches as he swaps places with Janus. We agree to the data-center-strewn Gobiz Desert for our terrain, and

I select a paralift for my mode of transportation. Janus chooses an electra-balloon. I beat him in eight moves.

"Wait, wait, wait." Janus holds up a hand. "I see what I did wrong. Go again."

We change up the terrain and our transports. He makes a few good moves, but I still manage to win in thirteen.

Janus laughs. "You really are incredible. Would you all mind if we played one more?"

He looks around the group. Donovan scratches his neck, but no one objects.

While Janus considers the next terrain, he runs a thumb across his bottom lip, drawing my focus there. "Remote island?"

I bet he would be a great kisser with full lips like those. I lick my own at the thought. "Sure." My voice emerges more breathy than usual.

The side of his mouth tips up. He leans closer. "Which transport do you want?"

His scent of clean linen makes me salivate. Is it getting hot in here? "You choose."

"No, you go first." Janus's smile is so seductively wicked, it stirs something in me.

How long has it been since someone tried this hard to beat me at a game? Years, probably. The thrill of the challenge fires all the synapses of my brain.

I examine my transport options. "I want the copter."

He chuckles. "I knew you'd pick the copter. I'll take the sub."

Brilliant choice. We might actually be evenly matched for this one. "Are you ready?"

Janus's eyes trail over my face, stalling on my mouth, then snapping to my eyes. "I sure as hell hope so."

I shiver with anticipation. "Let's go."

Donovan stands and heads toward the lavatory, but I can't pay attention to him now. This match will be the hardest I've played in a long time, perhaps forever. And I do not want to lose.

RAID

RAID—(raid) abbr. 1. Robotic AI domestic. 2. Robotic AI defender.

Wednesday, September 5, 236 A.K.—Guam

Our game still hasn't ended when Vivi and Corah's jet touches down in Guam. The two of them are napping, but Crosier and Donovan are still very much invested.

Sweat beads Janus's brow as he studies the board. I have only one path to victory. He cannot win. The best he can hope for is a stalemate. I examine my fingernails, already resigned to either fate. I may not win, but I won't lose either.

My biggest mistake was believing I couldn't make mistakes. Janus served up a much-needed slice of humble pie. And I kind of love it.

Janus sits up and grins at me. "Okay, just tell me. How can I win?"

"You can't."

He crosses his arms and focuses on the terrain again. As Vivi and Corah yawn and stretch, he moves his knight to take my bishop. "It's a draw."

I reach over and shake his hand, proud of him, exhilarated even. I can't remember the last time someone came so close to beating me. "Thank you, Janus. Great game."

Donovan rises to his feet with a subtle shake of his head. No idea what that's all about, and frankly, I don't care.

Vivi scratches her head, looking at the board, then me. "Wait. You didn't win?"

"I didn't win." I shrug. "No one won."

Corah hops to her feet. "Stop it. Are you serious?"

I laugh and wave at the board. "See for yourself."

Donovan and the other two Secret Service agents depart the plane, then Vivi and Crosier, who resume their earlier conversation about the origins of religions. Janus steps down next, leaving me and Corah.

"I called it," Corah says. "I said your soulmate would be the one who finally beat you at a game. Remember that when you two settle down and have lots of babies."

I smirk, taking one final look at the game board. "Well, you're wrong on both counts. Janus isn't my soulmate, and he didn't beat me." I take my first step down.

"Sivon," Corah says.

"Hm?" I pull up short, locking eyes with Donovan as he waits for me to descend.

"I know you just met, but the way he looks at you... I have this feeling he's about to change everything for you."

Donovan holds out a hand, giving me the kindest, most heartbreakingly beautiful smile.

I sigh, take his hand, and whisper back to Corah, "I sure hope you're right."

Even though our flight was only four hours, we lost fifteen as we shot through time zones. With the local time just after five a.m., the black sky is starting to take on hints of raspberry red.

Janus's two NASS agents claim the navigator seats in the two waiting hovers. Donovan insists on going with me, as does Janus.

"But we can't separate the soulmates," says Janus. "Crosier, you're with us too. It'll be snug, but it's only a fifteen-minute ride."

Janus sits in back with me, and I expect Crosier to take the third spot, but Donovan insists she ride up front. He squeezes into the back, sandwiching me between him and Janus. I click my tongue and try to focus on the passing scenery while my senses die on overload.

Linen or pine. Stimulation or security. My brain and heart fight one another for dominance. But my heart has no path to victory. Maybe I just need to give it a little nudge in the opposite direction.

I shift away from Donovan, leaning into Janus's arm. "Did I read that your vacation home is in the wildlife refuge?"

Janus slides his arm behind me. "That's right. On the Tarague Beach overlook. When the Air Force base closed last century, they parceled off ten hectares for the prime minister and returned the rest to the native Chamorro people."

He begins tracing lazy circles on my shoulder, sending electrifying tingles through my body. "I last visited a few years ago, but it's the most beautiful place I've ever seen. So peaceful and secluded. I hope you'll feel at home there. All of you."

I set my hand on Janus's leg. "Thank you for hosting us."

Donovan rests his elbow on the windowsill. The early morning light bathes his features in scarlet flames, accentuating his sharp jaw and darkening his eyes. His expression reminds me he's trained not only to protect people, but to kill them as well.

Janus lays his free hand over mine, entwining our fingers. Maybe I imagine it, but I swear Donovan growls under his breath.

"Crosier, have you ever traveled this far before?" Janus asks politely.

Her head turns left, revealing her perfect profile. "Sadly no, this is my first time out of Buryland. Before my trip to SKI last week, I'd never even left my community."

As Janus peppers her with follow-up questions, he skims his hand over mine and pulls me closer. It feels . . . It feels like I more than admire Janus. And that's enough for now. I'll take that as a win.

A few minutes later, we pull up to a vine-covered gate, which opens to reveal a modern two-story home. The wall-size corner windows are fully retracted, curtains billowing in the breeze. Our doors lift, ushering in the sweet humid air and distant roar of the ocean. After collecting my bag from the trunk, I breathe it all in. Paradise.

"I knew you'd like it. C'mon, let me show you inside." Janus holds out his hand.

The home's interior is spacious and inviting. The white couches match the curtains, barely offset from the ivory walls. But unlike SKI's sterility, their decorator included a jute rug and half a dozen potted plants, creating the coziness you'd expect from a vacation home.

The kitchen could comfortably seat a dozen people around the table, but the RAID standing next to it freezes me in place. This one has long auburn hair, wears a floral shift and apron, and holds an incap in its hands, pointed right at my heart.

Donovan leaps in front of me, taking the full force of the hit. His body seizes and drops to the floor.

"Donovan!"

The logical part of my brain knows he's only temporarily

incapacitated. He should recover in a minute or two, but seeing him defenseless on the floor strikes a primal nerve. He defended me. I will do the same for him.

Without formulating a plan, I lunge for the RAID before its incap has time to recycle the charge. I simultaneously barrel into its chest and the weapon, knocking the latter free.

"Carrefour, look out!" Janus lies underneath one of his NASS guards, struggling in vain to free himself.

A silver flash soars through the air, nearly slicing my neck, but thanks to Janus's heads-up, I dodge it just in time. The blade lodges into the floor a mere millimeter beside Donovan's twitching hand. Where did that come from?

A cry of pain comes from my right, but I can't tell if it's Crosier, Vivi, or Corah, and I don't have time to look. The RAID clamps a hand onto my shoulder, drawing out a yelp of my own.

"Creature," it says in a silky female voice. "Kill the creature."

"No!" Janus shouts.

I shove backward, but the RAID digs in its fingers. I scream in agony and push until it falls backward, bringing me down with it. The grip on my shoulder doesn't let up, and I'm involuntarily panting to clear the spots from my vision when its other hand grabs for my throat.

I manage to block it, pinning my right arm by my neck. The RAID doesn't let that stop it, using my own arm to cut off my airway. I try ramming my left elbow into its side, but the RAID doesn't have kidneys, doesn't feel pain. *Don't panic. Think.*

My left hand frantically searches the floor for the incap. It must be nearby. But the instant my fingers locate it, my hasty movements nudge it out of reach. *Dammit!*

"Help her!" Janus cries.

Across the room, more crashes and banging erupt, but I can't see what's happening. I can't see anything as the darkness creeps in. *No, don't you dare give up.* I get my feet under me and twist my hips, giving me enough leverage to turn my head. I pull in a short breath before the RAID shifts its own grip, cutting off my windpipe again. Fuck!

A primeval growl sounds behind me, followed by a metallic clank, then I'm sucking in a lungful of humid air. Donovan throws a barstool to the side and yells as he pries at the RAID's hand on my shoulder. He only succeeds in dragging me with it.

I cry out a pained sob. *"Stop!"*

"I've almost—" He grunts.

Blood flows back into my shoulder as the vise releases. I waste no time rolling onto my left side and grabbing for the incap. I stumble to my feet and point the weapon at the RAID. The robot's head is bashed in, but it's still fighting against Donovan, who has his arms and legs wrapped around it.

"Aim for the chest. Do it," Donovan orders.

"You need to move!" The electricity would travel through the RAID to Donovan. Could he even survive another shock?

The RAID jerks forward, reaching for me.

"NOW!"

I aim and fire.

Bruisedy

bruisedy—(BROO-zih-dee) n. A UV-activated topical ointment that heals contusions and scratches, typically within a couple hours.

An hour later, I'm slumped on one of the patio's chaise longues, waiting for the bruisedy to kick in and the RAID attacks to make sense. Two RAIDs. One programmed to attack me, one Janus. If it weren't for the quick thinking and self-sacrifice of our NASS agents, who knows what may have happened.

After our group entered the house, a RAID came out of the back bedrooms and struck one of Janus's bodyguards unconscious. When it started flinging knives, his other agent tackled Janus to the ground. Vivi and Corah went to work subduing the robot. Crosier tried to help as well, but the RAID broke her arm. Vivi and Corah took her to the infirmary. Despite my insistence he go too, Donovan refused to leave me.

He was groggy when he woke a few minutes after the indirect hit but seems to have fully recovered. He's now going through the kitchen pantry and fridge, tossing everything.

My mind continuously replays the pulling of the trigger, bringing on a swell of nausea. I could've killed him. I could've killed Donovan. I moan and drop my head into my hands.

"Does it still hurt?" Janus approaches with a glass of ice water in one hand and the tube of bruisedy in the other.

He hands me the glass, and I chug it down while nodding. The image of Donovan twitching on the floor flashes across my mind, squeezing my insides. Yes, it hurts very much. And I don't mean the bruise.

Janus sits beside me on the chaise. "It's been an hour. Want some help applying another dose?"

"Sure. Thanks." I hold the cold glass against my throbbing temple.

Janus sweeps the hair off my injured shoulder and hisses at the hoverball-size purple bloom. "I'm so sorry, Carrefour."

"What are your agents saying? This had to be an inside job, right?" Apparently, the two RAIDs have done the housekeeping, cooking, and maintenance on this estate for years.

He sighs and flips the tube open. "Not necessarily. They were sent for maintenance yesterday in preparation for our arrival."

Fucking RAIDs. If I never see one again, it will be too soon. "Did the ones protecting Flavinsky go in for maintenance too?"

Janus's hands fall to his lap. "They didn't." He ducks his chin. "I heard back this morning but wasn't sure how to bring it up. The medical examiner completed her investigation."

His eyes hold so much shared sorrow, I know what he's going to say before the words leave his lips.

"Death by suicide."

My chin wobbles. How can that be? I was so sure. . . .

Janus hugs me into his chest and runs a soothing hand over my arm. "I'll send you the report as promised but wanted to tell you myself first. I'm so very sorry, Carrefour."

I gulp and nod solemnly. "Thank you." I doubt I'll find anything incriminating but want to double-check all the same.

He rests his head on mine, and we stay like that for a long minute. A dizzying whoosh of déjà vu hits. I swear I've been here before, tucked into Janus while he comforted me. I sit up and look around the pool deck, trying to pinpoint what brought it on but losing grasp of it altogether.

"Are you okay?" Janus asks.

"Yeah." I catch sight of my ghastly shoulder and wince. "Well, not quite."

"Oh, shoot. Forgot why I came out here." Janus squeezes a cherry-size dollop onto his fingers while I gather my hair over my right shoulder.

His touch is warm and gentle as he applies the ointment, spreading goose bumps over my skin. Bruisedy works better when it's massaged into the injury, so once a thin layer is in place, he increases the pressure. "Tell me if this becomes too much, okay?"

I close my eyes, relishing the soothing relief. "It feels amazing."

Janus audibly swallows. "Carrefour, I . . . I feel so ashamed for not doing more to stop the attack. Or the one in the Fringe. Seeing you injured, having to witness it this time . . ." His hands freeze for a second before resuming their ministrations. "It's tearing me up inside."

I raise my head and turn to look at him. His eyes are bloodshot, his brows sagging with guilt.

"Janus, I don't blame you for either of those attacks. On the contrary. You were the first to come to my aid in the Fringe. And if you hadn't warned me earlier, I'd have a dagger in my heart right now."

His eyes squeeze shut.

I cup his jaw and sweep my thumb over his cheek. "I'm so relieved you weren't hurt. If the tables were turned . . ." I draw in a sharp breath, imagining Janus being attacked while I was unable to help. "I couldn't bear it."

Janus's lips part, and he leans into my palm. His eyes blink open, brimming with hope. "Carrefour," he whispers, trailing his fingers toward my neck.

My back arches at the tickling sensation, but I don't pull away. My words were true. I do care for Janus, quite a bit, and more with each minute we spend together. So as he nudges me closer, I don't resist. On the contrary, I slide my hand around his head and pull him toward me as well.

The subtle lift of his lips similarly lifts my spirits. This man who's enthralled me for years, who challenges me, and makes me feel truly alive has feelings for me. I'd love to go back and tell my thirteen-year-old self that she'd eventually get her wish. Was this our destiny all along? I sigh in willful acceptance as his lips brush mine.

A loud clang from the house brings us to our feet. What the hell was that? Another RAID attack? I search through the open archway to the kitchen, make out Donovan's silhouette, and press a hand over my racing heart. Apparently, he finished searching the pantry and moved on to the pots and pans. Not sure what he expects to find in there.

"It's just Shepherd. He—" I turn to face Janus, and he presses his mouth to mine.

Oh. *Oh my.* Janus knows how to *kiss*.

One hand slides into my hair while the other wraps around

my waist. He steps closer and angles my head to align with his mouth. I settle my hands on his hips and lean forward, pressing our chests together. Janus groans and deepens the kiss. It feels wonderful. Wonderful to be wanted. Wonderful to be wanted by someone so perfect for me.

A few seconds later, he slows, then pecks my lips once more before resting his cheek by mine. "We have an audience," he whispers.

I stiffen, feeling the eyes boring into my back. Donovan.

My heart twinges at the sight of him, leaning against the arch, arms crossed, and expression as sour as the morning he stormed into my room.

"Is everything okay?" I ask.

Donovan's jaw flexes. "You tell me."

I cluck my tongue at his insinuation that Janus might be a threat. We're both consenting adults.

Janus's screen buzzes against my thigh. He withdraws it from his pocket to read the message and shows it to me since it's addressed to both of us.

"Kitsune and Raposa are on their way back with Crosier," I announce to Donovan. "They want to know if we're still up for the trip to Kopar's ship this afternoon."

Donovan lifts one shoulder. "You're calling the shots."

What's that supposed to mean? Since when? "Wouldn't want to take you away from your soulmate."

His eyes narrow by a fraction. "I appreciate the consideration, but what do *you* want?"

What do I want? The subtle undertones to his question are obvious—him or me? But that's not even a choice. Even if Donovan isn't romantically attracted to Crosier, I won't put myself in the position of constantly wondering who he cares for most. Between the two of us, he'll always and forever choose his soulmate.

Janus rubs my shoulder, a reminder that I have a better alternative. But neither Donovan nor Janus are the reason I'm here. No, I came to Guam for answers. And if the attack this morning was meant to keep me from them, all the more reason to go now, before it's too late. "We should stick with our plans."

"Fine." Donovan's lips tug down, somehow taking my reply personally. He presses his earlobe and returns to the kitchen to confirm the arrangements. Whatever this is between us, it isn't healthy. I need to put an end to it.

I chew my bottom lip and turn to face Janus. "You know what? Forget what I said earlier about wanting Shepherd as my guard. Can I switch back to Mudak when we get home?"

I tug Janus in for a kiss so he won't see the tears in my eyes. Soon enough, he's made me forget why I ever wanted Donovan in the first place.

When we pull apart, gasping for air, he says, "Carrefour, I will give you anything and everything your heart desires. Just say the word."

Donovan.

Oh, shut up, heart. You fucking traitor.

X

X—n. A symbol representing any of the following: a choice, a wrong answer, the beginning or end of a path, a kiss, an unknown variable, the Roman numeral for ten, a crossroads.

"Look, Sivon." Corah's voice startles me awake.

I fought my drowsiness as long as I could on the copter, but the hum of the engine and peaceful ocean views must've won out. Vivi and Corah are all smiles as they peer out the front windows.

Janus, seated to my left, points out his. "Check it out."

I lean across him and gasp. "Corah, I thought you said Kopar had a *ship*. This is practically an island!"

The copter lands on a red X with a white circle around it, like it's my calling card or something. The coincidences keep piling up. Janus's NASS agent and Donovan disembark first and help the rest of us out. Crosier and the other agent stayed behind to recuperate from their injuries.

Kopar greets us up on deck, as gangly as ever, but with tawny sun-bleached hair instead of his usual dark brown. Vivi and Corah run to him, cheering. He scoops them up by their waists and twirls them in a circle before setting his eyes on me.

"Holy shit, Sivon, when did you become so beautiful?" He grabs me for a hug.

My cheeks blush from embarrassment. "It's great to see you, Kopar. Wow, this is . . . impressive. You *own* this vessel?"

He grins proudly. "Bought it with my inheritance. Why travel to the far reaches of the galaxy when so much of our own planet remains undiscovered?"

I pull Janus forward to introduce him.

Kopar shakes his hand. "Honored to have you on board. You're our first celebrity visitor."

"What about her?" Janus taps my nose.

"Doesn't count. Sivon will always and forever be my honorary sister." He knocks me on the jaw. "Bet you're still as much of a brat as these two are, huh?"

Behind us, Donovan snickers, but I choose to ignore it. "Only when necessary."

"Come on, I'll take you on a tour." Kopar beckons us to an elevator.

He shows off his living quarters, which are somehow even more luxurious than those at Mirovnik's vacation home. In the research lab, I finally get a moment alone with Vivi to ask her what we should do about Janus and our two NASS agents.

"Should I invent an illness to go back earlier?" I don't love the idea of having so many witnesses for their treasure hunt.

Vivi shoos away my suggestion. "Corah and I already discussed it, and we aren't worried. Our past lives wouldn't have hidden money. We have plenty of that already. So, given our previous occupations, we suspect it's sensitive information."

My hands grow sweaty. "Exactly why you don't need a crowd."

"But we wouldn't have buried reams of paper in the water. They'd never last. If we find anything at all, it'll be some sort of data-storage device. And who cares if they watch us retrieve the device if we're the only ones to see what's on it? Ensio is on standby in Indostralia with computers ranging from fifty years old to pre-kirling days."

Her reassurance does nothing to settle my nerves. I knit my hands together, drawing circles and Xs as we descend to the bottom floor and into a cavernous room, smelling strongly of sea water. In the center, a railing surrounds an open pool of black water. The perimeter glows aqua blue from underwater lights.

A bright yellow vessel is vertically suspended above the water, coming to a point at the top. The name painted over the hatch is *Justice*, and I take a second to honor her memory. She may have broken Kopar's heart, but she obviously held a place in it, even if only a reminder of what he lost.

I turn to Donovan, who's marveling at the sub. Perhaps drawn by my gaze, his eyes shift to me. I quickly look away.

"This is your sub?" Janus circles the railing. "It looks like a rocket."

"This shape disperses the pressure of the water, which at the bottom is about one tonne per square centimeter. But Kitsune and Raposa's coordinates lead to a wall of the Mariana Trench, which is on a bit of a slope"—Kopar holds his arm at an angle—"pinpointing a spot about eight meters below the surface."

Janus comes to a halt. "Coordinates?"

I try to think up some sort of excuse, but Vivi comes out and says it. "Apparently, our past lives always send the next on a scavenger hunt. Ours left coordinates to the Mariana Trench."

Janus breaks into a smile. "Seriously? That's amazing." He looks at me. "You didn't tell me that's why we're here."

My nose wrinkles. "It wasn't my secret to share."

Donovan tilts his head, studying me. I shuffle my feet, suddenly feeling as though I've been caught in a lie. I should've told Donovan my real reason for coming to Guam, not for a romantic getaway with Janus.

"Exciting stuff." Janus rubs his jaw while continuing his circuit. "Do we get to go in this thing?"

Kopar shifts his weight. "Not unless you have several years of deep-sea diving experience I don't know about."

"Not yet, but I'm looking into that as soon as we get home." Janus walks back over and shakes Kopar's hand. "Man, what a cool job you have."

Kopar leads us into a dark room with a wide, semicircular screen occupying one side.

"You can watch the dive from here. It'll take about an hour each way, so make yourselves at home. Got snacks in the cabinets and fridge, and a bathroom in the corner there."

He turns his focus on Vivi and Corah, his expression going solemn. "I want this to work out, but we need to be realistic. Your last deathspan was forty-three years. If you tack on the additional eighteen years since you were born, that means you buried this treasure of yours at least sixty years ago. And the Mariana Trench is incredibly seismic with shifting topography."

He lowers his head to their level. "The truth is these coordinates could very well lead to nothing now." He knocks them on the chins. "But I promise to try."

They sandwich him in a hug. "Thank you, Kopar."

Without even realizing it, my thumbs have resumed their familiar patterns, this time to the point of pain. I shake out my wrists. It would suck to get this far and find nothing, but an inexplicable part of me hopes we come away empty-handed. I don't know why Vivi and Corah found my symbol in their Last Letter. I'm no longer sure I want to.

Vivi and Corah claim the two chairs closest to the screen. I sit behind them, Janus and Donovan on either side. Once tucked into his sub, Kopar performs a few sound checks, rattling off some figures that mean nothing to me. Then he's underwater. I stand and walk toward the screen to get a better view.

Only seconds later, we spot a school of fish, which Kopar thoughtfully follows for a few seconds. But as he descends, the sunlight dissipates and eventually disappears. The screen dims, bathing our room in darkness. I return to my seat and tap my foot nervously.

Janus fills the silence by asking Vivi and Corah about their Last Letters, then their studies at NAIC, but I find it hard to focus. Growing more antsy by the minute, I stand and pace the back of the room, unable to calm my racing heart.

Donovan rises and walks to the refrigerator, taking out two water bottles and offering me one. I wave it away.

"What's the matter?" he whispers.

"I don't know. Claustrophobia, maybe? I can't describe it." I lean against the counter and press my hands to my knees.

He scrunches his lips to one side, studying me. "Want to go up to the deck?"

"No, I just"—my stomach clenches—"feel like . . ." I suck in a deep breath. "Like this is all wrong." The second I say it, part of my tension eases. That's it exactly.

Donovan crouches down to my level. "*Wrong?* What do you mean?"

My throat swells with pent-up emotion. "All of it," I whisper. I look at the screen, then back to him. "Everything, Donovan."

"Nearing the coordinates." Kopar breaks radio silence for the first time in an hour.

I squeeze my eyes shut against the waves of nausea.

"Oh no, are you okay?" Janus rushes over and kneels next to me.

"A bit seasick, I guess." As soon as I utter the lie, I hate myself for it. Why tell Donovan the truth but hide it from Janus?

Janus takes the unopened water bottle on the counter and presses it to my forehead. "Would it help to sit down?"

"Maybe."

He helps me to my seat just as a wall speeds into view on the screen. I jolt, anticipating a collision, but Kopar slows down just in time.

The rocky facade is marked by hundreds, maybe thousands, of holes. From our perspective, they appear to be about ten-by-ten centimeters each.

Another wave of nausea hits, making me whimper, but it just as quickly passes. Vivi and Corah eye me with matching expressions of worry.

"I'm okay," I say, not wanting to distract them. This is their big moment.

Kopar recites the coordinates while Vivi and Corah compare them to the numbers on their own screens. "Okay, we're here," he confirms.

Head pounding, I examine the wall and its crevices. Nothing out of the ordinary catches my eye.

"Kopar, can you aim a light into the holes?" Vivi asks.

As he illuminates them, it becomes apparent most are only a handful of centimeters deep, more like pockmarks than caves.

"Don't get discouraged," Kopar says. "We knew this was likely. I'll work my way around from this spot in a grid. Holler if anything catches your eye."

He drifts down half a meter, then moves in a slow, tight circle. Nothing appears out of the ordinary. I release a lungful of air and remind myself to breathe.

"Next circuit starts now. Going wider."

He gradually descends a full meter, repeating the process with a larger circumference. Nothing. My chest eases. It's okay. Everything will be okay.

I feel completely back to myself again by the time Kopar begins his fourth circuit and rise to stand behind Vivi and Corah, prepared to offer my condolences for a failed mission.

"There!" Corah shouts. She points to a spot on the rock straight ahead, a small X etched above a dark hole.

Donovan and Janus step up beside me just as my heart begins hammering again. I grab Janus's hand and squeeze it tightly while Kopar directs a light into the dark pit. Another mechanical arm extends with pliers on it, held open while they angle down to enter the little cave.

Please be empty. I don't want to be here anymore. We need to leave. "Janus, maybe we should—"

"This is as far as they'll go," Kopar says. "We're about thirty-five centimeters deep. Attempting to close the pliers now."

"Hmm?" Janus leans toward me, his eyes fixed on the screen.

Kopar's microphone crackles. "They won't fully close. I think we've got something."

Vivi and Corah cheer. A net extends under the hole, then the pliers slowly emerge, twisting them toward the camera. I tug Janus's hand. We shouldn't be here.

But he's hypnotized by the finger-size metal box in the plier's grip. *No.* I gulp, my vision narrowing as darkness presses in. Printed on one side is a white circle with a red X in the middle.

"X marks the spot!" Kopar shouts over the intercom.

Donovan whispers, "Carrefour," just before I black out.

Janus

Janus—n. The Greek god of doors and gateways, often depicted with two faces—one looking to the past and one to the future.

My eyes flutter open, then quickly shut against the brightness of the room. I lift to my elbows and squint, finding Donovan slumped in a chair of what appears to be a small infirmary.

"What happened?" I ask.

He bolts to his feet. "You're awake." He looks out the window, then steps in front of me. "You fainted."

I scoff and sit up. "No, I didn't."

He raises a brow. "I was there, and you absolutely did."

"I don't faint." I swing my legs over the gurney, hop down, and nearly fall on my ass.

"Whoa." Donovan catches my elbow and lifts me back onto the stretcher. He glances out the window again, then scowls at me. "Stay here until the doctor returns."

I wiggle toward the edge, but he plants his hands on either side of my hips. "Stay."

Kiss him. I shake away the intrusive thought and narrow my eyes. "You can't order me around."

He smirks. *"Protect me, Shepherd. Keep me safe."* He mocks my words from before Trevin's party. "Well, I'm doing just that. I never should've let you come out here. Not after that attack and on little to no sleep. No wonder you fainted."

"I didn't—"

"*Fain-ted.*" He brings his face in line with mine. "Get over it."

The scent of his skin nearly bowls me over. My eyes involuntarily go to his lips, their perfect bow calling to me like a sea siren. I swallow. "If I agree to stay up here, will you back off, please?"

A corner of his mouth lifts. "Why?"

He's toying with me, the NASShole. "Because I'm not—"

Donovan jerks to attention and steps against the wall. His gaze tracks someone as they walk past the window. The door opens and Janus steps inside, raising his specs to his head.

"You're up! Feeling any better?" He takes my hand.

"Much. Thank you." I pull his hand onto my lap in answer to Donovan's earlier question. "Where are Vivi and Corah?"

"I was just chatting with them. They're waiting for Kopar to return but suggested we head back so you can get some rest. They'll use their brother's copter. Sound good?"

I sigh in relief and lean into his support as I climb down. "Yeah, let's go."

Once we're safely buckled in, I rest my cheek against the cool glass, my thoughts spinning with the events of the day. The games, the attack, the kisses, the treasure hunt. Crossroads, crossroads, crossroads. I puzzle through it again and again, trying to pinpoint what I'm missing. What I'm forgetting.

Sensing I'm not up for conversation, Janus asks if I mind if he gets a little work done.

"Not at all," I say, returning to my thoughts, though I feel

Donovan's gaze on the back of my head the entire flight home.

When we reach the house, Janus gives me a goodnight peck. "Get some rest, okay? You'll feel better tomorrow." He heads into his bedroom, followed by the NASS agent who was tailing us all day.

Donovan takes the escalasteps to his bedroom, his shoulders rounded and weary. I sit on the couch and press my palms into my eyes. Zooming in on the details isn't working, so I follow Mom's advice and pull back on the day. *Look at the big picture, Sivon. What are you missing?*

The crossroads symbol, my kirling, the attacks, my connection with Janus, the déjà vu. None of it makes sense alone, but taken together, I start to see a pattern.

What if your soul knows you only need this one life?

Chills spread down my spine. The puzzle pieces begin falling into place. I can't believe I didn't see it before.

My brain whirs with adrenaline as I take the escalasteps to the second floor. I pause outside Crosier and Donovan's closed door, wishing I could knock, knowing I shouldn't. This will have to wait until tomorrow, but as soon as I wake up, I need to talk to Crosier.

I rise at five a.m., not an unreasonable hour, considering I went to sleep at eight last night. A hurried message from Vivi and Corah waits on my specs.

"First and foremost, we hope you're feeling better. We don't have much time but wanted you to know that Ensio came through again. This was inside the box Kopar dug up." Vivi holds up a silver rectangular prism. "It's called a USB drive, archaic data storage from centuries ago."

Corah leans over Vivi. "We just got to Indostralia, but we're pretty sure we're being followed. We're leaving our screens on the copter so we can't be traced. Do *not* worry about us. You know as well as anyone that we've trained for this all our lives."

The message ends. I blink rapidly, dread setting in. That's it? They're just gonna leave me hanging for who knows how long, not knowing if they're dead or alive?

I grab my neck and work the sore muscles. They're alive. They have to be. *Focus on your own shit and let them do theirs.*

I climb out of bed, shower up, and make it downstairs as the sky starts to lighten.

Donovan is chopping fruit in the kitchen. His eyes briefly lift to mine, but he doesn't stop whacking at the pineapple.

"Is Crosier up?"

He lays down the knife and slides the pieces into a small bowl. "She's on the patio." When I pass by, he nudges the bowl to me. "Will you give this to her?"

I take it and step outside, finding Crosier meditating, legs crossed and facing the rising sun. A white plaster cast surrounds her left arm.

I sit beside her and set the bowl between us. She peeks open one eye. "Good morning, Carrefour."

"Good morning. Sorry for interrupting."

"Not at all." She angles toward me. "Ooh, what's this?"

"Pineapple." Then I realize she's probably never eaten tropical fruit before. "It's tangy and sweet. You'll like it."

She chooses a small piece and sets it on her tongue. Her eyes glow with wonder. "Goodness," she says after swallowing and takes another piece.

"Sorry about your broken arm. How long till it heals?"

She chews and covers her mouth. "The doctor said a few days. But it doesn't hurt anymore. I'm heading back to the hospital shortly to have the cast removed."

"Good, I'm glad." I tap my knees, trying to think of the best way to move past the small talk. Just out with it, I guess. "Would it be okay if I asked you some questions about your community?"

She brushes her hands clean. "Of course."

While Janus and I were playing Chessfield on the flight over, Vivi and Crosier had a long discussion about religions. But it's the afterlife I'm more curious about. "Yesterday, you told Vivi that Christians and Muslims believed we answer to judgment when we die, sentenced to an eternity of torture or heavenly peace. But since criminals are typically reborn faster than others, then hell doesn't exist, unless being reborn is a punishment."

"Do you think life is a punishment?"

"No, we all have our struggles, but . . ." I look around at the bright green plants bearing fuchsia blooms and breathe in the salt air. "How can this world be a punishment when places like this exist?"

"Agreed." Crosier smiles.

"Okay. You said other religions believed in reincarnation and that we went into a dreamlike state in our deathspans. But it's hard to believe I've been floating around in the ether for centuries."

Crosier turns her body toward mine. "Why don't you ask me the question in your heart?"

My pulse thunders in my ears. Nothing I've ever learned about life and deathspans supports the theory I pulled together last night. So my compulsion to talk with Crosier must be driven by the belief she could prove it right. And if I'm right, I'll finally have the answers I've been searching for, not for weeks but for years.

This is why I needed to come to Guam with Vivi and Corah. Not to go on their treasure hunt, not to get to know Janus or help Mirovnik get reelected. This conversation right here, with Donovan's soulmate.

If my theory is correct, none of the recent coincidences will be coincidental, least of all finding one of the few people on the planet who can justify my rationale.

I turn to face her. Here goes. "You've spoken about other religions, but your community's philosophies must have evolved to fit the post-kirling world. What do *your* people believe about the afterlife?"

"I see." She eats another piece of pineapple while getting her thoughts together. "First, I should clarify we think of them as theories, not facts or guarantees for the future."

"Duly noted." I swivel to face her, my pulse racing.

"Based on what we've learned and observed, we expect that when we die, the truths we've sought are revealed to us—about ourselves, our loved ones, and those we have wrongly judged or harmed. When given that knowledge, our souls decide what to do with it. Some choose to be reborn right away, determined to make things right and see justice served. Others take time to reflect on their purpose and goals for their next lives."

My eyes prickle. "So rebirth is an individual's choice. We decide when to be reborn."

"Yes. Theoretically."

That explains why "bad" souls have shorter deathspans. They must be determined to set things right, but kirling holds them back, sending them into an inescapable spiral, Flavinsky worst of all. And their kirling is the trigger.

"Is there ever an end? Or do we just keep being reborn for eternity?"

Crosier smiles. "We suspect that when we learn all the lessons we want, we set ourselves free, not a judgment on us, but an individual's choice."

The sun crests the distant trees, bathing me in warmth. "I love that."

She cups my hands in hers. "I hope I am helping you."

"Yes, more than you know."

The theory I cobbled together last night settles into glue. Mom was right. My soul is so much smarter than me, but I'm finally catching up. I could cry with relief.

But like the clouds rolling in, the reality of my discovery soon overshadows the thrill of guessing correctly. Oh shit. This changes everything.

I need to talk with Janus. *Now.*

Movement in my periphery makes me jump. Donovan is sitting on the step leading from the kitchen to the patio, his back angled against the wall.

"Were you over there this whole time? You could've joined us." I stand and brush at my shorts, feigning nonchalance while my brain explodes.

He shakes his head. "I can tell when I'm not needed."

Janus rounds the corner and brightens at seeing me. "Goodness, you look more beautiful than ever." He removes his specs and slides them into his pocket. "Get some rest?"

He looks so relaxed and happy. Do I really want to ruin his day by telling him what I've learned? Not really, but I must. I can't start a relationship with him without being truthful about this.

I step into his open arms and hug him tightly. "Yes, more than enough sleep. Did you finish your work?" I need his undivided attention today.

"Yes, and then some. I arranged a sunset visit to Two Lovers Point for our group. After a few photos to appease my uncle and the insatiable public, we can all explore on our own before our redeye flight home."

Janus turns to Donovan. "I know you're worried about having your soulmate with you while on duty." He smiles at Crosier. "So if you don't mind waiting in the car until the photographer leaves, it'll all work out. I promise the view is worth it."

"Of course. No problem at all." She rises from the ground, prompting Donovan to stand as well. "Please excuse me, but I'm ready to rid myself of this thing." She holds up her cast.

"I'll see you out." Donovan follows her toward the entrance.

Now, Sivon, before you talk yourself out of it. I take Janus's hand. "Do you have someplace we could talk where we won't be overheard?"

His smile slips. "Of course. All the bedrooms are soundproof. And NASS checked mine for bugs when we arrived."

"Perfect." I pull him through the kitchen and into the primary bedroom tucked behind the escalasteps.

His forehead creases when I shut the doors behind us. "Is everything okay?"

"I'm not sure." My voice wavers. How will he react to my news? I'm not even sure how I feel about it.

"You're scaring me."

"I'm scaring myself." I press my palms to my cheeks.

Janus sets his hands on my shoulders. "*Hey.* Whatever it is, we'll work through it together. Come here, sit down."

He leads me to the bed, and we sit side by side.

I run through the facts again, reaffirming my conclusion. "This might sound impossible, but I'm pretty sure . . ." I shake my head. "No, I'm certain . . ." My eyes squeeze shut. He's going to think I'm joking or that I hit my head when I fainted yesterday. I say it anyway. "Janus, we're not new souls."

My longtime crush on Janus. My recurring déjà vu and feelings of forgetfulness. My improbable kirling results. The crossroads symbol. Janus's coincidental new soul. Our matching auras.

Crosier said our souls get to choose when and where and why we're reborn.

We strategically chose these bodies, and these aren't our first lives. We did something to make ourselves new souls. I don't know what exactly or why, but it makes so much sense.

We're playing a real-life game of Chessfield, in both life *and* death. And that's absolutely terrifying because I'm not sure who we're playing against.

Janus stares at me for a long minute. I study his expression, searching for hints of what he's thinking and coming up empty. "Janus . . ." I tremble. "Please, say something."

He leans toward me and presses a gentle kiss to my lips, then pulls back only enough to say his next words. "You are truly a wonder." He cups my cheek reverently. "Yes, Carrefour. I already know. We were together in our last life."

Krest

krest—n. Belarussian word for *cross*, *X*, or *mark*.

I lurch to my feet and back away from him. "What do you mean you already know?" Impossible. He couldn't have known this and kept it from me.

"When we were in the Fringe last week—"

My hands fly to my head. "You weren't meeting with constituents." How had I not suspected? If Yinbi kirled Bardou early in the Fringe, why not the prime minister's nephew?

He shakes his head, having the nerve to look chagrined. "I found someone there to do my kirling early. My SKI visit was scheduled for the next day, and I wanted a heads-up in case my past could hurt my uncle's chances of reelection, to give us time to get ahead of the messaging."

Janus stands. "Like you said, I'm not a new soul. I have four folies."

"Then why? How . . . ?" What was he trying to cover up? I take another step away as he approaches, kicking myself for sealing us in a soundproof room for this discussion. My pulse races. Donovan would never hear me scream.

Janus comes toward me. "That day in the Fringe, I accessed my Last Letter and learned about my past, about you, about us."

"Us?" My muscles tense, preparing to fight or flee.

"Hey, look at me." He tucks a piece of hair behind my ear. "You're upset, and understandably so. But please know I did this for you. Even then, twenty-four hours after we met, I was fully committed to you. I can't explain it, Carrefour, but from the minute I saw you, I knew you were the one I've been waiting for."

My fear subsides. Didn't I feel something like that too? Like my vision sharpened when Janus approached me at the gala? He cautiously takes my hand and raises it to his lips. The same sparks of awareness alight my vision as they had that night.

"In our last folies, we grew up in the Salt Flat City Fringe. Best friends turned lovers."

Lovers in our last lives? That explains my years of devout interest in him, how our connected souls naturally gravitated toward one another. Yes, he's telling the truth. I'm sure of it.

But he's also holding back . . . something. "What aren't you telling me? How did we become new souls?"

He clasps his hands behind my neck. "Your soulname was Krest."

I gasp. Krest is *X* in Belarussian, the language I studied in high school. The crossroads symbol. X marks the spot. I drop my head to his chest, relieved to feel his heart pounding as quickly as mine.

His hand slides into my hair. "You became obsessed with Mirovnik."

I pull back so I can see his eyes. *"Mirovnik?"*

Janus nods, his chest heaving. "It was nearly twenty years ago, so he wasn't my uncle or the prime minister yet, but yes, the same man."

This is also true. "Why Mirovnik?"

"My letter didn't get into details, so your motive I can only guess. But I think it had something to do with the Fringe. Even as a senator, Mirovnik was pressing parliament to unite our nation."

Teeth chattering, I zero in on one word of his reply. "Motive? Did I do something?"

He pulls me into an embrace. "You had to delete your soul from SEIK, Carrefour. To make sure you'd never get caught if something went wrong." He gulps. "And it went very, very wrong."

My body trembles in his arms. Yesterday's nausea returns. "What did I do?"

He takes a lifetime to respond, and when he does, his own voice quivers. "I'll never tell a soul. I promise."

My eyes brim with fearful tears.

Janus hugs me tightly. "I gave that man in the Fringe every bit of my inheritance for you. He deleted my soulid from SEIK, ensuring no one could ever trace me back to . . ." He swallows. "Back to the soul who attempted to murder Mirovnik."

My hands and feet go numb. I tried to murder Mirovnik? I'm a *murderer*? It can't be. Janus may have told the truth before, but this must be a lie. I wrench myself from his arms and take two steps back. "Say it again."

Janus's eyes are bloodshot, full of pain and concern. He reaches for me, but I back away. I need to watch him say the words.

"Krest has an outstanding warrant for their arrest. You were given a postmortem trial and found guilty, received a life sentence. That's why I couldn't tell you, Carrefour. I can't bear to hurt you." He covers his mouth, shaking his head. "I can't."

"No." A cold tear spills down my cheek. He's telling the truth.

I turn to the screen embedded in his bedroom wall and tap to waken it. I pull up SEIK, search for *Krest*. Nothing. But if I deleted myself, I wouldn't find my soulid there. I search for news stories. Still nothing. Krest is mentioned nowhere on Sociaty either.

The tension in my shoulders eases. Did Janus's past life make it all up? "If someone tried to kill the prime minister, wouldn't there be articles about it? Why hasn't Mirovnik mentioned it before? Seems like something he would leverage for sympathy points."

"Because *he* killed *you* in self-defense." Janus steps in front of me, pulls up the database of criminal investigations and judicial records and types in a soulid—*OOOXOOO*.

Circle X. That's me. That's Krest. I press the crossroads symbol into my palm.

Two reports come up. The first is the probe into Krest's death at the hands of Mirovnik. Opened and closed on the same day. He choked me to death after I slashed him several times with a knife. I shudder at the photos of the petite blond woman, trying to reconcile the fact that she was me. I am her. Dead at the hands of the prime minister.

Choking seems like a violent way to protect himself. Was this his red-and-black aura at play? Evil and dangerous? I saw hints of that side of him at our luncheon. Had he instinctually recognized my soul as the one who tried to kill him?

But protecting oneself isn't evil. And a red-and-black aura can also mean leadership and power. Love and elegance. Sensitivity and mystery. And Mirovnik has always lived up to his namesake—the peacemaker. A benevolent pacifist, the magical elf delivering goodwill. He did what he had to do to survive, but no wonder he buried this part of his past.

The second investigation provides more detail. Photos of the weapon. Samples of my DNA matching my entry in SEIK. "Look,

Janus. I was still in SEIK when this investigation happened. I couldn't have deleted myself."

"You must've hired someone else to do it once the dust settled."

"Who? You?"

"I doubt it. I probably would've followed your lead back then if you told me you were planning to become a new soul." His arms circle my waist from behind. "I'm just so relieved I went to the Fringe last week so I could do what was necessary to protect your soul."

I settle against him to read the report from start to finish. It briefly outlines my five former lives.

   Foli 1—Soldier in World War III.

   Foli 2—Died of exposure in Tokyo.

Did I live on the streets?

   Foli 3—Belarussian mafia princess.

What?

   Foli 4—

My heart stutters.

   General Molemo's spouse.

General Molemo? The soul Ladiron murdered during the war? *What?* How did I go from a Belarussian crime syndicate in foli 3 to the spouse of the most venerable soul of our time in foli 4? It doesn't make sense.

Foli 5—As Janus said, I lived in the Salt Flat City Fringe in my fifth life.

Soldier. Unhoused. Mafia. Molemo's spouse. Murderer. It's like I'm reading the foli histories of five different souls, not the same one. Where's the common thread? Besides Janus and the Belarussian language, how do I connect to any of them?

When I reach the end of the murder investigation, the date catches my eye. December 30, 216. I scroll back to the date of the attempted murder. November 10, 216. The same date as Flavinsky's last death. My stomach clenches.

Flavinsky, Ladiron, and General Molemo. Why do these names keep popping up? Ziva was Flavinsky. Trevin's mom is Ladiron. I was married to General Molemo. Soul networks at play or another coincidence?

I read the report again and again, waiting for the words to make sense, searching for a mistake, a way out of this new hell. My strategically adept brain can't fathom how my former self made such a cataclysmic move. *Attempted murder of a senator?* What was I thinking?

On the fifth or sixth time through, the utter disaster of my predicament sinks in. There's no coming back from this. The facts are clear as day. I tried to kill Mirovnik and erased my soul from SEIK to escape punishment for my crime. *I'm a bad soul.*

Me. A bad soul, just as I always feared. The room spins. I knew this whole time. The warning signs were always there—my elusive aura, the way I can mastermind a win against almost any opponent. I slip out of Janus's arms, falling to my knees.

That boy when I arrived at SKI, pleading for help, screaming that he couldn't possibly have done such a thing. A knife stabs my heart, remembering his pain, feeling it now myself. That would've been me if I hadn't erased myself. I should have suffered the same consequences.

And Mom. *Oh, Mom!* She'll be destroyed. All this time believing the best in me, her unwavering pride, only for her daughter to end up a violent criminal. I clasp my hands by my heart as tears of shame drip down my jaw. How can I tell her any of this?

Janus lowers himself to sit in front of me. "Carrefour, look at me. Nothing has changed."

"How can you say that? I have a warrant out for my arrest!" I can barely choke out the words. "Why didn't you report me?"

He sets his warm hands on my thighs, swishing his thumbs back and forth. "Because I know how deeply flawed the kirling system is for people with criminal histories. I visit the prisons, assist with reform programs, receive messages and videos every day from families pleading for help. How could I do that to you, to the soul I'm meant to be with?" He shakes his head. "I would never. Besides, your new soul is helping my uncle in ways you could never do behind bars."

I bring my hand to his cheek. "Janus, I have to turn myself in."

He leans into my touch. "No, Carrefour. I won't let you do that to your soul. You have this amazing opportunity that others in your position do not."

"*Exactly.* How can I walk around free when they can't? I wouldn't be able to live with myself." I stand and pace his room. "You forget that my best friends are Kitsune and Raposa. They know me better than anyone. That X on their treasure. They must've hidden evidence about my other lives. Don't you think it's strange for a former mafia princess to marry General Molemo? What if I was up to something back then too?" That explains why I fainted yesterday. My soul didn't want them to learn the truth.

"Are they back yet?" Janus looks out his bedroom window as if he expects to find them at the pool.

"No, and that can't be a good sign. Do you think they're rounding up people to arrest me?" I stop in my tracks and hug my shoulders, trying to contain the shivers. Even my best friends will turn against me. I'm about to lose everything and everyone I care about. "I'm so scared, Janus."

He rises and opens his arms to me. I step into his embrace, my arms still curled around myself. All this time I bemoaned my new soul, wishing I had past lives, and now I'd gladly return to the naive person I was yesterday.

He kisses my forehead. "Shh. You're jumping to conclusions left and right. If you take some time to process everything, you'll realize this situation isn't as bad as you think." He runs his hands over my back. "You're the most brilliant person I've ever met. And I know this thing between us is new, but I have a feeling that together we could move mountains. That won't be possible if you're behind bars. Please, Carrefour. I'm begging you. Give us a chance."

Janus lifts my chin so that I'll look at him. He wipes a tear from my cheek while I do the same for him.

"Let me prove it to you." He presses a chaste kiss to my lips, then cradles my head to his chest. "Why don't you take my room for the day? Rest. Do all the research you want. But promise me you won't make any decisions until you've weighed all your options and we work out a plan. You know better than anyone how essential a strategy is."

I swallow and nod, breaking into trembles again. "Thank you, Janus."

"Anything for you."

And I know he means it. He *would* do anything for me, the least of which is deleting his soulid to save me from myself. I press my lips to his. It's not a kiss of passion, but of appreciation. He could've had me arrested in the Fringe, but he got down on one knee and promised me everything I wanted.

"I love you, Carrefour. I think I always have."

Puntan Dos Amåntes

Puntan Dos Amåntes (Two Lovers Point)—n. A scenic cliffside overlook in Guam.

A buzzer sounds, saving me from having to respond to Janus's declaration. Janus *loves* me? I just learned neither of us are new souls and that I'm wanted for attempted murder. I don't have the mental capacity to consider whether I feel the same.

Janus opens the doors, and Donovan pulls his hands out of his hair and halts his pacing. He glares at Janus, then takes me in, his eyes going wide.

"What the hell did you do to her?" He pushes Janus to the side to approach me. "Are you okay? I turned my back for a second and you disappeared. What happened? Did he hurt you?" He grabs the back of his neck, studying my eyes.

I cover my face, bursting into uncontrollable sobs. This is too much. My heart can't handle it.

"Hurt her?" Janus rushes over and hugs me to him. "How dare you come in here flinging accusations?"

Donovan softens his voice. "Carrefour, what's wrong? How can I help?"

I hang my head, ashamed of my past. He can never find out. "Get out."

Donovan stiffens. "What?"

"You heard her." Janus raises his chin. "You're dismissed."

"You, too, Janus." I wipe the tears from my cheeks. "I'm sorry, but I need time to think."

Donovan arches his brows at Janus.

Janus narrows his eyes and steps in front of me. He thumbs away another tear. "Of course." He leans in and kisses me, deeply and possessively.

I know what he's doing, but I don't pull away. The temporary distraction feels wonderful, and if Donovan feels a shred of the jealousy I did when he left me to meet Crosier, so much the better. I hear him turn and walk away.

Janus pecks me once more, then follows behind. "I'll be here if you need me."

"Thank you," I say as he pulls the doors closed.

I spend most of the day curled up in Janus's bed, staring at the wall while my brain whirs through everything I've learned. When I finally come to terms with my fateful past decisions, I shift to the present, plotting out every possible move and countermove.

Could I go on pretending I'm an immaculate new soul while harboring this truth? No. I couldn't look myself in the mirror, much less face Mom, Vivi, or Corah again. And odds are Vivi and Corah know exactly who I am now. I have no way of winning. The best I can hope for is a stalemate.

By the time Janus returns with a plate of food hours later, I've stopped shaking in fear. Knowing what lies ahead is far less scary than uncertainty. And with some careful planning and mental preparation, I might just be okay. I set aside the sandwich and take his hands.

"I've come to a decision. Let's discuss how to best implement it."

With a steady voice, devoid of emotion, I explain the extreme unlikelihood that we'll live out our days without being caught. "I don't know what we did to SEIK, but at some point, someone will go searching for us . . . or at least for Krest. Or they'll arrest the person or people who deleted our souls. We can't trust criminals like that to keep our secret."

Janus opens his mouth to argue, but I cut him off. "I know you gave him all your savings, but what's stopping him from asking for more? He could blackmail you into doing horrible things. Do you want to give someone like that power over your soul?"

Janus crosses his arms. "What are you saying? You think we should turn ourselves in?"

"You're not the one who tried to murder someone," I say.

"Neither did you," Janus sits beside me. "You are Carrefour, not Krest."

"That's not true." I shift to face him. "This is hard to explain, but even though I don't understand her actions, I know they were mine. She's very much a part of me." I flip one of his hands over and draw the crossroads symbol on his palm. "Krest and I are connected. Just like you and me."

Janus tucks me up next to him.

I entwine our fingers. "I'll let you do what you think is best. Your secret is safe with me, no matter what."

"But I don't want to lose you. That's what I'm most worried about." He settles his head on mine.

"It's just for this life. Maybe we'll share our next lifespans too. If you still want me then, come find me."

"*If?* Carrefour, I'd walk through the gates of hell for you."

The saddest part about his declaration is knowing that's likely where I would be, if hell existed. "Knowing you, you'd find a way to pull me out of there."

"If only," he says before kissing me. His lips are reverent, paying homage to my jaw, cheeks, and even my eyelids before working their way back to my mouth. Neither of us wants the kiss to end.

Eventually, though, my determination wins out. We need to discuss my plan, and part of it hinges on one detail.

"How did the meeting with Ladiron go? Did she agree to endorse your uncle?"

Janus shakes his head. "She isn't ready to commit one way or the other. She's meeting with Senator Fahari today."

"Okay, then, I'll wait until after the election to ensure Mirovnik wins." I want that more for Janus than Mirovnik. It'll put him in the right position for what comes next. "Then you'll hire an investigator to figure out who I really am."

Janus tugs me onto his lap. "No."

I drop my forehead against his. "Mirovnik can accuse me of tricking him, trying to find another way to murder him."

Janus growls. "I won't allow it."

I run a comforting hand over his hair. This is the only solution. "You and Mirovnik come away heroes, and I serve my life sentence."

Janus's jaw flexes. "Fuck Mirovnik. Fuck the election. Stay with me, Carrefour."

I hang my head, heavy under the weight of five additional lives. "If Vivi and Corah return today and confront me, I'll share my plan with them, too, ask them to hold off on arresting me. I'm fairly confident our friendship will earn me that much." I press on Janus's shoulders to stand, then lean over to give him one last kiss. "I wish I could find a different way."

Janus tucks his head into my belly, his shoulders sagging. "So do I."

When I get to my room, I slide on my specs, both hoping for and dreading an update from Vivi and Corah. Nothing from either of them, but I have five missed calls and one message from Windrose. What in the world?

Carrefour, I urgently need to speak with you.

Sweat beads my brow. Did she figure out I'm not a new soul? I can't call her back, not now. We need to get through the election first. If the world finds out I've been lying about my new soul, Janus will lose credibility by association. The last thing I want is for my past to jeopardize Janus's future. I need to stall, at least until the election in six days.

In a panic, I block Windrose and slide my specs into my bag. The best thing I can do now is follow through with our visit to Two Lovers Point. When we return to CD tomorrow, I'll contact Windrose and tell her my plan to turn myself in, plead with her to give me a little time to atone for my sins. She's a reasonable person. Of course she'll understand.

With no word from Vivi and Corah, we leave for Two Lovers Point at five thirty p.m. Donovan, who quietly stationed himself outside my bedroom door all afternoon, sits up front in my hover with Janus in back beside me. Crosier rides in the other with one of Janus's NASS officers.

My mounting concern for Vivi and Corah has fully eclipsed my own dilemma. "What could be taking them so long?" I ask Janus. "Do you think they're okay?"

He rubs my hand. "I'll make some calls when we get back, send a team to look for them."

I nod and pull in a long breath.

The hover stops in the Puntan Dos Amåntes parking lot, and the doors lift.

Janus squeezes my hand to stop me from leaving. "Is your mind still made up? What we discussed today?"

Donovan's head turns by a fraction, his eyes narrowing.

I swallow hard. When we return to CD, I'll give up my security detail entirely. The person behind my attacks could be the same person Krest hired to delete her from SEIK. I endangered myself with my recklessness. How can I expect others to sacrifice themselves for me?

"Yes. It must be done." I release Janus's hand to climb out, walking straight toward the iconic bronze statue, a tribute to whom many believe are the first documented soulmates.

I've seen movies and read countless adaptations about the couple. But now that I'm here, their story feels even more real, ever more tragic. Donovan hangs back as the local photographer begins circling me. I ignore them to focus on the couple's entwined bodies, perfectly depicting their love and helplessness.

According to legend, during Spanish colonial rule, a wealthy businessman betrothed his beautiful daughter to a powerful captain. When she found out, his daughter was so distraught, she ran away to a secluded beach where she met and instantly fell in love with a young Chamorro man. She went home the next day after promising to return for him.

When her father learned of her new lover, he demanded his daughter marry the Spanish captain at once. She slipped away that night to meet her beloved, but the Spanish army chased them up the hillside to the top of this cliff, trapping them on the precipice.

The bronze statue, much taller than I imagined it to be, commemorates their final moments. The two lovers tied their long hair together, joined hands, and leapt over the edge, never to be seen again.

I press a hand to my heart, hoping their nelies found their way back to each other. Janus comes up behind me and places his hands on my shoulders. I lean into his chest, knowing the whole world is watching.

After a long minute, he turns me in his arms. Like all soulmates who visit this statue, we mimic their posture, wrapping an arm around each other's waists and joining hands above our heads. I look into his eyes with the same fear and resolve the couple above us must have felt, but unlike them, I'm determined not to take Janus down with me.

"I will find you again," he whispers. "I promise."

He gives me a chaste peck on the lips, then rests his forehead against mine. We still have six days until the election, but this feels a lot like goodbye. I set my jaw and nod. *Goodbye, Janus.*

When we break apart, the photographer thanks us and heads to the parking lot.

Janus sweeps a finger under my jaw, giving me a sad smile. "I'll be right back, okay?" He motions toward the parking lot. "My uncle has the worst timing, messaged me just as you got out of the hover and said it was urgent."

"Mm-hmm." I turn toward the cliffside overlook, drawn to the haunting beauty beyond.

I climb the closest terrace, heading out to the highest point, followed closely by Donovan. His presence settles my racing mind, and my shoulders relax for the first time today. I step up to the railing and breathe in the sea air.

Donovan quietly clears his throat. "Are you in love with him?"

I study the view as I consider his question. I love spending time with Janus, how he makes me feel about myself, his addictive desire. Janus is the man I *should* love, and perhaps, given the right circumstances, I would. But as wonderful as he makes me feel, I don't yearn for his touches or lose myself in his eyes.

Janus gave up his soul for me, but my heart still sings for another. I hang my head, despondent. Janus deserves someone who loves him back, who he can share a full life with. And that's not me.

Eventually, I work up the nerve to answer Donovan, truthfully, the only way I know how. I slowly spin to face him, a stone lodged in my throat. He turns his cheek, as if my next words might physically hurt him.

"No," I whisper. "I don't love him."

He closes his eyes and inhales. "Carrefour, I—"

Crosier steps between us. "Janus said it was safe for me to come over. Is that okay?"

Desperate to hear what Donovan was about to say, I want to shout that no, it's not okay. But her beautiful soul deserves none of that. And perhaps it's best I never find out. Because if Donovan still has feelings for me, it would only make executing my plan harder. He is a good soul. Crosier is a good soul. I am a murderer.

"Of course it's okay." I gesture to our surroundings. "Not a security threat in sight."

The three of us continue around to the lower deck, protruding a few meters from the face of the cliff.

I look over the edge, and my vision swims. The treetops below resemble miniature bushes. "Quite the view, isn't it?"

Standing beside me, Crosier admires the sunset, her face aglow in the golden light. "I've never seen anything more beautiful."

She must be an old soul, close to learning all of life's lessons. I'm the polar opposite—a worthless, conniving criminal. Hopefully, the actions I take over the coming weeks will set me on a path of redemption. I will use Ladiron and Mom as role models, making the best of my circumstances, learning from my mistakes. It will be hard work, but like them, I can prove myself worthy.

Donovan steps between us. "Can we back up a little, please?"

He takes hold of our wrists to guide us from the railing just as the cliff face to our left explodes with a deafening boom, rocks flying every which way. I shout and crouch into a ball. Donovan leans over to protect us from the debris. But the ominous creaking of metal sends the three of us scrambling. None of us find purchase before the platform buckles in half.

We crash into the railing, Donovan landing on top of us. Crosier cries out in pain as she's pinned between the metal and his body. I moan, having fallen on my arm. Donovan, still clinging to my left wrist, tries to ease his body off ours, but a second later, the railing begins bending under our combined weight.

"*No, no, no,*" he growls as first Crosier and then I fall into the abyss.

My short, single life flashes before my eyes. Mom. Vivi. Corah.

Donovan. Please no. This can't be the end. Not yet. I open my mouth to scream, but no sound emerges. The air is sucked from my lungs as my body comes to a sudden jolt, dangling over the expanse below, held only by the vise around my wrist.

Wide-eyed and gasping for air, I follow the hand holding me up to Donovan's anguished face. He hangs upside down from what remains of the platform, holding steadfastly to me and Crosier. Sweat beads my brow as panic fully sets in. The only things keeping me alive are his grip and the mangled railing wrapped around his foot. Either could give way at any moment.

I seize Donovan's wrist with my left hand to strengthen our hold and frantically claw above with my right arm, searching for purchase. *Shit!* Coming up empty, I grab his wrist with that hand as well and scan the clifftop for signs of life. My sightline only reaches so far. *Please,* somebody. Anybody.

If Janus survived the explosion, he'd come for us. Unless NASS forced him to clear the area. But they'd definitely send help. We just need to hold tight until that help arrives.

Beside me, Crosier groans. Her eyes are closed, face drained of color. Donovan whimpers from the effort of holding us both and pushes out several breaths before a long inhale. How long can he bear our weight? A minute or two? He couldn't possibly pull either of us up, suspended upside down the way he is.

The horror of our predicament fills my core with cold realization. One of us will have to go—either me or Crosier. Donovan may lose his job if I fell. But if he lost Crosier? How could he go on knowing he killed his soulmate?

No, I won't let that happen. She's too good, and I'm about to spend the rest of my days in prison.

I consider letting go. Could I do it? Could I sacrifice myself?

Tears spring to my eyes. Yes, I *must*. It has to be my decision, and I have to do this for Donovan. For both of their worthy souls. I choke out a sob, finally accepting the hard truth. I must save him from this horrible choice.

My brain commands my hands to release, but my body refuses, clamping even harder to Donovan.

Now, Sivon. Before it's too late.

I manage to pry one finger away. Then two.

"Shepherd," Crosier says. She takes a staggered breath. "Look at me."

My fingers snap back. *Coward!*

Panting, he meets her eyes.

"Let me go, Shepherd."

"No," he snarls. "I can hold you both. Help will come."

"Save Carrefour." Crosier releases her grip on his arm, leaving Donovan to support her full weight.

"No!" I shout. "Hold on to him!"

Her left arm is bent at an unnatural angle, hanging limply by her hip. Did it break again when Donovan fell on her?

I choke out a sob. "Hold on, Crosier! I'm not worth it. *I'm not worth it!*"

The platform suddenly drops another meter. My right arm flails to the side. Donovan lets out an angry yell as his body begins swaying. Despite his tight grip, my left hand slips a fraction. The scream rising within me emerges as a shriek as I fight against the fear. *Let go of him, Sivon.*

Crosier uses the momentum to twist her body, breaking his hold. She silently falls from sight.

"No!" Donovan grabs at the empty air.

"CROSIER!" I gasp with shame, my eyes filling with tears. I should've been braver, should've let go first. "No, no, no," I mutter. *Why didn't I let go?* Donovan is her soulmate. Now she's gone, and it's all my fault. *Oh, Crosier, I'm so sorry!* I release a pained cry.

"Give me your other hand!" Donovan demands. His now-free hand extends toward me. With a loud grunt of exertion, I grab hold of his other wrist. My right hand now secure, he yanks my left wrist higher to fortify that connection.

He closes his eyes in relief. "You will not let go. You hear me?"

I nod, sobbing, unable to find words. I don't want Donovan to live with losing both of us, but neither do I want another person to sacrifice themself for my awful soul.

The seconds tick by, and my shoulders begin trembling from the strain. The platform creaks ominously. It could go at any moment, killing us both. If I let go now, he could pull himself up before the structure collapses.

"Donovan," I croak through the thickness of my throat.

He shakes his head as if he already knows what I'll say, but my hands are growing clammy, my muscles weaker. I can't hold on much longer. Tears stream down my cheeks. "*Donovan,*" I whisper.

"No! Do not fucking let go! I'd never forgive you. Never." One of his own tears drips onto my face. He releases a pained gasp and squeezes my wrists even tighter. "Just hold on. *Please.* For me."

For him. I release a sob and adjust my slippery grip. That's it, then. We're either both coming out of this or neither of us will. My fingers, starting to go numb, fight to hold on.

When shouts ring out from above, I first suspect I imagined them, that I'm going into shock.

But Donovan calls out, "Down here!" sending a surge of hope through me.

I hold my breath, searching the rubble above for movement. A couple of men scramble onto the platform, much too quickly for my liking, but they must know time is of the essence. Straps circle their waists, the ends of which are out of view. At least if we drop, they'll be okay.

The platform creaks again, and I screech, getting a heart-stopping look at the shore below. My breathing accelerates, going erratic. We're not gonna make it. I can't—

"No, no, look at me," Donovan commands. "Breathe."

I lock eyes with him and inhale. He nods, and we exhale together.

We're awkwardly jerked upward bit by bit, making it harder to maintain my grip.

"Donovan!" I shout as one hand slips free, but he catches it just as quickly. My eyes squeeze shut, pushing out a torrent of pooled tears. "Don't let go," I beg.

"Never."

I listen for his next inhale and fill my lungs.

On the next tug, we're hauled over the edge. One of the men lifts me into his arms, then passes me up to another person I hadn't even noticed. I break into inconsolable, heaving sobs. The stranger carries me over mounds of rubble to the parking lot. They set me down and throw a blanket over my shoulders. A different set of arms encircles me. I know it's Donovan.

I curl my hands inward and tuck my elbows to my sides as shivers rack my body. We rock back and forth, crying together, trying and failing to come to terms with our loss. Another loss I should have prevented. Another soul who meant the world to him.

I can't believe Crosier is gone. I can't believe she sacrificed herself for my despicable soul. The guilt is unbearable.

NAIA

NAIA—(NEYE-uh) abbr. The North American Intelligence Agency.

The distant wail of sirens pierces the night, and Donovan pulls me to my feet. "We can't stay here."

As distraught and exhausted as I am, I also know he's right. Someone just blew up the platform we were standing on, and I'm not ready to let the world know I survived.

The list of possible culprits is as long as it is wide. With the public so eager to see me and Janus at Two Lovers Point, any fool could've guessed we'd get here eventually. Or, hell, the photographer could've let on exactly where and when we'd arrive.

Noticeably limping, Donovan guides us onto a vacant sidewalk.

"I'm sorry, Donovan."

"Uh-uh." He wraps an arm around me, head swiveling left and right. "You just survived an assassination attempt. You're not allowed to be sorry."

"But Crosier . . ."

Donovan releases a pained whimper, pushing me along. "I can't do anything about Crosier right now. Your life still hangs in the balance, so that is priority one."

A copter flashes through the night sky, then circles back and sets down in the parking lot. Donovan tugs me into the trees. "Stay quiet and don't move."

"*Sivon!*"

Vivi and Corah! They're alive! I burst into tears, throw off the blanket, and run straight for the copter.

"Are you *fucking* kidding me?" Donovan hobbles after me. "I just said . . ."

I slam into Vivi's embrace, and Corah hugs me from behind.

"Crosier's dead!" My knees buckle, but Vivi and Corah catch my weight.

"I'm so sorry, but we don't have time. You need to come with us!" Vivi shoves me toward the copter, from which a middle-aged man climbs out. Two others occupy the remaining seats.

I freeze in place. They came to arrest me. I stumble backward.

"I go where Carrefour goes," Donovan says.

"There's no room!" Corah pushes me from behind. "We need to take her with us."

Donovan grabs my arm, but I pull free. I don't want him to witness my arrest. "Stay here. Find Crosier."

The man who stepped out flashes his credentials and pulls Donovan aside, no doubt to tell him all about the wanted criminal he's been protecting for the past week.

Vivi helps Corah lift me into the copter, but I don't have the strength or energy to put up a fight. I buckle myself in, resigned to my fate, focusing on Donovan's expression. What does he think of my crimes? Attempting to murder the prime minister. Hacking SEIK to return a new soul. Fooling the world. Fooling him.

As the copter lifts, Donovan's lips part. He rubs his jaw and shakes his head, then looks directly at me. Before I can get a read on his expression, the agent points to the bystanders who helped save us. Donovan dips his chin, and they split up to approach them.

He knows the truth now. Who I am. What I've done.

I flop my head against the backrest as a tear runs down my face. With any luck, I'll never see him again.

I don't know where they take me. The copter flies for about an hour. Vivi holds my hand the entire time, but I can't bring myself to look at her. Words require too much energy. So do cohesive thoughts.

We touch down on a copterpad outside a one-story residential building. It's too dark to see much of anything, but the sound of the ocean means we couldn't have made it far. Vivi and Corah hook their arms around my waist and lead me inside. We're followed by the two men.

The beach house is decorated in post-war decor. The smell of dust and mildew suggest no one's been here since then either. My friends turned captors lead me to a sofa, peel away the vinyl cover, then sit me in the middle.

One of the men runs the faucet for a long minute, then fills a glass of water and holds it out to me. My hands shake too much to take it. It's only then I notice the raised purple welts on my wrists where Donovan held so tightly. I trace the marks with my fingers.

Vivi takes the glass instead and holds it to my lips. "Take a sip." She tips it slightly, and I allow the cool liquid to rush over my tongue and down my throat. She sets the glass on the bamboo coffee table and turns to face me.

"These are Agents Hawkshaw and Bukhali. They're with NAIA. Corah and I worked with them in our past lives as well, and we trust them."

I give the men a quick once-over. If Vivi and Corah trust them, that's good enough for me. We exchange solemn nods.

Vivi lays her hand over mine. "I'm so sorry about Crosier. Do you know who might be responsible for attacking you?"

I shake my head.

"Have you ever heard of Say It Co.?"

My head keeps swaying.

"It's like Sociaty but populated by criminals. People create fake profiles and brag about their misdeeds. Others hire accomplices." Vivi adjusts her position. "Well, your name is all over it today. Someone wants you dead, like now. And they're offering a tonne of money to make it happen."

"Sure."

"*Sure?*" Corah says. "Sure, someone is trying to kill you?"

I lift one shoulder. "Someone put threatening messages on the Advertitude, a man attacked me in the Fringe, a RAID shot at me yesterday, and someone just tried to blow me up. It's not exactly breaking news."

"You don't have any suspects?" Vivi skims her fingertips over my lumpy wrist and looks up at the two agents. "Can you find some bruisedy?"

One of them extracts a tube from his inside pocket. Vivi squeezes a pea-size amount onto her finger and begins massaging it in.

"I've narrowed it down to the entire world population except for you two, Donovan, and Mom." My words come out flat. "Donovan could've just let me drop if he wanted me dead. I ruled out Mirovnik before, but he's back on the list since I tried to murder him in my last life."

Everyone in the house goes eerily still, as if someone paused a movie.

"Could you repeat that?" Corah says.

"You heard me." I slump into the cushion. "Isn't that what this interrogation is about?"

Vivi trades confused glances with Corah. "You think we brought you to our private island to interrogate you? Sivon, we're trying to save your life. Hundreds of people were about to swarm Guam searching for proof that you died or trying to finish the job. Agent Qarsoon and Donovan are still at the scene, doing their best to contain the truth."

My brows pull down. "This is *your* island?"

Corah whacks me on the leg. "Wake up. I know you've just gone through some shit, but we need our friend back."

My head sways back and forth, back and forth, holding the emotions inside. *Don't let them see how much this hurts. They'll have to do the right thing here in a minute, and it'll only be harder if you're crying.* "I thought you came to arrest me because you figured out I'm not a new soul. My symbol is on your USB drive."

"Our USB drive held evidence about people manipulating SEIK."

I raise my hand. "And I'm one of 'em. I found out today that I arranged for someone to delete my soulid from SEIK after my last life. My real soul has a life sentence for the attempted murder of Mirovnik in 216. My ID was OOOXOOO. Soulname: Krest."

Corah jumps up and shouts so loudly, my soul nearly leaves my body. "Called it! You owe me twenty valuts."

"Do not!" Vivi stands. "I never agreed to that bet. The symbol Sivon draws on her hands was a dead giveaway."

Agents Hawkshaw and Bukhali circle the table to shake my friends' hands.

"What's going on?" My eyes flit from person to person, heart hammering. My soul fills with hope I hadn't thought possible.

Vivi and Corah sit on the coffee table facing me. They each take one of my hands.

"The USB drive we uncovered yesterday. It didn't hold our research, but yours. Krest's. You used to work with us at the South American Intelligence Agency."

My eyes fill with the emotions I've held at bay since climbing onto their copter. "I'm not a bad soul?"

"Of course not," Vivi says. "You're one of the very best. It's an unspoken rule among agents that the Krest name must never be uttered over a call, in a message, or posted online. We all assumed SAIA hid your soulid from SEIK searches so people couldn't figure out who or where you'd end up next."

Chills work their way over my body. This is the complete opposite to how I felt on Kopar's ship, when everything felt so very wrong. Yes, an intelligence agent. Working undercover explains my disjointed past lives. Soldier. Unhoused. Mafia. Molemo's spouse . . . *Murderer?*

"But I tried to *kill* Mirovnik."

Corah rests her elbows on her knees. "If Krest tried to kill Mirovnik, then that doesn't bode well for Mirovnik."

Vivi and Corah fill me in on their past twenty-four hours. They shook off their tail easily, a little too easily, which prompted them to send their holo doubles to the copter. It exploded the second their counterparts climbed on board.

Who is after us? Me, Vivi, Corah, and Janus have all been the targets of recent attacks. Someone who knows what Vivi and Corah are hiding? Someone who knows Janus and I aren't new souls? Could it be Yinbi—the SEIK hacker in the Fringe?

"Isn't that how you last died?" I ask Vivi. "In a copter crash?"

"A plane, but yes. Krest was on it too."

I rub my forehead. Only minutes ago I believed I was a murderer. Now I'm a secret agent, former colleague of Vivi and Corah? How can something too good to be true also feel so right?

"That reminds me." Corah withdraws a new screen and touches a few options. "Our jet will arrive in thirty minutes."

"What if someone tampered with that one?"

Corah waves off my worries. "If anyone gets within twenty meters of it, we get an alert."

Vivi slathers more ointment on my wrists. "We inserted the USB into this ancient computer Ensio dug up called a laptop. It had a different button for every number and letter of the alphabet and made weird whirring noises. Anyway, up comes a wealth of documents, videos, and bank records supporting your investigations. But even stranger was how often you mentioned Flavinsky."

"Flavinsky?" The hairs on the back of my neck prickle.

"Krest was *obsessed* with saving Flavinsky. And you weren't the only one. Kitsune and Raposa too. Flavinsky was one of our childhood friends."

My eyes bug out of my head.

"Yep." Corah accepts a glass of water from Hawkshaw. "Kitsune and Raposa included our transcribed history on the USB. In our foli 2, Flavinsky lived in our hometown, our birthdays only months apart. I won't share their birth name because it'll get confusing to keep calling Flavinsky by different names. So, just know we were good friends with Flavinsky in their foli 6, and, well, as you already know, they died after their kirling."

Vivi and Corah lost their own Ziva. "I'm so sorry."

Vivi pats my hand. "As you well know, their loss made a big impact, because eighteen years later, when Flavinsky was kirled again, we tried to visit her. She was in Australia. We were still in Brazil."

"We didn't make it," Corah says.

My lips turn down.

Vivi sighs. "Just wait. Eighteen years later—"

"You were fifty-four?"

"Yes, exactly." Corah takes a sip of water. "Flavinsky was kirled again, this time on Grand Cayman Island, and we got the news early. We flew over and used our credentials with the South American Intelligence Agency to visit him."

My pulse picks up. I know how this ends, but part of me still wishes for an alternative, some way for Flavinsky to have survived foli 7's tragedy.

Vivi scoots toward the edge of the couch. "We promised to pay off his fine, said we'd do everything in our power to lessen his sentence. He promised us he wouldn't take his life. We never would've left him otherwise." She sighs. "He was dead by morning."

"You think Flavinsky was murdered?" I was right all along. Ziva didn't kill herself, no matter what the death investigation says.

Corah nods. "We were convinced of it. A few years later, we paid off Flavinsky's fines and created a charity to pay the subscriptions of expired Foli Journals accounts. We couldn't do anything about Flavinsky's sentence, but we did that much. And today, we paid off Flavinsky's current balance. If Flavinsky *is* dying by suicide, we don't want money to be the reason for it."

"Flavinsky is *not* dying by suicide." But who is targeting that soul and why? Does this go all the way back to World War III and the murder of General Molemo? Is Ladiron behind this? I can't imagine telling Vivi that Trevin's mom, the incredibly popular leader of the Global Civil Liberties Union, is Flavinsky's serial killer.

Vivi places her hand over mine. "Krest was secretive about her own relationship with Flavinsky, but she vowed to save them from another tragic ending, to break the cycle."

The crossroads symbol spins in my head. Break the cycle. Save Flavinsky. Yes, that makes sense as well. Not even knowing my past, I yearned so desperately to save Ziva and felt like a complete failure for my inability to do so.

I slump into the cushion. "But I didn't. Flavinsky died five more times since then, all on the day of their kirling. The cycle hasn't changed at all." I clamp my mouth shut.

That's not true. This time was different from the others. Flavinsky was born the day after their death in every life. Except this one. Ziva was kirled one year and almost nine months later than expected. Not a coincidence. Nothing here is coincidental.

I temple my hands over my nose. *Pull back, Sivon. Look at the big picture. What are you missing?*

Krest and Flavinsky both died on November 10, 216. I was obsessed with saving Flavinsky and convicted of attempting to murder Mirovnik. Centuries of vindictive rage light a fire in my gut. "Mirovnik. Krest believed he was Flavinsky's murderer." The words feel truer than any I've ever spoken.

How *dare* he? He pulled me into his web of deceit, enticed me with his sticky promises. I spoke on his behalf, encouraged people to vote for him. *Flavinsky's murderer was mine as well.*

I pick up my glass of water and chug the contents to douse the flames. There's more to see here. I can't afford to let emotions undercut my reasoning.

Agents Hawkshaw and Bukhali come out of the kitchen and sit in front of the coffee table. I quickly explain my reasoning, then close my eyes, sinking into my mind.

If I was so determined to save Flavinsky, why delete my own soulid from SEIK? Why not erase Flavinsky's as well?

Because an infamous soul like Flavinsky couldn't just disappear from SEIK. They're probably the result of thousands of daily searches. People would notice right away if Flavinsky went missing from SEIK. A move like that had no chance of succeeding.

So I didn't delete Flavinsky. I did something else. Swapped Flavinsky for Ziva? No, as right as the previous revelation about Mirovnik felt, this conclusion feels wrong. I would never sacrifice one soul for another. But her late birthday . . . Ziva doesn't fit the pattern.

"Corah, call Ensio. Ask him to dive deep into Ziva's record in SEIK. Find the anomaly. There must be some sort of trace."

Corah makes the call.

"A trace of what, Sivon?" Vivi asks.

"Ziva isn't Flavinsky." Yes, I'm certain.

A second later, the tragedy of my realization crashes over me, eliciting a full-body tremor. *Ziva isn't Flavinsky.* I slap a hand over my mouth to hold back a sob. My friend. Dikela's friend. Sister and daughter of the sweetest family. *Why Ziva?*

The next epiphany brings me to my feet. Under a sudden onslaught of vertigo, I run out the door and fall to my knees on the sidewalk, vomiting up the meager contents of my stomach. Vivi,

Corah, and the two agents rush outside, but none of them touch me. And I'm grateful. This isn't the time for compassion. Because the second the words leave my mouth, I will forever hate myself for uttering them.

"It's Donovan. Donovan is Flavinsky."

Windrose

Windrose—(wind-ROSE) n. A diagram showing the strength and direction of the wind at a given location.

I suspected it a week ago. Donovan has an 11/11/16 birthday. His parents, who lived in the Fringe, abandoned him when he was five. They kirled a *five-year-old* boy and decided he was worthless. My eyes sting with unshed tears. People can be so cruel.

Vivi and Corah wrap me in a blanket to calm my shivering and guide me back into the living room.

"I think she's in shock," Vivi says.

But I'm not. I'm just unable to do anything but think right now. I need to play this game backward, figure out how our knights, bishops, kings, and queens reached these squares on the terrain.

Donovan is Flavinsky, which means Crosier isn't his soulmate. She shouldn't have come on this trip. She'd still be alive. . . . Her final moments flicker across my mind like a horror movie, her yelp of pain, disjointed arm, calm directives.

Let me go.

I should've been the one to let go, not Crosier. Whatever Krest did to Flavinsky's or Shepherd's souls put Crosier's death on her hands. My hands. I stare down at my obstinate, determined fingers and curl them into fists. Whoever blew up that platform, I will find them. I will never let them hurt anyone I care about again.

"Sivon, I have news. Can you hear me?" Corah leans into my face.

I meet her eyes.

"Ensio said Ziva's DNA was added to Flavinksy's record in SEIK *three months* before her kirling, artificially matching the two. Further, someone inserted code to discard any new soulid images for that DNA match. Because of those database manipulations, a search for Ziva's DNA will always return Flavinsky's record."

I nod to let her know I understand, then retreat into myself. Okay, this is helpful.

SEIK stores a DNA sample with our soulid, matching our bodies with our souls. But if Ziva's DNA was recorded months ago as a match for Flavinsky's, and reentering Ziva's DNA during her kirling triggered code to replace her soulid with Flavinsky's, then Ziva would appear to be Flavinsky through all the system checks. The SKI counselors had no reason to doubt the results.

So who did this to her? Forget for a minute that Donovan somehow got Shepherd's soul nearly two years ago. Go back one move at a time. Could Donovan have input Ziva's DNA into SEIK?

I won't ask if he *would*. I already know the answer to that question. *Hell* no. He desperately tried to get into her room that night, insisted her results were wrong, and tore out the oleander bush. Donovan protects the ones he loves.

But loving his family isn't an alibi. Everyone will assume Donovan did this unless I can prove otherwise. So *could* Donovan have done this?

Did he have access to her DNA? Yes, easy access. A hairbrush, her teeth nanorizer, a water glass. They shared the same bathroom.

Could he have added her DNA into SEIK? Himself? I doubt it. He's Secret Service, not a hacker. Could he have arranged for someone else to do it? I *guess*? But the "would" impossibility continues to overpower the "could."

I knead the crossroads symbol into my palms. *Save Flavinsky.*

Okay, Donovan technically could have done it. Who else? Why three months ago? What was three months ago? Tingles spread down my legs as a memory unfurls in my brain—the reception after Ziva's funeral, walking downstairs to find Windrose standing in Ziva's doorway, a handkerchief pressed to her eyes.

Only a few months ago we were chatting at Golds's birthday party. . . .

I never thought she'd do this. I just . . . I thought she was stronger.

She's worked with SEIK for over three dozen years. She *called* me five times today.

Carrefour, I urgently need to speak with you.

I stand, letting the blanket fall to the couch. "I need an in-person meeting with Windrose. As soon as humanly possible."

We're strapped into the jet three minutes later.

During our flight, I explain my reasoning to Vivi, Corah, and the two agents. As suspected, my argument on Donovan's behalf is met with skepticism. They promise not to report anything until we speak with Windrose, though, so all my hope rides on this conversation.

As we approach Langley, I press my forehead to the window, curious about the reportedly top-secret campus, but the only landmarks in view are trees and fields. "Where are we?"

"Just wait." Corah winks.

The jet descends, and seconds later, the fields and trees disappear, replaced by dozens of redbrick buildings.

Whoa. Was not expecting that. "The entire campus is hidden under a hologram?"

Corah bounces her brows. "Pretty cool, huh?"

We left their island at ten p.m. and touch down on their dedicated tarmac at noon the same day. I wish time really worked that way, that I could redo the past ten hours, knowing what I know now.

I squint against the bright sun when we step out. Vivi and Corah shut down their handheld screens and accept incaps from Hawkshaw and Bukhali. Since the two senior agents have earplants—unlike me, Vivi, and Corah—they have to stay behind. We're all three being targeted, perhaps by the prime minister himself, and Bukhali's and Hawkshaw's trackers could lead them straight to us.

"We'll report back in two hours," Corah says to them. "In the meantime, comb through Krest's research. We need to figure out who's after us."

We climb into their nearby hover and take off. Ten minutes later, we park inside a pre-kirling apartment garage in old-town Atomdale. The doors open, pouring in the pungent smell of trash. I cover my nose. Windrose lives *here*? I thought SKI paid their counselors well.

When she opens her eighth-floor apartment door, she sways slightly before pulling me inside. "Oh, thank you. Thank you." From her raw nose to her sunken eyes, she looks like she's been crying for days. Weeks, even.

"Yinbi promised me one more day, but I can't pay him more than I already have. I have nothing left." She gestures to her nearly vacant apartment. "You're my only hope."

Yinbi? The child-kirler in the Fringe? "Yinbi is blackmailing you?"

She nods.

I pull in a shaky breath and hazard another guess. "Because of Donovan?"

Windrose holds a fist over her mouth, sniffles and nods. I was right. I was right about everything. My knees go weak, but Corah offers her support, helping me to the raggedy couch.

Windrose perches on a wooden chair that's literally on its last legs. Vivi takes out her screen and taps a few options. "Do you grant your permission for me to record an official statement?"

Windrose stares vacantly at Vivi's screen.

"For Donovan," I add.

Windrose looks at me again, her eyes refilling. "Yes, I give permission. Donovan is innocent. He doesn't know what I did. He doesn't know who he really is."

My heart physically aches. Donovan is Flavinsky. If he finds out, the truth would destroy him, and not just because he's lived as the venerable Shepherd for years. His own sister was murdered in his place.

Vivi sets her screen on the floor between Windrose and us. "Did you enter Ziva's DNA into SEIK ahead of her kirling as Flavinsky's, thereby artificially linking the two?"

Windrose pulls in her lips. "I did. Or rather, I paid Yinbi to do it." She removes her specs and covers her eyes. "Ziva is my only regret. If I could go back and fix it, I would. I just . . . had to pick someone, and I knew she would never . . . I honestly thought Donovan could help her. I didn't know I'd be saving one life and ending another."

My throat clenches. I hoped we'd get a confession out of Windrose, but now I'm not sure I can handle hearing it. I should feel relieved. Ziva didn't take her life. But to be murdered because of a mistaken identity? It's too tragic, too unfair.

Vivi edges forward. "You also arranged for the true Flavinsky to receive Shepherd's soul instead?"

"Yes." Windrose squeezes her handkerchief. "But to understand why, it might help if I start at the beginning. And the beginning isn't in this life. It's in my last."

I scoot back on the couch.

"In the year 144, my sister gave birth to a precious baby boy. We lived on Grand Cayman Island."

"Foli 8," Corah states.

Windrose's brows lift. "Yes. My nephew was Flavinsky. Of course, we didn't know for those eighteen years. I worked nights as a crisis counselor and watched him every afternoon while my sister was at work. Without children of my own, he was my whole world. My Foli Journal is nothing but photos and videos of him from birth to eighteen years old.

"He was such a *good* soul. He dreamt of becoming a community protector, of helping others. His sudden death was devastating, especially since I could've helped him, if only he'd made it home."

She dabs at her eyes. "I think his death broke me. Ten years passed, and I let a completely curable disease take me.

"I was reborn only a year later. At my kirling, I received my Foli Journal, and my heart shattered all over again. If soul networks truly existed, I knew I'd meet Flavinsky again. And, it seems, someone else did as well. My journal included a plea, not from myself, but from a soul who doesn't exist. Not that I can find, anyway. Perhaps I made them up in the delirium of my illness."

Krest. I don't say the name since this confession is going on the record.

"What was the request?" Corah asks.

"Save Flavinsky. Get a job at SKI and do whatever it takes to save Flavinsky." Windrose shifts in her seat. "The directive became a mantra. I had a mission. Thankfully, my foli's profession was in perfect alignment with my new goal, and only a few months after becoming a counselor at the New Union SKI, I kirled Flavinsky."

My hand flies to my mouth.

"As you know, I failed. He died the night of his kirling. I assured him I'd do everything I could to help, and I thought he was okay, that he believed me. He reminded me so much of my nephew, had the same beautiful heart." She begins crying again.

"The next time Flavinsky was kirled, she wasn't in my group, wasn't even in my SKI. She was in Utah."

My stomach clenches. Krest lived in Salt Flat City at the time. We were so close.

"I tried to catch a flight out there, but boarding hadn't even begun when the news hit. Did you know her mother came to Ziva's funeral last week? Flavinsky is so loved by so many."

I gulp. Foli 11. Our shared death dates.

"As the years passed, I grew ever more anxious. The next kirling was approaching by the day, and I knew something had to change, or Flavinsky would keep dying.

"In my years at SKI, I'd witnessed a lot and heard even more. Souls came in from the Fringe already knowing who they were, not the least bit surprised at their results. I hoped whoever was kirling them could do more than match soulids with SEIK. Finally, one of my charges trusted me enough to tell me their name—Yinbi. You can't imagine my relief."

She breathes deeply. "So I went to the Delmarva Fringe and found him. It wasn't hard. He doesn't exactly advertise, but everyone knows who he is.

"When I told him what I wanted, he said he'd only ever pulled data from SEIK, never manipulated it. Told me it would take time, but he'd work on it. The fifty percent deposit took most of my inheritance. The balance took the rest and then some."

I take another look around her sparsely decorated apartment. She's lost so much weight over the past two weeks, withering away to save Donovan.

"As the months ticked by, I lost hope, but a year later, Yinbi messaged me to meet him. I took a day off and returned to the Fringe. He'd figured out how to swap soulids. He suggested giving Flavinsky a Fringe soul who'd recently died, close to the same age Flavinsky would be, a good soul."

"Shepherd," I say.

"Yes, Yinbi had kirled Shepherd when he was seventeen. He assured me Shepherd came on his own for his kirling, that no one knew who he was. Shepherd died only a few months later, pushing a child out of the path of a speeding hover rail."

I swallow a gulp of sadness. The real Shepherd was Crosier's true soulmate, and they each sacrificed their lives to save another.

"Shepherd had two long deathspans, so we agreed that soul was perfect. By the time they were kirled again, Flavinsky would've finished a full life. And, I must admit, I loved that Shepherd worked in community protection in both lives, like my nephew hoped to do. It seemed like fate."

A tear slowly treks down her cheek and drips onto her hand. She dabs at it.

"Yinbi inserted code to pull up Shepherd's soulid when Flavinsky's portrait was taken, switching one for the other.

"You can't imagine my terror when meeting the group of November eleventh birthdays. I was working at the Washington, CD, SKI and already on alert. We all were.

"Almost immediately, I pinpointed Donovan. Souls often recognize those they've loved before. So it wasn't surprising when his kirling came back as Shepherd. I was elated, actually, especially when he left SKI to join the Secret Service. The plan worked.

"I lived only a few kilometers from his family, so I arranged to bump into them one day. Donovan introduced me to his parents, and over time, I inserted myself into their lives. I wanted to know he was okay."

I shake my head. "But if everything was going so well, why did you set up Ziva?"

Windrose chokes on a sob. "Yinbi contacted me again four months ago. He said with Flavinsky so overdue for their kirling, people would get suspicious and start digging around SEIK. He threatened to take me down if anyone discovered what we'd done.

"I don't care what happens to me, but Donovan deserves a full life. So Yinbi made me choose someone. Told me to collect a sample of their DNA, and he'd take care of the rest."

"And you knew Ziva's kirling was coming up," Corah says.

Windrose inhales sharply. "Donovan was a Secret Service officer. Believing he could protect her, I called him after her kirling, let him into SKI, and directed him to her room. I never expected the patrols would turn away a member of the Secret Service."

My throat aches at the futility of her efforts. Ziva was poisoned that night. The RAID in her room probably hid the seeds in her meal. I'm lucky I had Raphaela or could've suffered the same fate by the person who's after me. *Creature.*

"Yinbi called after Ziva's funeral and demanded a hundred thousand valuts to keep Donovan's identity a secret. I don't have any savings left, and I own nothing of value. I can't pay him. I can't." She drops her head into her hands.

My heart begins racing. "When does Yinbi expect the money?"

"I asked him for two weeks to come up with it, but he wouldn't relent, no matter how much I begged. My deadline is midnight tonight."

Tonight? Dizziness washes over me. We only have hours to find and pay Yinbi, or the whole world will know Donovan is Flavinsky. If the truth comes out, Donovan will be arrested to serve Flavinsky's sentence. Or worse, he'll die at the hands of whoever has killed him in every life.

"No," I growl. *Save Flavinsky.*

I jump to my feet. Windrose does as well. She crosses to me and takes my hands. "That's why I called you, Carrefour. You're my only hope."

I thought she'd somehow figured out I was the lost soul who recruited her to save Flavinsky. But as far as I know, she still believes I'm a new soul. "But why me? You know I didn't receive an inheritance. I don't have a hundred thousand valuts, Windrose."

"I know you'll find a way. You must." She kisses my hands. "Flavinsky is your soulmate."

Bad Soul

bad soul—n. a person embodying one or more of the following characteristics: wicked, criminal, morally unsound, greedy, rude, disloyal, shameless.

Thursday, September 6, 236 A.K.—The Delmarva Fringe

We hop in the hover, formulate a plan, and start for the Fringe. Corah calls Ensio, asking if he can figure out how Yinbi is accessing SEIK. I stare out the window in disbelief.

This time yesterday, or today, I was kissing Janus, hoping to feel the same way he did for me, trying to get over Donovan. But Donovan is my soulmate. He's mine. I would cry with happiness if I wasn't so terrified. If we don't stop Yinbi, I may never see him again.

Donovan saved my life last night . . . tonight . . . whatever. Now it's my turn to save his. Hopefully once and for all.

I'm still in my head when the hover sounds a warning and comes to a stop.

"We're still twenty-five kilometers away," Vivi says.

Corah opens the door and steps out. "What the hell?"

"Oh shoot, I forgot they have different roads here." I climb out too. "Hovers can't go into the Fringe."

"That's one way to keep out unwanted guests." Corah slides back in and directs the hover to an adjacent parking lot with one other vehicle parked inside. Vivi and Corah join me on the road.

"Know anyone with a car?" Vivi crouches down and runs her hand over the rough surface of the road.

Corah kicks at a loose rock. "Should we start walking?"

"We don't have time to walk or run twenty-five kilometers. We need to get inside the Fringe, find Yinbi, and negotiate with him before he tells the world who Flavinsky is." I hold out my hand. "Can I use your screen, Vivi? I hoped to avoid this, but I guess we have no choice."

"*Ladies*, your knight in shining armor has arrived." Bardou rolls up in a beat-up first-century relic of a car. He coasts to a stop and leans out the window. "Damn, Sivon, you didn't say anything about twins. This just got way more interesting."

"I'm sitting right here, asshat." A hand knocks him on the head.

Bardou rubs the sore spot. "*Ow!* Quit doing that!"

"I'll quit doing it when you stop being an asshat," the female voice says.

"Okay, okay! I just said twins were interesting. *Jeez!*"

The passenger door opens, and Dikela steps out.

I break into a smile. "*Dikela?* What are you doing here?"

"I ask myself that every day." She rounds the car and embraces me.

Bardou brings a hand to chest and pouts. "You hurt-ed my heart."

Dikela rolls her eyes. "Get in. I'll catch you up."

Once we're buckled, I make introductions, then ask Dikela how she ended up in the Fringe. With Bardou, of all people.

"After you and I talked about Bardou at the funeral, I couldn't get him out of my mind."

"Aw, yeah." Bardou waggles his brows at Dikela.

Dikela grabs the dashboard. "Eyes on the road. Hands on the wheel." She shoots him a death glare and turns to face us. "So I called him up, and I know you won't believe me, but we actually had a good conversation."

I pinch my lips shut. She's right; that's hard to believe.

Dikela rubs her forehead. "He called me the next night, and I called him the following, and next thing I knew, I accepted his invitation to visit."

"Wow."

"I know. A bit cliché, I guess, two people bonding over a shared loss, but he really helped me push through." She glances his way and shrugs. "He's still a *complete dick* when we're around anyone else, but one-on-one, he's actually . . . sweet?"

"You got me blushing over here, mi amor." He brushes his lips over her hand.

She smiles, then snatches her hand away. "Two. Hands."

Bardou makes a show of gripping the steering wheel and leaning forward to stare at the road ahead.

Dikela rests her arm on the seatback. "Anyway, enough about me. Why are *you* in this hell on earth?"

Bardou hisses at the insult.

"We need to find Yinbi."

He slams on the brakes, and we all lurch forward. The rear end of the car fishtails before coming to a stop.

Corah kicks the back of Bardou's seat. "We need to make it there alive, buddy."

Bardou shifts into park and turns to face me. "What do you want with Yinbi?"

"Is that any of your business?"

"It is if you want me to take you to him."

I make a show of taking Vivi's hand. "My friends are worried about their kirling in a few months. So we're here to find out who they were, give them time to prepare."

Bardou narrows his eyes. "I'm not stupid. You told our group at SKI about your identical twin friends who are soulmates. You want me to believe you're friends with *two* sets of identical twins?"

"It's *possible*."

"But it's not true."

We don't have time for this. "Why do you even care?"

He drops his hands to his lap and turns to look at me. "Yinbi isn't a good guy, not even an okay guy. He makes his living off the fear of others. Do you get that? He kirls little kids. *Little kids*, Sivon. The child mortality rate in the Fringe is five times higher than anywhere else in the world. That's on him."

"Parents are killing their kids?" Vivi asks.

Bardou faces the roof. "Sometimes. They don't make 'em look like murders, though. One way or another, Yinbi is responsible."

The car falls into silence.

"Hell on earth," whispers Dikela.

"How can you *stay* here?" I ask.

She sighs. "It's a rough town; don't get me wrong. But it has good people too. They don't think or act like us. No one asks you who you were. You can be whoever you want. No one cares."

"Obviously, they care, or Yinbi wouldn't do what he's doing," says Corah.

Bardou squeezes the steering wheel. "I'm not taking you anywhere near that monster unless it's absolutely necessary."

I tap my foot. We need to get a move on, but I don't want to put the two of them through the pain of Ziva's death again. "Fine. If you insist, here's the abbreviated version."

I fill my lungs. "My soulid is new, but I also have a soulmate. But someone hired Yinbi to switch my soulmate's soul in SEIK, so everyone thinks my soulmate is dead. But he's actually alive, and if people find out my soulmate is alive, he'll be arrested for his previous suicide. Yinbi is blackmailing me to stay quiet about my soulmate's true identity, so we're going to confront him and make sure he never exposes the truth."

I cross my arms. "That's all I can say with my soulmate's life at stake, but if Yinbi thinks he can feed off my fear, he'll be sadly mistaken. If anyone should be scared, it's him."

Bardou snorts. "And you think Yinbi is gonna be scared of a few teenage girls?"

"Yes." Corah pulls out her incap.

Vivi brandishes hers as well. "We sure as hell do."

Bardou looks between the two weapons, then shifts into gear. "Well, *all right*. Let's go get the son of a bitch."

The compatibility issue with Vivi and Corah's hover was a blessing in disguise. We would've drawn a lot of attention asking for directions to Yinbi's, which may have tipped him off. Bardou drives us directly to Yinbi's place, located on the edge of a two-block town.

We pull up in front of the wooden building with peeling white paint just as a family is walking in. A terrified girl, no older than seven, wraps her arms around her mother's neck. The stone-faced dad glances around the street before closing the door behind them.

Vivi shifts to open the car door, but I stop her. "We can't do this with an audience."

Corah checks her screen. "We have to wait for Ensio anyway; otherwise the plan won't work."

Vivi stares out the window, her face a mask of worry. "But if we go in now, we could keep that little girl from being kirled."

"And then what?" Corah asks. "None of us want her to be kirled, but we must stick with Sivon's plan. It *will* work, but we have to wait."

Vivi covers her mouth with her hands, and we settle into our seats. I trace the crossroads symbol across my palms, taking in the town for the first time. As much as I hate to admit it, it's charming, like something out of an old movie. But the pastel-painted wood-and-brick buildings are a masquerade of cheerfulness, hiding secrets within. Upon closer inspection, the paint chips from most of them, the wooden steps sag, and the windows appear to be actual glass, their cracks sutured with some sort of adhesive.

The residents look friendly enough. A couple walks by holding hands and laughing. A boy runs across the street to an ice cream shop, followed by a smiling woman who wipes her forehead of sweat before following him inside. I imagine Bardou's life here and what it was like to learn he was a criminal at only ten years old. What stopped his parents from abandoning him at the hospital . . . or worse?

"Bardou, did any of your friends unexpectedly die growing up?"

He drums his fingers on the steering wheel. "Two. Three, if you count . . ."

Ziva. I yearn to tell him about Ziva's murder, but he might be tempted to confront Yinbi as well, which would screw up everything. The plan matters most. Donovan matters most.

I rest my hand on his shoulder. "You can't come inside with us. Don't hang around either. I don't want either of you mixed up in this."

"We'll call you when we're ready," Corah says.

"You do know I'm not a chauffeur, right?"

I squeeze his shoulder. "You're helping us save a life, Bardou. And for that, I'll be forever grateful."

Bardou looks at me through the mirror, no longer wearing his characteristic smirk. "It's kind of like we're getting a second chance, huh?" His eyes redden.

Dikela takes his hand, then reaches over the seat to hold mine as well.

My throat closes up, making it hard to get out the words. "Yes. That's exactly what it is."

"Then the honor is all mine. Go save your soulmate, Sivon."

"Do it for Ziva," Dikela says.

I nod, my chin wobbling. "For Ziva."

The family finally emerges from Yinbi's building, awash in smiles. I release a lungful of air. That's one thing we won't have weighing down our consciences.

We wait for them to drive away and for the sidewalks to clear before Vivi, Corah, and I exit the car. Ensio said he needed a few more minutes, but this is probably our best chance. Another family could come along any time now.

The steps creak on our ascent, threading unease through the cords of my muscles. I place my hand on the bronze doorknob, take a stabilizing breath, and turn it without knocking. The wide, musty foyer is painted a grayish blue with white trim but holds no furnishings. Dust moats hover in the ray of sunshine spilling through the arched window at the far end. Four open doorways branch off to either side.

We shuffle inside and close the door. I run through the plan again, which requires me to appear scared and uncertain. Convenient, since that's exactly how I feel.

"Hello?" I make my voice crack.

A man emerges from the first room on the left.

"Yinbi?"

"Why, hello. How can I help you, Carrefour?"

I'm not sure what I expected him to look like, but it wasn't this. He's the shortest of our group, thin and gangly, and in his late fifties or early sixties. His skin is an inhuman dark orange, and his confident smile reveals a missing incisor, features in stark contrast to his professional attire and coiffed hair.

He thinks he caught me off guard by knowing who I am, but I was banking on it. All part of the plan. "Windrose sent me."

He runs a thumb under his bottom lip. "Is that right? Now that Flavinsky has a soulmate, she washes her hands of the matter. I always wondered what her true motivations were. Loving nephew, my ass. More likely a lover she never got over. Don't you think?"

I swallow. He knows I'm Flavinsky's soulmate. A part of me worried that Windrose lied so I'd pay his ransom. She could've even called Yinbi to tell him I was on the way. *It's fine, Sivon.* The plan still works.

I place a hand on my chest, feigning distress. "How did you know Flavinsky is my soulmate?"

Vivi takes my other hand, and Corah wraps her arm around my waist.

"It's amazing what secrets are hidden in the depths of SEIK. Wouldn't you agree, Kitsune and Raposa?"

Vivi's hand tightens ever so slightly in my grip. Corah stiffens. We didn't expect him to know who *they* are. Shit. If we lose the element of surprise, that could derail things.

He laughs and walks into the adjoining room. An elegant couch stretches in front of an ornate fireplace. He rounds the mirrored coffee table and gestures to two Victorian-era high-back chairs. Despite their age, they're in remarkable shape. I motion for Vivi and Corah to sit, preferring to stand myself.

He lifts a decanter of amber liquor from the table, tops off his glass, and raises it to Vivi and Corah. "Given your impressive past, I'm surprised the two of you came here without actual agents in tow. I know you *students* can't arrest me." He takes a sip. "If you turn me in, I'll spill my guts about Donovan. If you kill me, one of my associates will."

He gulps down his drink, issuing a loud "Ahh" after swallowing. "I would offer you a glass, but I don't like to share."

I step toward him. "About the ransom—"

"One million valuts." He refills his glass, smiling wickedly at our baffled silence.

"Windrose said a hundred thousand," Vivi says.

"That's when I was dealing with a SKI counselor. Now I'm dealing with Carrefour. Flavinsky's market price just went up."

I hear the click of the front door and a few muted footsteps. *Dammit, Bardou.* He was supposed to stay in the car! I try to cover the sounds by pacing the room.

Yinbi clicks his fingernail against his glass. "And a million valuts every year after that."

My lip curls as I swivel to face him. "You're a monster!"

"A rich monster." He chuckles and downs another gulp.

Act meek, Sivon. Not angry. I round my shoulders. "Please, Yinbi, listen to reason. I didn't receive an inheritance. I don't have anywhere near that much money."

He points to Vivi and Corah. "Oh, don't you?"

Yinbi sets down the glass and settles his arms on the back of the couch. "Those are my terms. You want me to keep quiet about switching Donovan's soul from Flavinsky to Shepherd? Pay up."

A gasp comes from the foyer. We all turn toward the sound.

I clutch my throat as tears fill my eyes. *No, no, no.* This isn't happening. My plan crumbles into pieces, along with the walls of my heart.

"Well, isn't this nice? The gang's all here!" Yinbi breaks into an evil grin. "Welcome . . . Donovan."

Neli

neli—(NELL-ee) n. A soul's next life.

Donovan steps into the archway, his face ashen. Why is he here? I want to run to him, push him out the door, and catch the next shuttle to Thessaly together. But that's ridiculous. We'd never be safe, not anywhere, until this is settled.

Maybe we can still fix this, if Ensio comes through. I check with Corah, but she shakes her head. Shit! *Think, Sivon.*

"Thanks for coming all this way, Donovan." Yinbi rubs his jaw. "It's okay if I call you Donovan, yeah? Can't imagine you'd prefer *Flavinsky*." He sets his glass on the mirrored table. "I invited you because I had a feeling my secondary source of income wouldn't come through. Figured you'd be interested in picking up the slack."

Donovan's eyes have glazed over. He doesn't respond.

"He looks a little weary, ladies, don't you think?" Yinbi pats the cushion. "Come on in and sit down. I'll share a little story."

Donovan shuffles into the room. His knees seem to collapse when he gets to the couch. He covers his mouth, staring at the table. *Look at me, Donovan!*

Yinbi leans toward him. "Your parents brought you here fourteen years ago. Do you remember?"

Donovan inhales sharply.

Yinbi pats his shoulder. "Me too. Vivid memories of that day.

You're much taller now, but I'll never forget those adorable curls. You were all smiles. I think your parents promised ice cream if you stood still like a good boy."

Bile rises in my throat. They're evil. Yinbi. Donovan's parents. The whole lot.

"You were chasing my old tabby cat around the foyer when I told them who you were."

A cold tear rolls down my cheek. *How do I stop this?* "He's a criminal, Donovan. Don't believe a word he says."

"I remember the cat," Donovan croaks. He plants his elbows on his knees and drops his head into his hands.

Yinbi pats Donovan's shoulder. "Yes, she was a good girl. Putting her down was the hardest thing I've ever done. . . ." He clicks his tongue. "Sorry. Where was I?

"Oh, yes. It was no surprise when your parents hung up missing posters a week later. Said you'd run off during a camping trip. Park rangers searched night and day, copters circling. I thought for sure they'd find you in a creek bed somewhere, but apparently, they abandoned you at a hospital outside the Fringe. I guess their conscience got the best of them."

I grab handfuls of my hair. *Stop, stop, make him stop!* I'll never forgive myself for letting Donovan find out this way.

"You'll never guess who I heard from last week. Your loving parents! Seems they didn't forget that day fourteen years ago, either, and once your sister died—*adopted* sister—they came a'callin'."

I hadn't even thought of that. Donovan's parents would've known Ziva wasn't the real Flavinsky. Unless Yinbi had lied to them years ago. I take a stilted breath while Donovan shakes his head.

Yinbi squeezes Donovan's shoulder. "Now, don't you worry for one second. I didn't tell them who *you* were. They only knew Ziva looked nothing like their beautiful baby boy. They thought they could extort a little money out of me, but your secret is safe . . . for as long as you and Carrefour want it to be."

Corah catches my eye and nods. *Finally.* I bow my head and reconstruct my plan. We can still win, if I play my hand right.

I wipe my face free of tears, stand tall, and clear my throat. "I won't pay the ransom." Donovan's eyes finally snap up to me, but I keep mine focused on Yinbi. "You can't tell the truth about Donovan without exposing the child-kirling operation you're running. You'd end up in prison, too, probably with multiple life sentences."

Yinbi chuckles and applauds. "Is *that* the ace up your sleeve?" He stands from the couch and walks over to me. "You think I'd let them take me alive?"

His rotten breath stings my nostrils.

"No, no. I won't be coming back as myself. Once I figured out how to switch souls, I started making a list of my favorites." He pats my cheek, making me flinch. "To be honest, your name was near the top. But I'm rethinking that now." He turns to face Vivi and Corah. "After all, I could be an incredibly wealthy secret agent with a soulmate . . . to do with whatever I want."

Sneering, Vivi and Corah rise from their chairs in measured synchronicity.

"No. You won't." I cross the room to stand beside Donovan. *Save Flavinsky. Protect your heart.* They're one and the same. Flavinsky *is* my heart.

"You're right. I won't. As long as one million valuts hits my account within the next hour."

Donovan sits up. He draws in a slow breath and flexes his jaw.

I chuckle and take Donovan's hand, pulling him to a stand beside me. My body rushes with power. "Sorry, I chose the wrong word. What I meant was you can't."

Yinbi's smile falters.

"You see, once we learned what you did, we reached out to a good friend. He's a talented hacker himself. And he figured out how you were accessing SEIK and cut off your access." I snap my fingers. "Just like that."

Yinbi shuffles his feet. "Bullshit."

"Go ahead, try."

Donovan vibrates with tension. I squeeze his hand, offering reassurance, but instead of returning the gesture, he lets go. My brows furrow, but before I can read into it, Yinbi whips out his screen. My fingers and toes curl. If Ensio didn't fully close Yinbi's backdoor access, we're sunk.

Yinbi frantically taps at his screen, his expression changing from cool and collected to infuriated. "No! How did—"

Donovan's eyes shoot daggers at me. He nods toward the exit, then storms out of the room. Oh, shit, what now? Vivi, Corah, and I trade worried glances before rushing after him. When I reach the archway, I turn back toward Yinbi. "You're stuck with the soul you have. Guess you'll have to find a way to live with yourself."

Flavinsky

Flavinsky—Soulid: FLVZK3Y, an infamous soul who tragically, and inexplicably, takes their life after each kirling.

Donovan stomps down the steps to the large black car resembling the one Mudak drove on our last trip to the Fringe. He throws open the front passenger door and growls, "Get in."

I climb inside. "Are you *mad* at me?"

He slams the door and rounds to the driver's side. Vivi and Corah jump into the back seat. Donovan starts the engine and presses hard on the floor pedal. The car screeches onto the empty street.

I grab the handle above the door to keep from falling over. Why is he acting like this? Did he not hear me? "Are you mad—"

"Mad? No." He licks the inside of his cheek and pushes harder on the pedal, making the car accelerate. "I'm fucking *furious*. With all three of you."

"*Us?*" Corah scoffs. "What did we do?"

"You brought her into the Fringe. Without protection. To that maniac's place."

My eyes narrow. "They didn't *bring* me anywhere. We came here together."

"And we're her protection," Vivi says.

"*I'm* her protection. Me." His voice chokes with emotion. "And when you took her away, that agent assured me she'd be safe." He yanks the steering wheel to the right, taking the corner on two wheels. "Then I walk into the business of the most sadistic person I've ever met to find her standing there."

I sink into my seat.

He pounds the steering wheel. "*Dammit*, Carrefour. I didn't hold on to you with every bit of my strength for you to go running around in the open, searching out dangerous criminals. Every bad soul on this planet is hunting you right now, and the rest of the world just heard you died in Guam. You're not even wearing a disguise. Are you *trying* to get yourself killed?"

We barely made it to Yinbi's in time; I wasn't gonna stop to buy chromix on the way. "I'm *trying* to save your life. It's what I do. It's what I've done in every one of my six lives."

Brows furrowed, Donovan looks at me, then out the windshield, then into the mirror. "What the hell is she talking about?"

"Sivon isn't a new soul," Corah says. "Her soulid was deleted from SEIK after her last life."

Donovan huffs and shakes his head. "Now, why the hell would you go and do a thing like that?"

I sit up. "Oh, you just automatically assume I deleted my own soul?"

"Well, didn't you?"

"Yes, but that's not the point."

"*I know*. The point is you keep making decisions that put your life in danger."

I punch my index finger at him. "To *save yours*!"

Vivi leans between the two front seats. "Hey, why don't you pull over? I think you two could use a minute."

Donovan switches pedals, decreasing our speed, and swerves onto a stretch of packed dirt. We're probably five kilometers from town, without another in sight. The second the car stops, I unbuckle and climb out, slamming the door behind me. Donovan does the same and meets me by the rear end.

I settle my hands on my hips, trying to make myself as tall as possible.

Donovan crosses his arms. "Let me get this straight. You are not a new soul, and you have five folies."

"Yes. My soulname was Krest." I tap my foot in the dirt.

"Uh-huh. And you claim you've been trying to save my life. Which one? Flavinsky or Shepherd?"

"*You*, Donovan."

He presses his lips together. "Flavinsky, then."

I sigh, the fight leaving me. "Yes, you are Flavinsky . . . and Ziva was not."

Donovan rubs his mouth and starts pacing. "I knew she wasn't. Dammit, I knew it! You heard me telling everyone. I tried to stop her. . . ." He covers his eyes. "They wouldn't let me in."

I tug his hand down, my eyes welling with tears. "Because they *killed* her. We have reason to believe Flavinsky was murdered in every life."

His face goes ashen. "What?"

While it physically pains me to recount Vivi and Corah's and then Windrose's histories with Flavinsky, he needs to know the truth. He has to hear how many of us believe in him and are doing our very best to save his soul.

Donovan bends over as I tell our tales. By the end, he's crouching in the dirt. "They murdered Ziva because they thought she was me. How am I supposed to live with that?"

"I don't know, Donovan. I can't fully comprehend Crosier's death either. Ziva shouldn't have been Flavinsky. Crosier shouldn't have been in Guam." My voice cracks. "If I'd been smarter, or braver, they'd still be here."

I kick at a rock, then lean against the bumper. "We need to fix SEIK so they'll end up with the right soul and soulmate next time. And we must find who killed Ziva. And who bombed that platform."

He rises to his feet. "I found Crosier. At the bottom of the cliff."

My memories of her rewind and replay. Her kindness on the tarmac when I could barely contain my jealousy, bravely fighting the RAID despite her pacifist lifestyle, patiently answering my questions, radiating gentility and compassion in the glow of the setting sun. Then gone, as quickly and incomprehensibly as Ziva. How is it that people we only know for a few days can make such an impact on our lives? I cover my mouth as a tear slips free.

Donovan catches it with his finger then pulls my head into his stomach. "This will sound awful, but we told the locals Crosier was you. The lie will probably unravel any minute now. We brought her home with us."

Her poor family. Her community. They'll all be devastated.

He sits beside me. "When I met her, I thought there was something wrong with me. I'd waited all that time for my soulmate, and ..." He raises one shoulder. "I think deep down we both knew our match was wrong. Crosier is Shepherd's soulmate, and I'm not Shepherd."

I give him a sad smile. "Maybe she's with Shepherd now."

"I hope so." Donovan hangs his head, and we sit in silence for a long minute.

"Can we go back to your past lives?" he asks. "Why did you delete your soulid from SEIK?"

"I already told you." I shuffle my feet in the dirt.

"You became a new soul to save mine?" Donovan shifts to face me.

My heartbeat picks up, thumping in time to the pulse in his neck. "That's my understanding, yes. I haven't read my Last Letter. Don't even know if I have one."

"But Carrefour, I'm *Flavinsky*. Arguably the worst soul in the world. Why would your soul care about mine?"

I rise to stand in front of him. "First of all, stop calling me Carrefour. I only told you to because I was hurt and jealous. From now on, I'm Sivon. Got it?"

The corners of his lips curl up. "Whatever you want, Sivon."

Warmth spreads through my body. I step between his legs, and his arms circle my waist. "And the reason I care so much should be obvious. It's why my heart races whenever you're near, and my skin tingles when you touch me. It's why, for centuries, you've stubbornly reincarnated a day after each death, and why I'll fight for you until the end of time." I skim my fingers over his cheek. "We belong together. We belong to each other.

"I am yours, Donovan, and you are mine. We are soulmates." Another tear spills down my cheek, but this one from relief. He's here, with me, and my soul recognizes how rare moments like these are for us, how long we've been kept apart.

Donovan wipes my tear with his finger, while one escapes his own eye. His chuckle bears equal hope and pain. "My soulmate.

That explains why you drive me mad with worry." He hugs me to him. "But how is it possible? The world would've known if Flavinsky had a soulmate, and you've had five folies."

"Corah's boyfriend found some strange code on Krest's soulid in an old backup copy of SEIK. It negated the soulmate connection for both of us."

"But that was your old soulid." He visibly deflates. "Your new one would've matched with Flavinsky's at your kirling a couple weeks ago."

"It did." My hands run through his curls, like they've itched to do thousands of times before. "But Windrose decided it'd be too much to handle, finding out I was a new soul and also that my soulmate was Flavinsky, who died only hours before. She hid the match somewhere in the depths of SEIK."

"Sivon." Donovan rises slowly. He slips a hand into my hair. "But how can we trust Windrose? She could've made it up." He pulls me closer, clearly not caring one way or another.

"I was thinking the same thing, but I know of one way to check." Soulmate auras merge together. If I can somehow bring him home with me . . .

"So do I." He focuses on my lips, his hazel eyes pleading for permission.

I tip up my chin. His smile fills me with such happiness that I wish I could pause time, relish this moment for eternity. But when our lips meet, I'm grateful I hold no such powers. I see what he means now. This kiss doesn't just feel good, it feels necessary, like arriving home after centuries of battle.

His lips are warm and soft, and perfectly fit with mine. I don't have to think about what to do or when to breathe. We intuitively fall into sync with one another—caressing, tasting, and exploring. After centuries apart, we reconnect. We remember.

My heart leaps in celebration. My soul dances with joy, painting a swirl of colors across my vision.

Donovan is my soulmate. It's no longer a label, but a feeling, a promise as sure as his arms around me. My heart thunders against my chest, and the little moan he releases makes it burst wide open. I deepen our kiss.

Vivi and Corah cheer from the back seat, making us giggle, but that doesn't stop us. We've waited too long for each other, and our future holds no guarantees. I have a bounty on my head and a warrant out for my soul's arrest. He has a serial killer after him and fifty years of SCAR penalties to serve. We'll need to fight tooth and nail to stay together.

Game on.

Mirovnik

Mirovnik—Soulid: 31R072K, foli 1: chief executive of the Eastern Asian Alliance; foli 2: president of the European Council; foli 3: prime minister of the North American government as head of the Advancement Party.

Back in the car, I fill in Donovan on my past twenty-four hours and tell him about our new powerful allies—agents Hawkshaw and Bukhali. I decide not to reveal Janus's truth. He believed he was protecting me by deleting himself from SEIK, so I should keep his secret in return. But in no way can Janus trust Yinbi to do so. I need to warn Janus about the kind of man he sold his soul to.

"Mirovnik is the one killing me?" Donovan pulls into the parking lot where Vivi and Corah left their hover.

We switch vehicles and rows, Donovan and I taking the back. The quiet of the hover makes it so much easier to think.

"Yes, Mirovnik is targeting you, but I'm not sure why. Can you think of a reason Prime Minister Mirovnik or any of his past lives would hunt you down?"

Donovan scratches his jaw. "I'm not exactly an expert in Flavinsky's past lives, but nothing comes to mind. This is Mirovnik's first life in North America, so it couldn't have anything to do with the General Molemo thing during World War III, right?"

I shake my head, partially to clear out the cobwebs. *The General Molemo thing.* I was married to Molemo a couple of lives ago. My soulmate, Flavinsky, failed to protect Molemo from Ladiron during World War III. That can't be a coincidence.

"Give me a sec." I lean forward, resting my head in my hands.

"Are you okay?" Donovan pulls back my hair.

Corah looks over her shoulder. "She's been doing this all day. Working out some sort of problem. Any second now, she'll probably pop up with some proclamation like 'The prime minister isn't really Mirovnik.'"

"He's not," I say. "Now shut it so I can figure this out."

The hover falls quiet.

But I only need a second to work it out. It's clear as day. "Oh, easy. The prime minister is Ladiron."

Two minutes later, the three of them are still staring at me, slack-jawed.

"If you found that shocking, you should probably sit down for this next one."

Corah tilts her head, lips pressed flat.

I tap a finger against my mouth. "I'm pretty sure the prime minister was also General Molemo for a time."

"Explain," Corah says. "You're about thirty steps ahead of us."

I draw in a deep breath and gather my thoughts. This is gonna get complicated, so I need to break it down piece by piece. "Okay, first, a recap. Krest deleted her soulid, Yinbi switched Flavinsky's and Shepherd's, and he planned to hijack one of ours. SEIK isn't secure. Which means anyone with enough money and depravity can steal whatever soul they want. Enter Ladiron."

I pause, giving them time to digest my summary. "It'll be easier to follow the next part if you have a general outline. Ladiron has jumped souls twice. First by switching places with General Molemo, then stealing Mirovnik's soul."

Vivi turns to face me. "How are you so sure?"

I nod. "Let's start at the beginning. World War III. Ladiron and Flavinsky were friends, both serving under General Molemo in the Coalition Army. Ladiron turned traitor, killing General Molemo, who was under Flavinsky's protection. Then Ladiron and Flavinsky shot each other. That was Flavinsky's only death that wasn't declared a suicide."

Donovan narrows his eyes. "So whatever Ladiron and Flavinsky fought over was enough for Ladiron to kill Flavinsky eleven more times?"

"Seems a bit over the top, but yes, I believe so." I look around the hover. "Still with me?"

They nod.

"Okay, I'll come back to Molemo. Let's fast-forward to November 10, 216. On the same day of Flavinsky's kirling, my soul, Krest, comes out of the Fringe and tries to kill Mirovnik, who was a senator at the time. Since we know Krest's primary objective was to save Flavinsky, I suspect Krest believed Mirovnik was the culprit." I won't get into his evil aura, but that makes sense now as well. The prime minister is the murdering, traitorous Ladiron, not the peace bringer he claims to be.

"Senator Mirovnik 'defended himself' from Krest's attack by choking her to death, so he's certainly *capable* of killing someone. And when I met him for lunch a few days ago, he asked about Flavinsky out of nowhere."

Oh shit. I place my hand on Donovan's knee to steady myself. Was that the "top secret" intel Mirovnik learned during our luncheon? That I was Krest, the soul who once tried to kill him? No wonder he jumped at the chance to send me to Guam. He's probably the one behind the RAID attack and explosion.

Donovan lays his hand over mine. "What's wrong?"

His touch immediately subdues my fear, allowing me to think clearly again. "I'm okay. Just another revelation. But let's stick with one thing at a time." I pull his hand onto my lap, using it as my rock.

"Where was I? Twenty years ago, Krest tried to kill Senator Mirovnik, so she must've believed he was responsible for Flavinsky's deaths. But the real Mirovnik, the one who was chief executive of the Eastern Asia Alliance and the president of the European Council, had no beef with Flavinsky.

"Think about that résumé for a second. If you knew any soul in SEIK was up for grabs, *why wouldn't* you choose a leader with Mirovnik's peacemaker reputation?"

"Yep, called it," says Corah. "The prime minister isn't Mirovnik."

"Exactly. If he *deleted* the real Mirovnik's soulid from SEIK instead of switching them like he did with Molemo, that would've made the real Mirovnik a *new* soul. I bet if we compared soulids against an old server, we'd find a match between the real Mirovnik and Primus, the new soul who became the secretary general of the GCG."

A surge of pride swells in my chest. Krest's research must have given her the idea to become a new soul herself. She knew the senator was power hungry and would try to recruit and exploit any future new souls. Thanks to her brilliant move, I have a disguise better than even a *gallon* of chromix could provide. The prime minister unwittingly welcomed on to his staff the one person who, for centuries, has been intent on bringing him down.

I check their faces. Crap, I've lost them again. "Ignore what I said about Primus. He isn't our concern.

"We need to track the prime minister back to Ladiron. Here's what we know." I hold up one finger. "SEIK can be manipulated for the right price." I raise another. "The real Mirovnik has no connection to Flavinsky." I lift a third. "If the prime minister wanted to steal a soul, Mirovnik would be the perfect candidate." A fourth goes up. "Krest believed Senator Mirovnik was killing Flavinsky." My hand fully opens. "Who was it that first killed and has the best motive to continue killing Flavinsky?"

"Ladiron," they say in unison.

"You've got it." I pull in a relieved breath. "Then we're all in agreement. The traitor who murdered Flavinsky and General Molemo in World War III is currently masquerading as Mirovnik. Now let's go back in time. Who was the most celebrated soul of the war? Practically guaranteed a high-powered position when they returned from the dead?"

"General Molemo," they chorus.

I nod. "General Molemo was Ladiron's stepping stone to Mirovnik. And if you aren't already disgusted, remember that Ladiron was given a life sentence for killing Molemo. So by swapping souls, Ladiron made Molemo serve the sentence for their own murder."

"Fucking monster." Donovan leans into his seat.

I lay a hand on Vivi's shoulder. "Think about it. Doesn't it make sense that the inspirational soul who serves as the head of the Global Civil Liberties Union would be the acclaimed General Molemo, not the traitorous Ladiron?"

Vivi covers her mouth. "*Oh no*, Trevin's *mom* believes she's Ladiron."

"For now," Corah says. "But we will fix this."

I set Donovan's hand on my leg to rub my throbbing temples. "This sequence of events also explains why I married Molemo. Krest knew it wasn't the real Molemo. Keep your friends close and your enemies closer, right? That's the same life I worked with Vivi and Corah, collecting evidence of Ladiron's crimes. We buried it in the ocean, probably because we were about to be discovered, and our plane went down afterward." I splay my hands to the sides. "That's all I've got."

Vivi turns to face me. "Why did we hide our research, though? Why not turn it over to the agency to investigate?"

I work the Carrefour symbol into my palm. "We didn't trust them. How many other bad souls could be masking as high-ranking officials? And maybe we knew someone was coming for us, but we hadn't finished collecting evidence."

The hover goes quiet again. Who can we trust? My circle is pretty small. Mom, Donovan, Vivi, and Corah. They trust Hawkshaw and Bukhali. Ensio has proven himself many times over. Donovan trusts Mudak.

"So how do we prove any of this?" Corah asks.

I run a hand through my hair. "Well, first Corah needs to call her boyfriend and have him look through Ladiron's, Mirovnik's, and Molemo's records for anything suspicious."

"Not my boyfriend," Corah mumbles as she taps his name, but the smile on her face speaks otherwise.

"And Vivi will check in with the agents who are sifting through

Krest's research, see if we can expand our network of trusted souls."

"And you"—I lift Donovan's hand to my lips and kiss it—"are going to ask Mudak if the prime minister thinks I'm dead. Hopefully so, because we need sleep and time to work out a coherent strategy. I'm pretty sure Mirovnik is behind the attacks in Guam." Perhaps the one in the Fringe as well, but that was before his personality change at lunch. Did he have it out for the new soul all this time?

Donovan's lips turn down. "You know I'll have to go public about being Flavinsky, right? Yinbi will find a way to break the news without implicating himself."

"I'm well aware. And if you're arrested to fulfill Flavinsky's sentence, we could find ourselves back to square one, starting the cycle all over again." I hold his hand to my heart. "At least we have several things going for us this time."

"What's that?" he asks.

"We know who's after you. We have NAIA's help. And we have each other." I press a kiss to his fingers. "I like our odds."

NAIC

NAIC—(nack) abbr. The North American Intelligence College.

An hour later, Donovan is called in for questioning regarding my disappearance. They must've figured out Crosier's body isn't me, and since Donovan was the last person to see me alive, he'll likely be surveilled twenty-four seven. As much as we both hate it, we need to split up.

To alleviate our concerns, Vivi and Corah give us companion closed-network trackers. A thin, flexible chip adheres to my back molar and a smaller one hides within my ear crease. We can turn the microphones on and off with a good clench of the teeth and request location updates with three bites in quick succession.

Donovan cups my hands. "Before you do anything dumb, promise me you'll ask yourself whether I'd have an aneurysm over it, and if so, maybe don't do that. Okay?"

"Okay.... Maybe I won't." I wink.

Instead of chuckling at my joke, he looks me over as if he's memorizing my every feature, then kisses me on the forehead before climbing out of the hover. My relative calmness and clarity of thought leave with him. If anyone learns he's Flavinsky, he won't survive the night.

At seven thirty p.m., the White House sends out a correction to their earlier statement about my death in Guam, identifying the deceased as Crosier—C2O54ER, née Clarrah—of the Severed River Fringe.

"*Carrefour is considered missing and endangered. If anyone has information about her whereabouts, immediately contact your local authorities or the North American Intelligence Agency.*"

By eight p.m., I'm passed out on Vivi and Corah's dorm-room couch, the events of the past thirty-six hours finally catching up with me. I startle awake twice in the middle of the night, terrified Donovan's life is in peril only to locate him at his parents' house in Atomdale.

We're all awake by six a.m., gathered around Vivi and Corah's screens. They call out names to Ensio one by one, painstakingly adding to our list of trusted souls while occasionally identifying irregularities, like the deputy director of NAIA, whose promotion to director is expected within the year. Hawkshaw and Bukhali say they'll take care of it.

Ensio discovers dozens of booby traps protecting Kitsune's and Raposa's soulids, put in place by his own past life. Yinbi couldn't have stolen their souls without triggering hundreds of alarm bells worldwide.

But three hours later, we've lost steam. Corah is lying on the couch, staring at her split ends, when out of nowhere, she says, "Cadence."

We turn in our chairs to look at her.

"What's that?" Vivi says.

Corah sits up and tilts her screen. "Ensio, you there?"

Thirty minutes ago, we asked him to research the roster of NASS officers, but he always keeps the line open during his searches.

"Yep. Still here." His smooth tenor pings around the room. "Only found one so far."

"Can you check Cadence?"

Vivi and I exchange sidelong glances.

"Cadence, the *movie star*?" Ensio asks. "Of Cadence and Abernathy?"

"Yep. Has nothing to do with our investigation. Just a hunch." She chews her bottom lip, shaking her head.

Vivi pushes her hands into her hair. "You've gotta be kidding me."

But by now I've caught on too. Abernathy was always the more talented of the pair. And considering their frequent untimely deaths . . . Unreal. I tuck my joined hands under my chin, and we collectively hold our breaths.

Ensio huffs. "Yeah, you're right. The actor we know as Cadence isn't Abernathy's real soulmate. That's . . . some director who died last year."

My stomach bottoms out. Corah drops her head into her hands. I reach for Vivi, but she rushes into the en suite bathroom and shuts the door before erupting into sobs.

It was all an act. Justice's instalove, jumping into Cadence's arms, their passion-filled movies and interviews. I doubt she ever loved Kopar, because if she did, she never would've hurt him like that. Justice was an actress, and she was playing a role the whole time.

Her conversation with Kopar eight years ago and the Cadence and Abernathy soulmate reunion made us constantly doubt our own feelings and those of anyone we cared about, suspecting they'd change their minds in a heartbeat. Love can't survive without trust, and we never trusted anyone enough to let ourselves love.

I run my hands over my arms to abate the sudden chill, wishing I could hold Donovan.

Tears fill Corah's eyes. "Okay. Thanks, Ensio. Back to NASS, then."

"You okay?" he asks.

She releases a staggered breath. "Getting there." She studies his face on the screen. "Ensio?"

"Hmm?"

"In case you didn't already know . . . I love you."

I'm pretty sure that's the first time in eight years she's said those words.

By Saturday morning, our command center has multiplied tenfold. NAIA performs another kirling on me and matches me to Krest's soulid, granting me access to her Last Letter and Foli Journal. We sift through zettabytes of evidence, all of which need to be independently verified.

The most gut-wrenching part of my day is watching Mom's interview on the news. With unrestrained tears and a wobbly voice, she begs anyone with information about my whereabouts to come forward. I pace the room for thirty minutes afterward, in agony for making her worry, looking for a way to ease her suffering without revealing my location.

Amid everything else we have going on, my resulting plan is a bit clumsy, but it might just work.

Vivi calls Mom, and I position myself out of view. She asks all the normal things a friend of a missing girl would, then segues into our carefully scripted question, one she'd never really ask, given the circumstances. "I know you're dealing with a lot, but Corah and I are in disagreement over here, so we're hoping you'll settle a debate. Remember that orange-and-magenta portrait you painted of our joined auras?"

I press my hands to my mouth. *Please, Mom. Just go with it.*

"Of course." Mom sniffles. "Still one of my favorites."

I release a silent breath. Vivi knows better than to look at me.

"Great. So the indigo dot in the center . . . We can't quite recall, but Corah says indigo is safe, and I say indigo means healthy. Which one is it?" Their portrait doesn't have an indigo dot, but I am Mom's little Indigo.

Mom clears her throat. "I see. Actually, it's both?" The last word lilts up, making it into a question.

Vivi laughs and looks off camera. "Both! See Corah? Indigo is safe *and* healthy. We're both right."

Mom chokes out a relieved laugh. "Yes, safe and healthy." She pulls in a deep breath. "It's my favorite color of all."

I blow Vivi a kiss. An indigo aura means nothing of the sort.

Donovan pings my tracker early Sunday morning. He hasn't said much over the past two days, likely worried his house is bugged or his earplant is transmitting data even when it's turned off.

"Morning, Mom," he says. "What are you up to today?"

I sit up on the cot Vivi and Corah pulled into their room for me. Something's wrong. I close my eyes to listen in.

"Afternoon shift at the hospital." Lisabet's reply is muffled. "You?"

"I'm needed for more questioning at two. Then I'm off to the White House around six for the event tonight. Some sort of fundraising ball. Mirovnik is advertising a big announcement. Hopefully that means they've found or have a lead on Carrefour's whereabouts."

More questioning? A ball? What could Mirovnik know?

I crunch my chip to activate the microphone. "Has my location been compromised?"

"Yep, should be an interesting day."

Fuck. We were so careful! I jump up, prepared to wake Vivi and Corah, but they simultaneously stand and hurry over to me.

"How much time do we have?" I ask.

"Anyway, I think I'll go for a run in about fifteen minutes. Wanna come with?"

He's going to flee? My heart plummets to my stomach. They're coming for me in fifteen minutes. If I'm arrested under Krest's warrant, and Donovan was linked to either Flavinsky or helping Krest escape Guam, there'll be no coming back from this.

But it's too dangerous to run. And we're not the criminals here. Why should we be the ones going into hiding? We're so close to verifying my evidence. If I could somehow put myself in the position where I have the upper hand . . .

My lips curl. "No. We're not running. We're gonna beat them at their own game."

I turn to Vivi. "Call Trevin. I need to talk to Ladiron."

"My, my," Raphaela says as Stiletto and I emerge from her bedroom. "What a difference two weeks can make. Look at you!"

Getting away from NAIC undetected was tricky. I snuck out of Vivi and Corah's dorm by donning a holo head of one of their trusted classmates and borrowing her hover. Then five identical hovers, including mine, left the parking deck at the same time, all heading in different directions.

I needed to find someone I trusted who could offer added protection if needed. Not NASS, not NAIA, and not an obvious connection. As far as I know, this is the first life I've known Raphaela. She didn't hesitate to take me in.

I look down at my stunning ivory gown, off-the-shoulder with a steep plunge to my navel. My scarlet red heels counter my youth, giving me added height and a much-needed boost in confidence.

"Thanks, Raphaela." My shaky voice betrays me.

Stop stressing. The plan will work. It must.

Not knowing if Donovan is safe only makes this harder. We weren't sure where the leak came from, so Vivi and Corah recommended I turn off my tracker. That means I'm totally cut off here. My specs are still in Guam. And we have to assume Vivi and Corah are being watched, so they can't call either.

My fingers trace the bottom of the Carrefour Diamond necklace—*my* Carrefour Diamond—entrusted to the safekeeping of the Smithsonian until whoever held the security key came forward to claim it. That code was in Krest's Foli Journal, along with her other secrets.

The weight of the diamond presses against my chest, along with the burden of my past lives. I'm doing this for them. For Donovan. For us. *Protect your heart.*

The door chime buzzes. Raphaela checks her security cameras and nods. "All good."

With butterflies rattling my stomach, I open the door and am immediately engulfed in a hug. I laugh. "It's nice to meet you too."

Carrefour

carrefour—(CARE-eh-for) n. A crossroads.

Sunday, September 9, 236 A.K.—The White House, Washington, CD

Ladiron and I wait until all the guests arrive to make our entrance, arm in arm. As soon as I'm through the doors, I reactivate my tracker and bite down three times in quick succession.

"Donovan is seventy meters away. In the east wing of the White House."

Okay, good. He's here. I hold my head high as we round the corner. It takes only one startled shout to draw everyone's attention our way. After a few seconds of stunned silence, the guests break into wild applause.

I knew they'd be dressed this way, but my heart stutters nonetheless. Every attendee wears either a red gown or black suit. They surround Prime Minister Mirovnik like the very embodiment of his aura. I can't tell if we just walked into a firestorm or hell. The latter, I decide. But tonight, hell is *my* dominion.

Janus reaches me first, pulling me into an embrace. "You're alive. I can't believe it." He makes a sound that's part chuckle, part sob, then takes me by the shoulders and steps back. "Let me get a look at you. Are you hurt?"

"Never better," I say, beaming at him. Like the moment we first met, the room sharpens into focus.

Because he made daily pleas for my safe return, I knew Janus escaped the explosion unscathed, but it's good to see him again all the same. I just wish I didn't have to fully upend his world tonight. That's the only part of my plan I regret.

The prime minister's approach cuts off Janus's next question.

"Carrefour, Ladiron, how absolutely astonishing to see you both tonight." Mirovnik places Ladiron's hand on the arm of his red tuxedo and turns to face the crowd.

Just as I knew he would, he pretends *this* is his promised announcement. "Distinguished guests, our Carrefour is safe and sound. Please join me, Ladiron, and Janus in celebrating this extraordinary news!"

Whistles and cheers erupt around us, while drones assemble above. A string quartet begins playing a waltz, and the attendees step toward the walls, clearing an opening on the floor. Janus and Mirovnik lead us into the center.

I affix a smile to my face as Janus presents me to the room. As I turn, my eyes scan the perimeter, where NASS agents in white dress uniforms stand at attention. No Donovan. But the tracker said he was in the east wing, and I'm sure the Secret Service is stationed all over the building.

"May I have this dance?" Janus asks.

I hesitate, wondering if I should execute my plan now. But a quick dance to suss out how Mirovnik was acting the past few days couldn't hurt. "I'd love to."

I raise my arms into position, and Janus pulls me close. Mirovnik and Ladiron follow our lead.

"Am I dreaming or are you really here?" Janus says, sweeping his eyes over my face.

"I'm sorry for the shock. Kitsune and Raposa took me into hiding until we were sure it was safe."

His eyes bulge. "Kitsune and Raposa? I heard they died from an explosion in Indostralia."

NAIA has allowed that rumor to propagate while they investigate the explosion and review our evidence. As a whole, the agency has been incredibly supportive of all three of us over the past few days. We wouldn't have made it this far without NAIA's help.

"They're okay. I've been at the Intelligence College with them this whole time."

Janus frowns. "You were so close. I wish I'd known." He presses me to him. "So were they able to access the data they found? Did they learn anything about Krest?"

I sigh. "Unfortunately, the device they retrieved from the ocean blew up with their copter. They're pretty heartsick about it." It's not that I don't trust Janus, but I could put our investigations or lives at risk by revealing the truth.

"I don't blame them. But I must admit I'm relieved." He looks left and right, then whispers in my ear. "I hope this means you've reconsidered turning yourself in. Maybe now you don't have to."

This much I can give him. "Yes, that plan is no longer on the table."

He closes his eyes and inhales. "What a relief."

The melody ends before I can ask about Mirovnik. Janus lowers me into a dip and kisses my jaw to the delight of the onlookers. I hold back a wince. Oh gosh, he's gonna hate me after tonight. He passes me off to Mirovnik and sweeps Ladiron to the other side of the room.

Terrain—dance floor. Vehicle—secrets. Our game begins.

"Welcome home, Sivon." The prime minister's smile holds a conflagration of politeness, distrust, and pure evil.

Pretty weak first move.

"Let's stick with Carrefour. It's more professional, don't you think?" Point: me.

His grin widens. "Of course. Carrefour it is." He nods at the crowd, not having the decency to look me eye to eye. "I hope it goes unsaid how very relieved we are to see you again. You had us all quite worried."

"Yes, well, after the explosion, I wasn't sure who I could trust. And at least I didn't return empty-handed." I tip my head to Ladiron. Another point for me.

"And I'm grateful indeed. I knew I made the right decision by hiring you." His breath smells strongly of peppermint, tickling my nose. "As much as I wish I could repay you, I'm afraid I have some bittersweet news to share."

My mind flips through the millions of revelations I've had over the past couple of days. What does he think he's going to surprise me with? "Oh yeah, what's that?"

He leans closer. "Our intelligence officers apprehended one of North America's most wanted criminals last night."

My heart skips a beat. Flavinsky? But no, Flavinsky isn't a criminal, and Mirovnik still thinks Ziva was Flavinsky. "But that's great news, not bittersweet at all."

Mirovnik's lips twitch. "To be sure. He goes by the soulname Yinbi and was kirling children in the Fringe."

My feet stumble. "Kirling children?" Shit, this isn't good. Yinbi knows Donovan is Flavinsky.

"Sickening, I know." Mirovnik gracefully spins me around. "We received the anonymous tip from a woman in the Fringe. She claimed Yinbi kirled her son fourteen years ago and told her the boy was Flavinsky."

Bile rises in my throat. Yinbi didn't pay Donovan's mom's ransom, so she turned him in. I sweep the sea of guests and white uniforms, hoping to spot Donovan. *Where is he?* I gnash my teeth three times.

"Donovan is located two kilometers away, heading southeast on Pennsylvania Avenue."

Where's he going? Or is he being taken away? Cold dread seeps into my veins.

Mirovnik nods. "Based on the woman's tip, we had SEIK analysts do some digging into Ziva's kirling. Seems someone preemptively entered Ziva's DNA on Flavinsky's record, artificially linking the two."

Don't panic. He only knows half of the equation. They don't have evidence that could point to Donovan . . . unless Yinbi implicates himself and shares the truth. Perhaps Mirovnik's "bittersweet news" is just that Ziva, who he knows was my friend, wasn't Flavinsky. I sure as hell better act like this is news to me. And quick.

I blink rapidly, like I'm trying to digest everything. "Are you saying Ziva wasn't really Flavinsky?" I force my chin to quiver.

"I'm afraid she wasn't." He tightens his grip. "The news was upsetting for me as well." He spins me again. "Even more so when Yinbi finally confirmed who the real Flavinsky is, only minutes before you walked into the room tonight."

My eyes snap to his. *No.*

"Your recent bodyguard, Shepherd. Can you believe he'd do something like that to his own sister? I sent him straight off to prison."

I come to a halt. Donovan. I need to get to Donovan. I try to tug my hands free, but Mirovnik's tighten, refusing to release me. The more I struggle, the wider his sneer grows.

He leans closer and whispers, "That's where you'll be heading tonight as well. Yinbi and I are longtime associates. Gave him a little incentive to tell me if the soul who tried to kill me ever popped up again."

I stop struggling. *Focus, Sivon.* He's confessing.

Mirovnik presses me against him. "Deleted yourself from SEIK, huh? You must've known I'd be waiting for you. And you would've gotten away with it if Yinbi hadn't hacked into the tell-all Last Letter of my burdensome nephew."

I clamp down on my tracker to activate the microphone and allow my jaw to hang open as if I'm in shock. *Talk to me, Donovan. Let me know you're okay.*

"It's a shame," Mirovnik says. "The RAIDs should've taken out both your worthless souls at once. Impossible to find good help these days."

Mirovnik ordered the attack in Guam after all. I yank my arms free as furious tears spill onto my cheeks. "You heartless, evil bastard."

The music stops, and a hush falls over the room.

"Sivon, why are you at the White House? Get out.... Shit, no!" Donovan's voice grows muffled, then disappears. What's happening to him? My pulse skyrockets. But I can't leave now. If I proceed with my plan, I can save Donovan and bring down Mirovnik at the same time.

Before I have the chance to speak, Mirovnik steps forward, commanding everyone's attention. "Friends, I'm afraid I have some shocking news. Earlier today, I received confirmation that this woman here tricked us all into believing she was a new soul. She's actually Krest, the very criminal who attempted to murder me twenty years ago."

Gasps rise around the room, followed by a chorus of shouting and conversation.

"It's not true! He's *lying*." I spin around, trying to get their attention. "Listen to me! I have proof."

They can't hear me. Or won't. I turn to Janus. His eyes hold lifetimes of helpless sorrow.

Help, I mouth, but he seems to be frozen in shock.

Mirovnik motions to two NASS agents. "Gentlemen, if you will."

It's now or never. *Protect your heart. Trust your instincts. Seize your power.*

I yank my necklace off, twist the platinum dial three quarters to the right and one to the left, then press the diamond and throw it onto the ballroom floor. A second later, my arms are pulled behind my back.

A three-meter-tall holo shoots up from the gem. The entire room comes to a standstill. My chest heaves up and down as the footage begins playing.

A younger, fitter Mirovnik stands in the doorway of a hotel room, smiling at the person recording him. He runs a hand over his platinum-blond hair. *"Come on in."*

"We hit it off so well last night, I couldn't resist reaching out for a private audience." We can't see Krest, but her voice is sultry and

mature. By my calculations, she was thirty-seven when this was recorded, a couple years younger than Senator Mirovnik at the time.

He chuckles, twirls her into the room, and shuts the door. When he pulls her close, static erupts from the microphone, suggesting she wore the bug in place of a shirt button. The holo goes dark until Krest steps out of his arms.

"I was hoping we could talk. . . ." It's impossible to miss the tremor in her voice.

"Okay." It's impossible to miss the annoyance in his.

Beside me, the prime minister stalks up to the holo. "What the hell is this? AI-generated hogwash."

He raises his foot to stomp on the carrefour diamond, but Janus pulls him back.

"NAIA has already verified the authenticity of this footage," I state for the room.

Agents Bukhali and Hawkshaw step forward and flash their badges, nodding in acknowledgment. Where the hell did they come from?

On the holo, Krest perches on the bed. *"That's why I asked Cigacious to introduce us."*

I researched the soulname *Cigacious* immediately after first watching this. They weren't listed in SEIK under any possible spelling, but Ensio found them on a backup server.

In foli 1, Cigacious worked in military intelligence during World War III. Foli 2—Belarussian Foreign Intelligence. Foli 3—director of the South American Intelligence Agency. And foli 4—lived in the Salt Flat City Fringe.

Cigacious is Janus. And our two souls have orbited each other in every life, just as Janus said and our auras suggest. Not my soulmate, but almost as closely linked.

"*I want to talk about Flavinsky,*" Krest says.

Senator Mirovnik sits in the desk chair with wide-spread legs. "*What about Flavinsky?*"

"*I didn't give you my real name when we met. I've always gone by the soulname Krest.*"

Mirovnik's mouth falls open. He eyes her up and down, slowly dropping his elbows to his knees. "*You're Krest?*"

"*Yes.*"

"*Well, no wonder we hit it off last night. We were together during World War III. I proposed to you the night you died.*"

When I first heard this revelation, the final puzzle piece snapped into place. Ladiron and Flavinsky were not only at odds because of the Molemo betrayal, but over me. Sounds like a foolish reason to kill someone, but crimes of passion are a tale as old as time.

Krest clears her throat. "*Yes, I figured that out. You're actually Ladiron, the traitor who killed General Molemo.*"

At the ensuing murmurs around us, Prime Minister Mirovnik lunges for the necklace. Janus beats him to it, but the holo stops playing when his fingers curl around the gem. Hawkshaw and Bukhali slap handcuffs onto the prime minister's wrists.

Over the last minute, the Secret Service agents stepped away from the walls, worked their way through the stunned guests, and surrounded the five of us, forming a circle of white inside embers and ashes. I am the cross at the center, the end of the road for Ladiron's treachery.

The din of the crowd grows louder, but we haven't reached the most important part. I raise my voice to command their attention. "That's not the end of it." I nod at Janus. "Open your hand."

He studies me for a second, prompting doubts that he'll run off with the necklace. But then his palm opens, and the holo shoots up again, resuming the footage. I swallow hard, knowing what's coming and also fearing it.

Senator Mirovnik breaks into throaty laughter. *"Maybe Cigacious isn't such a prick after all. He delivered Krest straight to me."* He ogles her again. *"Holy shit."*

"About Flavinsky—"

The senator rolls his eyes. *"It's always fucking Flavinsky with you. What is it? Spit it out."*

"I came to make a deal. Spare her life this time, and you can h-have me . . . forever."

His lips twist up. *"You think I want you?"* He laughs maniacally. *"You think I've killed that rat bastard for two hundred years because I wanted their soulmate?"* He slaps his leg. *"Ha! That is rich."*

Now the world knows the truth. Flavinsky never died by suicide and shouldn't have a sentence. I clench my jaw three times.

"Donovan is located 6.4 kilometers away, at the CD penitentiary."

My knees tremble. They need to release him from custody. I try shrugging free of the agent holding my arms, but he won't loosen his grip. Does he still think I'm the murderer here?

On the holo, Senator Mirovnik rises and stalks toward Krest. *"I've already had you. Back when I was Molemo. And believe me, the only joy I got out of it was keeping you two scheming, traitorous souls apart. No, no, no. The only thing I want now, my dear, is the sweet satisfaction of knowing you'll never be together."*

Never together. And he's succeeding again, even as I make my winning move. If I can't get Donovan out of the penitentiary, he won't survive the night, just like his other lives, just like Ziva.

Krest's tears of frustration mirror mine. *"F-fine. I won't be with Flavinsky. Ever. You can stop killing them. I'll tell my soul to stay away, invent some lies about them."*

"Aw, that does sound lovely. What a perfect solution." Mirovnik slaps Krest across the face. I feel the sting as if it were my own.

A woman next to me cries out. Others cover their mouths in horror.

"Turn it off. Turn it off now!" Prime Minister Mirovnik shouts.

Agents Hawkshaw and Bukhali begin leading him from the room. They've already seen this footage, and Mirovnik was there. He knows what he did.

Senator Mirovnik pulls a screen from his pocket. *"Why does everyone underestimate me? I have a proven track record of success. Do you think just anyone could step into Molemo's and Mirovnik's shoes?"* He shakes his head. *"When I set my mind to something, I always follow through. Your darling Flavinsky? You're too late, my dear. She's already dead."* He holds up his screen, showing the dead body of Flavinsky's foli 11.

"No!" Krest's sobs echo my own. So many losses.

Senator Mirovnik smiles wickedly. *"I don't like owing Cigacious, but I might have to thank him for this."* He swipes a tear from Krest's cheek and licks it. *"Mmm . . . vintage 216. What a* fine *year this is turning out to be."*

Krest leaps toward the door but lands with a thud on her stomach. The holo goes black again, but Mirovnik's cheery voice rings crystal clear. *"Do you know how much fun it is, inventing new ways for Flavinsky to die?"*

Krest screams in frustration, rocking her body, eventually flipping over. The senator straddles her middle and grabs her throat. His face glows as red as his tuxedo tonight, his grin diabolical.

"My favorites are the painful ones. A little retribution for stealing my girl in foli 1."

Krest pushes against his arms, clawing for breaths until she resigns herself to her fate. She knows she must die at Mirovnik's hands. She knows his confession is uploading to her necklace, already stowed away at the Smithsonian. She knows she'll return a powerful new soul, as arranged before heading to Mirovnik's room.

She'll time her rebirth perfectly, when her teammates are in position—the pawns, bishops, knights, rooks—all eager to take down the evil king. The queen will sacrifice herself to save her own, to protect her heart. Next time will be their time. Yes, Krest will lose this life, but she's playing the long game. She's playing to win.

But if I don't get out of here in the next few minutes, I'll again fail at our primary goal. I must save Donovan.

Krest's gags can be heard for thirty long seconds before Janus closes his fist. The footage doesn't end there. The bug continued to record five more hours, including Mirovnik cutting himself with a knife, wiping his prints clean, and folding Krest's hand around the weapon. But the world has seen enough, and if they didn't, they can watch it in my interview with Ujjwala, recorded this afternoon and scheduled to run every hour until voting ends on Wednesday.

The NASS guard finally releases me, and I push through the circle of uniforms to dash for the door. Why hasn't Donovan said anything else over his mic?

Janus intercepts me, holding out my necklace. "Carrefour, that was ... incredible. I'm in absolute awe."

I shove the necklace into my pocket. "Janus, I need your help. It's an emergency."

He blinks several times. "Yeah, of course. Anything for you."

"How fast can you get me to the CD penitentiary?"

Incap

incap—n. Slang term for a targeted incapacitator, which delivers an electric shock capable of immobilizing humans for one to three minutes.

We climb aboard the prime minister's copter, Janus taking the navigator seat. As we're buckling in, three NASS agents run toward us.

"Carrefour!" Mudak shouts across the lawn.

Janus enters our destination on the console. "Should we wait for them?"

I make a split-second decision. "No. We don't have time." Mudak's soul was clean, but I can't say the same for the other two.

The door closes, and the copter lifts. Mudak frantically waves her hands. Just as we shoot forward, I realize I should've recruited her help to get Donovan released. Shit! How long will it take a judge to commute his sentences?

You'll make it in time, Sivon. We're only a few minutes away.

Janus pushes his hands through his hair. "I'm still in shock. You're alive? My uncle is Flavinsky's murderer? I can't believe it."

"I know how you feel. It's been a whirlwind few days." *Can't we go any faster?* "I guess you'll have some damage control to do. Won't be long until Yinbi tells everyone he erased your soul, or NAIA figures it out themselves."

"You didn't tell them?"

I turn to face him, brows drawn. "Why would I? You're one of the most upstanding souls I've ever met. But it was easy for me to figure out you were Cigacious. I doubt intelligence is far behind."

Janus smiles. "I do love you, Carrefour. Your brilliance, your heart. Only you would think of someone else at a time like this." His thumb skims my cheek. "I don't deserve you, but I promise to spend the rest of my days trying."

I rest my head against the seatback. How do I tell him I don't feel the same without ruining our friendship? "Janus—"

"But I've already figured out how to spin the new soul thing." He lowers his hand to take mine. "I'll tell them I did the same as you, deleted my soulid for intelligence gathering. My past lives are a testament to my character and experience."

I nod, filling my lungs. "That's really smart, Janus."

A corner of his lips turns up. "You don't have to sound so surprised. We're practically soulmates."

Practically. But not. Janus is wonderful. Anyone would be lucky to share his affections, but I can't string him along, treat him as some sort of consolation prize if something happens to . . .

I glance out the window and slowly withdraw my hand. We're approaching the prison, surrounded by a blue electromagnetic dome.

Donovan, please stay alive. You're the one I want.

The copter's intercom snaps on. "Permission to land denied. CD penitentiary copterpad occupied. Rerouting to the closest available, one block away."

I groan and clutch my stomach.

Janus lays a hand on my shoulder. "Hey, it's okay. We're gonna be fine. No matter what happens."

My neck prickles. I never told Janus why I needed to get to the prison. He never asked.

I close my eyes, partly to cover for my sudden unease, but mostly to make it easier to focus. Janus may have learned Donovan is Flavinsky from Mirovnik, but could he also know Donovan is my soulmate? It certainly seems like it based on his lack of questions surrounding our urgent departure. But how?

Yinbi. Fuck, of course. But why would Yinbi share that information with Janus? And how long has Janus known?

When I asked Janus why he hadn't turned me in that day in the Fringe, he said, *How could I do that to you, the soul I'm meant to be with?* If Janus believed we were meant to be together, and he'd already asked Yinbi to make him a new soul, why not ask Yinbi to make us soulmates as well? Bile scorches my throat.

The worst part is knowing I would've *believed* Janus, would've been relieved to call someone my own when the person I ached for had just walked out the door. I would've used our matching auras as confirmation, inventing some "new soul" excuse as a reason they didn't merge like real soulmates. Shivers rock my body. I would've pretended to love Janus for the rest of my life, playing the part I was given. Just like Abernathy.

But when Yinbi tried to make Janus my soulmate in SEIK, he must've seen I already have one. Flavinsky. And because of Windrose, Yinbi knew Donovan was the real Flavinsky, so he knew Donovan was my soulmate. And Yinbi, likely motivated by money, told Janus.

My stomach turns. Janus has known everything since the

Fringe—that I am Krest, Donovan is Flavinsky, and Donovan is my soulmate. *Holy shit.*

"We're landing." Janus begins massaging my shoulder. "On the ground in thirty seconds."

I nod as nausea builds, his touch reminding me of the day on the patio when we first kissed.

We have an audience.

Janus *knew* Donovan was watching. He kissed me again in the bedroom, rubbing it in even further. He *invited* Donovan's presumed soulmate on our trip, *insisted* they visit Two Lovers Point with us. That's not love; it's cruelty bordering on obsession.

And I *let* him. Trusted him. Kept his secret. I cover my mouth, rocking forward and back until the copter comes to a stop. The instant the doors lift, I kick off my heels, pull up my skirt, and run.

Run, Sivon. Run like your lives depend on it.

Janus calls my name, but I focus on the glowing blue dome, breaking into a sprint.

He's your mirror image, Mom said. *Separate but equal opposites.*

The sharpening of my senses when he's around, my adrenaline rush while playing Chessfield with him, maybe even my nausea at first meeting him. My soul recognized the truth this whole time; I just misinterpreted the signals. We *are* playing a game, but we're not on the same side. Janus is my opponent, my enemy. And also, it seems, my stalker.

He closes the distance by the time I reach the gate.

"Janus." The guard on duty shakes his hand as I fight to catch my breath. "Twice in one day?" He holds a fingerprint scanner toward us. "Can't say I'm surprised, considering our newest inmate. You love meeting the notorious ones, don't you?"

I press a trembling finger to the pad. His prisoner outreach . . . Did I misjudge that as well? If I've recruited Vivi, Corah, Donovan, Crosier, Mom, Raphaela, and a host of other good souls to my team, could Janus be doing the opposite? Assembling a network of criminals?

He said he deleted his soulid to protect me, that he'd do anything for me. Does that include *killing my soulmate*? The back corners of my mouth twinge. *You will not get sick, dammit. Donovan needs you.*

The guard checks his screen. "All right, head on in. They'll help you out inside." A door-size section of the dome dims by half. "Just don't back up unless you wanna get zapped."

I dart through, focusing on the double doors of the enormous granite building, eerily resembling the Semyon Kirlian Institute. Only fifty meters to go.

I'm here, Donovan. Hold on!

Janus catches up and takes my hand. I'm about to tug it free when the front doors open, and a gurney floats through.

I stop in my tracks.

No.

A white sheet covers the person on top. The body on top.

No.

One of the two paramedics following behind presses his earlobe. "Flavinsky en route. Alert the morgue."

NOOO!

I collapse to the ground, breaking into sobs. Donovan. *"DONOVAN!"*

I lost. I failed him again. *But we were so close!*

No, I don't believe it. I *won't* believe it until I see him for myself.

I punch my fist into the ground, then stagger to my feet and chase after the floating corpse of my soulmate. I reach the paramedics just before they load him into the waiting copter.

"Ma'am. What are you—"

Janus pulls them away, introducing himself, then asking questions. The ringing in my ears drowns them out.

My hand hovers over the white sheet, fresh tears coating my cheeks. It's not him. It can't be. With foolish hope, I fold down the cloth. My soul wails in pain. His face is bloated and purple, almost unrecognizable. But his black curls . . . his curls.

"Noooo!" I throw myself on him. "Donovan, wake up. Wake up." His body is so cold, lifeless.

No. He can't be dead. I rise back up and begin chest compressions. "Please, Donovan. I won't lose you again. *Please, please, please.* Come *back!*"

Tears drip from my face onto his. *Pump. Pump. Pump.*

"Donovan is located five meters away, to your right."

I freeze. What was . . . ?

Trembling, I sniffle once, then gnash my teeth three more times.

"Donovan is located four meters away, to your right."

Chills spread through my body. I look down at his face, splattered with my tears. Tears that left skin-colored trails through the purple.

Stop sweating, or your makeup will melt, Lepota warned before my debut.

His purple skin . . . is *chromix*? Heart racing, I clench my teeth three more times, easy because they're already chattering. *Please.*

"Donovan is located to your immediate right."

A warm hand settles on my right shoulder. "Breathe," he whispers in my ear.

I choke out a sob, then inhale. Pine. Donovan.

In disbelief, I cross my left hand to my shoulder. Invisible fingers lace with mine. I hang my head. He's here . . . but he's not. I'd suspect he was a ghost if it wasn't for the tracker. Doubt he'd take that into the afterlife.

One of the paramedics returns and frowns sympathetically. "I'm so sorry for your loss." He covers the body double and nudges the gurney onto the copter.

Donovan is free, invisible, and has a lookalike dead body. He couldn't have orchestrated this by himself.

"Vivi and Corah?" I whisper.

"Boo." The word tickles my left ear.

I roll my eyes. Had to be Corah.

Okay, Donovan is alive. They're all safe. I take a stabilizing breath. Then what the hell is going on? Why the charade? Why didn't they just release Donovan like any other wrongly accused victim?

Because if Janus is our real threat, that would solve nothing. He would kill both me and Donovan at the first opportunity, just to reset the board.

Janus likes collecting his players, making his calculated moves, dodging his opponents.

He doesn't love me. He loves the game.

His excitement over Vivi and Corah's treasure hunt . . . It's almost like he wanted them to find their plunder to give them hope, then blew up their copter. I bend over, clutching my stomach. He even asked me tonight if they retrieved the data. Ugh, I've been so *blind*!

But if the USB had something on Cigacious, we would've found it by now.

"He's coming," Donovan whispers.

Shit. I need more time to work up a strategy. It's clear they need me to get a confession out of Janus, but how? And for what crime?

The second paramedic climbs on board, and the copter lifts off.

"Stay," I exhale over my shoulder as Janus approaches with arms outstretched.

Donovan rests a hand on my back, just above my dress. His warmth centers me, bolsters my confidence. His palm remains there as Janus pulls me in for a hug. I allow my eyes to lose focus and jaw to slacken, pretending to be in shock. My arms remain at my sides.

"I'm so very sorry, Carrefour. I can't imagine how hard it must be losing your bodyguard like that."

My bodyguard. Ha. He must've finally realized he hadn't asked me why we were here.

I bite my tongue. Try waiting him out for a bit, see if he implicates himself in whatever this is. Why didn't Donovan tell me over the mic? Was a heads-up too much to ask?

"The paramedics said they found seeds in Shepherd's hand. Identified them as oleander seeds. Aren't those the same ones that killed his sister?"

Janus was here earlier today. Did he give someone the seeds for Donovan? I bet he thought the matching suicides would be poetic.

"He must've carried them since Ziva's death for a quick escape in case anyone found out he'd saddled his own sister with Flavinsky's soul."

The hand on my back tenses. *It's okay, Donovan. I've got this.*

"Ziva was murdered by your uncle."

Janus rubs his mouth. "In Flavinsky's previous lives, perhaps, but I heard Shepherd was at SKI the night of Ziva's death. He could've found a way to hide the seeds in her food."

Tears of rage spring into my eyes. "*Mirovnik* murdered Ziva."

I take a step toward him, punching a finger into his chest. "And *you* murdered Shepherd."

Okay, I guess my instincts weren't a fan of the wait and see approach. Attack it is.

Janus chokes out a startled laugh. "Carrefour, what are you—?"

"You did this. When you were here earlier today. You gave the seeds to one of the inmates, one of your new buddies."

Janus's mouth opens. "I'm here almost every day. That doesn't make me a mur—"

Rapid fire, Sivon. Don't give him time to invent excuses.

"You've killed before. Or at least attempted to. You blew up Kitsune and Raposa's copter in their last lives so they wouldn't implicate you."

"Implicate—?"

"You were the director of the South American Intelligence Agency at the time. Their copter went down immediately after hiding their research. Tell me, why would SAIA agents need to hide their research unless the director himself was corrupt?" The revelation crosses my lips as soon as I figure it out.

Searing hatred replaces every warm thought I've ever felt for Janus. He killed my best friends once and tried to do it again. The creature inside me claws its way out of hell, fully prepared for battle.

He backs away, looking around. "Stop, Carrefour."

"Tell me why you really deleted your soul from SEIK. It wasn't to protect me from Krest's arrest warrant. You only told me that so you'd have something over me, so you could play the hero. You wanted me under your thumb, to control me. You wanted to seize my power."

... you have a lot of power. More than you could've ever imagined. More than anyone in this world.

Raphaela's words pour into my brain, pushing open windows and doors I didn't know I'd closed.

I gasp. "*You're* the anonymous Advertitude buyer."

Janus shakes his head. "No."

"The threats. The insults. Creature. That was all you." We need evidence. "I bet if we cross-reference the Advertitude records with your bank accounts, we'll find a connection. If you didn't pay for them, you arranged for someone else to." Hopefully whoever's listening is taking notes.

Janus points his finger at me. "Be careful, Carrefour. You're crossing into territory we can't come back from. I didn't even *know* you then. I didn't know my own soul."

Be careful. *Son of a bitch*. He said the same thing during our first campaign stop. "Be careful, huh? What you meant was, don't steal my thunder. Stay in your place. You worked for years to ensure you'd follow in your uncle's footsteps, then along comes a new soul who could sweep the rug out from under you."

I pull back my shoulders, drawing energy from Donovan's touch. Fuck, this feels good. "And like your uncle, you tried to use me to boost your image, not by employing me, but by dating me."

My lips curl into a sneer. Here comes another revelation. "The guards who disappeared in Wilmington, the almost kidnapping in the Fringe. You wanted to scare me *just enough*"—I pinch my thumb and index finger—"to not run for office. And consequently gave yourself the opportunity to play my knight in shining armor."

A tear runs down his cheek. "That was before I knew how much you meant to me."

My hands form fists. That's one confession. Intimidation, maybe attempted kidnapping. It's not enough. Donovan taps my back twice, encouraging me to continue. *I know, my love. Stay with me.*

"Let's talk about that. You hired Yinbi to do your kirling early, got access to your Last Letter, and paid him to delete your soulid. You *claimed* you loved me so much you wanted to protect me from murder charges. But I bet jealousy brought you to Yinbi with another goal in mind. Not to spin potentially bad results, but to become a new soul as well, even out your odds a little. That kind of power would be worth an entire inheritance, wouldn't it?"

Janus's chin trembles as he looks down his nose at me. At least he's stopped denying my accusations.

"Admit it."

He lifts his shoulders. "So what." His voice cracks. "Wanting to be powerful does not make me a bad person. Every politician who ever lived enjoyed the power. You . . ." He runs a hand under his nose. "You do too. We're one and the same. Don't even deny it."

I huff out a laugh. "With one big difference . . ." I step closer. "I've never killed for it. You took down Kitsune and Raposa's copter before and tried to do it again."

"They'll come back," he says, as if he was sending them off on a weekend getaway. "They always come back. That's how this all works, isn't it?" He circles a hand. "We live. We die. We live. We die."

My throat swells with disgust. "You think reincarnation makes people *expendable*?" I scoff. "Wow. I can't believe I ever thought you loved me. You don't even know the meaning of the word."

"You're wrong, Carrefour. If I didn't love you, this wouldn't hurt so much." He pounds his chest. "I wouldn't try this hard. I wouldn't have begged you to change your mind about turning yourself in. We belong together."

I stagger back. "It was *you*." My eyes fill with angry tears. "You arranged for the explosion in Guam. You killed Crosier. You tried to kill us all." Donovan's hand slips from my back.

"I didn't *want* to! If anyone learned you weren't a new soul, it would've cast doubt on me too. I tried to talk you out of it."

"*You asked if I was sure!* That's *hardly* trying." I start pacing. "Crosier was still in the hover, and you sent her over. She was *innocent*, Janus." Tears spill down my cheeks. "*Why?* Why would you do that to her?"

"You won't like my answer," he says through gritted teeth.

I come to a stop, nostrils flaring. "You knew she'd be a distraction."

He lifts his hands. "If he had to pick one to save, which would it be? His fake soulmate or the real one?"

Janus killed Crosier. Not in some former life, but this one. Janus is a murderer, a serial killer, and he must be stopped. This ends now.

The collective sorrows of my past lives coalesce into a war cry as I barrel toward him. Janus pulls an incap out of his suit jacket, aims, and gets thrown to the ground by an invisible force. He manages to hit me anyway.

I look down at my stomach and fight to pull in my next breath. No, not an incap. Incaps don't make you bleed.

Suncture

suncture—(SUHNK-chur) n. A combination suture and tincture for treating puncture wounds.

Monday, September 10, 236 A.K.—Ashburn, VA

Heaven is a swirl of colors and smells like home. I'm just annoyed I can still feel pain in the afterlife. What's up with that?

My head pulses under relentless waves of agony. I groan and raise my hands to my temples. If this is what being dead feels like, no wonder we choose to be reborn.

"Welcome back."

Whoa. Okay, so there is a God, and he sounds a lot like Donovan.

I tighten my abs to sit up and nearly pass out as red-hot flames sear my insides. I hiss and fall back again. Not dead. Just shot in the stomach.

"Take it easy. The doctor said the pain will recede in a few hours."

"*Hours?* Shit, Donovan. I'm not sure I can bear the next few seconds." I prove my point by breaking into full-body shivers.

He glides the desk chair he's sitting in along my bed, tucking blankets around me as he goes. "She said the shivers will pass too. A normal side effect of the suncture." When he reaches my head, he leans over, sliding one arm above me to lay his cheek on the pillow.

I pull in his familiar, comforting scent and take a moment to appreciate the fact that we're still here, together and alive. "You brought me home?"

He dips his chin. "The crowd outside cleared out after they learned you weren't a new soul. And you've been saying you wanted to go home for weeks. Asked me again last night at the hospital."

"Did I?" I try to cobble together the memory but must've buried it under kilometers of ocean water. "I don't remember anything after the gunshot. How long ago was that?"

"About twelve hours." He closes his eyes. "I'm so sorry. If I'd been a split second faster . . ."

"Don't do that." I raise the hand between us to scratch the hairs at the top of his neck. "It was entirely Janus's fault. All of it. You have nothing to be sorry for."

"I almost lost you."

"I thought I *did* lose you." Another tremor shakes my body as the memory of the gurney flashes across my vision.

Donovan strokes my head. "Seeing you so upset tore me up inside. It was all I could do not to carry you out of there. The body-double RAID wasn't my idea, just so you know. NAIA didn't even want me to stick around. But no way would I leave you alone with Janus again, not after I learned the truth about him." He groans. "I can't believe you got on that copter without Mudak. You promised you wouldn't do anything dumb."

I hold up a finger. "I distinctly remember promising maybe. Besides, how could I be sure the other NASS agents weren't in Mirovnik's pocket? And why didn't you use your tracker to clue me into the plan?"

He winces. "I accidentally swallowed the microphone chip."

I rub my eyes. That explains why his voice disappeared. I thought someone was attacking him.

"For what it's worth, NAIA didn't tell me the plan until you were on your way. One minute I was in handcuffs, being led into the penitentiary, and the next NAIA agents are trying to force me onto a copter. Vivi and Corah stepped in on my behalf, hooked me up with a holoshield, and gave me a quick rundown of the plan. Next thing I know, you're running past me toward the gurney."

"The paramedics weren't paramedics, were they?" True medics can distinguish a RAID from a human.

"NAIA agents."

I try to puzzle out the sequence of events, but cross off every move as an impossibility. "How did NAIA coordinate this so quickly? They saw my video at the ball and immediately found a body double to catch whoever came to kill you?"

I hold up a hand as thoughts stretch and tug toward one another, making new connections. NAIA wouldn't need a body double to save Donovan. They must've already known Janus was pulling the strings and believed I'd be the best one to get a confession out of him. They could've easily predicted I'd go after Donovan, but taking Janus with me?

I click my tongue. No, they didn't predict *I'd* take Janus, they predicted *Janus* would take *me*, that he'd try to kill me . . . again. Hence, the three NASS agents frantically waving at me to wait for them.

I bunch my lips together and grunt. Yeah, that was dumb. I guess I'm lucky Janus took me to the penitentiary at all. He must've believed his plan to kill Donovan would succeed and wanted to rub the win in my face. And why not? He and Mirovnik had never failed before.

Another tremor runs over me. I tuck my hand back under the covers. "Maybe it's best if you just talk me through it in sequential order. Start with your warning yesterday morning."

Donovan runs a hand through his curls. "When Yinbi was arrested two nights ago, he thought you were behind it, not my birth mother. So he confessed he saw you with me, Vivi, and Corah after your reported disappearance, guessing correctly that Mirovnik would find you with us. Using his connections, Mirovnik traced you to the intelligence college and arranged for the Bureau to extract you."

Makes sense. The Bureau has authority to arrest an attempted murderer.

"Mudak alerted me after hearing the news from her wife, who works for the Bureau. Then I was called in for more questions, so I figured Yinbi also spilled I was Flavinsky." He rubs his jaw. "And Mirovnik started advertising a big announcement for his fundraiser. Didn't take a genius to figure out that would be the arrest of the real Flavinsky or the capture of his attempted murderer. Or both."

I nod slowly, processing his words. "Your heads-up was much appreciated. And super stealthy. Maybe *you* should become an intelligence agent."

He smirks. "The thought *has* crossed my mind. Especially considering NAIA is ready to roll out the red carpet to recruit you."

My heart flutters. "Me, you, Vivi, and Corah. We'd be quite the dream team."

"We already are." He winks.

NAIA wants me to work for them. Me. When Vivi and Corah

received their results, I never once imagined I could follow in their footsteps. My whole life I felt different—unsure and even fearful of who I was. Now I can't imagine any other path for myself. It so perfectly fits who I am.

I glance around my colorful walls and marvel at their beauty. For so long, I hated my aura, wished Mom could read mine like everyone else's. Come to find out, inscrutability is one of my most useful assets.

I smile at Donovan. He'll be the perfect partner. Like he said, he already is. "Okay. What happened next? Who called you in for questioning?"

"NAIA. They clamped a sound silencer to my earlobe and started firing a million questions. They already knew I was Flavinsky."

My heart begins pounding. "That must've been terrifying." If any of the agents questioning him were on Mirovnik's side, he wouldn't be here. Another shiver runs through me.

Donovan rises to tuck the blankets again. "Agents Hawkshaw and Bukhali were in the room, so I wasn't too worried. They had done some digging into Yinbi's accounts and found huge lump sum payments from both Windrose and Janus. They called in Windrose for questioning yesterday morning. She was promised immunity for her confession."

A weight lifts from my chest, allowing me to breathe easier. It was me, Krest, who got Windrose involved in the first place. "That's how NAIA connected you with Flavinsky."

"Mm-hmm." Donovan leans on his elbows. "After matching my soulid against a backup copy of SEIK, they granted me access to Flavinsky's Last Letter. Seems I had a Foli Journal of my own, but none of my past lives had seen it."

"Because they kept killing you." I stare at the ceiling while more loose ends knit together. The Prime Minister wasn't just trying to separate me and Donovan out of some long-standing vendetta. "You had evidence against Janus and Mirovnik."

"Yes. Otherwise known as Cigacious and Ladiron. My last journal entry was a video Flavinsky captured during World War III, coming upon Ladiron after he'd murdered General Molemo. I caught him radioing confirmation of the kill to Cigacious and asking for Cigacious to do his part in return."

Cigacious's part . . . deleting our soulmate connection in SEIK. Ladiron made a deal with Cigacious to ensure Krest and Flavinsky would never be together, and killed Molemo to fulfill his end of the bargain.

Unreal. So Ladiron kept me and Donovan apart as some sort of vindictive payback, and life by life, as I tried to save my soulmate, Cigacious grew ever more intrigued with the game.

We've been his pawns all along. Janus is the traitor. In each and every life. Killing the general of his own army. Working for Belarussian Foreign Intelligence, while supporting the mafia. Thwarting his own agents at SAIA. Trying to kill the one person he claimed to love.

"So Ladiron caught Flavinsky listening into their conversation and shot him?"

"He fired and missed, giving Flavinsky time to stream the evidence to our foli journal. He alerted Cigacious, then aimed to shoot again, and we both landed fatal blows."

My heart squeezes. They couldn't let Flavinsky release the evidence, so they worked together to silence them life after life, all the while running Flavinsky's reputation into the ground.

And Krest, in her tireless fight to save her soulmate, compiled evidence to expose the criminal network that was hijacking reputable souls to amass more power. I recall Mom's portrait of Mirovnik, his red and black aura. Evil, danger, death. She knew the entire time.

"NAIA didn't arrest you to serve out your SCAR sentences?"

"They were more interested in capturing actual criminals." Donovan pats the comforter, avoiding my eyes. "I agreed to be their bait."

"Donovan!" I bolt upright and immediately regret it. Vertigo plus the whirling colors on my walls do not make a winning combination. I close my eyes until the nausea passes.

He jumps to his feet. "How can I help?"

I wince. "Maybe start by not baiting the people who've murdered you for two centuries?" I double over and moan as the burning in my gut intensifies.

"Sivon, lie down. *Please.*"

"I'm too upset to lie down!" My fingers curl into the sheets as I release a measured breath.

Donovan rests his hip on the bed. "NAIA never let me out of their sight. Hawkshaw and Bukhali came to the White House with me, wearing their invisibility holoshields. And NAIA agents accompanied me to the penitentiary. I was safe the entire time. You, on the other hand . . ." He looks at my stomach.

I show up uninvited to one murderer's party and fly off alone with the other one. I purse my lips. "Touché."

"NAIA released my true identity to Mirovnik just as the ball started, making it sound like it came from Yinbi."

"Yinbi didn't talk?"

"Yinbi is dead."

My chin juts forward. "What?"

"Death by suicide no more than twelve hours after his arrest."

"Suicide?" I raise a brow. "Like Flavinsky's suicides?"

Donovan lifts one shoulder. "The report said he strangled himself with his pants, but who's to say? Janus and Mirovnik have plenty of experience covering up their crimes. The guy who attacked you in the Fringe also took his life in jail."

I cover my eyes. "Jeez. They must have people working for them everywhere. Will we ever be safe?"

Donovan chews his lip. "I wish I could say yes. The good news is Janus's and Mirovnik's secrets are out in the open, no longer hidden by the four of us. We grew our team roster a hundredfold over the past twenty-four hours and are adding to it by the minute.

"And keep in mind it's now Mirovnik and Janus who're hiding secrets. They'll likely be targeted by the same souls who've been doing their dirty work. NAIA has them on round-the-clock suicide watch, especially given Janus's attempt to turn the gun on himself after shooting you."

Janus tried to kill himself? My throat swells with unexpected grief. Until twelve hours ago, I counted him among the few people I trusted, even cared about. I probably did so for many lives. His deceit physically hurts, much like, well, a gunshot to the stomach. "Where did Janus even get a gun? They've been illegal for over a century."

Donovan's brows form sharp peaks. "Are you really asking if Janus would do something illegal?"

I snort, then press a hand to my stomach. "Ow. It hurts to laugh."

"Lie down," Donovan says sternly. "You need to get better so I can give you your surprise."

I let him ease me back by the shoulders. "What surprise?"

"If I tell you it won't be a surprise."

I narrow my eyes. "You're insufferable."

He huffs and tucks the blankets around me again. "Don't even. You can't lie to me."

I open my mouth to lie about not lying, but Mom chooses that moment to poke her head into the room.

"You're awake!" She holds a canvas behind her back, a glimmer in her eye. "How's my little Indigo?"

"Feeling better by the minute."

Donovan presses his lips together, silently calling me out on my fib. I roll my eyes.

"I'm so glad to hear it." She takes a step forward. "Sorry I wasn't here when you woke up, but I knew you were in good hands. And I haven't been this inspired in ages."

She pulls the canvas from behind her back and turns it to face us. I gasp, almost sitting up again, but Donovan presses on my shoulder to stop me.

"Mom, is that . . . ?"

She nods, tears filling her eyes. "This is what your aura looks like when it merges with Donovan's."

He takes my hand as we admire her masterpiece. The two of us as one. A combination like none I've ever seen before. Another shiver runs through me. It's the most beautiful portrait I've ever seen.

Indigo

indigo—The spectral color between blue and violet, as designated by Sir Isaac Newton. Having the smallest electromagnetic spectrum, optical scientists argue indigo is indistinguishable from its neighbors and therefore doesn't exist.

Thursday, September 13, 236 A.K.—The Lincoln Memorial—Washington, CD

Completely starstruck, my mouth hangs open as the iconic singer Lavonne walks away, surrounded by her entourage. Norine told me Lavonne was scheduled to perform at Fahari's victory celebration today, but the fact that Lavonne sought me out blows my mind. *Lavonne* wanted to meet *me*.

"Was that your big surprise?" I ask Donovan.

He snorts. "How in the world would I know Lavonne? No, that's not my surprise."

"I've waited three whole days. When are you going to tell me?" I take his arm as we meander through the central chamber of the Lincoln Memorial, gawking at celebrities who gawk back at us in return.

The corner of his mouth lifts. "It will be today."

"When today?" My heart starts racing. The mystery is killing me.

He shakes his head and waves as Vivi and Trevin approach hand in hand, followed by Corah and Ensio.

Trevin gives me their third hug of the day. "This one is from Mom. She's about to go on with Fahari but wanted me to say hi and to thank you once again for clearing her soulname."

"I only wish we could've done it sooner. She's going by Molemo now?"

Trevin tips their head side to side. "She's trying it on for size, but I bet she'll return to Ladiron. It took three lifetimes and almost inhuman persistence to make Ladiron into the reputable soul it is today. The last thing she wants is for Mirovnik to reclaim his first soulname, pretending to be her."

Ensio raises a hand. "We could assign Mirovnik a new ID. Make him choose a different soulname."

"That would essentially give him a new soul, though," Corah says.

"Hmm." I study the ground, trying to work out the right solution.

Donovan lays his arm across my shoulders. "How about we save that problem for another day? Molemo's going on now."

As she takes the stage, I wave back at Norine, who granted us backstage access today. Donovan points out his family and Mom standing near the front, beside Vivi and Corah's parents, and we wave at them as well.

Trevin's mother gives a rousing speech, reliving the history of this historic site—hundreds of years and dozens of marches by people who knew we could do better, and be better, if we worked together and believed in ourselves. She challenges everyone to imagine themselves a new soul, their pasts wiped clean. "Who would you become if you followed your dreams? Flip the lid, free your soul."

The newly elected Prime Minister Fahari thanks Molemo before announcing the policy changes her administration will make over the coming months, provided negotiations with the GCG continue moving forward. She promises to abolish the kirling mandate. Every North American will have the right to choose whether to be kirled. If they do, their results will remain private unless they elect to publish them.

A not-so-small part of me is nervous about her proposed reforms. If Mirovnik or Janus kill themselves, they could escape all culpability for their centuries of murder and misdeeds. But could I condemn another eighteen-year-old for the crimes of their past lives? Never. Their future selves deserve the freedom to carve a new path, to learn and grow. The same is true for all of us. Otherwise, why are we here?

Vivi and Corah step up next to me, one on either side.

I take their hands. "If you could've chosen to be kirled, would you have gone through with it?"

Vivi considers for a few seconds. "I don't think so. I already knew who my soulmate was and what I wanted to do with my life. What about you, Cor?"

"*Hell* yes. I wouldn't pass up all those valuts. It was worth going just for that."

I chuckle and elbow her in the ribs.

"And you?" Vivi prods.

"I've been thinking about Ziva a lot. I know she would've turned it down. Hopefully by the time she turns eighteen again, the GCG mandate will be gone worldwide. Maybe in her next life, she'll be a dancer or a baker ... or a dancing baker."

I snort at my dumb joke and turn my gaze to Donovan, who's listening intently to the end of Fahari's speech. My heart swells with pride. We suffered so many painful losses, but we never gave up on each other. And we never will.

"As for myself, I'd like to think I would've turned it down, but if so, I wouldn't be who I am today."

Donovan catches me staring and winks, making butterflies dance in my stomach.

"Two months ago, I had no clue what I was capable of, or that I'd ever love and *be* loved so completely. So yeah, I'd do it all over again. I wouldn't change a thing."

Vivi pumps the air. "Yes! I have never, in my entire life, been so happy to lose a bet."

By the time we hug our friends and family goodbye, cicadas are chorusing, and twilight has settled onto the streets of Washington, CD.

I step out of Mom's arms. "I'll see you at home."

She wears a bright smile, despite the strain of the past couple days. After filling her in on my past lives, Mom solved the last mystery—who was responsible for erasing my soulid from SEIK.

Twenty years ago, a few days before her death, Krest hired an up-and-coming artist to paint her aura, likely knowing her husband was a data analyst at SKI. But after they all had dinner together, Mom never saw her again. Dad took Krest's unclaimed portrait to work with him, and Mom never gave the silver-and-indigo-blue aura another thought.

After my dad died two years later, his entire database-integrity department lost funding and was dissolved, allowing the system to go unchecked. On the rare occasions questions arose about SEIK's accuracy, the whistleblower would be similarly "dissolved."

We no longer believe Dad's death was accidental, especially given Mirovnik's questions when he first met Mom. Mirovnik must've suspected Dad had evidence that would reveal his true identity. And he was right. Ensio found a file Dad planted on an old backup server, connecting the real Mirovnik with Primus's new soul. It was signed with a crossroads symbol.

I wish I knew why my soul picked Mom and Dad to be my parents. The cynic in me figures Krest planned to use Mom's aura-reading skills and Dad's connections to SEIK to save Flavinsky. But I like to think that dinner with two remarkable and loving souls convinced her. Without Mom's example and unconditional love, I wouldn't be the person I am today.

Her gaze flits to Donovan so quickly, I nearly miss it. "Yep, see you, Indigo." She hugs me again and giggles as she walks away.

Oh, they are *up to something*. It's time for my surprise. I practically bounce on my feet as Donovan escorts me to his hover in the heavily guarded garage.

"Is it a party?" I ask when he climbs in beside me. "Like, a belated-eighteenth thing?"

He blinks several times. "Do you *want* a party?"

"*Hell* no. I want to wrap myself into a blanket burrito and stay there until we start at NAIC next week."

"I figured." He buckles his seatbelt and types a series of coordinates into the navigation panel.

"Ooh, coordinates. Where are we going?"

His eyes twinkle from the street globes as we turn out of the garage. "It's a surprise."

I whack his arm playfully. "Can't you give me a hint?"

"If I did, you'd figure it out within seconds. I know my girl."

My heart flips. His girl.

"But I can be reasonable." Donovan scratches his jaw. "How about this? I'll give you a three-second heads-up."

I bite my lip, holding back a smile, and shake my foot. We soar past block after block, taking the same route we would to get to my house. I run through the list of possibilities. Mom is in on it, but it's not a party. A present, then?

Stop, Sivon. It's way more fun not knowing, and he can barely restrain his prideful grin. *Let him have his moment.*

I can't believe I once thought Donovan's aura was gray and beige. Nothing about this man has ever screamed boring or indifferent. But when Mom told me his true colors, I thought she was joking. Red and black.

She assured me his aura doesn't in any way give off the horrifying energy of Mirovnik's. But to me, Donovan embodies every interpretation. I bet Janus and Mirovnik would describe him as evil, and Donovan's soul knows the very meaning of death. He's also loving, powerful, sensitive, strong, mysterious, and yes, even dangerous. That one might be my favorite of all.

I take his hand, and he smirks. "You still haven't figured it out. Am I actually beating you at this game, Sivon?"

I narrow my eyes. "It's more like I've decided not to play."

"Uh-huh. There you go again, trying to lie to me." He tsks.

The hover makes a few sharp turns, and I no longer have any clue where we are. The unmarked road is lined with trees. My knee starts bouncing. *Where is he taking me?*

A few kilometers later, nothing has changed. We pass no landmarks, hovers, or signs of life. But we're getting closer. I feel it now, deep in my bones, settling in like a hug from an old friend. And just like that, I know exactly where we're going. It's both a surprise, and it's not. And I'm more excited than ever.

"Three, two, one."

The hover makes a sharp left turn, not onto another street or driveway, but straight into a grove of pine trees. I scream and throw my arms over my head, but we pass right through them.

"They're holos?" I twist to look at the trees illuminated by the rear lights.

"Realistic, right?"

"Unbelievably so." They're the perfect cover.

The hover winds down a narrow path for another hundred meters and comes to a stop. The doors pop open, and I climb out. We're still surrounded by trees, but I doubt they're all real.

He rounds the hover, wearing a cocky grin. "Ready?"

Smiling giddily, I nod quickly, and he taps my chin before taking me by the shoulders and leading me to the far corner of the path. "Stand here. It's a soulid reader." He steps away from me.

Two seconds later, three peaceful notes chime through the woods. Like something out of a fairy tale, a hundred square meters of trees vanish, revealing a house. My jaw drops. It's gorgeous.

Donovan threads his fingers with mine. "It's constructed of recycled steel and reclaimed wood. The entire front window retracts, along with the matching one out back."

"How did you—?"

"I was saving up for a dream home with my soulmate, remember?" He kisses my knuckles.

My heart flips again as I take in every perfect detail. "How much did NASS *pay* you?"

He chuckles. "I also made an advantageous real estate deal with a couple of good friends." He points to the right. "Vivi and Corah have a place about three hundred meters that way."

"Are you serious? But we can't accept this. It's too much!"

He laughs. "I told them you'd say that. Don't worry, they already have grand ideas for how we can repay them."

"Oh, *really*?"

He tugs my arm. "Come on. I wanna show you inside."

The second I step into our home, it becomes a part of my soul. It smells like honey and pine, much like Donovan. The walls match the exterior—gray steel beams, amber planks of wood, and stainless-steel fixtures. Cream-colored couches, a cozy pouf, and a few leafy plants make up the sparse decorations.

We walk through the living room and onto the back deck. I place my hands on the railing, close my eyes, and listen to the rustling leaves and burble of a nearby stream. Donovan hugs me around the waist, and I lean against his chest. This is it, the reason I fought so hard and for so long, for this very moment in time. We did it. We're together. We won.

"It reminds me of the forest in the Holusion Museum." I entwine my fingers with his. Being with Donovan feels as natural as breathing.

"Do you love it? If not, Vivi and Corah have an island off the coast of Japan that's ours for the taking."

I spin to face him. "I have *seen* said island, and trust me, it doesn't hold a candle to this." My hands skim up his arms, finding their way into his hair. "I love it. I love *you*, Donovan."

He rests his forehead against mine and closes his eyes. "No way can I be this lucky." He caresses my cheek. "The most incredible woman I've ever met is my soulmate." He draws in a long breath. "I don't deserve you."

"You've got it all wrong. If one of us isn't deserving, it's—"

Donovan silences me with a kiss—gentle yet firm, liberating yet possessive. One hand cups my head while the other holds me against him. He's still too far away. I tug at his shirt hem and slide my fingers up the bare skin of his back. He gasps, his lips skimming my jaw before bringing them back to mine.

After another minute, he draws away, panting. "Do you have any idea how much I love you? How *long* I've loved you? You can't imagine how hard it was to leave that day to meet Crosier, how wrong it felt. I think I've loved you since you braided Linzy's hair."

I huff, remembering how fearful and insecure I felt at his parents' house, and so very frustrated with Donovan's behavior. "You were so mean back then."

"I *couldn't* love you back then. What could I do other than push you away?"

"And now?" I press myself against him, reveling in the tingles spreading over my skin.

Donovan moans and kisses me again, then scoops me into his arms. "Now I'll never let you go."

He carries me into our home and directly into the bedroom, where our kisses become vows—to love one another, protect one another, and fight for each other until the end of time. Bit by bit, we remove the barriers separating us, and bit by bit, we maneuver closer together until finally, our souls unite and our souls ignite.

Flavinsky's Last Letter

My soulmate, Carrefour, isn't leaving her neli anything. I fully support her decision, but you need to know what you're up against.

In our foli 1, I screwed up. From my Foli Journal, I learned that I didn't think I was good enough for her. When Ladiron asked her out, I supported him, despite her confusion and my irrepressible feelings. He and I had been friends for years. He was a good soul once. Perhaps his villainy grew by trying to hold on to someone he could never have. Maybe if I confided how I felt from the start, he wouldn't have become so vindictive. We'll never know. The biggest takeaway here is to trust your instincts, and trust Carrefour.

I've worked out the following by pulling together information from Carrefour, SEIK, and Sociaty:

In foli 2, Carrefour and I grew up in Tokyo and started dating at fifteen. Ladiron killed me at SKI, and Carrefour stayed by my grave day and night, eventually dying of exposure. I know, dramatic. I've already begged her not to do anything like that again.

In foli 3, my best friend's younger sister had a rare kidney disease, and I was the ideal donor. We scheduled the surgery for the day after I was to leave SKI. I didn't leave SKI alive. She succumbed to her disease a year later. Since she didn't have a kirling, I can only guess this was Carrefour.

I died twice during her foli 4, never meeting her. She was born into a Belarussian crime family. Ladiron was the kingpin. Carrefour became an informant, hoping to bring them down. Her bullet-ridden body was discovered soon thereafter.

Carrefour's foli 5 was their longest life. Ladiron assumed General Molemo's identity, married Carrefour, and killed me three more times. Carrefour worked at the South American Intelligence Agency alongside Kitsune and Raposa, uncovering the soul-swapping operation. Convinced someone on the inside was hindering the investigation, they hid their data in the Mariana Trench. Their return flight went down with all three on board. Cigacious/Janus led the SAIA at the time.

Carrefour's sixth life was in the Fringe. She grew up friends with Cigacious/Janus. After his kirling, he introduced her to his "business acquaintance" Senator Mirovnik. The rest, including everything you need to know about Carrefour's foli 7, can be found by searching Sociaty for "New Soul Carrefour" and "Prime Minister's arrest," both in 236 A.K.

I'm sharing this so you'll appreciate the depths Carrefour went through to fix the kirling system and save us. Maybe database audits will prevent future soul swapping and expose every criminal who switched identities. Maybe kirling will end as we know it. But realistically, when fortune and power are at stake, bad souls will do whatever it takes to seize it.

So love Carrefour while you can, with everything you are, but watch your backs. I doubt we've seen the last of Ladiron or Cigacious.

Folijournal.com—
Username: ElevenKey Password: sivonovan

ACKNOWLEDGEMENTS

Though but one name appears on *Soulmatch*'s cover, writing and publishing isn't a solitary endeavor, not by far. I owe so much to so many, and while I'll try my best to name them all, there are dozens, likely *hundreds*, more—from mail rooms to executives, from early reviewers to librarians—to whom I offer my sincere gratitude.

Thank you to my agent, Michelle Wolfson, for pulling me out of the slush pile and seeing this project through to the end. I couldn't have done this without your expertise, guidance, and persistence.

Thanks to Michelle and a healthy dose of good fortune, I ended up with the best publishing team ever assembled. My editor, Nicole Ellul, made me a better writer all around. What a joy to find someone who shares my affinity for exclamation points!!!! The keen eyes of my copyeditor Marinda Valenti, proofreader Ela Schwartz, and production editor Morgan York rooted out grammatical errors and mind-blowing inconsistencies. The immensely talented Katt Phatt designed *Soulmatch*'s drool-worthy cover art, and Alex Kelleher and Lindsey Ferris set a high bar against which I'll measure any future publicists.

Soulmatch touches on some difficult and complex topics—namely suicide and religion—which I sought to handle with sensitivity and accuracy. Thank you to my authenticity reader, who prefers to remain anonymous, and Dr. Martyn Oliver for lending your insight and expertise to those passages.

I couldn't have navigated my debut year without the camaraderie of my fellow 2025 debuts, notably Veronica Bane—my agent sibling who I now call friend. Be sure to pick up her YA theme park murder mystery, *Difficult Girls*!

Pitching a novel requires entirely different skills from writing one, but I learned those with the help of M.M. Finck, Sylvia Young's "Pitmad Hatters," and Kathy Ver Eecke's "Pitch to Publish" community. Authors Constance Sayers and Jenny Hale gave me primers on the publishing industry and provided much-needed encouragement. Constance has continued her valuable mentorship throughout this lengthy process. Please read her magical novels. You won't regret it!

Soulmatch went through dozens upon dozens of revisions over the past five years. With each round, I found new readers who gifted me with their time and suggestions. My critique partners were Ginny Carlberg, Miranda Combs, Angie Paxton, and Stefanie Medrek. I won partial critiques from Rin Chupeco and Carolyn Tara O'Neil, and I honed *Soulmatch*'s first chapter(s) with feedback from Kristin Kutrieb, Simeon Care, Clare Draycott, Sarah Burchett, Lucia Scarano, Sue Newton, Marcy Holle, Meghan Perry, Kathy BeMiller, Nic DiSalvo, Sonia Hartl, Rachel Loertscher, and Heather Robb.

My much-loved beta readers include Mark Danzenbaker, Meghan Corbitt, Hannah Corbitt, Tim Corbitt, Chase Danzenbaker, Tracy Cronin, Heather McDade, Jennifer Viselli, Maureen Sidor, Elizabeth Ross, Megan Lamb, Jon Lamb, Carri Light, Whitney Rutz, Kristin Pascual, Beth Cook, Maddie Wasaff, Gabi Pritchett, Kaitlyn Balovich, Tiffany Perry, Jill Nolton, and Britt Cooper (my apologies if I missed anyone!). Without your validation, I would've given up years ago!

My street team is the very best! Thank you for your enthusiastic support! LET'S FREAKING GO!!!

To my dear friends and family, I can't begin to tell you how much your comments, shares, and messages have meant to me.

From lending an ear when I needed comfort to celebrating my every win, no matter how big or small, you kept me moving toward the finish line, one foot after the other. I love you all so much!

My lifelong friends, Whitney and Carri, are just as awesome as Vivi and Corah, their fictional counterparts—sympathetic, intelligent, down-to-earth, and goofy as hell. I hope we find each other in our next lives.

To Meghan and Mark, my biggest cheerleaders, who read this story way back when I was drafting it in Evernote (tip for new writers: do not do this), you have propped me up, one on either side, since the summer of 2020. You continued to believe in *Soulmatch* when I had given up hope. If it weren't for you two, this book would not exist.

Meghan, I'm looking forward to our double room in the nursing home. When should we submit our deposit?

Mark, it didn't take a kirling to figure out you are my soulmate. I've known since the day we met. I love you. I love us.

Chase and Clara, I hope my publishing journey inspires you to pursue your own dreams, no matter how difficult, no matter how lofty. When the day comes that I'm no longer able to tell you myself, simply open *Soulmatch* to this page, close your eyes, and feel how proud I am of you. I'm so honored you chose me to be your mom.

Carry forth,
Becky